TOP OF THE WORLD, MA!

Michael Guinzburg

CANONGATE

First published simultaneously in Great Britain,
the United States of America and Canada in 2001
by Canongate Books Ltd, 14 High Street,
Edinburgh EH1 1TE.

10 9 8 7 6 5 4 3 2 1

British Library Cataloguing-in-Publication Data
A catalogue record for this book is available
on request from the British Library

ISBN 0 86241 946 8

Typeset by Hewer Text Ltd, Edinburgh
Printed and bound by CPD, Ebbw Vale, Wales.

www.canongate.net

For Bruno Fonseca

We have art in order not to die of the truth.
—Friedrich Nietzsche

Look at me now, Ma! Top of the world!
—Jimmy Cagney in *White Heat*

IN CASHAMPTON BY THE SEA they still tell the story of Jackson Pollock — how he lived and how he died, and how he lives forever, in the paintings. They tell of his heavy drinking and his bad driving, his pain and his poverty and his brooding whiskey glooms. They tell of Lee, long-suffering, childless Lee — wife, mother-figure, anchor, victim — their love of the land, of the sea and the sand, and their sunrise walks through the winter woods.

They tell of rainy days and smoky bars, of clambakes, friends, and fast cars, of three-day bebop-and-beer blasts alone in his room.

And they say he was mad, demented and violent and brilliant and beat — impotent those last years, unable to paint, a balding bloated shadow of the graceful catlike genius whose extraordinary explosions onto canvas now command vast millions of dollars at auction — a tragic rag-souled drunk in the sad shabby dregs of his life.

And they tell of death, violent car-crash death, two girls along for the ride (one died), on Fireplace Road in Cashampton — over and over, they tell it. They tell it. For it, too, is part of the legend.

But there are cracks in the myth, whispers in the night . . .

As in any small town, there are whispers . . .

One

WHEN I WAS younger and even more of an asshole, making my first assault on the Manhattan art scene – driving a cab to pay the bills and still quite happy to attend every opening at every gallery – I was gleefully swilling wine at an early Keith Haring show in Soho when a suave older man wearing a splendid cream linen suit and raspberry ascot (with not a single nose hair on display) tapped me on the shoulder and gave me some very sound advice.

'Appearances,' he said, 'can be deceiving.'

'Well then, gramps,' I said, thinking I was deflecting some crusty chickenhawk's advance, 'perhaps I should disappear.'

And I did. I turned on my sneakered heel and took my flushed face and bad manners to another part of the crowded room.

My wine-soaked head swirled with the possibilities: Should I talk with the red-headed woman over there with the thrusting chest? She appeared to be a super-rich collector, maybe even a Whitney or a Vanderbilt or a Mellon (what double-luck that would be: Mellon melons!), who might take me home and subsidize the writing of my imagined master-piece of art-criticism. How about you mustachioed man with the powder-streaked blue jeans and the dusty hair? A famous Bulgarian sculptor in search of a biographer?

I buttonholed an acquaintance — a fellow taxicab-driver — the now celebrated Martinican monochromatic painter, Les-ter Valboges. (Perhaps you have seen his work from that period? — drab yellow canvases that resemble crashed-in automobile doors hastily slapped with house paint?)

'Lester, who's the redhead?'

'Her name's Kelly Swett. Last week she was a blonde.'

'She must be really fucking rich,' I said, saliva pooling in the pit beneath my tongue.

Lester laughed. 'Fucking rich is right. She fucks rich guys for a living. See, she makes what she calls Art-Bras. Cast-iron tit-holders with toy soldiers welded on. No one will buy one, so she gets by selling her ass.'

My first Art World assumption: shot down by toy soldiers.

'How about that sculptor over there? The one with all the stone-dust in his hair?'

'Roger, that's the guy who works in the bakery next door.'

Strike two.

But Roger Lymon knew art, right? And the Keith Haring pictures were awful and amateurish — pale suburban deriva-tives of marvelous ghetto graffiti — not worth the spray-paint they'd been made with. Right? So I had some more wine.

'And what do *you* do?' I asked a fellow in jeans and work boots.

'I'm the artist's brother.' He offered me a hand. 'Ted Haring.'

'Red Herring?' We shook. 'And how is your other brother, Pickled Herring?'

'Why are you being so nasty?' Ted Haring whined. 'This is my brother's *moment*. There's no call for that.'

And, of course, there wasn't any call for that. It was strike three. Red Herring told Keith Haring, who told Raspberry Ascot, the owner of the gallery, and a very large security guard very firmly and very politely escorted me very much outside.

So I learned, the hard way, that in the Manhattan Art World and its contiguous fields of play, not only could appearances be deceiving, *they could be completely fucking befuddling*, and that if I wanted inside the candy store with carte blanche to finger the sticky-bun yummies, instead of having to stand outside in the cold with my drippy nose griming the window, then I had better get with the program and learn to dress well and act politely and be ready to plant a wet fresh smooch on whatever wrinkled ass presented itself. I couldn't have cared less about the dreck that passed for art in the contemporary Art World – but I liked the glamor, I liked the glitz, I liked the free wine and cheese: I liked *The Scene*. There was money to be made, women to make. You didn't have to get your hands dirty or use your brain; all you had to do was get in. In the worst way, I wanted in. And though I was woefully unprepared for the position and duties of art-critic – barely able as I was, then, to discern Dada from Surrealism from Non-Objective Gobbledygookism, let alone tell a baker apart from a sculptor – that in itself was no real obstacle, because it was clear (as an empty stretch of outer space) that in the Art World there is always room for one more phony.

So the next week I purchased a fashionable suit of clothes with appropriately padded shoulders, I retired my sneakers in lieu of a proper pair of snakeskin shoes, I cut down on the alcohol in public, and eventually – after some shameless brownnosing here and there around town – landed a job as a reporter for *Artnews*.

Ah, the heady years of the 1980s, when Reagan dollars and Japanese money and Arab cash flooded the market, creating instant superstars out of talentless imbeciles – I was right in there, going with the flow, part of The Scene. Keith Haring became an industry; Kelly Swett sold her soldier-studded Art-Bras to Madonna and Nancy Kissinger and Mrs. Norman Schwartzkopf, then branched into Art-Girdles; the baker bought the bakery and turned it into a gallery (I'm sure you have heard of, if not visited, The Bakery) and now makes reputations and money as he once made baguettes and bagels. Kostabi and Bleckner and Fischl and Schnabel (no, they are not onomatopeic flu-season throat-clearing noises, they are famous moneyboy artists) – they have all shown at The Bakery – and I have met them all, I have listened to their stylish bullshit, I have dutifully recorded their incomprehensible aesthetics for posterity. (Perhaps you remember my interview with Bill Wegman's favorite photographic subject, the dog Man Ray? The Weimaraner was on its death-bed and I was dispatched by the magazine to cover the passing of an Art World luminary. I snapped pictures of the wheezing pajama-clad pooch and, as Wegman wept great sincere tears of sorrow, I tape-recorded – and *Artnews* triumphantly published – the dying dog's Molly Bloomish last words: 'Arf,' Man Ray said. 'Arf arf and arf and arf and arf arf.' On editor's orders I counted Man Ray's 'arfs' ten times to insure accuracy.)

For a while there, things certainly looked good for old Roger. Not only was I romantically linked with the noted performance artist Sharon Timlin, but I had just published my biography of Sammy Stillman, the gay autistic fourteen-year-old Crayon-Primitivist. Things looked excellent. The dinner and cocktail invitations were just flying in. My mailbox was stuffed. I never paid for coke. I was in demand. Yes indeed, I could pick and choose. Uptown and Downtown, I was a comer, a real comer.

But then, like a hog-farm wind blowing into a rose garden, came Sharon's big night – her breakthrough, my fall from grace – that fateful first performance she stood on stage jaybird-naked and stuffed a baking potato into her succulent red-fringed matrix while singing the national anthem. I was front-and-center in the audience. My God! how they cheered and yowled! (You'd have thought it was Charlie Parker up there playing godlike harmonies or Allen Ginsberg reading *Howl*.) And I felt myself blushing a dramatic Turner sunset shade of red. Put yourself in my shoes: Imagine what it feels like playing second-banana to an Idaho potato.

At the party afterward, I was speechless with provincial embarrassment, my ears burned scarlet as Hester Prynne's panties – cuckolded by a humble tuber! The shame of it! And everyone saw my distress, the whole Art World knew it – and Sharon, sweet, mad, ambitious, red-haired Sharon, now clothed like a Victorian virgin in Laura Ashley ankle-length white frock, Sharon knew it too. So right there, right then and there, she cut her losses and dumped me (like a hot potato) for Rawlings Black – kissed him full on the lips, ground her vegetable-loving pelvis into his gargantuan gut to the strains of Laurie Anderson's 'O Superman!' And Rawlings Black, no prudish suburban boob he, Rawlings Black knew what to do: In front of the whole Art World he seized the moment – he ate that damned half-baked potato raw, licking his lips, drooling potato juice, baying at the spinning disco crystal ball like a blood-slaked Yukon wolf. And in consuming that cursed second-hand spud he absorbed the power of the night: He graduated from a simple spinner of monologues – a pretender to the throne of the great Spalding Gray (how many potbellied pale pretenders emerged that year? all trying to capitalize on Hollywood-gone Spalding's success, all copying his style and his name: surname a color, Christian name a sporting goods brand? There was Rawlings Black, Adidas Ocher, Brunswick Brown, Wilson White – a gimmick a gimmick, my kingdom for a gimmick!) – to become Sharon's consort, the chosen one, anointed to suckle at the breast of her success, a serious player on the Downtown Scene.

I had missed my moment. My edge no longer cut. Dull, dull Roger Lymon. I was not ruined, no, but my reputation sank like a stone cast into a deep polluted lake, and the ripples of failure spread across my life. There were fewer and fewer invitations, fewer and fewer freebies. Some nights I'd sit at home in my Greenwich Village dump, staring at the phone, willing it to ring, ordering out for Chinese food, then engaging the delivery boy in conversation while the broccoli in garlic sauce cooled and congealed. Well, I consoled myself, I still had Sammy Stillman. For a long time I ate out on Sammy Stillman. But it did not lead to other biographies. Why not? Because success cured Sammy Stillman of his autism and he invested his Art Dollars in five McDonald's franchises back home in Sarasota, Florida, and is at present a very normal college sophomore at Florida State University, an equipment manager for the football team, with huge hamburger holdings.

Which brings us to John Dough and the town of Cashampton. Perhaps my last chance at the proverbial brass ring. John Dough appeared from nowhere that spring. Appeared on The Scene like a fully formed rose. No budding or blooming for John Dough. One minute it was business as usual, the next it was, John Dough this, John Dough that.

I remember very clearly my first impression: Here was a

lion, I thought, a beautiful powerful man to fall in love with. Oh, no, I do not mean that in a homoerotic way (I don't do gay); I mean, this was a man to admire, a man to emulate, a go-get-'em guy with looks and a story and obvious class.

I first saw John Dough at Sotheby's in late April, some days after the *Post* reported his story, at the exclusive auction for the pearls that he had plucked from the Bosporus. Everyone who was anyone in the overlapping art and Social Worlds was there, to purchase a piece of a modern legend. He had lived, the catalogue informed us, 'in Turkey for some years, diving with the local divers, eating their humble fare, sleeping in a shack on the beach.' Some whispered that he was a POW MIA who had escaped his Vietcong captors and walked across Asia to fight with the Kurds. A blonde Rambo. Some speculated that he was born an English aristocrat or the son of Paraguayan Nazis.

He cut a dramatic figure. Hair: perfect, wavy, golden, falling sun-streaked onto his shoulders. Eyes: green and glowing as center-court at Wimbledon after a midday rain. Body: shoulders broad as a limousine; hands large and gnarled from opening oysters; arms huge; wrists corded with sinew; legs bursting with muscle; chest proud with vitality, puffed from diving. A man to make women swoon and men envious, the kind of fellow pictured on the covers of romance novels. What is commonly termed 'a hunk.' I suppose if I were gay – and I'm not – I would have loved him. He had everything: looks, style, confidence, and charm; and by the end of the afternoon, after Sotheby's had auctioned the three-hundred-and-twelve pearls that he'd managed to smuggle back from Turkey tucked inside his guts in home-made lambskin con-doms, pearls ranging from tiny and perfect to hen's egg-sized and rough as igneous rock, from white to rose to pale blue, John Dough was eighty-seven-million-dollars richer and the instant darling of the Gilded Set.

'My God,' I said to Hiroshi Koyabashi, the Japanese businessman I was having dinner with that night at Robert De Niro's Raging Bull Steakhouse in Tribeca. 'That John Dough is something.'

'Magnificent,' Hiroshi said, daintily chewing his two-hundred-dollar Kobe steak. 'But that is not why I asked you to dinner . . .'

I smiled, allowing my smile to say everything: The food is delicious, the wine is superb, the ambience is enchanting. The room is peppered with a Who's Who of Hollywood, the Mafia, the Social Register. Why, there's rap-impresario Leroy Buggins with Georgia blue blood Myrtle Spiddle-Sparrow and comedienne Sandra Bernhard; there's Ruffino crime boss Bonzo 'The Carp' Mancini with ex-Senator Cranston of California; there's brat-pack writer Tama Janowitz with National Endowments of the Arts watchdog The Reverend Doctor Jasper Jurkbaitt (Pronounced *Yoork*-bite) and super-model Jezebella Mussolini. Why have you invited me to dinner? You know that I am, in the parlance of street and stream, a bottom-feeder – a very minor art-reviewer from the un-chic provinces of New Jersey, mired in mid-career crisis. And you, Hiroshi, you wear two-thousand-dollar suits, you represent a consortium that buys Van Goghs and Rembrandts and owns a publishing house and a film studio and the world's largest toaster-oven manufacturer. Thanks for the feed and what, pray tell, do you want?

'You know, Roger, there are three films about Jackson Pollock slated to come out later this year. I have managed to see the rough cuts, and these films are very good, very dramatic, very insightful – but all three lack something. . . . They fail to address the rumors . . . the rumors of Pollock's . . .'

'Pollock's what?'

'His possible, umm . . .' And here Hiroshi took a large Adam's apple-bobbing swallow of wine. 'His possible bisexuality. His philandering. His—'

'Excuse me, Hiroshi, it's well-documented that Pollock had an affair with a woman called Ruth Kligman that last summer of his life, but the gay thing—'

'You have heard, of course, that he was incapable of painting those last years, that he was in fact impotent, dried-up as an artist and as a man, an empty shell of the great Pollock who created *Autumn Rhythm* and *Lavender Mist* – but Roger, hear me out, we have reason to believe that those last few years he *was* painting and that he *was* having affairs and that he was *even* a . . . How do I say this without sounding crass or sensationalistic . . . that Pollock was a pederast.'

'You must be joking.'

'Not at all.'

'But Hiroshi, that's ridiculous. This isn't Shakespeare who lived four-hundred-years ago in the dim pre-mass-media past, where you can speculate that the dark lady of the sonnets was actually the dark laddie or that Willie was Wilhemina. No, my friend, this is Jack The Dripper, born 1912, died 1956, a modern genius whose every flatulence and vomit and violent episode was noted and catalogueed. Lost paintings? Strange women? Little boys? Please.'

'But would it not make for a wonderful film?' His dark almond eyes glittered brightly and he poured more wine.

Yes, I thought, it most certainly would. A wonderful film. A fabulous biography. Money, success – controversy out the wazoo!

'A toast.' I raised my glass. 'To Jackson Pollock and little boys.'

Two

COUNTESS BABY LUEGODAGO, the tall stately wife of South American beef billionaire Count Hugo Luegodago, hopped out of her quarter-million-dollar Lamborghini Range Rover, looked at the seagulls swirling about the soggy gray sky above the Upton Riding Club in Cashampton By The Sea, farted loudly and muttered:

'Anuddah fuckin' day like dis, Rog, an' I'll slit my fuckin' wrists.'

I had met Baby – I should say, I had maneuvered to meet Baby – at the Kelly Swett show at the Solly Holliman Gallery the day following John Dough's electrifying debut at Sotheby's. That morning, after I had arranged a leave of absence from the magazine, Hiroshi had paid my rent for four months, bought me a new wardrobe, and set up a small expense account in my name at the Cashampton Savings and Loan – certainly not enough to rent in Cashampton (he proposed that I become a sort of floating houseguest), but an adequate amount to keep my head above water, to buy people drinks here and there, to pick up the odd brunch check. He wanted me in the mix, wangling invitations, up-close and cozy with the Pollock collectors and locals. Like a knife-man or a prostitute, I did my best work up-close.

At the show Baby had plunked down a forty-three-thousand-dollar check, outbidding Oprah Winfrey and Princess Margaret for an original Kelly Swett ensemble: an Art-Bra – a frightening, gleaming bustier covered with gold-plated thumbtacks – and an Art-Girdle, an equally dangerous matching chastity belt. Her husband Count Hugo Luegodago, was in Uruguay that week, attending to the beef business, so I was invited to the Fifth Avenue triplex palace for a drink. The drink led to a private fashion show.

'Magnificent!' I said, attempting to unhook the porcupiney Kelly Swett bra, stabbing my fingers on tacks. 'Ouch!'

'Seff segz,' Baby said in her thick Uruguayan accent, wagging a long silver fingernail in my face.

'How do I get them off?' I asked.

'Vary carfoolly.'

So Baby and I became lovers. Yes, she was older, in her late fifties to my early thirties, but the body was hard (from riding horses) and the breasts were rocky (from her surgeon) and the accent was a complete fake.

'I'm a wop from Bensonhoist,' she told me, after double-jointed sex, as she put Mickey Mouse Band-Aids on my punctured fingers. 'I met da Count back when I was just a kid in da chorus line in Vegas. He's da only one what knows I ain't a spic. Even my son Diego don't know. Ya bettah not rat me out.'

'My lips are sealed with Krazy Glue,' I said, making a lip-zippering motion. 'I hear Cashampton is lovely this time of year.'

'Ya little fuckin' snake, ya tryin' to glom an *in*vite?'

'Why, Baby, I'd love to visit . . . that is, if it's alright with the Count.'

'Dat peanut-dick? He does what I tell 'im.'

So there I was, a guest at the Upton Riding Club, swimming in the chubby Count's baggy riding clothes. It was, in fact, my first time on horseback. Growing up middle-class in snobby Westfield, New Jersey, the son of an accountant father and a librarian mother (both dead now), the closest I ever came to the Horse World was watching television re-runs of that four-legged poetic genius Mr. Ed: 'I grow old I grow old/ I shall eat my sweet oats rolled.' But, as I kept telling myself, Baby Luegodago is my host, and I cannot offend my host. She is providing me with food and drink and shelter from the *Sturm und Drang* – not to mention the varied treasures of her surgically-augmented Las Vegas-trained body. Plus, some of the foremost collectors of Pollocks keep their horses here. And this is where Pollock lived. This is Pollock country.

'Mr. Lymon, this is Count Hugo's horse, Gandhi,' said Kurtis, the chief groom, passing me the horse's reins. He was tall and handsome – a muscular Bob Marley with short hair.

'What the hell did I get myself into?' I asked, watching Baby ride Pancho Villa out the stable door into the drizzle.

'I don't know, pal,' Kurtis said, whacking Gandhi's rump and sending the huge horse on its way. 'But if you fall off, try not to land on your head.'

Oh, my sore posterior. I was sitting beneath a large Pollock mural, sipping brandy, at the exquisitely appointed dinner table in the glassed-in dining room overlooking the dramatic whitecapped ocean, at the extraordinary home of Big Barton Snitbread, the pharmaceuticals magnate.

The house – more castle than house – was near the Upton Riding Club in Cashampton By The Sea, and the grounds were immense and green, blocked from prying eyes by twenty-foot-high hedges. Upon arrival, Big Barton (he insisted on being called Big Barton, and truly the man merited the moniker) had given me the grand tour. As we putt-putted about the dusk-draped rain-heavy fields in a golf-cart, he pointed out fifteen fat shaggy buffalo, a pair of camels, five ostriches, and in a special field an old solitary horse. 'My pride and joy,' my host explained. 'Trigger's grandson, Fred. Bought him from Roy Rogers.'

Dinner had been delightful. To start with: fresh crab-salad, goldfish sushi, and tender slivers of Louisiana alligator pro-sciutto; followed by Long Island duckling with an Albanian bruised-cherry sauce and a warm baby-ginger and leek salad; for the main course, tender filets of Kobe-style buffalo steak ('They're fed with imported beer,' Big Barton had boasted, 'and receive a Swedish full-body massage three times a week!' No wonder they'd seemed so relaxed) and lightly-blanched asparagus tips, with a dollop of creamed purple Peruvian potatoes on the side – wine, wine, and even more wine throughout – and for dessert, guava sorbet; topped off by Cappuccino made with coffee from Borneo and fresh frothing organic goat's milk; and for each guest: a handcarved antique whalebone toothpick, a sample two-pack of Big Barton's Speed-Lax, and a ten-inch length of Zimbabwean silk dental floss which, according to our host, had been 'created for your flossing pleasure by the hardiest damn silk-worms on the planet.'

There were twelve of us there, digging and flossing bits of 'gator and goldfish and buffalo from our teeth: Big Barton and his wife Sarah (puffy-faced, dozing-eyed, she fell asleep twice before the main course), their daughter Muffy Snitbread-Gritz (a very pretty blonde in her late thirties) and her husband Jonas Gritz (the thin-lipped blonde scion of the Gritz Electronics fortune, with a bandaged broken nose — 'I fell off a goddamn horse,' he'd said with a grim laugh over pink gins), Egon Bibble-Booth (the public relations flack and famed walker of presidents' wives — brother of Evan Bibble-Booth, the opera-critic), Baroness Sonja Dreckenzorfer (widow of the late German automobile kaiser Baron Klaus Dreckenzorfer and mother of the famed Dreckenzorfer Quintuplets), Clara and Reggie Spoon (art dealers I knew slightly from the Sharon Timlin days), John Dough (dubbed by the *New York Post* 'The Pearl Man,' by the *Daily News* 'The Man of Many Pearls' — he had just bought the former Mulrooney Estate (furnished), and all through dinner had sat silent, fumbling a bit with the silverware, sneaking glances at Muffy Snitbread-Gritz), Auralee Emeraldstein-Bittburg (thirty-something widow of the late ex-Nazi Austrian prime minister), Baby Luegodago (in her Art-Bra — she wouldn't stop feeling my thigh with her hard horny hand), and yours truly. Me! Roger Lymon! Dining under a Pollock! With the Gilded Set! The big-time!

'So, Roger, how is Sammy Stillman these days?' asked Clara Spoon with an impudent coral sneer.

'Quite well. I've just had a letter from him,' I said, shaking my head No to the brandy-refill offered by Pancho, the Mayan-looking butler. 'He has high hopes for the Seminoles' chances next autumn for a national championship.'

'Hear you're a writer,' said Big Barton Snitbread, spitting the word 'writer' as if it were a clot of ugly phlegm caught in his throat, then lighting a cigar.

'Yes,' I said. 'I'm doing a biography of Jackson Pollock.'

'Jesus, not another one!' crowed rail-thin Reggie Spoon in dismay. 'Enough about Pollock. I'm sure Big Barton doesn't care to dredge up the past. Why, at the *Spoon Gallery* – 42 East 57th Street, third floor, take a right off the elevator – we've mounted a terrific exhibition of some lovely, quite-reasonably-priced Neo-Platonic sculptures by Edison St. Pierre, the seven-year-old nephew of the late Jean-Michel Basquiat.'

'Pollock,' – said Big Barton with a fond faraway smile, ignoring Reggie Spoon completely – 'was one of the most interesting and irascible fellows out here.'

'Did you know him well?' I asked.

'Hell yeah. Knew Jack, knew his wife Lee Krasner – Jesus, there was a face that'd make a Mack Truck pull a 360 – knew 'em all. De Kooning, Gracie Hartigan, Franz Kline, Larry Rivers, Phil Pavia. Bill de Kooning's still out here full-time. He's a guinea-pig in a study we're doing on Alzheimer's. Those Action Painters loved to drink – but Pollock! Talk about your original tortured wacko. Pollock was a lulu. You see that picture?' With a casual hairy hand he indicated *Number 3, 1949*, behind me on the wall. 'I had the local pharmacy then – still do – and Pollock ran up a large bill – aspirin, Benzedrine, tranqs – the man was a pharmacist's wet dream, but the poor lush never had a dime to pay. So I took the painting in trade. Considered it charity. Didn't like the picture then – still don't – but last year it was appraised at twenty-two million smackeroos.'

'Niggers,' said Jonas Gritz bitterly.

'Excuse me?' I said, taken aback (to the Old South).

'Goddamn niggers.'

'Jonas, please . . .' beseeched wife Muffy. The faces around the table were blank, but John Dough's lips were flat and angry, a twitch was working his left eye.

Muffy Snitbread-Gritz spoke to the table at large: 'Please forgive my husband. It seems that our daughter has a crush on one of our local black Indians and—'

Sarah Snitbread jolted from her slumber. 'Did somebody say Indians? Ya wanna play that immigrant game?'

'Game?' I asked.

'Sure,' Sarah said, yawning. 'It's a board game from Porker Brothers called "The American Dream." Everyone draws a card that gives them an identity. You could be a Russian Jewboy or a Haitian with AIDS or a Bosnian with a perforated heart and one leg or a Pakistani with eczema, or lots of fun things. You come over to America and then by spinning a wheel and drawing other cards you work out your – how do they say it in the booklet, Big Bart?'

'Your manifest destiny.'

'Right! You know, all sorts of fates. Attend Harvard, live in a slum, drive a taxi, win Lotto, have sex with Madonna, get deported, get AIDS, open a pizza-parlor. It's lots of fun. Last time we played I got to be a Sudanese Muslim who worked in a Jimmy Dean pork-sausage factory in Chicago and married a Mormon beauty queen and ran for Congress but lost then got syphilis and went insane but won Lotto!'

'Look, Mother Snitbread,' Jonas Gritz said, downing his brandy in one shot. 'The *Negro Question* isn't a game that you can just play and put away at the end of the evening; it's a deadly serious subject.'

But Sarah Snitbread was not listening; her head had nodded forward, her neck was now lolling, and great oceanic snores were crashing from her nose and mouth, making the hardy streamer of Zimbabwean floss stuck in her teeth flutter like a flag in the breeze.

Jonas addressed the table: 'I saw one of them on *Nightline* the other night, telling that little Howdy Doody Koppel kike about how when they take over America completely they won't let whites have babies. They'll put us in camps – make us pick cotton as some kind of symbolic punishment and then lynch all the men who don't pull their weight, castrate the good workers, and screw all our women!'

'Mr. Reagan had the right idea,' said Egon Bibble-Booth. 'In fact, it was yours truly who found the autographed first edition of Malthus that Nancy gave to him for Christmas. He always read a few lines before bedtime. . . . Ronnie had the right idea: Contain them in the slums and let them destroy themselves with drugs and AIDS and guns, or else they'll be everywhere.'

'Yah!' yahhed Sonja Dreckenzorfer. 'Zee blocks are eff-ree-whar!'

'Een Souse Amayrica,' said Baby Luegodago, spooning the phony accent on a bit thick, I thought, 'we hov a tay-reeble nee-gair pro-plem.'

'It's true,' said Jonas Gritz. 'Everywhere you look. Jesus, the Upton Riding Club just accepted Diana Ross as a member. Terrific. What next? Free crack and welfare checks with your first ten riding lessons?'

'Personally, I find zem fascinating,' said Auralee Emerald-stein-Bittburg, biting an apple with her large square teeth, a gob of appled spit rolling down her chin. 'Zee sexiest, loffliest people on zee planett – absolutely beautiful.'

'Look at fuckin' Somalia!' Jonas Gritz spewed. 'Those skinny black ants are gonna bite the hand that feeds them – mark my words.'

'You make it sound like a cannibals' picnic,' I said, truly disgusted.

'Picnic my ass,' snorted Jonas Gritz. 'It's a fucking world-class food-fight.'

Clara Spoon jumped in: 'Yes, but do you know that Susan Sontag is over there in a refugee camp outside of Mogadishu, staging *Porgy and Bess*? What a brave woman.'

All of a sudden a chair scraped and John Dough stood up.

He hadn't said two words all night, but now he was staring with volcanic anger at Jonas Gritz.

'Outside, Gritz,' he said. 'You and me, you piece of shit racist motherfucker.'

Bravo, John Dough! I wanted to kiss him. Oh, not like that – I told you, I don't do gay.

Gritz got to his feet. 'I know Scottish Kung Fu, you fucking interloper.'

'So what's it gonna be, boys?' Big Barton soothed them with a smile. 'Guns or knives or bagpipes at dawn?'

Jonas Gritz and John Dough stood staring at each other, breathing loudly.

'You know,' I said, hoping to diffuse the tension. 'You know that Pollock—'

'Shut the fuck up!' yelled Jonas Gritz.

'Johnny?' said Auralee Emeraldstein-Bittburg to the Pearl Man in a strangled whisper, followed by a small rasping cough. 'I feel wiggly.'

'What are the symptoms?' asked Big Barton Snitbread, assuming a professional manner, though it had been many years since he'd donned the pharmacist's smock.

'My head . . .' said Auralee, shaking her blonde pageboy and hiccuping loudly. John Dough patted her back with a gentle callused hand. 'My head . . .'

'Dreenk *agua*, my deah,' suggested Baby Luegodago, the thousand thumbtacks of her Art-Bra shimmering in the candlelight. 'Poot a knife een da glaz an' hold da knife weet yer nose.'

'No,' said Reggie Spoon, as Auralee's hiccups came barking fast and loud. 'A mouthful of peanut butter with a slice of jalapeno pepper will do the trick.'

'*Nein*,' Sonja Dreckenzorfer interjected. 'Ven der Kvintz vere *leibchin* and zey had zee hee-kopfs, vee gafe zem beeyah.

Pancho!' she called for the butler. 'Bring Mrs. Emeraldztein-Bittburg zom beeyah. Cherman beeyah.'

'Now, Auralee,' said Big Barton to the stylish woman whose head snapped and chest heaved with every bark, 'listen to Big Barton. Hold your breath and count to thirty.'

'One Mississippi . . .' counted Clara Spoon.

Auralee's face went from white to pink, and a few of the other guests joined in. Baby Luegodago took the opportunity to massage my disinterested manhood.

'Five Mississippi . . .'

Sarah Snitbread snored on, undisturbed, as the former First Lady of Austria went from pink to red – and now the whole table, except for John Dough and me, were counting. Millionaires and billionaires counting Mississippis as if it was a game of hide-and-go-seek, while Pancho poured a perfectly-headed glass of Heineken beer and placed it in front of Auralee.

'Zat' – screamed Sonja Dreckenzorfer – 'iz not Cherman beeyah! Take it back, Pancho.'

'Yes, Madame.' Pancho's face colored slightly.

'Don't worry Pancho, I'll drink this one,' Big Barton said. 'Get Mrs. Em-Bitt a Dinckelacker.'

'Twelve Mississippi . . .'

Auralee's face was now a deep dark, almost brown shade of red – almost like one of Gauguin's South Sea girls.

'See, she stopped hiccuping!' said Big Barton proudly.

'You can start breathing again,' said Egon Bibble-Booth.

'Take deep breaths, darling,' said Muffy Snitbread-Gritz.

Auralee's skin tone had now deepened to the lush purple of a ripe eggplant, but she hadn't yet drawn breath.

'Maybe she swallowed some fruit wrong!' cried Reggie Spoon.

John Dough lifted her from behind, joined his oyster-hard

hands below her brassiereless breasts, and thumped. The whole party watched with fascination, some sitting, some standing, some wringing their stained napkins, as he thumped again, and again, and again – but no fruit popped forth.

Auralee's eyes bulged froglike with fear. Her neck seemed to lengthen – a la Modigliani on LSD. Her arms shot straight out and she clawed air. Twin jets of crimson flushed out her nose and spilled onto her Donna Karan blouse, and a thin ribbon of red leaked from her lips.

Muffy Snitbread-Gritz and Reggie Spoon screamed.

'*Mein Gott!*' Sonja Dreckenzorfer moaned.

'Holy fucking shit,' said John Dough, echoing my sentiments exactly, lowering Auralee into her Louis XIV teak chair.

'Call a Doctor, Pancho!' I yelled.

Auralee's body stiffened, her face, plump as a gorged tick, quiverered, and – I hesitate to relate this but I must, I must – two thick geysers of blood gushed out her ears and streamed down her neck, one eye swelled out, large as a fried quail's egg, the contact lens sparkling, and then, as if in a Stephen King story – but this was no twisted fiction, it was a shocking real-life medical emergency – the eyeball burst from its socket with such force that all connective tissue tore free and, like a perfectly launched Michael Jordan jump-shot, the blue-yolked orb described an exact parabola above the table and plopped with a high-diver's baby splash into the crystal bowl of melted guava sorbet.

I had to look into the drip-dotted Pollock to keep from fainting.

'Here's your German beer, Madame' said Pancho, entering the dining-room and expertly pouring a Dinckelacker.

'Well, everybody' said Sarah Snitbread, waking from her nap with a start and pulling her bloody Zimbabwean floss from her teeth as Reggie Spoon retchingly deposited duckling and goldfish and 'gator onto the tablecloth and Big Barton grabbed and inhaled the Dinckelacker — 'who wants to play "The American Dream"?'

Three

'WE ARE HERE today to say goodbye to Auralee Laurelai
Bratwurst Emeraldstein-Bittburg, beloved widow of Kurt
Bittburg, devoted daughter of Fritz and Hilda Bratwurst,
treasured mother of Christian and Courtney Emeraldstein,
snatched from the prime of life by the cruel unwashed teeth of
death, leaving a gaping painful cavity in all her loved ones'
lives . . .'

Finally, a sunny day. I stifled a yawn and burped a bit of
caviar omelet as the society minister, The Reverend Doctor
Jasper Jurkbaitt — a former dentist — of the non-denomina-
tional 42nd Street Church, rattled on about the life and the
proposed afterlife of the late lamented Auralee. The faces at
graveside were somber, if perhaps a bit bored. Twins Courtney
and Christian, eleven, standing with their father, Auralee's first
husband, the noted divorce lawyer Marvin Lorca Emeraldstein,
fidgeted and pinched one another. They hadn't known their
mother well. She'd been divorced from Marvin Lorca for

years, hadn't even fought for custody — something about being caught on videotape performing aerobics *au naturel* with a fitness instructor from Klaatu's Studio — perhaps even Klaatu himself. And then she'd married Kurt Bittburg, right before the scandal about his Nazi past had hit.

Auralee's parents, who looked like Bavarian hillbillies, resplendent in matching K-Mart-style brown pantsuits, wept openly. A good crowd, many of them socialites and members of the Upton Riding Club, riding hats in hand, wearing appropriately black jodhpurs and boots, all stood about with sad blank faces. The emergency room doctor at Cashampton General had said the cause of death was the most massive brain hemmhorage he'd ever encountered.

There was my hostess, Countess Luegodago, with her husband, Count Hugo, who'd flown into Cashampton Airport on his private jet the night before, exiling me to a guest room and some well-deserved rest for once; Mariah and Fergus Frankfurter; Muffy Snitbread-Gritz; Big Barton and Sarah Snitbread; author Jay Macaroni and his wife, the actress Oma Munson; the blind writer of lifestyle books, Bertha Seward; Klaatu the Serbian fitness expert (who squeezed a Spaldeen ball throughout the proceedings); John Dough; Marmalind and Portius Pleistocene; Hank Upton, the owner of the club, and some employees, Kurtis the chief groom, Maria the instructor, and a few young female grooms.

I peeled away from the crowd and wandered the cemetery. Green River Cemetery. Where Jackson Pollock and many other famous artists were buried: Jimmy Ernst, Ad Rheinhardt, Elaine de Kooning, Stuart Davis — just a few who'd followed Pollock, the pie-eyed piper, to the sleepy little field of graves.

A huge boulder on a rise marked the site of Jackson Pollock's grave. A brass plaque bearing Jackson's signature was tacked to the rock, identifying the occupant as the tortured Babe Ruth of Abstract Expressionism. Atop of the boulder had been placed three Camel cigarettes, an empty bottle of Jack Daniel's, and a softball.

'They buried Lee at his feet,' said a thin, tall, very old man with an accent who had appeared silently at my side, pointing to a smaller stone. 'She'll be pissed off for all eternity. Yah, very ironic. And the softball – now that is a nice touch.'

'Pollock liked softball?'

'No, Jackson liked wrestling. He was indifferent to games that required coordination. A bit clumsy. But when he painted, then he was graceful. But the softball refers to a day in '54, a softball game we had . . .'

I gave a start: My God, it was Willem de Kooning – Pollock's friend and greatest painting rival. Along with Jackson and Franz Kline, one of the three kings of the New York School.

De Kooning chattered on:

'The historians mark that as a turning point, the day the movement started to die. We had stayed up late the night before, drinking too much, blowing up balloons and tying them to trees. Painting the pennies gold and scattering them on the lawn. Listening to the jazz. Elaine painted a grapefruit just like a ball, white with the stitching red, the Spalding label, everything. It was Franz Kline's idea. Yah! She also painted a coconut. Next day Franz was catching. Pavia was batting. Franz walks out to the pitcher, Esteban Vicente, and gives him the grapefruit-ball. Now it would not have worked if Philip had not been such a good batter. Vicente pitches, Pavia swings – boom! – grapefruit all over! Ah, Philip was so angry, the pulp in his eyes and hair. Everyone laughs. "Please, Philip, it was a joke," we say. "Don't be angry." So he wipes his face and goes back to the bat. Franz confers with Vicente, slips him the coconut-ball. Vicente pitches, Pavia swings – crack! – the coconut splits open. We were rolling, rolling. Funniest thing I ever saw. What a moment! The last happy time we were all together. After that, down the hill it went.'

'I've read about that,' I said. 'But I was of the impression that the second ball was also a grapefruit.'

'Coconut. Take my word, sonny; it was a coconut.'

'Was Pollock there?'

'Yah, Jackson was there. He wandered off with a girl—'

'Ruth Kligman?'

'No no. Before Ruthie. This one was young, and really' – his long white painter's hands gracefully traced the universal hourglass shape – 'really someone delicious, a young, young woman.'

'Do you recall her name?'

'Jackson and the girl walked off into the woods,' he said, ignoring my question, lost in the memories, smiling. 'Lee was so mad.' He sighed. 'Who could blame her? What she put up with. Yah, but she could be a real ball-buster.'

'Mr. de Kooning, you might not remember me . . .' I looked at the pale blue eyes. The old guy must have been ninety. They said he had Alzheimer's and hadn't even been aware who the guest-of-honor was when his ex-wife Elaine was being interred down the slope. 'I met you a few years ago with Sharon Timlin.'

'The crazy redhead with the potato?' His Dutch accent was fine and lilting, and when he grinned, I blushed. 'Yah, I remember; you are the reviewer, the *Artnews* boy. Elaine said you had great potential. Roger Lemon.'

Lemon, Lymon, what did it matter? A genius – a living silver-haired immortal – knew me!

'Actually, sir, it's Lymon.'

'Yah, Lymon: the fellow who wrote the Sammy Stillman biography.'

'You know it, Mr. de Kooning? I'm honored.'

'You seem surprised, Mr. Lymon. Sure I know it. The premise that Stillman was the perfect post-Pop Pop-artist – no ego, no nostalgia, no training, no talent. Very amusing. Since I began taking my new medication I do not forget anymore.'

'That's remarkable.'

'I thank young Barton Snitbread for that.'

'Big Barton?'

'The miracle drug – Alz-Well it is called – he developed it. I am one of the first patients in the experimental program.'

'Did you know Mrs. Emeraldstein-Bittburg?'

'Yah, she was one sweet kid. She came to me recently and wanted a small picture. Offered me two-million dollars. I did not accept. It was Nazi money.'

'Nazi money?'

'Yah, from that Bittburg, the husband. But Auralee was persistent; she got the painting. We bartered.' He looked happy as a child telling a friend about a new puppy. 'I gave her a picture and she gave me a taste of her precious little plum.'

'I'm not sure I understand.'

'Don't be dense, Lymon,' de Kooning said irritably. 'I went down on her. I may be old, yah, but I still have a taste for the women.' His pale, long, handsome old-man's face broke into a sneaky grin and he reached into his baggy paint-streaked pants' pocket and fished out a half-pint of gin. 'And I still have a taste for the gin.'

'I thought you quit,' I said, surprised.

'Sssh.' He placed a finger to his lips, looked around. A pair of birds chirped and flew about trees still stripped for winter. A lone dark figure limped a ways off. It was Kurtis the groom.

'This is a no-no. My daughter will kill me. "Daddy, paint," she says. Always: "Daddy you must work." Am I a painter or am I a mule? But this morning, I feel so good,' he said, nipping from the bottle, passing it to me, and then performing a spry little jig. 'Yah! Have a drink with old Bill. Have one for Jackson.'

'To Jackson Pollock,' I said, and drank. 'To Jackson Pollock and little boys.'

'Little boys?' De Kooning looked at me curiously.

'Yes,' I said. 'I have heard that Pollock was fond of youngsters in his last years. Do you recall any boys he had a thing for?'

'Yah, Jackson had a boy.' He put a finger to his mouth conspiratorially. 'It was a secret.' He drank again.

'Do you remember the boy's name?'

'Boy?' A blank look came over his face.

'Yes, Pollock's little friend.'

'Pollock?'

'Yes, your friend, Jackson Pollock.'

'Pollack is a kind of fish, no? I do not like fish.'

'Father!' An angry vibrating woman had snuck up on us and batted the bottle out of de Kooning's hand. 'You know that alcohol ruins your medicine.' She looked at me with loathing. 'If he dies, I'll have you up on murder charges.'

'Now, look here, lady, it was Mr. de Kooning's bottle—'

'Come, Father.' She steered him away. 'You have to paint after lunch. We're having fish for lunch.'

'Fish?' He looked at the sky. 'I do not like fish.'

'Goodbye, sir,' I said, picking up the bottle; and the old man – deconstructed by time and booze and now reconstructed by Big Barton Snitbread – turned and grinned at me. I finished his gin and placed the empty on Jackson's boulder.

'I do not like fish,' he called, 'but I love Pollock.'

*　　　*　　　*

The Emeraldstein-Bittburg service was over and people were meandering about, reading the names of dead artists.

'I paid two-point-eight mil for a de Kooning sculpture,' said Mariah Frankfurter to Muffy Snitbread-Gritz with a sigh. 'When he croaks I'll sell it for ten-plus; but now it's on my lawn and the birds use it for a toilet.'

'Hello, Muffy,' I said to Big Barton's daughter, falling in step with the shapely blonde as she trod the grass. 'Are you feeling okay?'

'Oh, hi there, Roger. I'm a bit rocky. I haven't been sleeping well since . . .'

'Me too,' I said, though my sleeplessness had more to do with the nightly ministrations of Nurse Luegodago than Auralee's grisly goodbye. We walked along the cold ground in silence, losing Mariah along the way. The air was crisp, and the breeze tangy with Cash Bay salt.

'There's Kurtis,' Muffy said. 'He and Auralee were close.'

Kurtis was standing in front of a trio of graves, his face streaked with tears.

'I'm sorry about Auralee, Kurtis,' said Muffy, placing a delicate hand on the groom's bulging shoulder. The horsy set was very democratic when it came to death. 'She was a terrific girl, and she cared for you deeply.'

'I know,' Kurtis said.

We stood in silence. The three graves were marked with simple, inexpensive stones. Leonard Heathcliff Schwartz, Valerie Foote Schwartz, Gilbert Schwartz. There were fresh flowers on all three graves; and judging by the lack of grass in front of their headstones, Gilbert and Valerie Schwartz were fairly new residents of Green River Cemetery.

'And I'm sorry,' said Muffy, 'about Specs. He had a hard life.'

'Yeah,' said Kurtis, and his eyes welled. 'Here lies Gilbert

Schwartz, twenty years of shoveling shit at the Upton Riding Club, died a virgin suicide with pimples.'

'Leonard Schwartz?' I asked. 'Wasn't he a painter? One of Pollock's gang?'

'Specs's father was a gardener,' said Muffy.

'Step-father,' said Kurtis. 'Leo painted too. Never made a cent at it.'

'It's nice of you to bring flowers,' I said. 'Were you and Specs close?'

New tears spilled from Kurtis's eyes. I could have kicked myself.

'He was my cousin. My uncle Josiah adopted his mother and her sister. But it wasn't me brung the flowers. Probably his aunt Esther.'

'But you really cared for Specs,' Muffy stated. 'That's what counts.'

'And he was in love with you, Muffy.'

'Me?' She seemed surprised. 'I never knew.'

'The three of us went to Cashampton High together,' Kurtis explained to me, wiping his eyes, sniffling, taking a big breath and letting it out in a long sad sigh. 'Muffy was the Queen, I was the Jock, and Gilbert—'

A muffled sob came from behind the grave of Valerie Schwartz. I went to investigate. It was John Dough.

'Mr. Dough . . .' I said. 'Are you okay?'

'My mother,' he said, standing. 'My mother, she died a while back.' John Dough wiped his tears and joined us in front of the graves. 'All these graves got me thinking . . . I guess I'm still mourning my mother.'

'Kurtis, meet John Dough. John Dough, this is Kurtis . . . ?'

'Kurtis Swimming Otter Cash,' said the Pearl Man.

'Do I know you?' the groom asked.

'No, but I know you. Five years in Attica. I read about it in the newspaper.'

'Fuck the newspaper,' said Kurtis.

'Kurtis,' said Muffy. 'None of us at the club thought you did it, and you received a full pardon.'

'For what?' I asked, but Muffy dug a sharp elbow into my ribs.

John Dough broke the silence: 'How did Gilbert Schwartz die?'

'Dumb motherfucker took a midnight swim,' Kurtis said, laughing. 'They never found his body.'

'Look, how about we all get a drink?' I suggested, because damned if I was going to stand around all day in some cold cemetery, talking about some suicided horseshit-shoveler, when I was looking for clues to the Pollock puzzle.

'Thanks, but I got to get to work,' said Kurtis, shaking my hand, shaking John Dough's hand, shaking Muffy's hand, shaking a leg.

'I'll take a rain check,' said Muffy Snitbread-Gritz. 'My daughter's cat has a psychiatrist appointment.'

'Nothing serious, I hope?'

'We're not really sure yet,' said Muffy. 'The psychic thinks—'

'I thought you said psychiatrist?'

'The psychic recommended the psychiatrist. Madame Szabo picked up some very strange vibrations from Tabby — "cosmic queerness" she called it — possibly related to psychological trauma experienced in kittenhood. Anyhow, I can't be late. This the first session and you know how Freudians are about being late.'

'Of course,' I said. Though the closest I'd ever been to a shrink was the 1990 show at Barry Nogosian's gallery of the pipe-cleaner mandalas of the famed cross-dressing Jungian, Dr. Everett Silt.

'Mr. Dough?' I asked. 'A drink?'

'Hell, yeah,' said John Dough, shivering. 'Right about now I could use a drink.'

'That Muffy Snitbread-Gritz is gorgeous,' John Dough proclaimed over shots of Wild Turkey 101 with Budweiser chasers at Fish Head Danny's, a countrified dump on Fireplace Road, not far from where Jackson Pollock had died.

'She certainly is,' I agreed.

'Her husband's a troubled man.'

'He certainly is.' Now this was Roger Lymon territory – up-close and cozy. 'That's the kind of asshole who needs complete reprograming.'

John Dough's handsome face broke into a wide happy grin. He clapped a large hand on my shoulder and gripped hard.

'You're a decent fucking guy, Roger.'

'Thanks, Mr. Dough,' I said.

'Call me John.'

'John.'

'Bartender,' called the Pearl Man, 'Another for me and my friend here. And drinks on me, for the house.'

The house consisted of a few old men in overalls drinking their lunch, and a few young men who appeared to be still drinking their breakfast.

'They're called Bonackers' John Dough explained – 'because their ancestors fished the Accabonac Bay before it was renamed Cash Bay.'

'Yes, I recall reading a review of a Peter Matthiessen book on the subject.'

The Bonackers nodded demure thanks as the bartender slopped beers and shots of bar-brand liquor in front of them.

'What's your name, buddy?' John Dough asked the geezer who refilled our shot-glasses and took our cash.

'Fish Head Danny,' said the pasty-skinned septuagenarian. The name suited him. He looked remarkably like a pouting albino trout.

'Have a drink with us,' said John Dough.

Fish Head Danny surveyed our fancy dark suits and said, 'Why the hell not?' 'So what are you swells doing in a dive like this?' asked Fish Head Danny as he sipped a Lite Beer.

'Havin' a few pops after a funeral,' said John Dough, admirably slipping into the working man's vernacular.

'Ain't you? ain't you the fellow what fought in Vietnam and then got all them pearls from over there in Arabia?'

'Meet John Dough,' I said.

'An honor, pal.' They shook hands.

'No, man,' said the Pearl Man, 'the honor's mine.'

'And who are you?' asked Fish Head Danny.

'Roger Lymon, from *Artnews*. I'm—'

'Aw Christ, is Billy de Kooning sick again?'

'No, he's fine,' I said, 'I'm doing a piece on his friend Jackson.'

'Reggie Jackson's got a place in Montauk.'

'Not Reggie Jackson – Jackson Pollock!'

'Excitable little cuss, ain't he?' Fish Head Danny winked at John Dough.

'Aw, he's alright,' the Pearl Man said, draping my shoulders with a massive arm. 'Little fucker's been in The City too long. I think I'll take him home and make him mow the lawn.'

This was not going well.

'Don't get so excited, Art-Snooze.' Fish Head Danny poured me a shot. 'You wanna know about Jack The Dripper? I'll tellya: Jack was like a goddamn cowboy or a football player or a wrestler in a sensitive guy's body, and it tore him up inside. You could never tell how many he'd had. Not until he'd slugged somebody, or put a stool through the window, or asked some guy's wife to fuck. He was a lousy drinker, a lousy painter, and I liked him a helluva lot. He was finest kind. I still miss him.'

'Did he have a lover?'

'Hell yeah.'

'Who?'

'Himself.'

'C'mon, Mr. Fish Head, you can tell me.'

'You know what Jackson's favorite expression was, junior?'

'Tell me.'

' "Fuck off!" '

'How about this Gilbert Schwartz guy?' John Dough asked, laughing at Fish Head Danny's wit – though I found no humor therein. 'We saw his grave over at Green River. What was he like?'

Fish Head Danny shook his head. 'When other guys had kids in high school, that poor fucker still had pimples. But he took good care of his mother, Specs did. She passed on recently. A fire.' Fish Head Danny made the sign of the cross. 'Y'know, back in the old days she was a real looker. Her and her sister. Valerie and Esther. They was in one of them Nazi camps, then got adopted by a colored sergeant from Cashampton, Josiah Foote. . . . Esther married-up well, a Wall Street WASP-type, but Val had it rough, 'specially after Leo Schwartz bought it in a car crash. And Specs . . . well, the kids teased Specs kinda brutal-like when he was a young, y'know – called him Pizzaface. But whaddaya expect? Guy with pimples and glasses, and bald like he was before he could vote. But still, suicide's a fucking shame.'

John Dough smiled sadly and said: 'Maybe he's happy now.'

'Maybe so,' admitted Fish Head Danny.

'Well,' I said, 'if you remember anything about Pollock that I might use, please give me a call at—'

'Call him at my place.' John Dough threw an arm around my shoulder. 'The Mulrooney Estate. I'm adopting this little bastard.'

'The Mulrooney spread,' Fish Head said. 'That's where Specs Schwartz lived. He was the caretaker.'

'No shit?' said John Dough, but he didn't sound very surprised.

Four

I AM HONEST enough to admit that I am basically a very dishonest man. Which explains what I was doing snooping around John Dough's desk some three weeks after I'd moved into his mansion. But, gentle reader, I'm getting ahead of myself.

Since those tantalizing little crumbs of hearsay which the resurrected, if unreliable, Willem de Kooning had thrown my way, I'd had nothing but fruitless sniffing. Everyone in Cashampton, it seemed, told the same fatigued stories: Pollock the bad driver; Pollock the impoverished moody genius; Pollock the kind, crazy, sensitive, frustrated, agonized, doomed drunk; but none of the juicy Jackson-with-his-pants-down follies, co-starring jaunty juvenile buttocks, that Hiroshi had hoped for. And when I phoned de Kooning's home, my very politely-worded request for an interview with old Bill was met by his daughter with a hostile, resounding, downright Pollocky 'Fuck off!'

Which is not to say that I wasn't having a fine time – I was. The weeks with John Dough had been highly amusing. The man could drink, and he kept the house stunningly stocked with Wild Turkey and beer (domestic beer, like any good patriot who might have been a POW), and women were drawn to him like flies to . . . well, like pigs to truffles, and he took his pleasure with the various models and socialite sweeties compulsively, rarely allowing his contented con-quests a second night, though they tried – inspired by visions of snagging the Pearl Man and becoming Mrs. John Dough – Lord knows they tried.

John behaved as you would expect a handsome man in his late thirties with over eighty million dollars to behave: he was a conspicuous consumer. Free with his money, loaning me his wine-red Jaguar on request, buying a ten-thousand-dollar membership for me (along with his own) at the Upton Riding Club (though he refused to attire himself in the elaborate outfits that the Uptonites wore, choosing, instead, to ride in jeans and sneakers and a New York Yankees cap), sending out to The Pregnant Duchess gourmet-food store each day for hundreds of dollars worth of finger-food delicacies – he would introduce me to his female visitors (who I came to think of as his string of pearl-girls) as 'my little buddy, Roger.' Not that I was small – I was six-foot-tall and a well-toned hundred-and-sixty pounds (from jog-ging) – but poolside, next to John's sculpted mountain physique, 'little buddy' was, I am sad to report, a rather apt description.

His most curious attribute, though – besides mowing his own lawn, sweeping his own tennis court for the guests, refusing to hire servants, and a decided unfamiliarity with such recent modern conveniences as the phone-answering ma-chine, microwave oven, and VCR – was a seemingly inordinate curiosity about the Upton Riding Club's late stall-mucker Specs Schwartz. At every bar we drank in – be it Billy Truck's (a polished-wood bar much-favored by the horsy set) or the rough and tumble Iggy BooBoo's or the hip and stylish Timothy's Talkhouse (where Dustin Hoffman, the actor, introduced himself to the Pearl Man and asked for an autograph) or the yuppified barnlike Danceteria – he'd ask – waitresses and bartenders and patrons – had they known Specs? 'What was he really like?' Every groom who saddled our horses, he'd question about poor Specs: 'Did you hate him? Did you tease him? What did you really think of him?' And Specs, in contrast to John Dough, seemed such a sad, comical, wretched figure, the direct opposite of the glorious Pearl Man. I wondered, Why the interest? Was he writing a screenplay?

As the month of May trickled along, trees budding, flowers blooming, air growing warm and sweet-smelling with summer's promise, we attended all the local events of importance: the fundraising galas (including Mariah and Fergus Frankfurter's bash for the Cashampton Equine Family Planning Organization), the society weddings, the cocktail and dinner to-do's; and of course, how could we miss the lavish funeral for Pumpy The Pony? – The Reverend Doctor Jasper Jurkbaitt presiding, Billy Joel and Paul Simon singing a duet of 'Nearer My God To Thee' – who'd tragically passed away and been cremated, after a brief illness at a special clinic for horses in Connecticut. As they buried the Grecian urn-enclosed ashes of the late Pumpy in a plot out behind Hank Upton's house by the stables, the Uptonites wept. Huge, hot, sobbing tears of sorrow. It was understandable – many of the younger equestrian generations had taken their first rides on old Pumpy. He was a sentimental link to their childhood, to a time of long-lost innocence, to sexless broken maidenheads. But why, I wondered, why was John Dough wiping his eyes?

As the days slipped by and the quest for Pollock gems seemed more and more a remote quixotic dream, I began to consider a biography on the Man Of Many Pearls; but John Dough was vague about his past, never validating or discounting any of the rumors; and though he was a walking-talking multi-million-dollar mystery, the man was a veritable oracle on the subject of Cashampton history. Upon purchasing the Mulrooney Estate, he told me, he had combed the local library for books pertaining to the area and its past.

From him I learned that the portion of Long Island which comprised Cashampton (the township that encompasses the villages of Montauk, Amagansett, Sag Harbor, The Springs, Cashampton, and Cashampton By The Sea – perhaps the richest of the rich enclaves) had been known until the early 1960s as the South Fork or the East End. All that Cashampton business came later, with the locust-like invasion of the swarming summer hordes.

The town's history was a microcosm of the American Experience. Go back four hundred years: Take a few tribes of peaceful Indians living in harmony with nature – a plentiful supply of fish, corn, ground nuts, whales, and wildlife – add a few handfuls of English, led by the voracious moralist Tiger Edgar Cash, who eliminated, for the most part, the male Indians by the standard Christian methods of smallpox and gunfire, while bedding and impregnating the surviving females, throw in, over time, slavery, farming, piracy, maritime trade, whaling, war, and tourism, alternately bake and freeze and soak with rain, whip with the occasional hurricane, add some more agriculture (eventually mostly potato farms), some clamming and scalloping and fishing, retain a few Indians, mix them with the freed blacks, add some artists, sprinkle with rich summering New Yorkers, then bring in the developers, build and build and build, pollute the waters, decimate the aquatic industry, spray the whole area with moneyed New York Socialites and Art World types – and *voilà*: modern day Cashampton.

'License and registration,' said the Cashampton cop who stopped us for going one mile per hour above the limit on the two-lane Sag Harbor Highway in the Jaguar. John Dough leaned over me, his blond hair crazed from the wind, and dug in the glove box for papers.

The sandy-haired cop looked at the registration with slitted eyes.

'This car is registered to Punck and Pinck, Attorneys At Law . . .' The officer scratched his razor-rashed neck. 'Which one are you, sir, Punck or Pinck?'

'Neither,' said John Dough. 'I'm—'

'License,' he ordered.

'I must've left it at home,' the Pearl Man said.

The cop unsnapped his holster guard and lightly fingered his gun.

'I'll have to ask you gentlemen to step out of the vehicle – slowly.'

We got out.

'Name and address?' he asked John Dough.

'John Dough, Mulrooney Estate, Hither'n Yon Lane, Cashampton By The—'

'The Pearl Man?' the cop asked. Oh shit, I thought, now we're in for it. These small-town cops hate the rich.

The cop broke into a grin. 'Holy Christ! You *are* him. Shit, Mr. Dough, it would be a real honor to shake your hand.'

'Call me John, Officer,' said the gracious Pearl Man, shaking the cop's hand.

'Hell, John, it's an honor. You're a real frikkin' hero. Took a whole platoon of gooks out before they gotya, huh?'

John Dough stared at his feet and blushed slightly, shuffled a bit in the roadside gravel. How fucking humble can you get?

'And that POW camp up in Laos! And those heathen Turkey dudes and the pearl-diving! You've had some life. I read all about it in *Stan's Paper*.' Ah, the local newspaper article which had been headlined 'THE PEARL MAN CO-METH'. 'C'mon, I'll give you an escort.' He blushed a little, hemmed a bit and asked: 'If it ain't too much to ask, John, could I get an autograph?'

'No problem,' said the Man Of Many Pearls, climbing in the driver's side and reaching for a slice of paper from the dash. It was the engraved invitation to the Pumpy The Pony farewell.

'Who do I make it out to?'

'To . . .' The cop blushed again. 'My son's name is Bobby, my wife's name is Bobbie – short for Roberta – my name is Bobby too.'

'To the Bobbies,' said John Dough, writing and reading. 'The world is your oyster. From your friend, John Dough.'

'Gee thanks, Mr. Dough.'

'By the way,' said John Dough, starting the Jaguar purring, 'if you have some free time one of these days, I'd love for you to come out to the house. There's some questions I'd like to ask about Gilbert Schwartz.'

'Pizzaface?' Bobby the cop asked, puzzled, then, seeing the Pearl Man's frown, breaking into a sweet innocent grin. 'Why sure, John.'

And then we drove, at ninety miles-per-hour, the cop's siren blaring in front of us, past newly-nubbed corn fields, past potato fields in spring flower, past greening woods where baby deer nibbled sweet fresh leaves, all the way to shore of Cash Bay.

* * *

'Ahoy, Pearl Man!' called Big Barton Snitbread from behind the wheel of a gleaming sixty-foot-long gold cigarette boat called *Speed-Lax 1*. Thick black smoke spewed with a tubercular rumble from the idling boat's rear end.

Sag Harbor Wharf – which, according to John Dough had been a hustling bustling whaling port in the 18th century, the world's largest, conducting more seafaring trade with Europe and the Caribbean than even New York City – was near dead in the mist. A few listless dirty seagulls sat on pilings.

'What's shaking, Mr. Snitbread?' asked John Dough, pumping the hand of the man who'd parlayed a nation's constipation into a billion-dollar fortune.

'My friends call me Big Barton.'

'You look very sporty today, Big Barton,' I complimented. He resembled a bloated Kennedy-clone: elephantine white duck pants, Docksiders the size of flippers, a blue Lacoste shirt, and a white yachtsman cap with gold braid.

'*You* can call me Mr. Snitbread.' He handed me a limp fish of a hand to shake – or perhaps kiss. The seagulls watched hungrily. 'You like the boat, John?'

'How many knots does she do?' I asked, but the billionaire ignored me.

'You look good today, John. I think you'll be very excited by the lab. We're always open for new investors.'

'You know, Mr. Snitbread,' I said, 'in the film I'm writing I foresee some truly meaty scenes between you and Jackson. You and Pollock, in your first drugstore, discussing life and art and aspirin—'

'So, John,' Big Barton broke in, 'have you thought of investing anywhere?'

'I see someone like, say, Luke Perry playing the young Big Barton,' I persisted.

'Have to be bigger.' Big Barton never took his eyes off John Dough. 'Bigger star, bigger man. Someone on the order of a young Gary Cooper, someone like the Pearl Man here.'

'Hmm.' I scratched my head. 'I'll have to think about it. But it will be a strong juicy role worthy of Academy Award consideration. That I can guarantee.'

'In that case, Ralph,' he said, goosing the motor. 'Call me Big Barton.'

'The name is Roger,' I said, as we docked at the pier on Cash Island.

'Had to contribute big units to the Retired Bonacker's Association to expedite a zoning adjustment,' said the billionaire to John Dough, hoisting his heft onto the dock, nodding at the armed sentry. 'Welcome to Cash Island. Cost me seventy-five mil, just for the land.'

The island, six miles in length, three miles at its widest – a mile-and-a-half off the mainland – appeared to be peaceful and green and uninhabited.

'I've read about this place,' said John Dough. 'The Indians used it as a graveyard, called it the Island Of The Dead.'

'Well, John, as you'll soon see, Cash Island is now dedicated to the fabulous adventure of life.'

'Isn't this where Captain Kidd buried some treasure?' asked the Pearl Man.

'Correctamundo,' said Big Barton, seating us in a golf-cart driven by a young black man in hospital whites. 'William Kidd was a Wall Street banker who did a little pirating on the side. He struck a deal with Medgar Cash, the grandson of Tiger Edgar Cash, our town's founder. Traded him some captured Africans and a couple of barrels of rum for six sheep, a barrel of cider, a new pair of socks, and the right to bury his treasure here. Then Kidd surrendered to the English Crown, himself and the treasure – thought he could work a deal. Dumb move: They executed the poor bastard. You hate to see a versatile fellow like that get the shaft.'

'I read that he raped one of the African women,' said John Dough, as we passed another sentry.

'I suppose it depends on your definition of rape, John. Who's to say? After giving birth, the woman hung herself. Kidd's daughter grew up here, ended up one of old Medgar's concubines. He called himself Lord Medgar, was partial to Indian squaws. They say even as an old man, when Lord Medgar took a bath in the Bay, the fish quit swimming – to keep from getting rear-ended.'

The cart crested a ridgetop and there was the old Cash Mansion, a plantation-style manor guarded by a pair of uniforms with guns.

'Lord Medgar loved his subjects dearly,' Big Barton pronounced. 'Which explains why so many blacks and Indians around here have the Cash nametag sewn into their sweat-suits.'

'Like Kurtis Swimming Otter Cash,' said John Dough.

'Like Kurtis,' concurred Big Barton. 'If bloodlines meant anything, Kurtis would own most of Cashampton, plus sizable chunks of Ghana and Wall Street.

'And now,' he said, disembarking from the cart, tipping the driver a quarter, while John Dough slipped the man a C-note. 'The grand tour.'

The original mansion, our host informed us, had been burnt down in the 1940s for the insurance money by the 'white-trash Bonacker' branch of the Cash family, who had invested the proceeds in – and still ran – the Cashampton Bowlarama. When Big Barton purchased the Island, he rebuilt the outside of the mansion exactly as it had been during the time of Tiger Edgar Cash; but inside, going several levels down into the ground, it was high-tech all the way, gleaming metal modernism and white antiseptic walls.

'Human testees stay in the west wing,' Big Barton said. 'Staff stay in the east wing. More comfortable than a Ramada Inn.'

We penetrated the interior and descended via elevator.

Big Barton inserted his ID card in a slot. The door quietly whooshed open.

'Now this,' he said, 'is the Fertility Room.'

Around the large room, men and women in white suits mixed potions in test tubes, cooked concoctions in Bunsen burners and ovens, hunched over computers. The activity resembled a Hieronymus Bosch rendition of a four-star-hotel kitchen.

'Aren't there enough hungry mouths to feed already?' asked John Dough.

'That may be true, Pearl Man. And for those poor wretches we've developed a time-release birth-control implant that keeps them reproduction-free for five years. At present it's being tested at inner-city junior highs in Philadelphia and Tampa. I'm happy to report that the youngsters are having condom-free, fertility-free sex. Everybody involved hopes it'll contribute to downsizing the welfare rolls.'

We stopped by a glass tank in which two rats were making squeaky love.

'On the other hand,' Big Barton continued, 'the high-stress of the modern white-collar lifestyle makes reproduction a virtually impossible equation for our more financially-stable citizenry. Worldwide, sperm-counts among the upwardly mobile are in the toilet. Now we, the caring professionals here at Snitbread Pharmaceutical – we've developed a safe, inexpensive solution. Let me show you.'

Big Barton led us over to where a pretty Korean woman was packaging items in a box. A card clipped to her breast identified her as Miss Kim Kim. Big Barton put his Yeti-sized hand on her petite back.

'You know the current craze in making beer at home?' he asked.

'You're going into home-brewery kits?' I asked, thinking: Get the yuppies drunk and maybe they'll breed.

'No, Ralph, home-fertility kits. FDA trials start next month.'

The box showed a fabulously happy white couple, soap-opera handsome, all but drooling with joy over a plump pink Gerber's-jar infant. Miss Kim opened the box and pulled out a Petri Dish, a packet of powder labeled INSTANT FERTI-LITY, a pint of Evian water, a copy of *Hustler*, a small egg-whisk, and a turkey-baster.

'Behold the future of sexuality!' exclaimed Big Barton with parental pride. 'The subject pleasures himself with the aid of the erotic literature, mixes his dud sperm with a spoonful of powder and a little shot of designer water, stirs it with the whisk, and then with the baster he injects the bambino-batter into his dear wife, and bingo! Buy the baby-buggy!'

'Mistah Snitbread,' said Miss Kim. 'He true genius.'

'No, Miss Kim, just a responsible man of science. And now for thirty-nine ninety-five anyone can experience the joy of parenthood!'

'What's in the magic dust?' asked John Dough.

'My own secret recipe, John. Crystallized glandular ex-tractions and Chinese herbs – powdered rhinoceros horn and rabbit prostate, among others.'

'Pollock and Krasner were childless,' I mused. 'They could have used one of these kits.'

'If you think Pollock didn't have any paint in his brush, Ralph, you're way off base. Jack was buying twelvepacks of raincoats from me up until the day he died.'

'Ruth Kligman?'

'So they say.'

Now we were getting somewhere.

'Who else?'

'He could've been doing waitresses at the Cashampton Poon Tang Chinese Restaurant for all I know,' he said, patting Miss Kim's haunch and leading us out of the Fertility Room, down the hall, and through another mechanized sliding door, this one marked Alcoholism Room.

'You see this beagle, John?' He indicated a sad caged dog lying with his head between his paws, hooked up to an IV of clear, dripping liquid. 'This little fellow lived for the sauce – we had him up to three sixes of Beck's dark beer a day.'

Big Barton reached under the counter into a fridge and cracked a bottle of beer, took a belt, then poured it into a clean bowl and slid it though the cage slot. The melancholy beagle sniffed the beer and tentatively licked at it, then yowled horribly and scrunched into a fetal ball, kicking and howling, and then suddenly lying there, silent, legs pointing at the ceiling, stiff as a statue.

'It stabs you right in the kidneys – excruciating pain! – then induces a half-hour paralysis, so that even if you were foolhardy enough to drink some more, you can't. When the paralysis wears off, we offer the subject a choice between a fine imported beer and a bowl of water. You'd be surprised how fast he goes for the water. The marketing boys call it "Instant AA." Terrific, huh?'

The dog stared blankly.

I had to jog to catch up with Big Barton and John Dough.

'Now here' Big Barton led us into a room whose door read Anti-Aging Room, 'is where Snitbread Pharmaceutical is making the horrors of the golden years a dim memory.'

Around the cavernous room: dogs and cats and rats and monkeys and goats and sheep; some with shaved skulls and electrodes taped to their heads; many penned or caged, barking and bleating and meowing and screeching; some dead on tables, being dissected by scientists with gleaming silver instruments in their gloved hands; some just lying there, anesthetized, barely alive, eyes open and terrorized.

'Yes indeed!' Big Barton had to yell to be heard. 'It was in this very room that Dr. Guberstein developed Alz-Well! The original name was Alz-Well That Endz-Well, but on Marketing's recommendation we shortened it! Our first human studies are going wonderfully!'

'I know!' I yelled, as a goat with a shaved head and a black beard broke free from an attendant. 'I met Willem de Kooning! He's sharp as a tack!'

'C'mon!' Big Barton steered John Dough out of there, and I had to turn sideways to make it through the sliding door. 'There's lots more to see.'

Next stop: the Intestinal Room.

'Y'know, John, my folks were Bonackers — finest kind — poor farmers. After the War I attended Pharmacy School on the GI Bill. Worked the local pharmacy. When old man Smithers retired, I bought it from him with a bank loan. Muffy was eight or so when I invented Speed-Lax.'

He opened the door and guided us in.

The smell of animal feces was overwhelming. Big Barton handed us each a gas-mask from a rack. He, himself, went unmasked.

Miserable caged animals, standing or sitting or lying in their own shit, stared at us, their faces strained and sad.

'Those were the halcyon years of this nation's economy, and everybody ate meat, lots of red meat. People just didn't know that meat was a killer; but Big Barton knew.'

Big Barton stopped by a cage where a skeletal orangutan stared dolefully through the bars. The tycoon reached into the sub-counter fridge for a bunch of bananas. He peeled and handed them to the famished simian, one by one.

'By the time the average American hits fifty, five pounds – five *pounds*! – of red meat will be accumulated and rotting in his rectum.' Big Barton shook his head sadly. 'Makes you want to rush out and buy some tofu, I know. But, if everyone took just one capsule of Speed-Lax every night after supper, we could eat all the burgers and bacon and steaks we wanted!'

He walked over to a cabinet and came back with a trial-sized packet of Speed-Lax for John Dough. The package bore a picture of a speed-blurred racing car and a checkered flag being waved.

'Use it in good health, John. New and Improved High-Octane Speed-Lax. The ultimate digestive aid. Look for it next fall.

'Watch,' he said, opening a packet and stuffing a capsule inside a peeled banana. 'Regard the miracle of spontaneous intestinal-rectal relaxation.' He passed the banana through the bars and the monkey hungrily scarfed it down.

'One,' he counted. 'Two, three, four, five – stand back,' he said, guiding us to a distance of ten feet. 'Seven, eight, nine . . .'

The monkey's face took on a surprised and shamed look, and at 'ten' his banana-packed bowels exploded.

'I'm looking Nobel Prize for this.'

We passed other wards. Cancer Room. Circulatory Room. AIDS Room. Pediatric Room. Flu Room. (An attendant led the frisky geriatric skinhead goat with the black goatee through the whooshing Flu Room door.) Feminine Hygiene Room. Genetics Room. Skin Room.

'From what I hear,' said John Dough, 'Gilbert Schwartz could have used a trip to the Skin Room.'

'We tried, Pearl Man,' Big Barton said sadly. 'But nothing short of a miracle would have helped that old boy.'

John Dough and I were both silent and rattled as we guzzled mint juleps on the veranda. It was a velvet-aired seaside sunset. Pink skies. Soft, warm, beautiful. Birds wheeled overhead. Fishing boats and pleasure crafts plied the waters.

'It's very different above ground,' said our host, pouring refills from a pitcher. 'Makes you appreciate being a healthy human being. Life's simple pleasures.'

John and I nodded and guzzled. Our complimentary Louis Vuitton leather satchels, packed with Speed-Lax, Sensuous brand condoms, Snitinex sleeping tablets, and home-fertility kits, lay on the Italian-tiled veranda floor.

'Do the animal-rights activists give you any trouble?' I asked, because if they didn't, PETA could expect a long anonymous letter very soon.

'A bit. And I'm sensitive to their position. No one loves the beasts of the field any more than Big Barton Snitbread. The Bible very clearly gives mankind dominion – it's right up front, in Genesis; and when I met that man in Pittsburgh last year, the one with the baboon liver, and I saw him breathing and smiling and bitching about the hospital food just like anyone else, I knew, I truly knew, that God had blessed the good work we do here at Snitbread Pee.'

'But he died,' I said. 'His body rejected the liver.'

'Doesn't matter, Ralph. His life was extended. God appreciates the effort.'

There was a sad plangent wailing and barking from out back, and Big Barton answered my unasked question.

'Those are animals we keep outside,' he said. 'As a reward for services rendered.'

There were no women at the Mulrooney Estate that night, no deliveries of fresh gourmet goods from The Pregnant Duchess. We sat there in the living room, lights low, a soft rain clawing at the windows, sat there downing Wild Turkey, drink after drink, depressed.

'Well, good night, John,' I said, finally.

'G'night, Roger,' he mumbled.

'We'll have fun tomorrow,' I said, injecting some false hope into my voice. John Dough sat silent, staring at his drink.

'We'll have fun the day after tomorrow,' I said.

But I knew it would be a while before either of us felt like having any fun.

Which brings us to what I was doing snooping about John Dough's desk. I had looked in on John after a long shower during which I had scrubbed and scrubbed and scrubbed, attempting to wash away the stink of Cash Island. And there was the Man Of Many Pearls, passed out on the floor, dried trails of tears on his face, the snot of sadness bubbling out his nose, an empty bottle of Wild Turkey at his side, an empty tube of Duco Cement in his hand, a dark-stained, glue-stinking paper bag by his body. I made sure he was breathing and then cleaned up around him. He whimpered in his sleep like a baby. Poor John Dough, I thought, sniffing glue like a ten-year-old to escape the sorrow of the day.

And then, like the reporter I was . . . no: Then, like the nosey bastard I was, I snuck into his den, opened the desk drawer – looking for a passport, a license, anything which might illuminate his mysterious past. But all I found was a thick sheaf of hand-scribbled legal-pad pages.

I mixed myself a tall drink, sat down, and I read:

'Once upon an April, in a fabulous land of fun and sun known as Cashampton By The Sea . . .'

A fairy tale, I thought. How sweet. The Pearl Man's writing a fairy tale.

CASHAMPTON
BY JOHN DOUGH

ONCE UPON AN APRIL, in a fabulous land of fun and sun
known as Cashampton By The Sea, on the shank end of a
particularly cold and heartless winter, a month after I'd
planted Mama in the Green River Cemetery next to my
stepfather Leo – dug the frozen earth myself, cheeks salty-
slick with tears and sweat, the antifreeze of grief – and one
aching year after my brief tragic unconsummated marriage to
Lindsay LaRouche, I stood in the cobweb-beamed riding barn
of the Upton Riding Club, leaning on my trusty rusty
pitchfork, at my side a wheelbarrow brimming with steaming
golden nuggets and mounds of pee-soaked sawdust. At the
overripe age of thirty-nine I carried hard muscles from
twenty-one years of Herculean labor as the resident horse-
manure technician. Through my thick glasses I was watching –
with the heart-pounding awe of a virgin (which I unfortu-
nately and frustratingly still was) – a blonde teenaged girl

riding around the indoor dirt ring. A sweat-stained Cleveland Indians baseball cap topped my bald birthmarked head — was pulled low to cover the knoblike pimples of my lunar fore-head, the zits and pits and craters of my outrageous fortune.

Just another morning. Mustard-gas hangover. Two beers and a joint for breakfast. The house quiet. No Mama to remind me what a nothing I was. So I'd just sat there, smoking the herb and drinking the brew, painting a fresh coat of buzz onto my permanently-pickled Swiss-Cheese brain. The nostril-tickling stink of charred wood still strong from her bedroom; her final screams still sizzling in my brain-pan; my useless leap through the orange wall of dancing flame fresh as oven-hot bread in my memory; the look of peace on her smoked-ham face as I lay her down dead on a fluffy bed of snow, smudged skin suddenly smooth and untroubled as a newborn baby's behind — all this: food for the guilt-monster. But was it my fault? I hadn't asked her to stay awake late watching wrestling re-runs, I didn't suggest spilling a bottle of vodka and tripping over a space heater. It wasn't my fault. But if I hadn't been over at Fish Head Danny's getting plastered, if I'd hidden that vodka. . . .

And now work. Manicured green fields sparkling with winter drizzle. Cold wind blowing wet. Richfolk riding sleek well-fed nags. A damp dog happily gobbling a fresh-fallen field-turd. Muddied parking lot packed with Range Rovers, Benzes, Beamers, Bentleys, Jags and Saabs. Grooms groom-ing. Hank Upton in the office, staring at wall-photos of forty years worth of Cashampton cuties jumping fences, forty years of bluebloods' blue ribbons. Horses in their stalls, eating, drinking, snorting steam, pissing garden hose streams and lifting their tails to drop pungent fecal bombs.

In the off-season, Cashampton By The Sea is like any other vacation community in the USA: among us working locals drug use and the suicide rate skyrocket. It's my favorite time of year. All those depressed faces make me feel part of the community. The roads are clear, the beaches are empty and you can walk and think and stew in your blues, can even hang in a bar and get a drink without being stared at. It's almost like being free.

But local businesses live for summer, when glitzy City suckers migrate from Manhattan, hogging the roads, packing the bars, lying and frying on the beaches, running in the surf, splashing in the cold salt waves, making the cash registers sing with the ding-a-ling-ling of sweet greenback music.

After a morning shoveling horseshit and ignoring hordes of buzzing shitflies I'd walk to the beach to eat my sandwich. Sitting in the sand fully clothed, chewing the tasteless lunchmeat, I'd longingly watch the long-limbed lotion-greased wealthy women, the knock-kneed near-naked Nox-ema-nosed sunbathers of summer, lounging on towels, sipping iced libations from shining thermoses as sandpipers sprinted stiff-legged in the blinding raw-silk sands. I'd rubber-neck the heartbreaking hardbodied teenage girls as they jogged, apple-breasts and bonbon butts abobble, past freckled blonde children splashing and yelping in the surf, as they strolled, elegant as adolescent antelope under fluff-clouded blueskies, combing the waterfront rim of white foam – like a mustache of milk on a kid's upper lip – for shore-washed shells, distant ship-shapes hugging the hazy horizon, sus-pended by vague balloonstrings of smoke.

Driving home in the afternoons, the air spiked with the sweet summertime smells of saltwater and fresh-cut grass, birds twittering, I'd pass sprawling white houses – swim-ming pools packed with nubile young sexpots wiggling in and out of Nautilus-pumped weightlifters' embraces like greased pigs. In the dying sun of summer their skin glowed orange as barbecued ducks. I'd pass the long-lawned mega-mansions of the power-brokers, the movers and shakers of Manhattan society, incapable of changing a flat bicycle tire or a light bulb without calling in specialized help. For years I'd picked up extra bucks – aside from my normal duties that had gotten me and Mama free rent and a hundred bucks a month on the Mulrooney Estate: pool and tennis court maintenance, clipping hedges, pruning trees, mowing and watering lawns, raking leaves in autumn, shoveling snow in winter (a tenure I'd inherited at age fifteen when Leo died in a car crash) – helping the cultural elite change fuses or set up their sprinkler systems. Off their abstract clouds, the rich were all thumbs and dollars. But oh those Mercedes cars! Those Jag-u-ars! Those Rolls-Royces and Beamers! The power dudes loved their automobiles. Some even washed them themselves! They spent more time with their cars than they did with their kids – little wonder – spoilt ice-cream-eating brats who spouted cultured obscenities and aped their parents' speech patterns ('Terrific!' they'd exclaim when happy; 'Terrific,' they'd whine sarcastically when their keepers – delectable young nannies from France or Sweden, or underpaid local girls, wouldn't buy them the exact video or toy their greedy little hearts desired). And the mothers! Oh, the mothers – twenty, thirty, forty years younger than the men, how I dreamed crazycream dreams of being their helper! They zipped about Cashampton in sporty convertibles, wearing skimpy white tennis togs or wispy Band-Aid bathing suits under diaphanous beach caftans, exhibiting so much rich soft glowing flesh that I was mixmastered into a frothing frappe of sexual frenzy which could only be relieved by speeding home in my pickup truck, slamming the bedroom door and brutally tenderizing my meat, imagining those slinky slim gaudily-jeweled bodies squirming joyously beneath me, diamond rings scratching my back, aerobically streamlined liposuction-butted silicon-titted dreambodies gyrating in acrobatic ecstasy as I kissed their surgically-sculpted noses, their collagen-puffy lips (once shaggy but now shorn by the magic of electrolysis), as I stroked their Kama Sutrically-contorted legs with my work-rasped hands, licked their hairless velvet bellies with my whiskey-fragrant tongue, plumbed their champagne-douched juice-vaults with my proud solitary unpimpled joystick.

And then in the afterglow — as I lay there smoking a joint, listening to Mama squawk parrot-like for the beer I'd neglected to pick up in my haste to spank the carrot — I realized that were it not for some unlucky roll of the celestial dice, some ineradicable karmic snake-eyes of the soul, some fundamental inequity in the distribution of life's goodies, it would be me in the mansion (boffing the Icelandic nanny (me putting it to the Ecuadorian maid (then a few hours later the Haitian housekeeper (me getting my ashes hauled by the British-born lady of the house (me rising late in the morning to play tennis or watch Geraldo on the big-screen TV (me drinking im-ported booze and gobbling gourmet snacks (me having the skid-marks of my monogrammed hundred-dollar designer silk jockey shorts lovingly scrubbed by some delectable delovely Oriental downstairs maid who'd bring the snow-white pressed undies back folded on a silver platter alongside a glass of fresh-squeezed orange juice, then kneel before me and place her willing practiced lips on my irrepressible millionaire wang)))))))). Hell no, you can't keep a good man down! It would be me to an infinite power. Me. And I was not alone in this envy. As a class we locals 'yessirred' and 'yesma'amed' the moneybags all summer long, and in accordance with the laws of Nature and the American Way everyone made out, made out to such a degree that when business was booming and the customers got extra-snotty they got snotted right the fuck back; but when summer was over and most of the richfolk were back in their luxurious City caves, we The People experienced deep pangs of guilt and remorse for our summer-long circus of servility and we spent the desolate winter hating ourselves for having smiled and scraped and demeaned ourselves so obviously in pursuit of the Almighty Dollar. But that was the cycle: kiss ass in summer (so that the sacred greenbacks flowed into town) and then blow it bitterly in winter, the long depressing months of drugs and booze and shotgun blowjobs.

The pear-buttocked blonde up top the clip-clopping gray stallion was rich, very rich. She wore six diamond studs in each ear. A black velvet-domed hardhat capped her flowing yellow hair. I loved the way that hair smelled. Whenever she passed close to me in the barn I'd take a giant whiff and my nose hairs would tingle with excitement. The fragrance was intoxicating, exotic, made my juices run electric, completely drowning the smell of horseshit. Sort of a cross between cinnamon toast and Brazilian rain-forest orchid.

Round and round the dirt ring, the horseshoed hooves thudding like lovers' heartbeats, the strong slim legs gripping the steed's muscled flanks, the anti-gravity chest-mangoes dancing braless under a red-checked work shirt, the blonde hair bouncing on the ramrod back above ripe-fleshed ass cheeks sheathed in faded jeans — perfect gluteal blue moons rising and falling, making the polished leather of the saddle creak on the downthrust. Round and round, rising and falling, the horse's black tail curving rigid above its proudly puckered anus, the long hanging horsehair swishing in harmony with the long blonde girlhair, the horse's steaming breath fading in the sharp April air. I felt the blood rushing groinward and I groaned with lust.

No, Specs! No! Not Jennifer Gritz. She's only fifteen! Down, boy, down! Not Jenny. Not Muffy's kid, not Muffy Snitbread-Gritz's baby!

'What the fuck are you staring at?' asked the sneering rich man.

He had a milk-white unblemished complexion with pores tight as an ant's asshole, cold blue eyes, a thin slash of pale pink lips, carefully coiffed blonde hair. He sported a black riding habit, the requisite black velvet-domed hardhat, black knee-high boots, and he was metronomically whacking a riding crop into the palm of his pale soft hand.

It was Jonas Gritz. Muffy's husband, Jenny's father.

The blood flowing to my loins stopped on a dime, reversed directions, sprinted to my face, pumping my pimples purple, making them throb with pain. I was mute . . . Blond old-money Jonas, with a skin as clear and white and untouched by time and grime as a field of fresh-fallen snow, handsome as a young wartless Robert Redford, a face so perfect and cruel it cried out for the sharp kiss of a broken bottle – a face that had never known failure.

I scratched an itching pregnant pimple on the fleshy part of my neck, a walnut-sized lump I'd just a week earlier nick-named Mt. Pinatubo. Swollen to the point of bursting, Pinatubo was the stuff of legend – yet no juice was forth-coming, no gunk apparent, just an ever-growing lump, long past due, so full of promise, so disappointing, with a dead blue-white eye staring sorrowfully back at me blind like some cataracted Cyclops. Call me sentimental, but I had harbored high hopes for that pimple. Apple pie hopes! Nothing in the world quite came close to the white liquid spurt of relief.

Years back Mama had been the Gritzes' maid, and while the old lady scoured the rambling oceanside mansion – the daylong scrubadubdub dance of dusting and polishing and mopping and waxing, of laundering clothes and making beds – young Jonas and I had gone swimming, we'd bodysurfed, whacked tennis balls or shot his BB gun. Once to my eternal shame I hit a mother wren in its nest and the nest tumbled from the hedge; I cried at that broken birdbody and I stroked the baby wrens, but wicked Jonas, my daytime playtime buddy, had mocked my tears, he'd laughed at my weakness and when I took the birds home they died. But that was ancient history, before zits and class and time had erected an insurmountable barbed-wire barricade to friendship.

I scratched at Pinatubo. Hadn't had a good gusher in weeks, just these petrified pimples that sprouted and itched but never spurted. Hadn't had a good session in front of the mirror since Mama—

'I'm talking to you, Pizzaface!' Jonas yelled, staring directly at Pinatubo, lips curling with undisguised revulsion, meaty chin thrust forward like the prow of a destroyer.

Pizzaface! I hadn't been called that since high school . . .

. . . back when all the pretty girls and perfect boys were cruising in cars, whooping at the moon with the juice of youth, throwing empty cans at mailboxes, testing testosterone and exploring the possibilities of their freshly-fuzzed genitalia, puking up bellies full of Budweiser and booze onto innocent rose bushes and swapping Marlboro-flavored spit, I was at home popping pimples, pressing whitecapped purple pustules and shuddering with near orgasmic pleasure at the explosions of lily-white pus onto the mirror.

'Please, Mr. Gritz, call me Gilbert. Call me Specs, call me Schwartz. But please don't call me . . .'

'Pizzaface?'

Pizzaface! I quivered with anger and shame. Cashampton
High. How the halfway dudes had daily trashed me in their
hormone-happy voices: 'Hey Pizzaface, how's the pepperoni
hanging?' I'd blush behind my mask of acne, pull my ballcap
lower, adjust my glasses, stick my nose in a book and
stumblerush down the hall, blurrily blind with tears, past
endless rows of tombstone lockers.

At night in my bed in the gateman's shack on the
Mulrooney Estate, with my inebriated widowed Mama snoring beerily away in a cooling puddle of pee on her rubber-
sheeted bed in the next room, I dreamt in vivid Van Gogh
Technicolor that my face truly was a pizza, the skin bubbling
with rich red sauce and sebaceous blisters of mottled mozza-
rella cheese, bursting with ripe black pitted olives and charred
chunks of smoking onion and pepper, seething with greasy red
slices of sausage, sprinkles of sizzling brown hamburger
droppings and wriggling live anchovies; and I'd stand there,
naked (shamed and baking) under relentlessly cruel fluorescent lights, surrounded by a mob of barbell-bloated jocks, lab-
rat nerds, groovy bell-bottomed stoners and pointy-breasted
pom-pom-waving cheerleaders, all laughing at my skinny
body, mocking my fear-shriveled penis (my testicles having
judiciously scampered up into my belly to hide), jabbing at my
steaming mug with sharpened claws, grabbing for slices,
tearing the sensitive skin and stuffing it dripping into their
grinding-piston teeth, and I would scream scream scream
scream scream . . .

. . . and awake in a cold sweat, weeping with loneliness
and shame, shivering at the prospect of the fresh horrors
awaiting me that day in the corridors of Cashampton High.
Would they again drag me kicking and pleading into the Boys'
Room? hang me by my feet and shove my head into a toilet
bowl and flush? – cold turdlets swirling in my face like vicious

mini-piranhas until I snorted and swallowed and choked on their malevolent mingled pee? — a Whirlie they called it. Would they form a hallway gauntlet and one by one boot my sorry ass as I tried to make English Lit. class? Would they have a hot gooey pizza delivered COD to my desk in Biology Lab? I'd lay there in bed, quivering with dread, gnashing my teeth midst the battlefield sheetstains of adolescent juiceletting, huffing lighter fluid or glue from a paper bag, smoking pipes of hashish and pot, holding onto my unzitted pecker for dear life, and I'd run through a Sears Catalogue of fantasies: Specs scoring the winning touchdown; Specs hitting the halfcourt jumpshot; Specs swatting a home run beyond the horizon; Specs heroically riding atop the sturdy shoulders of adoring fellow students, through throngs of backslapping handpumping worshipers; Specs being deposited in front of the girls' locker room and told: 'Go get 'em, boy!' — and then Specs singleglandedly satisfying the girls' field-hockey team atop the soap-slick tiles of their steam-shrouded shower-room, lathering their ripe panting pimpleless chests, licking droplets of water from betwixt their glorious gapped thighs, feeling the darting tongues, the ready hot lips and tickling tonsils giftwrapping my unpimplified manhood. And finally, the cherry atop the banana split, the Shangri-la of unattainables, the image that brought forth the creamspurt crescendo, the grand gonadial gush: getting Muffy Snitbread as . . . (dare I say it?) . . . as (dare I dream it?) . . . as my girlfriend — having Muffy as (oh great cosmic laugh!), as my lover!

Muffy was blonde and stacked, a lonely loser's jerkoff jamboree — you know the one — the long-legged cheerleader who dates and then dumps the captain of the football team, drives a powder-blue Mercedes sport-convertible, wears tit-hugging sweaters, butt-clinging skirts, LL Bean duckboots, takes horseback-riding lessons — always laughing, always happy, always showing you her Pearl Drops-perfect teeth, her crimson hairless nostrils, always with the in-crowd, sucking down a cheeseburger or a milkshake or some football player's dong – she was pampered and perfumed and pimple-free, the richest year-round girl in Cashampton, the prized only child of Sarah and Big Barton Snitbread.

Big Barton, former pharmacist, inventor of Speed-Lax – tabbed by the tabloids as 'the man who makes America go') – had built a bulky gaudy eyesore of a mansion, right next door to Count and Countess Hugo and Baby Luegodago of Uruguay and across the way from Larva and Sherman Shinsplintz, and he'd bribed and connived his way into all the 'right' clubs. Rumor had it that Muffy lost her cherry to the Luegodagos' polo-playing son, the dark dashing Diego Luegodago. And even though Big Barton could easily have shipped his darling to any one of a hundred-and-sixty-nine high-priced East Coast all-girl schools at which a snub-nosed WASP princess learns the refined ropes of upper-crust bitchery and puts the finishing touches on her education of entitlement, he couldn't bear to be separated from her, so he kept her close, sent her to Cashampton High, where she flourished, a carefree confident young goddess who served as a constant reminder to me of my insufficiency my abject nerdiness, my freakish pitiful home-liness.

'Look, Specs,' Jonas said, his tone now charitable, 'don't you have work to do?' Lock-jawed, the product of superior inbreeding, Jonas reverted to form and with a nasty little grin added: 'Turdburglar.'

Sure I have work to do. Another thirty years of mucking fifty stalls a day. The Upton Club pays me five bucks an hour and they charge twenty-five-hundred-a-month room-and-board per horse. Yessir, I loves my job. It's a science! It's an art! It's poetry! Y'see, no two horses shit alike, no two pee alike. Some pee in one spot, so all you

have to do is dig a three-foot-square six-inch-deep trench of pissy
sawdust. Some pee in three or four spots, some pee all over. Some shit
in one big pile – bless their souls. Some shit in three or four piles.
Some shit in piles then stomp it into little horseshitbits and kick it all
over. Some lift their tails right in your face and give you a snootful of
the old equine intestinal perfume, then let loose a torrent of turds or
pucker up and release a few thick bricks of shit or a single massive
brain-ridged shot-put or——

'Don't you like your job?' Jonas asked, flaring nostrils
sucking in horseshit-fragrant air; and, as he stroked his hardhat
with a gleaming manicured fingernail, Jennifer kept right on
riding, Zentent on becoming one with the horse, oblivious to
the hubbub her jutting buttocks had caused.

I stared from my beat old urine-cracked work-sad boots to
Jonas's shiny thousand-dollar knee-highs, then jammed my
pitchfork into the wheelbarrow and answered the sneering
rich man with the politeness of one who fully understands that
despite over twenty years of shoveling shit and taking shit,
over twenty years of minimum wage and minimum respect,
one wrong word could land me smack-dab on the unemploy-
ment line, shit out of a job.

'Sure, Mr. Gritz,' I said, picking up the handles of my
wheelbarrow. 'Horseshit is my life.'

I flung the dung into the barrow, uncapped my trusty pint of
Southern Comfort, wiped my dry chapped loveless lips and
took a healthy swallow of the thick sweet firewater, staring out
the open upper half of the door into the chattering teeth of a
cold-spray wind, across the wet green fields, past the freshly-
furrowed brown ground of the potato farm, to the seagulls
winging over the ocean. Soon it would be summer.

I mucked, working with speed and fury, as if running late
for a dermatologist appointment. Those skin docs never did

help much; their popping techniques hurt like a sonofabitch. First they'd steam my face, then a large-breasted assistant with a foreign accent would puncture my zits and press them with tissue-papered fingers, all the while leaning over, humming Romanian or Hungarian or Ukrainian folk ditties and breathing her lunchsmell into my face (salami sandwich, spaghetti with garlic bread, 7-11 burritos: it became a game, guessing their meals) – they made me bleed and ache and left ugly purple sores that, within days, festered into fresh mounds of gunk. Their drying lotions only served to cake my face into a concrete mask of agony. Antibiotics, Retin-A, Collagen, Acutane, 'Wonder Creams' from the Orient, fresh cucumber peels, lumpy oatmeal masks (not to mention the over-the-counter ointments and pads, old staples such as Clearasil and Stridex) – over the years I'd tried them all, and most of my disposable income had been disposed for treatment – yet still I bore a remarkable resemblance to a prize Hawaiian pineapple. Once I sank six months' savings into having my face surgically sanded till it was pink and raw as salmon sushi, but back the pimples came, loyal as a beaten dog, faithful and plentiful as swallows regurgitating to Capistrano. The doctors would make new appointments, milk me for more cash, until my bank account was shriveled and dry as an octogenarian cow's udder – but back I always went in the feeble hope that science might conquer nature.

It was the May 1990 issue of *Derma Quarterly* that alerted me to the fact that I'd become famous in East Coast skin circles. The article reprinted portions of two scholarly papers that had been presented as lectures to great acclaim at an Atlanta convention under the titles 'Acne Vulgaris In Middle Age' and 'Zits That Don't Quit.' Though my name was not mentioned – I was called Patient X – I had no doubt the poor sorry crater-faced sonofabitch they were describing was me.

(But why the kudos? Why the fame? Why the acclaim? They hadn't cured me, hadn't done squat.) The details were all on the money: the zits, the scars, the alcoholism, the despair. Man, I could just see them, those skin doctors, those soft little men with their soft little smiles, rubbing their soft little hands when my name popped up on their appointment calendars. So I was not surprised when I reached the centerfold spread: an obscene two-page photo showing jolly Dr. Shuvindar Rimjob of Bayshore by way of Bengal (my Doctor Rimjob!) sipping frosty margaritas with his topless Hungarian assistant (goulash-eating Marta!) on a yacht in a Palm Beach marina, a yacht that had been paid for by the pain of my face, by the angst of my soul, by the sweat of my muscles, by Himalayan mounds and pounds of horseshit, by endless hissing streams of horse-piss – a yacht that had very likely been christened with a bottle of medicated Sea Breeze astringent. And looking at the picture I didn't need a magnifying glass to read the yacht's name, for it was very clearly marked: SS *Specs Schwartz, Sucker*.

'Hey there, Specs!' yelled Big Barton Snitbread from across the barn as I forked a grapefruit-sized offering just jettisoned by Caesar, the chestnut gelding 'owned' by Cassandra Phlebitis, the voluptuous scimitar-nosed wife of Greek-born shipping and armaments magnate Socrates Phlebitis. Gelding. The Gilded Set loved gelding.

The laxative tycoon was breathing hard. Three-hundred pounds of dumb lucky meat, dressed in the same absurd riding costume as his son-in-law.

'You seen Kurtis?' he asked.

'Not lately.'

Kurtis Swimming Otter Cash, my cousin and best friend, had been doing hard time in Attica prison the past five years for a rape he hadn't committed.

'He's out,' Big Barton said. 'Ernie Hedges over at the *Sun* just called me with the news. Judge Merkin, Court of Appeals, got the results of that DNA check he ordered on the semen on the bimbo's underwear.'

'Back up a second, Mr. Snitbread. He's out? He's home?'

'I shit you not, Specs. He was seen getting off the Cashampton Jitney last night. Seems the alleged rapee broke down finally. Word is Kurtis just drove her home from a bar. The stuff on her panties was Doberman's sperm.'

'But Harry Dubermann moved to Bali ten years ago.'

'Not Dubermann, Specs. Doberman – as in dog.'

'As in woof woof?'

'As in they were barking up the wrong tree. Seems the girl didn't want to get hitched to her fiancé, so she cooked up the rape story. Had a one-night stand with a broom handle to approximate the bruises and then smeared herself with canine ejaculation. The happiest attack dog in Cashampton.'

'I'm glad I didn't eat breakfast.'

Big Barton eyed me curiously, sniffed and then said: 'Bit of a booze problem?'

'Only when I'm too broke to buy any.'

'Look here, Specs,' Big Barton said, the penultimate pitch-man smelling sucker, 'if you've got any vacation time . . . come on over to the Island.' Ten years back, Big Barton had rebuilt the old Cash Mansion on Cash Island into a futuristic drug-testing lab. Sit by the shore of Cash Bay on a windless night and you can hear caged dogs wailing across the water.

'Now Specs, I know the Snitbread Zit-B-Gone didn't work for you.' Big Barton wiped the slate clean of past disappointments with a flick of his wrist. 'But lick your booze problem, change your diet, get a little pussy – maybe your skin will improve.'

I shook my head. Except for the sex-with-another-human-being angle, I'd tried it all: low-fat diets, macrobiotic menus, no reefer and drink. Nothing had worked. And it wasn't just my face that was pizzafied. My back and chest and shoulders and thighs had been clotted and dotted and glutted with these natural wonders.

'Tell you the truth, Mr. Snitbread, I'm kind of fond of my drinking problem. It keeps me company nights.'

'Think it over. And if that one doesn't appeal to you we have a whole shitload of other projects. Cancer, lumbago, whatever – you catch it, we'll take care of it.'

Big Barton split and I went back to my work. Caesar's tail arched, his anus quivered and bloomed and gave birth to a fragrant steaming brown softball.

'Hail Caesar,' I said aloud, forking.

Commotion in the parking lot. A horse trailer had pulled up and Linda the groom, under the direction of Hank Upton, was leading old Pumpy The Pony out. Pumpy was resisting and Linda was pulling him by his halter. I could see this, looking through a knothole from Martin Luther King's stall where I was taking silent secret pipehits of weed and nipping from my half-pint of Southern Comfort. King, my host, a black gelding – swaybacked, knobby-kneed, white-whiskered, with teeth the color of 19th-century piano keys and joints gummed with the rust of years – was no longer spry enough for the jumping prancing proud-bodied preening of the horse-show world, not much good to his so-called owners for anything more strenuous than a walk on the beach; and because his people, Mariah and Fergus Frankfurter (Mariah was the daughter of Wall Street whiz Elliot Quinchard and his socialite wife Dorcas), rarely visited him, King's stall was a safe spot for me to cop a buzz.

'Where'th Pumpy going?' lisped a little girl in junior

riding-uniform – it was Verushka Grimstory, daughter of Lexus and Halley Grimstory.

'Pumpy's going to the clinic in Connecticut for his check-up,' answered Hank Upton kindly, as Linda yanked the halter with force.

More like check-out. Age and infirmity and the high cost of room-and-board at the Upton Club spelled one thing and one thing alone for Pumpy The Pony: a trip to the slaughterhouse. Instead of the accustomed friendly pat on the nose, Pumpy could expect a swift hammer between the eyes; and after being drained, gutted, skinned, chopped, hung from a hook and then packed in plastic, Pumpy The Pony – proud little Pumpy who'd never nipped a child, never bucked a baby, gentle little Pumpy with his twitching oak-leaf ears and velvet nose, brown-eyed Pumpy who loved licking packets of sugar with his hot wet sandpaper tongue, sweet little Pumpy, considerate little gentleman who always shat in his corner and peed in one precise spot as if he knew how hard my job could be if he didn't – within weeks, Pumpy The Pony would be boiled, stewed, sauteed or fried; the Blue Plate Special at the finest restaurants in Paris, France.

And as Pumpy was led up the ramp I patted the old oat-chewing Martin Luther King and whispered, 'Parly-voo Français?'

'Deformity is in the eye of the beholder, my brother,' Kurtis once told me on the phone from prison. 'Skin color, skin texture – it doesn't matter why they dump on you. A dump is a dump is a dump.'

All his life Kurtis had been dumped on for the two-scoop sin of being dark and good to look at, his childhood a quiltwork of name-calling and social-snubs. When he was a senior in high school, in the same class as me, the same class as Muffy Snitbread, the *Cashampton Sun* called him 'the greatest athlete in Cashampton history.' College football scouts and fawning female flatback fans scurried to him like ants to a picnic basket. He had even signed a letter-of-intent to attend USC, full-boat scholarship, the next OJ Simpson. But when the sons of Cashampton realized the extent to which their girlfriends and sisters dug his looks, as they watched him scoring right and left, on the football field and off – even the jealous boys' little brothers, too young yet to be infected by their elders' racism, worshiped him, pretended to be the great Kurtis Swimming Otter Cash as they juked and sprinted their way through lawnfront football games – they decided enough was enough. One evening after practice, Halloween Night it was, as twilight sprinkled violet light and the early stars twinkled through the gloaming, a gang of them, all wearing gorilla masks over KKK sheets, stopped us in the parking lot. And while one of them grabbed me, they set upon my cousin with baseball bats, hockey sticks, chains and boots. 'Take that you niggah-injun, you filthy cuntlappin' cocksucker!' – breaking bones with brutal home run swings, mashing inner organs with swift steel-toed kicks, crushing his testicles so that sweet cuddlebabies might never be his, fracturing the fingers covering his face, splitting his skull so that his brain was exposed to the cool November breeze. Bloody and broken, spitting teeth and chunks of tongue, the lights in his head dimming, he said, 'The fleas sure are biting tonight.'

After high school – Kurtis never graduated, spending the last six months of the school-year in the hospital – we both went to work at the Upton Riding Club. And though my handsome cousin would never again play football, he practiced another sport: Over the years he scored more rich white ass than a Daughters Of The American Revolution office toilet seat. Movie stars, models, normal rich-bitch clients, it seemed that

every woman who mounted a horse at the Upton Riding Club
– be she married, lesbian, menopausal, or pre-pubescent –
every horse-loving lassie between two and ninety-two in
Cashampton By The Sea was attracted to him.

But for me, the eternal geek, life squirmed along like a
dust-bowl worm. I was granted an exemption from the
military draft because I was Mama's sole support (Kurtis
was 4-F from the Halloween beating), and as well as working
the horseshit racket at the Upton Riding Club, weekends I
pumped gas at the Hess Station on the Montauk Highway.
That's where I was when Radcliffe honey Muffy Snitbread
married Harvard stud Jonas Gritz. The long procession of
white limousines heading for The City passed dreamlike as I
dry-swallowed a Quaalude and jammed a pump-nozzle into a
burgundy Jaguar I could never hope to own.

For a few years the newlywed Gritzes called Dallas, Texas
home and only once in a while graced Cashampton with their
blonde shining presence. One night, smoking a joint on break
from washing dishes at Captain Larry's Surf 'n' Turf (I'd taken
the night job in the vain hope that the megadoses of steam
would help my skin), I read the newspaper announcement of
the birth of Muffy's first child, Clark Stanton Frankfurter
Snitbread-Gritz. Four years later her daughter Jennifer Sus-
anne Snitbread-Gritz was born. On occasion, before the
Gritzes moved back East for good, I would see Muffy in
town or at the riding club and I would gauge my own failure
by her triumphs. In dermatologists' waiting rooms I read the
New York gossip columns, learned of her golden perfect life.
She'd published a bestselling romance novel, she'd dined with
the President, Jonas had won a huge government contract for
his family's computer firm, Big Barton had branched into
hemorrhoid cream. I'd go on a bender, drink myself silly in
the bars, end up stumbling home to Mama's endless beer-

soaked harangues – how tired she was, how her fingers and feet ached and itched with the memory of frostbite. So I'd pour a tall glass of Southern Comfort on the rocks, fill a paper bag with lighter fluid, huff the sweet acrid fumes, get a good dizzy buzz-on and then massage Mama's 'arthuritis.' And when she'd finally passed out and I'd carried her into her room and tucked her in, when the lights were out and she was merrily sawing bronchial wood, only then would I go in my room, smoke a joint and play spank-the-monkey, visions of Muffy Snitbread dancing in my head.

Now I was older, now I was wiser, now I was balder – cue-ball bald – and I didn't need a newspaper to keep track of Muffy. She was a permanent resident of Cashampton By The Sea, and she spent much of her time at the Upton Riding Club. She barely seemed to notice me, rarely deigned to speak to me, and then only to ask me the time or because McBride – or Rastus, the horse she 'owned' before McBride – was sick or in a testy mood. Nope, Muffy was all business. And why should she pay me any attention? My job had nothing to do with talking to clients. That was for grooms and instructors. That was for Hank Upton. My job was shoveling horseshit. And in the realm of horseshit I was The Man.

Unlike most of the rich people who own or rent property in Cashampton, the horse-people were a breed apart: They were year-round pests. They'd enter the barn, sniff the shit-stinking air and then sigh with pleasure. Though fastidious about their own odors, the rich loved the smell of horseshit. Changing light bulbs in their homes, I had used their toilets. Sachets of dried lavender and bowls of patchouli masked whatever excretory stinks went unsucked by overhead jet engine fans. But back in the stables, all bets were off. There was dirt, there was sweat, there was stink – and most importantly: There were the massive horse dicks that fueled their sick mad dreams.

Sometimes they'd waylay me to discuss an individual horse's bowel movements. 'He's a little runny today, eh Specs?' or 'Nice and firm!' I'd mumble something like: 'He's off his feed' or 'Organic hay from Wyoming' – anything to satisfy their cursory need for a human bridge into the wonderful world of horseshit.

And anyway, what would I talk about with the clients? Dermatological theory? Latvian eczema treatments? The Cuban cure for vitiligo? The classic novels and books of poetry I checked out from the library? The latest horse world gossip of who was shtupping who? Nope. With a flunky like me, horse people talked about one thing and one thing alone: horseshit.

So weekdays, while their husbands were slaving away at the office, generating the big bucks it costs to keep a horse in hay and oats and leg-wraps, in shoes and blankets and haircuts, in sawdust to shit on, as soon as their freckle-spackled spawn had been delivered to school, soon as they'd instructed the cook about the evening's menu, the rich bitches would jump in the Land Rover or the Benz, speed on out the Expressway, feed their baby a lump of sugar or chunk of apple, sniff the aromatic air and then mount on up and get a serious gruntcake thumping in the saddle.

I emptied a bag of fresh sawdust in Gandhi's stall. Motes of beige danced in the gloom. I crumpled the bag, threw it outside the door, then exited the stall, snicked the bolt – and there she was: Muffy Snitbread-Gritz, holding a carrot, nuzzling her stallion McBride, cooing sweet somethings in the expensive gluebag's twitching ear, kissing his bristled velvet nose, admiring his sleek chestnut flanks, the cropped Mohawk mane, the impressive underbelly mound.

Muffy! Blonde delicious Muffy! Barely changed from high school. Crotch-hugging jodhpurs delineated her sex, accentuated her wasp waist. Long blonde hair spilled from her hardhat and fell onto her sharp-shouldered jacket. (How many drunken nights have I snuck into the stable to sniff her saddle? Once I had a cold and left a spoor of snot, and the next day Gail the groom was blamed and yelled at and made to clean it.)

'Hello, Specs,' she said, not at all unkindly, her normal snottiness smoothed to friendly country syrup as I walked over to the plastic garbage can and tossed the bag.

'Mrs. Gritz,' I mumbled, coming back to my barrow and starting to wheel it toward the old Ford tractor outside the South-facing doors where I dumped each load. When the tractor was full I'd rev it up and drive the thirty yards across the dirt parking lot to the huge dumpster and unload it all. Every other Monday a truck would come and haul the dumpster away, bring it back later empty. That was the routine, my ancient and honorable routine.

'Specs, don't run away,' Muffy spread the butter, stopping me in my tracks, smiling a perfect smile. 'We used to be close.'

Yeah, we sat two seats away from each other in biology class, over twenty years and twenty million pimples ago.

'Call me Muffy,' she poured more syrup. 'That's what you called me when played together as little kids.'

'I don't think your husband would approve, Miss Muffy.'

'You don't like him?' Her good-humored gaze focused on Pinatubo. People rarely met my eyes.

I looked at her movie-star face, saw the small crow's feet of mirth bookending her blue eyes, the laugh-lines joining her lickable lips to her can-opener nose. She bared her small white teeth and spoke to me slowly, as you might to a little child or

to a dog you're training, kind yet firm, smiling as the wet
Canadian wind blew through the North doors, flapping a wisp
of honeyed hair into her puffy red-candy mouth:

'Tell Muffy the truth. She won't bite.'

I cracked a grin, though it hurt the zits around my mouth to
do so. The monster was throbbing in my shorts.

'He's a real prince,' I told her, the sarcasm dripping like a
hound dog being teased with a T-bone steak.

All the grooms and instructors were off having lunch. Hank
Upton was in the office, smoking cigarettes, fielding calls for
lessons, leafing through back issues of *Playgirl*. It was just me
and Muffy and the horses in the barn. So quiet you could have
heard a turd drop.

The megabucked blonde peeled a leather-palmed velvet glove
and sucked a fingertip – seductive as a lonely harem girl on the
night the sheik tells her she'll have to wait another six weeks for
her turn in the rotation because he's going bowling with the
boys. Then she whispered, 'I think Jonas is cheating on me.'

What was I supposed to say?

'I've got stalls to muck,' I said, lifting the handles of my
wheelbarrow.

Muffy's birdbone hand landed on my shoulder – *oh ache of
pleasure!* – and for the first time in twenty-five years she
looked directly into my eyes. 'Is he fucking one of the little
girl grooms?'

*The girl grooms? Those little horse-crazy bitches who never talk to
me, who snidely snicker when I pass them by, call me an ax-murderer
behind my back, who've been teasing me extra-hard the last couple
months, ever since I got that Valentine's card – my first ever that
wasn't sent by Mama (it wasn't her writing!) – that I found tacked on
the bulletin board and opened in front of everyone? 'Specsy's in lo-
ove!' they sing-songed. 'Specsy's got a girlfriend!' A Valentine's
card? It couldn't be real. Who'd send me a Valentine?*

'Tell me,' Muffy ordered. 'Or maybe the bastard's doing one of the instructors. That Maria looks like she needs a good hard fuck just to get her pea-brain working in the morning.' Muffy's eyes went arctic, focused on my forehead field of zits. 'Is it that Lana bitch? Is it Linda? He comes home from the stable absolutely reeking of sex. Like he dipped his wick in pussy soup. Who's he fucking, Specs?'

What do I look like, some kind of fink? He could be fucking Maria, the grooms, the tractor's exhaust pipe or Pumpy the fucking Pony for all I care.

I said: 'How long you been working as a longshoreman, Mrs. Gritz?'

'Go to hell, Gilbert' said Muffy, turning on her booted heel and leaving both me and McBride open-mouthed in her wake. *She called me Gilbert!*

And then she pirouetted, smiling graciously – and my heart and hard-on strained to hear her words.

'See you at the Easter Party . . . Pizzaface.'

According to the hospital report, Leonard Heathcliff Schwartz died of massive head and neck injuries at approximately nine o'clock on the Friday before Christmas in 1968 on icy Lily White Lane in Cashampton By The Sea. Leo had picked Mama up at the Gritz Mansion – that would be the old Colonel and Miz Goody Garlick Gritz, Jonas's parents (now pasturing down in Palm Beach for good) – after she'd spent the day sweetening the house in preparation for the Gritz winter family-reunion.

Tired. That's what Mama had been. Tired as bone, stiff as stone. She arrived at seven that morning and under Miz Goody's direction she sparkled the house top to bottom. So by the time the house was ship-shape and she'd called Leo to pick her up, her feet ached, her fingers throbbed, her nose was clogged with moldy dust and her neck was cricked from standing on a stepladder with a broom, craning to reach cobwebs spun up high in the corners.

Leo wrapped her in a bearhug on the steps. His old Dodge Dart must've looked out of place as a coal miner at a Beverly Hills cocktail party 'midst the Benzes and Beamers and Porsches. He couldn't have liked her working hard all day for a paltry twenty dollars. His landscaping clientele had grown and he was even almost ready to show his paintings again, after years of work, after getting over the disaster of that last show back in the early 'Sixties when a critic had written, 'Leo Schwartz has missed the boat. Abstract Expressionism is dead. Long live Warhol!' After reading that to me, we carried a bunch of Campbell's soup cans to the dunes by the bay. I lined them up and from a distance of fifty feet, he took aim with his .22 and popped them all. 'Fuck you, Andy Warthog,' he said, as pea soup and chicken broth and tomato soup streamed into the sand. But now he was ready to show again, and that was good, might even mean some bread. He was looking forward to giving Mama some of the finer things – maybe a vacuum cleaner – was even talking about us taking a vacation to the Adirondacks or buying me my first stereo.

So Leo and Mama got in the car. For the short drive to the end of happiness. Well, she hadn't known that. Hadn't known that two minutes later a speeding car would bear down on them, that the Dart would hurtle off the road, the front end sucked into a ditch, that Leo would jolt forward, head wedded to the wheel, neck snapped like a stalk of celery, that she would be catapulted through the windshield, face shredded into coleslaw, that she'd spend the next ten hours lying there on a lonely oceanside road, freezing and bleeding in a ditch, both legs, an arm and her back broken, being slowly filmed over then caked with snow, listening to the crash of waves and the whistling wail of the wind as the frostbite gnawed her fingers and nibbled her toes, thinking about me going to bed without supper that night, about her husband going without supper for a lot longer than that. She hadn't known that after the snowplow found them the next morning, after the cops and ambulance came, after they dug her out of the drift and rushed her to the hospital, after all the tears and plasma, after they planted Leo over in the Green River Cemetery with Jackson Pollock — yeah, he'd finally made it — after all the tears and praying and plastic surgery, after the eleven operations and all the physical therapy, she didn't know that her life would fade into a hum-drum malaise of beer and TV and sorrow, devoid of joy — no she didn't know, she couldn't know, and so when she and Leo got in the car that night (that night that night that long-ago night) she was happy.

Could be it was the accident that made the zits kick in big-time, that precipitated my hair falling out. After Leo died I started to lose my curly locks at an alarming rate. That's when I discovered the birthmark — the hieroglyphics on my head, the strange dark squiggles and dots. That's when I took to wearing a ballcap.

Some mornings I'd struggle to surface-consciousness from a Duco Cement or Ronson Fluid-induced dreamfog peopled by multiple Muffy Snitbreads and I'd have to spit refugee hairs from my dry crusty mouth. All I could do was cry. My tear-stained pillow resembled a bloated sick dog, sparsely covered with hair, but the salt water streaming from my eyes brought no comfort, only stung the open oozing gunksores of my face. So I gave up weeping, just sniffed more glue, resigned myself to my lot (my little) in life.

I'd ask Mama about this weird cranial birthmark, did it run in the family?

But Mama was mum, refused to spill. About my birth-mark, my birth, about her early life. What I knew was this: Polish-born, the product of a Warsaw ghetto, she'd been shipped with her twin sister and parents to Buchenwald and had spent four years of her girlhood in that Nazi hellhole. Mama and Aunt Esther were the only family members to make it out – and after the war they were adopted and brought to America by one of the camp's liberators, a black soldier from Cashampton named Josiah Foote.

That was it.

The night Mama died had been like every other night since Leo's adios. Wearing her tattered bathrobe, her silver-shot black hair expertly curled as if it was 1951 and she was expecting some stud in a Studebaker to pick her up for a night of reefers and whiskey and backseat groping, Mama had been in the living room, watching tube and drinking beer. Remote control and cable had vaulted her into a new realm of videocy. She'd flip through the forty-channel menu at warp speed, rejecting every offering save for the sweaty steroid-bloated behemoths of the pro-wrestling circuit. Only then would her gnarled fingers ease their stranglehold on the channel-changer, only then would she relax, pop a Thorazine, swig a brew, open a fresh bag of Cheez Doodles, lean on back in her couch and scream right along with all the yahoo-hooing goons in the studio audience.

I walked into the living room, yanked a beer from Mama's sixpack, popped it and guzzled, making my washboard belly dance as I sucked suds.

It was a small house, a cottage really – a goddamn sharecropper's shack to tell the truth – hidden in the trees off to the right of the gate leading into the Mulrooney Estate. Eustace P. Mulrooney was the CEO of a giant credit-card company. What with the economy gone to horseshit, the house and grounds were up for sale. The Mulrooney kids were all grown up – and though they still visited once in a while, winter weekends it was usually just old man Mulrooney, his wife Beatrice and his plump-breasted secretary, Mary Jo. I'd hidden in the bushes many a night, watching naked Mary Jo in the heated pool, cutting the moonlit water like Esther Williams sans swimsuit.

My bare spare room. Like a monk's cell. From out in the living room I could hear televised noise, could see the shadows of jumping video images.

Mama surfed from channel to channel, eating through basketball games, hockey games, news, sitcoms, old movies, news, animal kingdom shows, spring training baseball games, MTV, documentaries.

I came out of my room wearing clean jeans and jeans jacket over a T-shirt. Stood behind Mama, watching what she watched.

Snippets of commercials flashed by, showing perfect white people pitching product, happy dippy yuppies with masses of shiny clean hair, straight noses, cellophane-clear skin, selling luxury cars and soft drinks and life insurance – the only things they let a dark-skinned brother sell were malt-liquor, underwear, sneakers, The Army, fried chicken. The only things they let an African sister sell were feminine deodorants, aspirin, cheap cars and doughnuts. Implying what? Toxic love canals? Killer headaches? Rattletrap cars? Atrocious eating habits? And the Jews were the buffoons, the bald anteater-nosed foils to the handsome lordly WASPs.

But Mama just kept the images moving, on and on, never stopping. Tube without end, amen. She was waiting for the wrestlers.

'Hey, Mama.' I popped a fresh brew, but before I could

raise it to my lips she grabbed it and set to sucking suds. 'Muffy Snitbread talked to me today.'

'What do you want, schmuck, a medal?' she asked in her Polish accent, and then she giggled and burped and licked her lips. 'You still goin' on about Snuffy Shitbreath? All these years? Get a life.'

I cringed and scratched a shoulder-zit.

'Hey, Mama, I got a life, I take care of you.' I flashimagined Mama flying solo: no Cheez Doodles, no ice cold frosty Old Milwaukees, no cable. She'd crash-land in an institution for good, out there somewhere where the buses don't run. 'You don't like it?'

'Sure I do, Gilbert, but it doesn't keep my dentures from slipping.' Mama let her upper plate fall out of her mouth and she grinned at me, prune-like.

I sighed, sad replacing mad. 'So who's wrestling tonight?'

'Brutus Beefcake and Jake the Snake.' Mama's eyes glowed. She was savoring the confrontation: the sweat, the hair, the theatrical summit-meeting between Jake's nose and Beefcake's crotch; and the TV images kept on zipping by – from foreign war to sit-com to movie to ballgame. A melting kaleidoscope of color and motion.

'Stop it!' I cried. I wrestled the remote and flipped backward to baseball.

The Mets versus the Yankees from spring training, and the pitcher was backing off the mound as a cartoon-breasted woman ran toward him. She grabbed the guy and swallowed his thin form in her busty grandness, planted a fat smacking smooch on his lips, loud as the crack of the bat on the ball.

I felt a twinge in the belly, a mixture of lust and sorrow. It was Lindsay LaRouche.

A year earlier Lindsay LaRouche had been a normal-breasted girl who came to work at the Upton Riding Club

as a groom. Over the years I had seen hundreds like her —
pretty white girls from middle-class Bonacker families, all
saddled with the same horse-obsession. Sure they were nice to
the ponies, mares and geldings, but when it came to an intact-
penised horse they became downright possessive, arguing
over who got to curry him, who got to hose him down, who
got to trim his mane, who got to swab his wiener. But Lindsay
was different. She treated all the horses with equal care. And
to further separate her from the pack, she was unilaterally
friendly — to co-workers and clients alike. If Lola wanted to
brush Shaka Zulu, the pylon-penised 'property' of Auralee
Emeraldstein-Bittburg, Lindsay gracefully allowed her. If
Deborah wanted to saddle Caesar or Woodrow Wilson, that
was cool too. Was she content with currying and washing and
feeding and saddling horses? Was she there for the minimum
wage or the free riding lessons? Not likely. Lindsay LaRouche
gave off the not-so-subtle odor of ambition. Ambition to
what? To join the upper classes by copping herself a rich
horse-lover? Sure she flirted with club members, but then
again so did all the girl-grooms. And though client-groom
flings were as normal as buzzing shitflies in summer (such
harmonic hormonal convergences of bankbook and booty
were expected), and though it was fairly common knowledge
that she'd done the wild-thing with Fergus Frankfurter, in
Cashampton By The Sea inter-class marriages were rarer than
a freshly slaughtered rump-roast. So even if she was fucking
Fergus Frankfurter's prostate into a humongous salted pretzel, even if Fergus was gifting her with the occasional bracelet
or false promise, Lindsay posed no real threat to Mariah: It
would be a rainy day in Phoenix before the jelly-bellied failed
TV-game-show producer ditched his wife in favor of a lowly
groom, because Mariah Frankfurter, the two-piglets-fighting-
in-a-duffel-bag-butted daughter of Elliot and Dorcas Quinch-

ard (Elliot's daddy had founded the Wall Street brokerage firm of Quinchard Frères), Mariah was holding all the chips.

Nonetheless, it was clear that Lindsay was angling for something extra.

And baby did she ever get it. Fifty-eight Triple-X-cup-inches worth.

One night, three months into her Upton career, over a year back, I ran into her at old Fish Head Danny's bar and was more than surprised when she snuggled up against me and tearfully confided that she thought she was ugly.

'No no!' I said emphatically. 'You are a pretty woman, inside and out.'

'You think so?' she said, weeping onto my shoulder, honking into a hanky. 'I'm ugly. I'm poor. I have this bump on my nose. The clients all think I'm cheap. Fergus Frank-furter dumped me. No man would want me.'

'No man?' I scratched a cheekzit. 'Why a guy would have to be crazy not to want you.' I caught Fish Head Danny's eye and signaled for more drinks.

'Do you see this?' She rolled up her sleeve and showed me freshly healed scarred wrists. 'I tried to commit suicide when Fergus gave me the heave-ho.'

She snuggled close. Fish Head Danny slopped the drinks – shot of Southern Comfort with a beer-back for me and a double vodka-rocks for Lindsay – and he turned his face so she wouldn't see him grin. Specs Schwartz with a girl! A Cashampton first.

I hugged her and felt a shudder in my crotch that spread upwards till my whole body was shaking – but she pulled away.

'What's wrong?' I asked, mortified.

'I can't be touched. It makes me feel cheap.'

'I'm sorry. What can I do? I'll do anything to make you feel better.' I meant it. This was the first girl who'd ever allowed me this close.

'You mean that?' She sniffled. 'You really mean that?'

'Anything.'

'Well,' she said, leaning close and whispering, a small smile brightening her tear-mapped face. 'If you marry me I'll make your liver shiver and your bladder splatter.' My unzitted pecker snapped to attention and I grabbed her wrist, licked the puckered flesh of her failed suicide attempt.

And that's how I ended up, without a kiss, marrying Lindsay LaRouche.

Mama objected. Lindsay's folks boycotted the ceremony. Hank Upton and his dying brother Frank were our witnesses.

When the justice said, 'You may kiss the bride,' Lindsay turned her head and my lonely lips landed on her sprayed-stiff hair-helmet. When she tossed the bouquet, Frank and Hank both grabbed. Hank got it.

On our nuptial night at the Commack Motor Inn, after I'd bathed in the heart-shaped hot-tub, when I stood before my pink-pajamaed princess in my own brand-new flagpole-proud Caldor jammies, she laughed. She tried to gag her laughter in a pillow, but it came out, choked and snorting and cruel.

'I know I'm not handsome,' I said, with whatever dignity a baldheaded blushing pizzaface with a hard-on could muster, 'but you are the cherry atop the banana split and I am a virgin for you.'

She whinnied with unbridled mirth and chucked the pillow at me. 'On the couch, Specs.'

'But Lindsay, through sickness and health and all that.'

'Specs,' she said, tears of laughter running down her cheeks. 'Dear sweet disgusting Specs, I need five-thousand dollars for an operation.'

'What's wrong?'

'It's a female thing,' she said. 'When it's better, then I'll make love.'

So the next day I emptied my bank account – the bread I'd been saving for the new laser acne-surgery – and Lindsay went off for her operation.

When she came back, she had tender untouchable rivet-nippled watermelons for breasts, a new bumpless nose, a chin with 'character' and an upcoming job dancing topless in Bayshore. The first thing she said was:

'Specs, you're on the couch until the divorce.'

And that was that. Married and divorced without a kiss.

So there I was, still a virgin, still shoveling shit for a living, and there was Lindsay LaRouche, now nationally famous – the 'Kissin' Banshee' who had scurried onto the court to kiss Michael Jordan in the second game of the NBA finals, the platinum-blonde breast-monster who could have suckled a silicon-chip factory, who'd been arrested for causing a near-riot last summer at Yankee Stadium – my ex-wife, being escorted off the field by a pair of grinning stadium security men (I could have sworn that one of the rent-a-cops copped a feel) to the thunderous applause of the multitudes – and the back of her T-shirt read: APPEARING AT DANTE'S SEX-WORLD NYC Easter Day thru May 17.

I bent and kissed Mama's cheek, fitted a fresh brew in her hand, opened a bag of Cheez Doodles and placed it on her lap.

'I told you so,' Mama said.

'I don't think she has a bad heart,' I said.

'Boy, you talk more shit than Hitler.'

I stood there a long time.

And Mama just switched channels.

Big rain raked swollen puddles with machine guns plops. I turned off the two-lane highway onto the rutted road of the

Reservation, passing the shut-down shop that in summer sold Native American tourist junk — moccasins and dolls and jewelry the Montauks imported from other tribes — and I stopped in front the stand that sold tax-free cigarettes.

'Hello, Dawn,' I said through my unrolled window to the girl in the booth. A black/Indian of eighteen, brown-skinned, long-haired, plush-lipped, full-bodied — she was wearing a faceful of pretty bad acne herself. 'What's up?'

She blushed and her lovely zitscape clouded dark. I could feel my own pimpleology itching in empathy. It seemed just yesterday she was a kid, playing and running and giggling, kicking a can, chasing a dog, but now Dawn Cash was a young woman, so serious, so shy, so all-fired curvaceous. So many lovely ripe pimples.

'Uncle Kurtis . . .' she managed. 'He's back.'

'I heard,' I said, eyeing her cheek-zits jealously. 'The usual.' I exchanged two dollars for a pack of Marlboros, tossed them on the floor of my old Dodge pickup. There were twenty or thirty packs of cigs there. I didn't smoke. Just bought them to give me a reason to stop and chat. 'Well, see ya.'

Beat-up paint-peeling wooden shacks. Rooftops warped. Porches sagging. Yards decorated with old washing machines rusting alongside car carcasses. Faded empty beer cans bobbing like buoys in puddles. Just a gunshot away from the mansions.

Clarisse Cash, Kurtis's mother, my granddad's cousin, sat on an old sofa in her bric-a-brac-cluttered living-room, watching a *Cosby Show* re-run.

'Do black people really live like that?' she asked. I hadn't seen her since Mama's funeral. She wore an old bathrobe and her thick dark hair was plaited in long braids. Her aging pretty face was haggard. I kissed her cheek. Sweet baby-powder smell, and something else: illness.

'Not fucking likely,' came the familiar voice. 'And if they do, they're not black anymore.'

Kurtis Swimming Otter Cash stood in a bedroom doorway smoking a cigarette. Muscular — more than ever after his five year bit — and handsome, Kurtis limped over to me.

'You really did get out!' I said, giving him my hand to shake.

'No shit, Sherlock,' he said with a smile, scorning my hand and hugging me. 'Damn, Gilbert, you been pumping iron?'

'Pumping horseshit.'

'Let's blow this popcorn-stand.'

'Gilbert,' Clarisse called, 'go see Billy. He hasn't left his room in a month.'

Billy was Clarisse's second son. Darker than Kurtis and gay, Billy Cash was a twenty-year-old loner who dreamed of going to The City and becoming a fashion designer. He took in sewing to pay for his *Women's Wear Daily* subscription and was in the seventh month of a sympathetic pregnancy.

'Hey, Billy,' I said to the thin boy lying in a fetal position on the bed.

'Hi, Uncle Gil,' he said softly, not looking up.

'How you feeling?'

'Baby's kicking.'

I handed him an old copy of *Vogue* that Cassandra Phlebitis had dropped in Caesar's stall. One corner of the magazine was mangled, horse-tooth impressions marring some anorexic cross-eyed model's footwear.

'Thanks,' Billy said.

'Well,' I said, looking around the neat room with the two sewing dummies draped with material for baggy dresses — maternity outfits — and walls plastered with fashion pictures, 'take care, Billy. Anything you need, call.'

'I hope it's a girl,' he said softly.

*   *   *

'I'm sorry about your marriage,' Kurtis said.

'It was a pretty sorry marriage.'

'And I'm real sorry about your mother.' He swigged from a bottle of Wild Turkey as we drove the backroads of Cashampton, mansions looming dark and distant behind high hedges. 'She was good people.'

'It was a helluva funeral,' I said. 'Me and my rich Aunt Esther and old Billy de Kooning the artist, we were the only white folks there.'

'Still think you're white?' Kurtis asked. For years he'd been insisting that in America white was a state-of-mind, not a color. 'Your mama was a nice lady.' Kurtis hit from the bottle. 'Look, Gilbert, I apologize for not writing. I was kinda caught up in my own shit. I hope your feelings weren't hurt.'

'Hell, I understand what you were going through, being locked up for something you didn't do.' I took a swallow of Turkey. 'Are you bitter?'

'As Lord Nelson said on his deathbed, ''Fuckit, I ain't got time to be bitter.'' '

We stood smoking a joint in the horseshit-mudded stable parking lot, next door to the annual Easter Party at Hank Upton's. For grunts and grooms attendance was mandatory.

I sucked a monster hit of Hawaiian. The pineapple-sweet smoke circulated in my bloodstream, ventilating my brain, easing my anxiety, greasing the nooks and crannies of my cranium.

'And then Muffy asks me if Jonas is boffing Maria.' Unloading the day's horseshit helped. The less I kept bottled up the better I felt.

Kurtis toked off the joint.

'Jonas Gritz is one horny WASP. What you might call a

blue-blood with a white liver. A sperm bank with a stock portfolio.'

'But I don't get it. Muffy's so gorgeous.'

'Figger it's like Lay's Potato Chips. No one can eat just one.'

I yanked my emergency half-pint of Southern Comfort from inside my jeans jacket, took a healthy gulp. Kurtis pulled on the herbstick, the joint sending dense snakes of smoke into the sprinklemist. Smokeclouds billowed from his blemishless brown face. Kurtis was my brother, a few months younger in age, centuries older in experience. I drained the final glug, then threw the dead soldier into the trees. It crashed through branches, thudded in mud.

'You been hitting that Sudden Comfort kinda hard.'

'Wanna get shitfaced for the party,' I said, meditatively fingering my zitfarm. I pulled the crinkled-soft Valentine's card from my inner breast pocket and stroked the worn paper, the goofy dog on a skateboard with a bunch of balloons in its paw, saying, 'I wheelly think you're sweet!'

'Someone's got a crush on you.'

'Horseshit. Probably one of the girl-grooms.'

Kurtis picked up a stick and touched it to both my shoulders and my cap, saying, 'I hereby dub thee Sir Gilbert, Knight Of Horseshit Stable. Last of the romantics.'

'Man, this party's gonna be hell,' I said, lightly scratching Pinatubo.

'When you look at those rich fucks, just imagine them tomorrow morning all hungover on the toilet, taking a big fat squirrelly dump. Gotta learn how to hate creatively, baby.'

A Rolls-Royce with monster-truck wheels and a roaring dual-exhaust sped into the parking lot. The giant wheels sloshed through puddles of muck, sending rain-soft horseshit and mud splashing onto my face and chest with a wet solid thwack, missing Kurtis completely. Cold brown gook dripped down my chin. Kurtis pulled a fresh bandana from his pocket, gave it to me. I wiped my glasses, nose, cheeks, chin, clothes.

Big Barton Snitbread opened the door and hopped down. He was dressed in an LL Bean duckhunting outfit. 'Welcome back, Kurtis,' he boomed. 'I knew you didn't do it.'

'That why you refused to be a character witness at the trial?'

'So I made a mistake.' He shrugged. 'I'm human. How do you boys like the new ride?' He stuck a hand down his pants and rearranged his business.

The vanity plate read RUBBAS.

'The British would take you out back the barn and shoot you,' Kurtis said, kicking a massive wheel. RUBBAS was obvious. Snitbread Pharmaceutical had opened a prophylactics division.

'Hey Kurtis, maybe you can use these.' The billionaire tossed a box of Sensuous brand condoms.

Kurtis caught them. 'They might come in handy.'

'I hope so.' The tub-o'-guts laughed, a wheezy wounded-donkey bray. 'You can never be too protected.'

Kurtis said nothing.

'Use them in good health.' Big Barton squeezed another burst of nervous chuckles from his bright red mouth. 'Kurtis, how would you like to come over to Cash Island and guinea-pig some new drugs?'

'I've already had that pleasure.'

'And you made good money. By the way, Dr. Guberstein would like you to take a follow-up for long-term minor side-effects from that flu drug.'

'I'll tell you one side effect, Barton: no more tests.'

'Now what kind of attitude is that?'

'A healthy one.'

'I'd say it was a hostile one.'

'That's me, an A-numba-one hostile mothafucka.'

'Anyhow, welcome back and Happy Easter.'

Big Barton headed into the party.

I dabbed at Pinatubo with the handkerchief.

'Eat the rich,' said Kurtis.

We were watching the horsepeople drink and dance and shove cocktail wieners down their throats. When we'd entered the party the whole place had crowded around Kurtis, clapping his back, each uttering some variation on the 'I-knew-you-didn't-do-it' theme. Now, turbo-charged by a few glasses of Wild Turkey 101 from the bar, I was on a roll. The years of bitterness stored in my heart were seeping out my mouth. I'd already told socialite Auralee Emeraldstein-Bittburg that her newest nose job looked like the seventy-meter ski jump at the Sarajevo Olympics. She'd stormed off in a huff to complain to Hank Upton.

'Have you ever wondered why major disasters rarely hit on the white and wealthy?' I was bending the diamond-studded ear of Cassandra Phlebitis. She was gobbling mayonnaise-gloopy crab-salad, washing it down with gulps of wine. With every oversized bite I could see the copious gold of her molars.

'No, Specs, I haven't,' she said between chomps, rolling her eyes at Kurtis who stood smoking a cigarette and coolly eying the crowd, dancers gracelessly gyrating out of synch with the music, flapping arms like spastic birds. Boozy sweat-smells and expensive perfumes blended to form a gas that'd make a bull elephant hump a sewer pipe.

'Have you noticed anything strange about my Caesar's doo-doo?' Cassandra asked seriously. 'Do you think my love is getting fat?' Caesar the gelding was partial to the chocolate-chip cookies her maid baked.

'His shit is shit,' I said. 'And he's starting to look like your husband, especially around the crotch.'

Cassandra flushed and her eyes glazed with an angered incredulity.

I could just see her the morning-after, squatting on the throne extruding crab salad, makeupless, dyed hair a mangled tangled bird nest, face contorted, groaning grotesquely with the effort. I laughed aloud.

'And how's his fan club in Cyprus?' Kurtis asked. Some years back Sock Phlebitis had committed the unpardonable sin (for a Greek) of backing the Turks – selling weapons to his birth-country's dread ancient enemy when they annexed a chunk of Cyprus. He'd been ostracized by his countrymen and been forced to become an American citizen.

'Kurtis, just because you're privy to some family secrets there's no reason to be rude,' Cassandra said haughtily.

'I'm being honest,' Kurtis said. Before prison Kurtis had been going by Cassandra's place regularly to 'fix things' – wink wink. 'Sock's a motherfucking crook.'

Cassandra spluttered: 'Bu-bu-bu-but—'

'And why' – I raised my finger like Moses Heston preaching to the Israelites – 'doesn't a biblical plague of frogs rain down upon Cashampton?'

Cassandra sighed loudly and scooped crab-salad into her mouth. Mayonnaise pinking the red of her lipstick, she asked: 'What in the name of Robert Mapplethorpe does that have to do with me or my husband or my horse?' She turned to Kurtis for support.

'Everything, Sandy baby. You're pretty democratic when it comes to giving up the gruntcakes – and don't get me wrong, sis, the sex was outstanding, especially that little stunt you do with the golf balls. I thought about that a lot of nights Upstate. Even told some of the hardcases about it and they tried it out on each other with frozen meatballs. But when it comes to compassion? Hell, you care more about that dickless wonder-horse of yours than you do about people starving to death right outside your Park Avenue apartment.'

Cassandra's face turned dark. The hand holding the forkful of crab-salad up to her mouth shook. A small bubble of spit ballooned at the corner of her twitching pink lips. The crab-salad slid off the fork and dove into the space between her half-exposed breasts.

Kurtis held her wrist. She shuddered as the crab slid slimy cold down her silk-covered belly.

'What about that boat that sank last week in the Red Sea? Three-hundred pilgrims going for Spring Break at Mecca. Boat only supposed to hold a hundred-and-fifty. All drowned. Y'know who owns that boat?'

Cassandra shook No – but she knew, of course she knew. Everyone knew. It was in the papers, on the TV. Sock had been on the Upton office phone all morning that day. He'd even delayed his riding lesson.

Cassandra's head kept swiveling: No-No-No-No-No!

'You know,' Kurtis said.

'Then so what?' she spat angrily. 'We have insurance.'

Kurtis let go of her wrist and she scurried off to her beetle-browed butterball of a safari-suited husband, Socrates, who was dancing the Lambada with Lana, a seventeen-year-old blonde bubbleheaded Bonacker groom.

'Hey, I'm sorry,' I said, 'if I ruined your thing.'

'She'll be back. And don't be sorry; it would take a hundred-thousand of their hearts to fill your chest.'

We got refills and stood in a corner.

There was Marmalind and Portius Pleistocene, bopping like a pair of sock-hopping teens while designer Larva Shinsplintz, in an African muumu, nuzzled her teenaged Finnish chauffeur Lasse and spoke with tuxedoed Egon Bibble-Booth as Egon snuck leering looks at the pumping plump rump of Diego Luegodago who danced close and sweaty with black-haired Maria the instructor. And check out the Dreckenzorfer Quints — Titi, Bibi, Kiki, Fifi, and Lili — and their twin cousins from Dusseldorf, CeCe and Mimi — seven bionic Teutonic automobile heiresses — not a one of them under six-foot-four in their lizardskin boots, not a one of them wearing a bra — shaking their leather-panted booties with Big Barton Snitbread while Sarah Snitbread and grandson Clark stood guzzling Stoli on the rocks, talking to cover-girl Chessy Hinckley and morose novelist Jay Macaroni, while Jay's wife, giraffe-necked movie star Oma Munson, talked script with director Terry Tuba, as Musgrove Messerschmitt and Cleo Klamlapper and Mariah and Fergus Frankfurter toasted something or someone or other and lovely Muffy Snitbread-Gritz sprawled on a sofa with Count and Countess Hugo and Baby Luegodago of Uruguay.

We drifted over near Muffy and the Luegodagos.

Muffy: 'I don't see Jennifer or Jonas, but I just have to tell tell you, Baby, because I'm so proud: Last week in Maryland, Jonas took first in dressage for his division and Jenny took a second!'

Baby Luegodago: 'Dot's mahvluss, Moffy.'

Hugo Luegodago: 'I seenk dot's fahbooluss, Moffy.'

Me: 'Howdy, folks!' My pimples were pulsating and I rubbed Pinatubo for luck.

Kurtis: 'Say, Count Luegodago, how's the beef biz? Plow down any rain forests for grazing land today?'

Muffy: 'Now, Kurtis, the Count is the Chairman of the International Committee for Rain Forest Preservation. I think you owe him an apology.'

Kurtis: 'For what? Every time a cow farts the ozone layer gets that much thinner and some poor fuck who can't afford Big Barton's Sunblock 57 gets his slice of the melanoma pie.

Each fucking hamburger you Nazis make deprives a child of a year's worth of grain. Let 'em eat cancer, huh?'

Muffy Snitbread-Gritz and the Luegodagos stared at their drinks, their faces taking on a boiled lobster hue.

Me: 'And you, Muffy, while people are starving to death and shitting their guts in the dust, you're living on filthy fucking Speed-Lax dollars. Your whole damn life is built on diarrhea!'

'Shut up!' Muffy screamed. 'Shut up, Pizzaface!'

'Ahem.' It was bony bowlegged Hank Upton. A former top equestrian, he'd given up competitive riding for instructing and drinking and pursuing rosy-cheeked young men – or if none were available he availed himself of certain collectible photographs he bought through the back pages of the North American Man Boy Love Association magazine. I'd seen him reading it in his office, seen the half-blind postman Jerry deliver the plain brown-wrapped envelopes. 'May I borrow these gentlemen for a moment?'

'Pliz,' Countess Luegodago hissed, her jowls shivering with rage.

Hank led us outside the party.

'Party's over for you guys.' He lit a twiglike More cigarette.

'No sweat, Hank,' Kurtis said politely.

'Look, Kurtis, you've been away – and of course your job is open – but as long as you're a guest in my house I don't want you torturing the clients.'

'We wouldn't want you to get in any trouble,' I said.

'If anyone's ass is potentially grass, Gilbert, it's yours. And if our clients insist, I'll serve it to them. Diced, sliced or in the can.'

'Blame me, Hank,' Kurtis said. 'It was my fault.'

'Kurtis, you've got an excuse – you've been through an ordeal – but Gilbert knows better. What's gotten into you, son?'

'Hank, I been shoveling their horseshit and taking their bullshit for two fucking decades. Ain't that worth anything?'

'Sure. About five bucks an hour.' Hank fixed his thin lips to his glass of iced vodka, sipped, then chose his words carefully. 'Here's the scoop. The price of hay is rising, the price of oats is way up, we're booking fewer lessons, and more of our clients are selling their horses to French meatpackers. Ridable horses. And we're accepting people as members we'd have told to go piss up a stick a few years back. We're even considering Bertha Seward's application. So listen, Gilbert, if you want to be around to watch that poor sightless biddy learn how to ride you're going to have cool out. Just take care of the horseshit, guy.'

Hank turned on his booted heel and pounded back into the house.

'Fuck all that noise,' I said.

Kurtis sparked a joint and we walked, feet sloshing in mud, smoking.

'Cheer up, nigger,' Kurtis said, passing the pot. 'Least he didn't flog you.'

'Don't talk like that.'

'What? Nigger? Nigger ain't nothing but a word. It isn't about color, nigger. It's about class. You're just a pale liberal pisspot nigger and tonight you forgot to play the game . . . and now you're Bogarting that joint.'

I gave him the joint and he looked at it. 'You nigger-lipped it,' he said, and laughed.

A pack of wet yapping dogs ran up to us. A motley crew of pure-breeds – a Rottweiler, a Dane, a Yorkie, a Lab, a poodle – all goofy and muddy in their frolic.

'A dog don't know bigotry,' Kurtis said, as Musgrove Messerschmitt's poodle Kerensky humped his leg. 'Not unless it's taught. You know what Malcolm said about dogs? He said that while the white man in Europe sat up in the trees at night watching the mouth of his cave to keep predators out, the white woman opened her legs for the dog. That's why they're so hairy and that's why they treat their dogs better than they treat us.'

'Kurtis, you've got white in you too.'

'Maybe that's why I like cave bitches so much – I'm a dog motherfucker.' Kurtis sighed and shook Kerensky off. From his pocket he pulled a penknife and one of Big Barton's rubbers. 'There's only one way to beat bigots,' he said, delicately jabbing through the condom package. 'Only one way to fight fire, my negro.'

A car's headlights bathed us in light. I shielded my eyes but Kurtis didn't even blink. It was a Mercedes. The driver was Auralee Emeraldstein-Bittburg.

'Koortiss?' Auralee rolled her window down and the smell of perfume and gin wafted into the wet. 'Can you drife me home? I yam dronk.'

'No problem, Aur.' He winked at me and pocketed the condom. She opened the door and scooted across the seat as he climbed in; and before he'd even closed the door her jeweled claw had glommed onto his thigh.

'You know what you do when someone hates you?' Kurtis asked, smiling, as the late statesman's widow ran her blood-red nails along his crotch. 'Hate them right back,' he said, patting Auralee on the head. 'Fight fire with fire.'

Auralee Emeraldstein-Bittburg showed horse-teeth and loosed a schizoid chicken cackle.

'Come on bapy' she purred Germanically. 'Come on, bapy, light my fiya!'

Five

TWO WRITERS UNDER one roof? It wasn't going to work out. We'd drive each other mad. In the Art World I've seen solid lifelong friendships destroyed that way. Two artists just cannot live together. They end up mooching materials, cannibalizing ideas, bickering over whose idea it was originally or who didn't flush the toilet. And if one half of the equation reaches the promised land of success before the other – watch out. Witness: Pollock and Krasner (or, from a feminist standpoint: Krasner and Pollock). During her years with Jackson Lee barely painted; she was muffled into muteness by the loud thunder of his creativity, bitter and frustrated by his needs and neuroses; but after he died she came into her own and painted prodigiously. Well, at least John Dough and I didn't have any overweight love-baggage to drag around; and we weren't mining the same territory. The Pearl Man was a fictioneer, a quasi-Joycean satirist, obsessed with pimples and horseshit and class. I was but a humble journalist, researching the hidden life of one of the world's great dead artists.

I had awakened hung over and very disturbed. From Big Barton's tour, from the Wild Turkey, and from the Specs novel. The pages I'd read had triggered an unconscious identification process, and all night long I'd had anxiety-ridden dreams of high school. Not that my teenaged life had been as sad and painful as John Dough's Specs Schwartz's, but, as I thought in the sunsplashed kitchen, watching dark droplets of espresso drip from the Lavazza machine into a white china cup, there were similarities. I supposed that was what John was after, the *Everyman* quality of Specs. Fearful, pissed-upon, with the self-esteem of a castrated fieldmouse, there was a bit of Specs Schwartz in all of us. I was impressed by the prose, by the breadth of research and imagination – a bit jealous, I must admit; and though the novel seemed plotless, I wondered where it was going.

Like the fictional Specs, and like most Americans of a certain age, I had, in my youth, taken more drugs than was good for me. Walking in the woods out back of Westfield High – alone or with fellow-travelers on the rocky road to adulthood – before, between, and after classes, I'd puffed marijuana pipes, smoked joints, eaten downers or speed, dropped acid, drunk beer and vodka and sweet wine. When I couldn't afford weed, I used to scrape resin from my brass chamber pipe; I'd smoke that foul tar and cough my lungs out – but it was worth it, I'd get buzzed. And being buzzed I'd be less obsessed with the great troubling questions: When will I get laid? What will I do with my life? How can this middle-class kid get away from boring Westfield, New Jersey and a pushy mother? Putting a joint-roach between two matches, lighting it, letting it flare and burn, blowing it out and then taking nose-hits of smoking sulfur, paper, and resinous weed –

I can see now how desperate I was – all I cared about was getting off. The black kids called me 'Smoky,' told me to buy a pumice-stone and some lemon to sand the yellow stains off my fingers. No girlfriends and only an average athlete, not much interested in school and lost in cheerleader fantasies, I'd had a serious Specs Schwartz syndrome.

'Good morning, Roger,' said the Pearl Man, entering the kitchen wearing a silk dressing gown, his blond hair a wild forest.

'And good morning to you, John,' I said, vowing to not speak of his secret work. 'Did you sleep well?'

'No, I didn't,' he said, 'Those poor fucking animals.'

I nodded my head.

'Were you ever in jail, John?'

'Why do you ask?'

'Curious. About what it feels like to be, you know, locked up. Imagining isn't knowing, is it?'

'No, I guess not. But isn't existence a kind of jail?' he asked, artfully side-stepping my question. 'Maybe you should talk to Kurtis about it. Were you?'

'I never was. Oh, once when I got caught throwing iceballs at a fire engine I was in the Westfield station for three hours before my mother came to pick me up.'

'What do you feel like doing today?' he asked. 'No iceballs this time of year.'

I shrugged.

'I know,' he said. 'Let's go to The City, let's get away from this hellhole.'

'Hellhole? It's Memorial Day weekend in Cashampton. People would kill to be out here now. Let's go riding. There are a few Pollock collectors at the club I've yet to speak with.'

'You go ahead, Roger. I'm just gonna hang here and write some letters, maybe fix the sprinklers.' John reached into his robe pocket and extracted a Bic lighter and a perfectly-rolled joint. 'Do you smoke?' he asked.

'I haven't for years,' I said, feeling a familiar adrenaline rush.

'You know what they say in the mountains of India?'

'No, what do they say?'

'They say, ''Smoke ganja and honor your ancestors.'' '

He sparked the joint and inhaled.

'Were you in India?' I asked.

'Do you think,' he said, passing me the joint, smoke billowing out his mouth into the sun-flooded room, 'that Muffy Snitbread-Gritz loves her husband?'

'I don't know, John,' I said, taking the joint and smoking for the first time in years. 'Why don't you ask her?'

'Maybe I will,' he said, giggling. 'Maybe I will.'

They were all at the club. All of John Dough's main characters: Kurtis, Hank, Muffy, Jenny, Jonas, Big Barton, the Luegodagos, Cassandra. All except the dead: Specs, Mama, Pumpy The Pony – and the missing in action: Lindsay LaRouche.

'Where's John Dough?' asked Muffy Snitbread-Gritz in the dirt parking lot of the Upton Riding Club. Muffy's blue BMW had trailed the bumper of John's Jaguar all the way from Smithers' Pharmacy on Main Street in Cashampton, where I'd bought a pack of gum for my cottonmouth.

'And good morning to you, Miss Muffy,' I said – à la Specs Schwartz – with a giggle, still high from the pot.

'Oh' – she blushed – 'hi, Roger.'

'John's at home catching up on paperwork. Where's your husband?'

She pointed to a pair on horseback heading for the beach. 'He has a lesson with Maria on the beach.' She sighed.

'I don't think he and John care for each other.'

'They're very different. Jonas . . . has changed so much. People change, Roger. Sometimes I don't know him.'

'You know, Muffy, when I came to Cashampton I thought I'd be meeting a lot of liberals, but it's just the opposite. People here seem very reactionary.'

'What was it they used to say? "It's the economy, stupid." '

'The economy doesn't seem to have affected Big Barton.'

'No, it hasn't; even in hard times people still need laxatives and hemorrhoid cream and other staples. We're fortunate, I suppose.'

'I think that's called understatement.'

'I heard Daddy took you to Cash Island yesterday.'

'They should go back to calling it The Island Of The Dead.'

'I know what you mean,' she said. 'And I'm sorry.'

'Don't be sorry for me,' I said, as we entered the stables – and yes, as John Dough had written, Muffy seemed to sniff the air and sigh with appreciation. 'Be sorry for those poor animals.'

'I know, I know. But like Daddy says: "It's for the greater good." '

'That's what Dr. Mengele used to say.'

'Dr. who?'

'Oh, just a dentist I used to know who wouldn't use Novocaine.'

'Ya bin hidin' from me, Rog, ya little fuckin' peanut-dick.'

'Baby, if I've got a peanut-dick, what do you need me for?'

'I don't mean it dat way, Rog,' she said quickly. 'I miss ya. Why ya gotta stay ovah by da Poil Man's? I miss owa little tit-a-tits.'

She wore too much make-up, her age showed, and I felt for her. It's not nice being dumped on your home turf.

'I miss you too; but Baby, with the Count around, I don't

think it's such a great idea.' I just didn't have the killer instinct to deliver the knock-out blow.

'Mother?'

'Aw Christ, it's fuckin' Diego.'

Portly handsome Diego Luegodago and chunky Count Hugo approached us, three horses in tow, including Gandhi and the magnificent gelding Pancho Villa.

'Come, Mother,' Diego said.

'Yess, Baby dolling, we hov a lessong,' said the Count.

'*Vamanos, Mamacita*,' Diego said.

Baby's eyes flashed and she raised her riding crop.

'Whot deed I sez so many time, Diego?' Baby's south-of-the-border brogue was turned on full-blast. I wished she would drop the pretense. Christ, the guy was her son. Forty years of pidgin English to convince the kid his mother was a countess. Did Uruguay even have royalty? 'I estowped espeakin' Espaneesh an' Porchagoose whan I moof to Amayrica.'

'Yes, Mother. Sorry, Mother.'

'Say hallo to Meester Lemong.'

'Lymon,' I said. 'Roger Lymon. Hello, Diego, and hello again, Count Hugo.'

'Chommed ass de furs time,' the debonair elder Luegodago said, clicking his heels. If he knew anything about my little 'tit-a-tits' with his wife, he wasn't saying.

'By the way, Count,' I said, ever the responsible member of the working press. 'Did you know Jackson Pollock?'

'Yackson Polyp?' He looked puzzled. 'Ees whot, a disease?'

'*Parlez-vous Français?*' I asked the old horse, Martin Luther King.

King just stared back at me, chewing his oats, swishing his tail at flies, his eyes sad. He knew.

*   *   *

The lesson went well. My instructor, Vivian, knew her stuff. An hour of going around in a circle. No jumping for me yet. It was hot out. Flies buzzed. My butt no longer hurt.

Hank Upton was in the office smoking a cigarette, reading. When I knocked, he shoved the magazine in a desk drawer.

'Yes, Roger?'

'Hank, I wanted to ask you: Were you here back in the Jackson Pollock era?'

'I'm a Bonacker, thirteen generations – Cashampton born and raised. Finest kind. I was around, yes, but just a teenager.'

'I'm doing a film and a biography on Pollock and, well, this is a delicate subject, but do you know if he was gay?'

'You think that because I'm gay I'd know if someone else was gay?'

'Something like that.'

'Well, if he was, he never put the moves on me. Anyhow, I was pretty young.'

'That's what I mean. Young.'

'I don't know, Roger. Sure he liked kids; who doesn't? Back then it wasn't like these repressive days, when parents keep strange men away from their children for fear of the unknown natural. I saw Jack with boys, with boys and girls. Even remember him with a baby once. In Jungle Pete's. The tyke was up on the bar drinking Pabst Blue Ribbon from a baby-bottle while Pollock got sozzled on whiskey. Cute little thing was wearing one of those old-fashioned bonnets. Was Jack doing anything *wrong* with any of them? Who knows.'

'Well, Hank, I just heard that he liked boys,' I said, trying to imagine the great painter visiting ghastly atrocities upon some drunken cherub. 'Maybe he liked them and didn't act on it.'

He laughed and lit a smoke. 'All those dots and splotches and drips . . . You thinking what I think you're thinking?'

'I guess I am.'

'Here's a title for your book: *Handkerchief Dreams.*'

Six

'AMONG THE WORKING poor and the middle-class, there is little or no worry about caloric intake, no concern about preservatives or hormones, and a decided attraction to saturated fats. To quote Mrs. Seward, "They eat, therefore they die." '

I was explaining Chapter ten of Bertha Seward's bestselling *Eating For Success* book, titled 'How The Other Half Dies', to Cassandra Phlebitis, who was wolfing down crab-salad in the bright sunshine at Terry Tuba's Memorial Day party for Beverly Hills-based swimming-pool-art-impresario Simon Splatzstein. The bottom of Terry's pool was covered with sculptures and waterproofed canvases, and a few of the guests were treading water, wearing masks and snorkels to inspect the art at close range, their checkbooks and jewelry sitting in plastic bags on poolside chairs.

Among the partygoers, I saw the Luegodagos, the Snitbreads, the Gritzes, the Spoons, John Dough, Kurtis Cash,

Hank Upton, the Shinsplintzes, the Pleistocenes, Musgrove Messerschmitt, Egon Bibble-Booth, Sonja Dreckenzorfer, her five tan tall daughters and their two cousins – all the usual suspects and then some.

Simon Splatzstein, the nephew (and some said lover) of Solly Holliman, had been the receptionist-gofer at the Pelt gallery on Greene Street in Soho back in the early Eighties and, since moving to LA and finding his Art World *modus operandi* as the P.T. Barnum of Pool Art, he'd gone quite potbellied and completely bald, almost resembling one of the dolphins his girlfriend, a fifty-something woman of Amazonian proportions named Vera, trained for television shows. ('Flipper was a female,' she'd told me earlier, keeping a sharp eye on Simon Splatzstein as he splashed about, showing Muffy Snitbread-Gritz some sculpture, 'who got so stressed-out and despondent doing retakes that she sunk to the bottom of the pool and refused to eat and eventually stopped breathing. Suicide. It was rilly rilly depressing.') Simon's laminated plastic catalogues requested only three things of Terry Tuba's guests: that they 'please shower before taking to the water, in order that sunblock and suntan oils do not cloud the visual medium,' that they not touch the pieces until 'financial arrangements are concluded – all major credit cards accepted' – and that they 'please refrain from introducing into The Pool urine or any other noxious foreign agent which might offend The Art.'

'Mm ugg flbrngluh!' Cassandra said.

'Pardon?'

Cassandra swallowed her jumbo mouthful and said:

'I'm a Democrat. My husband, Socrates, is a liberal Republican. But we both eat carefully and believe strongly in political correctness – when it doesn't conflict with business. When I heard that your beloved hero Jackson

Pollock beat his wife Lee, I made Sock sell our Pollock. And that was in '88, a very soft year, so we took a bath.'

'But there's no evidence he beat her,' I said, sipping a perky little Chablis from Bertha Seward's Cashampton Winery.

'It's there,' she said, forking another load of crab. 'In the work – the violence, the hatred, the ugliness, the misogyny. All those splashes and splatters – like a snuff film. Why do you think they called him Jack The Dripper?'

'Remember the times, Cassandra. The man was working in the shadow of Hiroshima and Nagasaki. Perhaps he was painting a snuff film for the human race? Shattering the boundaries. Kissing the sky before it fell on his head. *I* see the work as a depiction of the random beauty and confusion of the Universe, both inner space and outer space, with, at times, ghostly human figures dancing in the void. Pollock used to say, "I am Nature." I find the work magical.'

'Hogwash,' she said, applying Sunblock 57 from one of the complimentary tubes provided by Big Barton Snitbread. 'Now this,' she indicated a large red sculpture shaped like a blooming pockmarked vulva, sunk in the shallow end of Terry Tuba's pool, '*this* is Art. The forms are feminine and graceful, and the message is quite feminist and PC.'

I checked the catalogue and read, '*Drowning Cunt On The Half-Shell – A Self-Portrait In Kevlar*. Mindy Boil. $50,000.'

'It's a powerful statement,' she declared, 'by a *woman* artist.'

'I think if my name was Mindy Boil I might be a tad bitter myself.'

'But exactly, Roger: it's a cry for help – for all woman-kind.'

'I'd have to agree – a drowning bulletproof rendition of your own abused vagina is a *serious* cry for help.'

'You *do* understand.' Cassandra glowed happily and bussed

my cheek. 'I think that somewhere deep inside all men there's a woman just screaming to get out. Can you keep a secret, Roger?'

'My lips are sealed with Krazy Glue.'

'I've taken a lover.'

'Congratulations.'

'Isn't it terrific? Guess who?'

I followed her love-soft eyes.

'Kurtis,' she said huskily, pride and passion lighting her from within. 'Before he went away, he and I were very, very close.'

'It's lovely to be in love,' I said, though I doubted very much I would know. The experience with Sharon Timlin had ended up making me bitter. I hadn't eaten a baked potato in years.

'Yes it is. Oh, Roger, I'm like a schoolgirl – giddy in love. Kurtis has taught me so much. Marriage is the ultimate prostitution, no? You know, at least the hooker on the street gets something in return for her slavery.'

The diamonds sparkled on her fingers and ears.

'Like what?' I asked. 'A drug habit, a beating from her pimp and a social disease?'

'No, her body is her own. She's chosen her own fate. Like Mindy Boil's cunt.'

'But what good is choosing something if you can't stick around to enjoy it?'

'Oh, Roger, haven't you read Dostoyevsky's *The Possessed*? Suicide is the ultimate act of willpower. A freeing, a cleansing. I learned that at Sarah Lawrence, the year four freshpersons took their lives after Glenn Close performed a dramatic reading of Sylvia Plath's poems while dressed as Bozo The Clown.'

Musgrove Messerschmitt's poodle Kerensky scampered

over, dripping water from the pool. He climbed aboard my leg and started to hump. I shook him off.

'Don't be zo broodle, Mr. Lymon,' said Musgrove, wearing a waterlogged nineteen-twenties ladies' bathing outfit and a mask and snorkel, picking up the dog (around whose neck hung a string of brilliant pink pearls). 'Kerenzky loff you.'

'He's a very friendly dog,' I said. 'But I'd prefer to keep it Platonic.'

'I love your swim-suit, Muzz,' said Cassandra Phlebitis. 'It's very *chic*.'

'*Danke*. It once belonged to Zelda Fitzgerald. It waz in diz fery zoot she had her lazt menztrool periot.'

'And I like Kerensky's necklace,' I said. 'Are they *faux*?'

'My dear Mr. Lymon, zey come vrom Toorkey, vrom Chohn Dough'z augtion!' Musgrove planted a wet smooch on Kerensky's lips. 'Now, my dearz, if you'll forgiff uz, Kerenzky mozt vinish fiewing ze show.' And they hopped in the pool.

'Hello there, Sandy,' said a man getting out of the pool, drying his hairy body with a Ritz-Carlton, Paris towel, taking off his mask and snorkel, a dripping catalogue in his hand. In the hot Cashampton sun his short mop of brown hair instantly crinkled dry and stood up on end. He looked vaguely familiar.

'Oh, Guy!' Cassandra kissed the man's cheek. 'Have you met Roger Lymon from *Artnews*? Roger, Guy Gattling.'

'I've admired your commercials for years,' I said, now recognizing the familiar face and rug of the Make My Hair-Day Club president. I quoted his oft-repeated slogan: ' "I'm not just the President of the Make My Hair-Day Club, I'm also a socially satisfied former baldie." '

'And I've read your biography of Sammy Stillman at least ten times. It's terrific. I was lucky enough to acquire three of his earliest Crayon works.' We clasped hands and shook.

'Ah,' I ahhed. 'From the Sarasota Pre-School Series, I presume?'

'You really know your Stillman!' Guy Gattling was impressed. 'I understand you're doing a film on Pollock.'

'A film and a bio.'

'I've got a few Pollocks, some Hoffmans, David Smiths, Rothkos, Motherwells, Joan Mitchells, Hartigans, Krasners, de Koonings, a few by Gorky, one of the lithographic stones that Larry Rivers and Frank O'Hara made, a Baziotes – and of course, the gorgeous blood-red Philip Guston—'

'Not *Type O?*'

'You know it?'

'Only from reproductions.'

'You must come and see it some day. I'm in the book. We'll talk Pollock.' His eyes wandered over to John Dough. 'Who is that man? He looks familiar.'

'That's John Dough, the Pearl Man.'

'Ah, *that's* John Dough.' He scratched his head. It was uncanny: I couldn't at all tell that his hair wasn't real. 'This is a terrific show, eh Roger?'

'Terrific,' I agreed, utilizing the jargon *du jour*.

'I especially love that Natalie Turner piece, the mustard-colored one.'

I tried to identify the object of his admiration, but the water was distorted by dog-paddling patrons, including Big Barton Snitbread and his Great Dane Speedy.

Guy Gattling handed me his mask, and I lay on the hot tiles at the pool's edge. Through the mask I could see clearly.

The piece in question was in the deep end, beneath the white kicking legs of Egon Bibble-Booth: A yellow plastic figure of a powerful, loin-cloth-clad African man, with tendrils of plastic seaweed fashioned into dreadlocks, his body wrapped with rusting chains, a plastic Uzi in one hand, and the upper half of his giant yellow erection jutting from his loin-cloth. Another drowning victim. I stood up.

'What's it called?'

'Ms. Turner calls it *I Am A Curious Fellow, Yellow*. I'm buying it for my hot-tub in The City.'

'A good buy,' said the black woman who appeared at my side.

'A *terrific* buy,' said Guy Gattling, barely looking at her. 'I'll have a gin and tonic, Miss.'

'Hello, Natalie,' I said.

'Roger,' she said, standing tippytoes to kiss me.

'Guy Gattling, meet Natalie Turner, the artist.'

'You're . . .' Guy Gattling blushed. 'I'm so sorry. I thought you were—'

'Think nothing of it.' Natalie let him off the hook with a laugh. She was small and pretty and feminine, with large cat's eyes. 'Art, like life, is all about perceptions and ironies. You thought I was a maid and my Curious Yellow Fellow will be in your hot-tub.'

'The heat of the hot-tub, it won't damage the work?'

'Honey, at a hundred-thousand dollars you could boil and whip and castrate that nigger and I wouldn't give a shit.' She laughed, and then added: 'And neither would he. His spirit is eternal.'

'But the message of the chains is that slavery still exists, no?' Guy Gattling asked, still blushing.

'But the yellow indicates what?' asked Cassandra. 'Solidarity with the students in Tiananmen Square? Or cowardice on the Negro's part, his unwillingness to use his weapon to change his lot in life – no? By the way, I'm Cassandra Phlebitis, Ms. Turner. I've admired your work forever. You're terrific.'

'Sugar,' said Nat Turner to Cassandra, winking at me. 'That *Negro*, as you so quaintly put it, is moving on up to the

East Side, free and happy and ready to exercise his curiosity —
he's gonna do a little poking about with his johnson before he
gets on to rocking the house with his Uzi.'

'The message is—' Cassandra started.

'The message is the revolution is not only on your doorstep, Mrs. Pee, it's taking a leak in your motherfucking
swimming pool.'

'Terrific!' said Guy Gattling.

'Terrific,' said Cassandra Phlebitis, with less conviction
and a noticeable shiver.

A hundred-thousand dollars, I thought. Now *that's* terrific.

'By the way,' Guy Gattling said to me, appraising my
hairline, 'you're a bit thin on top, Roger. Maybe you ought to
see me professionally.' He grinned at Natalie Turner. 'Help
me recoup some of the worthy dollars I'll be spending today.'

Natalie and I had known and liked each other for years. Unlike
most in the Art World, she'd been exceedingly sympathetic
when Sharon Timlin ditched me for Rawlings Black – perhaps
because all during the months I'd spent in the redheaded
potato-lover's bed she and Sharon had continued to be an item
and I hadn't objected. Women were Sharon's meat, men her
potatoes, and potatoes just the tools of her trade.

'Sharon's in a down period,' said Natalie after we'd caught
up on career stuff – my Pollock mission and her *Curious* phase
– as we sipped wine and ambled about Terry Tuba's broad
lawn, avoiding the croquet game. 'We stopped playing when
she and Rawlings got hitched. He's the jealous type. I wasn't
even invited to the wedding.'

'Neither was I, but I read about it. Performed at three-
thousand-feet in mid-air by a skydiving Unitarian minister.'

'That's what's called taking the plunge,' she said, and we
had a laugh.

'Who's that luscious brother in the jeans?' Natalie asked, pointing across the lawn to Kurtis Swimming Otter Cash, who sat smoking a large spliff with John Dough, Simon Splatzstein, and Vera.

'That's Kurtis Cash,' I said. 'He works at the Upton Riding Club and recently graduated from Attica. Governor Cuomo granted him a full pardon for a cry-wolf rape.'

'He's built. Him and that white boy. Yummy. Make me stop creaming over those stringy-haired bikini girls.'

'You still on the white-girl kick?'

'Affirmative.' She laughed. 'My version of affirmative action. . . . Speaking of government, have you heard about Sharon and Rawlings and the NEA?'

'Last I heard they'd cut off her potato-grant after she took the show to Russia and Gorby gave her the keys to The Kremlin.'

'That's ancient history, Roger; she's got a fresh grant.'

'What's the new work about?'

'You know about Sharon and Rawlings getting divorced?'

'I read about it in the *Times*.'

'Well, when Senator Helms and The Reverend Jurkbaitt got wind of it they devised a long-term performance piece for them. It's called *The Sanctity Of Our Vows*. Sharon and Rawlings have to stay married, handcuffed together and living outdoors, for a year. No cash to live on and they gotta make it homeless. If they do the year, without affairs or going indoors or getting rid of the handcuffs or taking cash from friends *or* divorce, they'll get two-hundred-thousand dollars. If she conceives a child, another hundred G's. Viet Jane Sak is videotaping it all – his hundred-grand is guaranteed, plus he gets a weekly check for expenses and a Chevy Astro Van to live in, with a solar-powered hotplate and a porto-potty, but he can't help them out; and periodically the NEA people are checking up on them. They were last seen two weeks ago living under the Manhattan Bridge, begging food in Chinatown and fighting like a couple of un-neutered male pit bulls.'

'Are they allowed in restaurants to use the bathroom?'

'Negatory. The piece is all about marriage surviving homelessness. Pretty swift idea for a couple of cracker politicos.'

'It's brilliant.'

'I think Sharon'll be ready for Bellevue by the end of the year.'

'Sharon was born ready for Bellevue,' I said. 'At least she has her Ben Wah balls.'

Natalie broke into a howling, thigh-slapping laugh.

'You didn't hear, Roger?' Natalie wiped a tear. 'Where you been?'

'Right here, the fashionable boondocks. What happened?'

'Before the NEA would okay the two hundred large, Sharon and Rawlings had to testify in front of Congress about how art was not antithetical to the American Way of marriage and Family Values and all that bourgeois bullshit. The day they're supposed to appear, they take the Metroliner to Washington. Sharon has her Ben Wah balls up where potatoes go to fry, and when they walk through the metal-detector at the House o' Reps, she sets off the alarm. The guards make her take out her keys, they search her pocketbook for a gun or a bomb, and finally, an FBI lezzie takes her to a back room, does a strip-search and finds the Ben Wahs.'

'That's fucking priceless.'

'Isn't it? So now it's in the grant contract: If they catch Sharon playing gynecological billiards during the year, or if they have sex with a condom, the Potato Head Family forfeits the bread.'

*   *   *

Twilight came and went, and all of Simon Splatzstein's Pool Art was sold. The party repaired under the shelter of a large striped tent on Terry Tuba's lawn for a sit-down dinner. Bertha Seward (whose membership to the Upton Riding Club had been approved just that day), wearing dark glasses, was given the place of honor at the head of the long table. I was seated next to her. Good-looking tuxedoed waiters of both sexes served swimsuited and bathrobed and casually-dressed guests. A few had shown up from late-afternoon jaunts at the riding club, still in riding habits.

John Dough and Muffy Snitbread-Gritz exchanged surreptitious glances of mutual attraction as a vichyssoise was served. If John didn't watch out he'd have to deal with Jonas Gritz; but at present, Jonas, his nose-bandage gone, seemed preoccupied, possessively watching Egon Bibble-Booth chat-up his daughter Jenny. But I was happy for the Pearl Man. Falling in love with Muffy. Living Specs Schwartz's dream. Ah, love. I spooned vichyssoise and thought of Sharon Timlin. Cold potato soup always makes me think of Sharon, always makes me sigh.

'I'm opening a store of Bonacker fashions later this summer,' Bertha Seward told me, spilling soup on her shirtfront. 'And next door to it I'll have a Bonacker restaurant.' For such a renowned style-maven she was rather unkempt, wearing a Red Sox baseball cap over her white hair, a faded Carl Yazstremski sweatshirt (John Dough had told me that the famous Yaz was Cashampton-born, potato farm-raised), baggy blue jeans with gardening dirt on them (I'd been informed that Bertha pruned her own dahlias and rose bushes), mismatched socks (despite her sightlessness, my source had confided, she insisted on doing her own laundry and dressing herself), and a pair of chewed-up old blue Keds.

Shlurp shlurp, went Bertha's soup.

'What exactly is Bonacker fashion?' I asked, watching Musgrove Messerschmitt, down the table a way, spoonfeed soup to his laptop poodle Kerensky.

'Oh, you know, terrific items: used jeans and fishing waders and work boots and T-shirts and such.'

'Bonacker cuisine?'

'Baloney sandwiches on white-bread, Spaghetti-O's, hot dogs, chips, Cool Aid, soda pop, Jello. Fresh local fish when available, if PCB levels and dioxins are low.'

'Sounds, uhh, terrific.'

'It's a living. Rich people will buy anything.'

That I knew. Witness Pool Art.

'Did you, by chance, know Jackson Pollock?' I asked.

'Know him?' she said with a snort. 'I gave that nut the best blowjob he ever had.'

'When was this?' I asked, trying to keep the happiness out of my voice.

'I think it was '55'

'But he was supposed to be impotent by '55.'

'Wrongo, Roger. Jacko was like a jackrabbit.'

'Where did the blessed event take place?'

'Y'know, out there in his studio. He used to pick me up from high school.'

You can imagine my excitement. I was honing in on the truth. I had visions of the Hollywood premiere. Red carpets, *People Magazine*, money, fame. . . .

'So you and Pollock had sexual congress right under Lee's eyes, in the studio by the farmhouse?'

'No, no, the secret studio. The one in the woods.'

'Which woods?'

'Woods. You know. Trees and shit. Out in Springs, *near* where he lived, near where he died.'

'Could you tell me how to find the place?'

'I can do better; I'll take you there. My daddy owned those woods. When my fucking eyes were working, I played there all the time.'

'I'd be most honored, and I'd show my appreciation with a prominent thank-you in the book and some very meaty scenes about your affair in the film.'

'I want Julia Roberts to play me.'

'That can be arranged. Tomorrow?' I asked eagerly. 'Can we see the place tomorrow?'

'There's nothing there, just some old rotted lumber and shit.'

'I'd just like to get a feel for the place.'

'No sweat.'

'Were there any . . . other girls?'

'A few.'

'Can you recall the names?'

'Now that would make me a gossip, wouldn't it?'

'No, it would make you an oral historian.'

'I'll have to think about it.'

'How about a young man or a boy. Did Jackson have a thing for boys?'

'Back then I'd have said there wasn't an AC/DC boner in that man's body; but now I don't know. You know what they say about extra-macho guys.'

Bertha Seward finished her soup, and I blotted her vichyssoise-dotted shirt with my napkin.

'Are you feeling me up?' she asked.

'No, I'm—'

'Well, if you're not, you better be,' she said, taking my hand and putting it on her thigh. 'Let's take a walk, Roger,' she said removing her dentures. 'And I'll show you why *I* called him Jack The Dripper.'

'But Bertha—'

'You want oral history, yes?'

'Yes,' I said, feeling glum but not showing it, as Tito Puente's big band tuned up on the lawn. 'I certainly do.'

I felt drained, emotionally and physically drained, as I watched Bertha Seward being packed into the ambulance, flashing red lights strobing the curious crowd. On our way back from my history lesson on the beach – 'Now *that's* eating for success,' she'd said, wiping her lips – Bertha, who'd refused my helping hand, had tripped over one of Terry Tuba's lawn jockeys.

'Broken leg, possible fractured collarbone,' said the cigarette-smoking paramedic from Cashampton General.

'Are you sure?' I asked.

'These old Bonackers dames are tough as nails, bud,' the man said. 'Your girlfriend'll be up and running a marathon by August.'

'She's not my girlfriend,' I said.

'Girlfriend or not,' the guy said, pointing at my pants with his cigarette, 'you better close the barn door.'

'What happened?' asked John Dough, as I zipped my fly. Muffy Snitbread-Gritz was out on the portable dance floor, shaking it up with her husband Jonas as Larry Rivers took a saxophone solo with the band. Rivers, whose return from Paris I'd been looking forward to for weeks, had earlier drunkenly told me and Natalie a wild story – 1952 vintage – of him and Pollock getting stoned and laid in a Harlem whorehouse ('Jackson loved black girls,' he'd said, winking at Nat), and I'd had the distinct feeling my leg was being pulled.

'What happened?' John Dough asked again.

'History,' I said, not wanting to discuss it.

'Holy shit!'

I followed his gaze.

It was Willem de Kooning in a John Travolta white disco-era suit, dancing with a wildly voluptuous woman whose extraordinary breasts barely moved as she twisted and shimmied and epileptically whipped her long blonde hair.

'It's de Kooning!' I said. 'And that's—'

'Lindsay LaRouche,' he said. 'The Kissin' Banshee.'

'Oh, Christ!' he cried, running out onto the dance floor as Tito and Larry and the gang pushed the beat into hyperdrive, and I followed.

Cassandra Phlebitis was doing a herky-jerky Frug, her face dark and full of fear in a sea of pale happy dancers, while her husband, small round Socrates, unaware of her distress, wiggled up close to her, grinding, lost in the ecstasy of the Lambada. John Dough grabbed Cassandra, held her shoulders. Blood ran from her nose, down over her chin, and her color was quite dark – Tito Puente had the boys soaring and blasting and the dancers whooped and wobbled and whirled – and then Cassandra's arms flailed, her ears sprayed, and her eye strained from its socket and shot out of her head like a Nolan Ryan fastball, bouncing twice and skipping among the dancing feet, and, quicker than you can say Auralee Emeraldstein-Bittburg, Cassandra was dead.

The ambulance driver smoked while his fellows put poor Sandy in the meatwagon.

'Another one of your babes?' he asked me with a wink.

I said nothing. Tito Puente and the band were packing up. Larry Rivers was drinking black coffee. De Kooning was telling a story to the thinning throng. Lindsay LaRouche, her massive breasts drawing male eyes like a strong magnet sucking little ball-bearings, hung on his every word, looked at the Abstract Expressionist with the light of love in her eyes. Simon Splatzstein smoked a joint with Terry Tuba. Big Barton

Snitbread gathered his brood and split. John Dough searched the edges of the deserted dance floor for the lost eye.

Socrates Phlebitis was burbling – who could blame him?

'Don't worry, Sock,' I said, holding his quaking shoulders, knowing that nothing I could say would ease his pain. 'She's dancing in heaven now.' Sock sank to his knees, held his wet face in his little jeweled hands, and wept.

Kurtis Swimming Otter Cash came up from the beach with Natalie Turner.

'Koortiz,' said the one of the seven weeping blonde Dreckenzorfers. 'Can you drife uz home. Mama took zee Rollz.'

'No problem, girls,' said the handsome chief groom.

'You two missed all of the excitement,' I said to Natalie.

'Looks that way.'

'You and Kurtis—'

'We just talked politics and toked a spliff. He's on a white-girl kick too. There's a certain kind of brother' – Natalie explained, as we watched Kurtis help the seven giant Germans up into the bed of his pickup truck (poor Specs Schwartz's old truck) – 'that likes breaking white girls' hearts. Historical payback.'

I looked about for John Dough. He was chasing Musgrove Messerschmitt's poodle Kerensky, who chewed while he ran.

Socrates Phlebitis stood now, staring at the ambulance as it drifted off into the night, red ember taillights fading into the dark.

'I'm sorry, Sock,' I said.

The little Greek shipping magnate gulped and coughed and wiped his eyes. The train whistle blew soft and sad in the distance.

'I don't feel so terrific,' he said.

'I don't blame you,' I said sympathetically.

'No, Roger, I mean I really feel bad.'

He hiccuped.

'Perhaps if you hold your breath . . . ?' I suggested, but as his face turned dark under the radiant Cashampton moon and stars and his chest jerked up and down and the hiccups burst forth like Cypriot semi-automatic gunfire, I kind of had the feeling that Socrates Phlebitis had danced his last Lambada.

Seven

IT WAS NICE having Natalie Turner around the Mulrooney Estate the next week. She and John Dough made each other happy; but sadly – for yours truly (horny) and perhaps for Nat – the Pearl Man had banished the chippies from his pool.

The three of us fell into a pleasant routine. Mornings we'd wake to an early splash in the pool, followed by espresso and marijuana (like the mountain-people of India, we found it necessary to regularly honor our ancestors) and fresh bread from The Pregnant Duchess, and then John Dough would disappear into his den 'to do paperwork.' I assumed he was laboring on the Specs Schwartz *oeuvre*. Natalie and I would take the Jaguar to the beach for some sun and swimming, ritually slathering our bodies with Big Barton's Sunblock 57. I'd make tape-recorded notes on my Pollock search and Natalie would check out the bodies and collect seashells and driftwood for future sculptures. After a few hours we'd return to the mansion for lunch, finding John performing some mundane task he could easily and cheaply have hired a Bonacker lackey to perform – mowing the lawn, pruning the hedges, cleaning the pool.

'Gotta keep in shape,' he'd say, corded muscles bulging and gleaming with sweat in the sun.

After lunch, John and Nat would disappear for a few hours into his bedroom to engage in a private dialogue on race-relations in America, and I would borrow the Jag to pursue my Pollock quest. Later, after I'd returned home from my afternoon lesson at the Upton Riding Club, Kurtis would come by. Though he'd become very chummy with John Dough (the Pearl Man had presented Kurtis with his samples bag from Cash Island and a healthy check for expenses; apparently Kurtis's mother and brother were ill), he and I were not close. He seemed a bit put-off by my presence; but I knew he was an excellent source for John's novel, and Natalie liked him, so I did my best to get along.

Hiroshi Koyabashi was itching for results. I informed him, via telephone, that I was making progress.

'How soon, Roger?'

'These things take time, Hiroshi. I've already established that Pollock had a lover – a young female lover who doesn't show up in any of the biographies; that he perhaps liked prostitutes; and that he may well have been enamored of a boy – or boys – or even, God forbid, a baby. Not too shabby for such a short time.'

'A baby? Why, that's wonderful news! But, Roger, the first Pollock film will be premiering in less than a month. Right there in Cashampton. We must strike while the iron is hot.'

'Patience, Hiroshi. The deeper you dig, the richer the dirt.'

*   *   *

Guy Gattling's Stillmans radiated innocence and wisdom, their shiny crayoned surfaces gleaming brightly behind glass; and the gilded frames – perfect.

We'd eaten some watermelon sorbet and, after he'd shown me a small museum's worth of priceless Abstract Expressionist art, I'd signed his dog-eared copy of my Sammy Stillman biography, *Crayola Payola: What Makes Sammy Paint*. 'For Guy,' I'd written. 'What a guy. Keep buying. Roger Lymon.'

'Thanks, Roger,' he said, tossing the book onto a couch. 'I'll treasure this.'

We moved into the living room and stood in front of a Pollock mural.

'Where's the Pearl Man?' he asked.

'Working on a project.' I'd left the Cashampton Thoreau up a ladder in a tree, sawing a Dutch Elm-diseased branch he'd been staring at all during lunch.

'I can't wait to see what Hollywood does with Pollock's life,' Guy said. 'You know, the premiere of the first film will be at the Cashampton Cinema. An unknown is playing Jackson, Matt Dillon is de Kooning, Danny Glover as Franz Kline, Julia Roberts plays Lee, and Drew Barrymore is Ruth Kligman.'

'I know, I know,' I said. 'Have you heard that Jackson beat his wife?'

'I've heard it, Roger, but I don't buy it. You want a woman-beater,' he said, leading on, 'try David Smith. Without art, Smitty would have been a serial rapist.'

The Smith piece was a powerful metal sculpture, a twisted abstraction of the female form, a stake driven directly into her matrix.

'Horrifying,' I said.

'Ain't it lovely, though?'

'I have heard rumblings, Guy, that Pollock had a homosexual lover.'

'You would know.'

'Me? How so? I don't do gay.'

'That's not what I heard, Roger. Oh sure, you do the occasional woman – the Sharon Timlin and the Baby Luegodago, but those are just career moves. The word is you're a bit light in the loafers. You had wonderful insight into Sammy Stillman.'

'Excuse me, Guy, I haven't even a scintilla of an idea what you mean.'

'Okay, be that way.' Guy Gattling shrugged and guided me to the dining room.

Surrounding the table were some very old and primitive mechanical objects.

'From the Spanish Inquisition,' he explained. 'A lotta Jews bought the farm on these devices.'

'Great for the appetite,' I said.

'My feelings exactly. Makes you appreciate a good juicy steak, eh?'

'You seem fascinated by violence.'

'Suffering. Contortion. The rape of space. That's why I love the New York School. They were professional sufferers. Iconographic masochists. All great art is born of suffering, no? Essentially, art is concerned with questions of the spirit – don't you think? Maybe I'll hire you to write a monograph – "From the Spanish Inquisition to the New York School: Five-Hundred Years Of Pain And Suffering." Catchy, eh? Or how about "The Emphatic Positive Of The Negative"?'

'And all this is funded by toupees?'

'Such delicious irony, no? My interest in suffering financed by alleviating the psychological trauma attendant to baldness and thinning hair. If I'd been around to fix Jackson Pollock up with a half-assed weave or a high-class suture job or even a cheapo rug, I doubt very much his madness would have flourished as wonderfully as it did. And we, the art-lovers, would have been deprived: *We* would have suffered because he *wouldn't* have suffered. He never would have found his voice, so to speak, his pipeline to God.'

'And you've found God?' I picked up a pair of rusted shears.

'God is everywhere.' Guy smiled.

'And torture devices and Pollocks and Smiths are—'

'Religious totems. The Jews wanted circumcision,' Guy said, reaching and stroking the shears I held, 'and by God the Spanish gave it to them – in spades.'

I put down the pair of shears.

'And what's this?' I asked, at the head of the table, examining a heavy wooden chair with metal wrist- and ankle-clamps and an adjustable circular ring the size of a Frisbee attached to the chair's back at head's height.

'An Andalusian trepanning chair. I paid ninety-thousand for it at auction.'

'A bargain, I'm sure.'

'What they'd do is they'd sit the subject in the chair, immobilize him, drill a few holes in his noggin, and then, with a very sharp surgical instrument that attached to the head-band, they'd play connect the dots: open his skull to check for demons. Go ahead, take a load off – see what it feels like.'

'I think we should walk some, Guy.'

'Speaking of walking, Rog: Have you heard that Sharon Timlin and Rawlings Black are walking to Cashampton?'

'Why ever would they do that?'

'To visit Jasper Jurkbaitt, their sponsor.'

'Who told you?'

'Jasper did. He's a friend. We met years ago – before he found Christ and before I found television. He'd do my teeth and I did his hairpiece. Barter-system.'

'Why do they need to see Reverend Jurkbaitt? Gingivitis?'

'Jasper hasn't worked teeth since Jesus came into his life. No, they simply want to go swimming in his pool, to get clean. And Cashampton's a terrific place to beg food. All the liberals leave The City in the summer. I just hope they're careful hoofing it through Queens.'

'Their art is their life.'

'If they know what's good for them, they better run for their art. As Jasper says, "Suffer the little children." Now *that's* visionary. He truly understands how God and art and pain walk hand in hand.'

'In handcuffs.'

'Don't tell anyone, Roger, that was my idea.'

'Brilliant, Guy.'

'Thanks,' he said. 'You, of all people, should appreciate my hypothesis.' We stood in front of an intricate dripped Pollock. 'After all, wasn't it you who wrote, and I quote: "Stillman's homoeroticism – born at the age of two in his family's trailer park, when he was sodomized by a retired asthmatic Belgian mime – metastasized, through his singular use of quivering crayon brushstrokes, into a vibrant, evocative, ever-growing memorial to the pain and caged suffering of the pre-teen gay in Middle-America." When I read that, I flipped, Roger. You helped to validate my collection, my curiosity about the fragility of mortality.'

'You really know your Stillman.'

'I'm his biggest fan. It's a shame Sammy's creativity is in remission.'

We passed a series of concentration-camp photos in a hallway and made our way into the master bedroom. Over the huge bed hung a glorious explosion of twisted forms – a Pollock I had never seen!

'And this,' said Guy Gattling, 'you must promise not to write about.'

'My lips are sealed with Krazy Glu,' I said, breath short, heart racing.

'This is *The Rat King*.'

'I've never seen this,' I said. 'When did Pollock paint it?'

'August 11, 1956. The morning of the day he died, Roger. It's his last work.'

'It's it's – it's stupendous. It's beyond . . .'

'Ain't it, though?'

'I've never seen reproductions, photos – nothing! Never even heard of it!'

'Not many have. It's been in private hands since the day he died. I lucked into it. I can't divulge its history at present. That was the deal I made. That, plus a helluva lot of money.'

It was, without a doubt, the bleakest, the saddest, the most frighteningly beautiful abstraction I'd ever seen. Faces appeared, then disappeared, faces and bodies, and the faces were crying and smiling and screaming and laughing, and the bodies were twisted and thrashing and bleeding and dancing – all this in black and red on a white background – human forms and animal forms tangled in love and struggle and death . . . and if you squinted, the forms became stars and planets and moons, meteors colliding and exploding, quasars and breasts and suns and limbs, white light, black velvet, red blood – the whole horrible gorgeous mosaic – human life and star life – a river of time and light and interstellar orgasm. It was the Question and the Answer. It was the end of art.

I am not ashamed to admit: I cried.

Bertha Seward was still in Cashampton General, her Bonacker bones healing much more slowly than I would have liked. The few times I visited, bringing wildflowers I picked on the roadside and containers of crab-salad I charged to the Pearl Man at The Pregnant Duchess, she was drugged and un-communicative, fighting infection in her shattered leg, her 'appetite' thankfully hampered by her broken collarbone – so off I'd go, no wiser on the Pollock front, to my lesson at the Upton Riding Club.

Baby Luegodago seemed to be accepting the new status of our relationship. In fact, around the barn, she wore the same goofy look on her face as when she'd had a crush on me, and I caught her more than once glancing at Kurtis with infatuation.

Maria, Maria, I just had a lesson with Maria!

Her name had come up in such a titillating fashion in the Specs tome that I'd specifically requested her as my instruc-tor.

Dark-haired, with a handsome face hardened and reddened by drink and wind and rain, I asked Maria, after a strenuous session in which I had taken my first jumps, if I might pose a personal question.

'Go ahead, Roger.'

'Are you and Jonas Gritz an item?'

She flushed. 'Who said that?'

'Just a rumor.'

'It's none of your scummy business, but I'll tell you this: that Muffy hasn't given Jonas a ride for a year now. Put that in your fucking feed-bag and chew on it.' And she clomped away across the green field.

Ah, so that explained . . . what? It explained nothing. Forget about the Gilded Set and their dilly-dalliances, I said to myself. Forget about John Dough's fictional take on the sex lives of the rich and horsy. Keep the focus on Pollock.

As I came in from the lesson, I espied Kurtis limping into the annex. There were only three of four horses there – recently returned from Palm Beach winters.

'Thank you, Kurtis,' I said from behind, as he entered a stall taking a large syringe filled with red liquid from his Luis Vuitton samples bag.

'For what?' he asked, petting a goat – the once shaven-headed goat from Cash Island, who now sported a crew cut.

'For taking over Baby Luegodago's English lessons.'

'Yeah, well, she's been having some trouble with the word "enough".'

'I hear that,' I said. 'What're you going to do, barbecue that goat?'

'Barton's giving him to his granddaughter for her birthday on Saturday.'

'Why the shot?'

'He's got the flu,' Kurtis said, massaging the goat's neck.

'The flu's a bitch,' I said.

'And then you die.' He found an artery in the back of the neck and plunged the huge needle home. The goat bleated as the red juice exited the syringe and entered his body.

'Forgive me, little guy,' Kurtis said sadly, twin tears running down his handsome face.

'Kurtis, why are you crying?'

'I hate to see anyone sick.'

'It's just a goat with the flu.'

'The flu can be a real motherfucker.'

'What's that stuff you gave him?'

'Antibiotics,' he said, pulling the syringe out and patting the goat, then putting the syringe back in his samples bag, next to a bunch of Sensuous brand condoms, a pack of cigarettes, and another jar of red liquid. 'Just to be safe.'

'It looks like blood.'

'Appearances,' he said, lighting a smoke, 'can be deceiving.'

Now where, thought I, had I heard that before?

*   *   *

As I said, it was a pleasant time. In the early evening, Kurtis would come by the Mulrooney Estate for poolside drinks and reefer – he seemed to be supplying the pot; and after we'd sat around awhile, smoking and drinking and laughing, listening to the crickets sing their ancient melodies, when our appetites were honed to a sharp edge, the four of us would venture forth for dinner. Italian food one night; seafood the following night; a weenie-roast on the beach the next; and finally, on Friday, Natalie Turner's last evening in town, Chinese food at the Cashampton Poon Tang Chinese Restaurant.

As the fiftyish proprietress seated us I recalled Big Barton's pithy comment on Cash Isle, and I asked her, 'Excuse me, by any chance did you ever know Pollock?'

'Pollock? Pollock? You ask me about Pollock?' This is it, I thought – I've hit the jackpot! Artsnoop Lotto! 'We use King Crab from Alaska, guaranteed crab – no pollack! You want fake crab made with pollack, go to The Pregnant Duchess!'

Natalie Turner was slated to leave for South Carolina the next morning, to babysit a piece being shown at the annual Charleston Backyard Art Exposition. The sculpture, titled *I Am A Curious Fellow, Blue*, an azure version of the piece that Guy Gattling had bought and shipped to his City hot-tub, was designed, unlike his seafaring Pool-Art brother, to be hung by the neck (nylon rope included) from a tree.

'You know who's going to be at the show and has expressed interest in *Fellow, Blue*?' Natalie asked over (guaranteed) crab soup. 'Justice Clarence Thomas. Now *that's* ironic, 'cause that nigger's so black he's downright blue.'

'He's not black,' said Kurtis, biting a spring roll. 'That's what you call an African-featured cracker.'

'He's got a white wife,' I said, snagging a sparerib. 'And his politics are white, and undoubtedly he's a right-winger who from time to time enjoys a pubic hair in his Coca-Cola, but he, himself—'

'Makes you look like Huey Newton,' Kurtis said, lighting a cigarette off the Pu Pu Platter's flame. 'His skin is just an accident of melanin. 'He's no more a nigger than Lester Maddox.'

'What's up, Johnny D?' Natalie tenderly brushed a lock of hair out of John Dough's eyes. He seemed distressed. 'Spareribs going down wrong?'

'I just don't like that word.'

'I told you, man,' said Kurtis, 'nigger ain't nothing but—'

'A word,' I said, completing the dialogue from the Specs Schwartz novel.

On Saturday John Dough drove Natalie to her apartment in The City to pack, and then on to Newark Airport. Before they left, as John raked the gravel driveway smooth and the Jaguar warmed up, Nat and I had a chat.

'Good luck with Pollock, Roger; but don't be fooled by the Japanese dude's bullshit. That ricepacker couldn't care less if Pollock was fucking chickens. You and I both know where the real green is in dead artists.'

'In the grass on top of their graves?'

'In the work, smartass. If Sammy Stillman croaked tomorrow you'd have collectors crawling around his motherfucking nursery school for his fingerpaintings and dried puke. You're just what they call a stalking horse.'

'Horseshit,' I said, employing a favorite Specsism.

'Money talks, horseshit walks. You take care of yourself, Roger. And take care of the Pearl Man. He's a sweetie.'

'You like him too?'

'Yeah, man. He's got innocence. And in the bedroom – yo, look out! – he's like a teenager who never got laid. It's been quite the pearl jam. He wore my little ass out. I'm looking forward to Myrtle Spiddle-Sparrow and all those Southern butch-belles. I like the Pearl Man a lot, Roger, but he's missing something.'

'Maybe it was all those years in Turkey.'

We watched John Dough put his rake in the shed and walk across the lawn, shirtless perfection, running his fingers through his hair.

'Maybe he never was in Turkey,' said Natalie, kissing me.

'You ready, Nat?' John Dough asked.

'Ready or not,' she said.

'Good luck in Carolina,' I said. 'Give my regards to Justice Clarence and tell him to lay off the Coca-Cola.'

The Jaguar crunched gravel and passed the little half-burnt Schwartz cottage nestled amongst the trees by the gate. Ah, solitude.

I went inside the mansion and made my way into the den.

The phone jangled.

'John Dough's residence.'

'Hello?' came the female voice. 'Roger Lymon, please.'

'Speaking.'

'Mr. Lymon, you may not remember me, and I must, absolutely must apologize for my behavior out at the cemetery and on the phone—'

'Ah, Ms. de Kooning.' Hold a grudge, eat no fudge – that's what Grandmother Lymon used to say. 'No problem. How can I help you?'

'It's my father. He hasn't painted all week. He's got a woman here with him and I'm very afraid that he'll never paint again.'

'He's had an over sixty-year career, Ms. de Kooning. History will remember Willem de Kooning as one of the gods. I think a little R and R isn't such a bad thing. Recharge the batteries.'

'We're not talking about the Energizer Bunny here, Mr. Lymon, this is my father, a great, great painter. This Lindsay LaRouche bimbo he's locked in with will blow his gaskets and short-circuit his whole system if something's not done.'

'You mean he's experiencing the splendors of the golden years?'

'I mean she's fucking him to death!' Ms. de Kooning yelled. 'Listen, I want you to come out here, interview him, whatever, just get him interested in painting again. And come soon. He's sober today.'

A large crashing noise filled my ear.

'Are you okay?'

'I've got to go now; they've broken the bed again. Please come.'

'I'll be there with bells on.'

'I don't care if you wear a fucking pink jockstrap, just no liquor.'

Well well well, I thought. Old Bill and Lindsay LaRouche were making sweet sheet music, singing the body electric. I made ready to go and then thought, what's the rush? Let the venerable fellow have some 'gruntcakes.' John Dough would be gone only six or eight hours and I had some reading to do.

Ah, solitude.

But not so soon. A car honked, out on the drive.

It was an old Chevy Nova from the age of Nixon. A man hopped out – Bobby the cop in his off-duty clothes. Inside the car: his wife and son. The three Bobbies.

'Is John Dough here? I wanted Bobbie and Bobby to meet him.'

'I'm sorry, Bobby – and Bobbie and Bobby,' I said. 'He's gone for the afternoon. But you're welcome to use the pool. Can I offer you something to drink? Or how about some crab-salad from The Pregnant Duchess?'

'Nah, that's okay,' said Bobby the cop. 'They use fake crab – crab-sticks. Hey, I got somethin' for the Pearl Man.' He opened the trunk of the car and took out a brown paper bag full of clothes.

'Thank you, but John already has his own wardrobe.'

'Nah, man. The Pearl Man was askin' about Specs Schwartz, and I took the liberty to empty the evidence locker and bring him Specs's clothes. This is what old Pizzaface was wearin' before he jumped in the ocean.'

'Well, I thank you, Bobby, for John. You sure I can't offer you anything?'

'Nah, you take it light, New York. We're goin' to the Bowlarama.'

He got back in the car.

'Goodbye, Bobbies,' I called, and the young Bobby waved and Mrs. Bobbie Bobby nodded and Bobby the cop honked, and then they were gone. Ah, solitude.

I went back in the house, into the den, emptied the bag of clothes. A pair of jeans and a jeans jacket – brown-stained – a white T-shirt, white Jockey shorts, some white sweat-socks, some old yellow odoriferous work boots, a battered Cleveland Indians cap. The pockets revealed little. A soiled bandana. Kurtis's? Ah, the Valentine's card, the mysterious Valentine's card. The paper was smudged and smooth from constant fingering. A canine on a wheeled board, his tongue wagging, a caption above his head saying, 'I wheelly think you're sweet!' Kurtis must have told John about that. Poor lonely Specs, I thought. How about the wallet? Three dollars, a library card, and a driver's license. The vital statistics. Date of Birth: 6/26/53. Height: six-foot two. Weight: two-hundred-and-fifteen pounds. Eyes: brown. Hair:——. Poor Specs. No hair color to speak of – no hair. Oh cruel statistical universe. Poor Specs. And then I examined the photo closely, and I said it aloud: 'Poor Specs.' The poor bastard. If anything, his face was more grotesque than John Dough had described. The acne was horrible, purple and pink connect-the-dot pimples spreading relentlessly – obscenely – across his face and neck like a topographical map of rocky country, like . . . like a pizza. Poor Specs. And the birthmark, only partially visible – a strange collection of dark dots and splotches. I much preferred the fictional Specs. At least *he* had a sense of humor. This sad dead man's face would break any mother's heart.

Well, I thought, no wonder he took his own life.

Now thoroughly happy to smoke pot like a teenager, I rolled a fat one from John Dough's stash, fixed a drink, fluffed a few pillows on the sofa, dug around the desk for John's chickenscratch novel – the fictional Specs Schwartz – and I lay down lit up and I read.

CASHAMPTON
(continued)

THE SKYSPRAY TINGLED my zitmask. I wiped my fogged goggles; touched the pocket over my heart where the Valentine's card lay. The Jag's brakelights were snuffed by the fog. I took my cap off and the drizzle coated my skull. I felt a crablike scrabbling on my leg: Musgrove Messerschmitt's poodle Kerensky was humping my calf. I shook him off.

Lights and music poured out of Hank Upton's windows. A world I could never belong to.

Into the barn. The smell of horseshit, so familiar. Bare bulbs dim. Dirt floors dark. Horses loosing dreamsnorts, soft whinnies in the moist night.

I took my wheelbarrow and pitchfork, went into Squirrel the pony's stall. How long before she made the trip to France? Her large liquid eyes recognized me and her breath blew warm on my hand.

I plucked a few dark plums of dung from the corner of the stall.

'Good Squirrel,' I said, stroking the satin-soft nose.

And then from the annex: a wild keening sound . . . like a hyena standing above its dead mate, caught in the confusion of hunger and mourning.

Squirrel snorted, backed into the wall, kicked it.

I ran cross the barn, out in the drizzle for a second, into the annex. No horses there. Some in Palm Beach for the winter. Some gone for good. Poor old Vishnu, poor old Hannibal. Sold for food to the French.

Banging, pounding – thumps against the wood of a stall wall – thumps plus grunts and squeals.

In the dark I made out Jonas Gritz humping furiously from behind at a blonde-haired woman, her head bucking against the wall.

'Bitch!' he cried, his face wild in the night light. 'Take it!'

'O-o-o-o-oh Jo-o-o-o-o-nas!' she moaned, and I stared with bog-eyed wonder. Then she turned her head. Her mouth was a red sensuous O, her lips bright with drool, her unbuttoned-buttondown-shirted body straining and – Oh God, it was Jenny! Jennifer Gritz! Old-money Jonas was raping his own daughter!

I unbolted the door, dropped my pitchfork, grabbed a handful of Jonas's mussed coif, pulled him off the wiggling double-teardrop buttocks, dragged him by the lank hank of hair across the stall as he yanked his pants over his pink dogbone erection. Jenny whimpered – and I clubbed his aristocratic nose, putting all my mucker muscle into it, the bone giving, blood spurting, and the rich man tumbled back into the sawdust, screeching and clutching his face.

'Are you through, Specs?' asked Jennifer, her breasts bobbing free in her open white shirtfront.

'I imagine I am. I'll probably be fired for this.'

'You interrupted a very special moment.'

'He was raping you, Muff – I mean Jenny.'

'You're mistaken,' said Jennifer calmly, stroking my arm muscle. 'We were fucking, Specs. Good old-fashioned all-American fucking. That's what civilized families do.'

Jonas whined and moaned through bubbles of blood.

Jennifer knelt so that her head was near my crotch, her hot breath stirring my lust-root, and she looked up at me with innocent blue eyes through a tangle of blonde hair, a carbon copy of teenage Muffy Snitbread. And that hair – how sweet it smelled.

'We fuck, Specs. Jonas and I fuck. Sensual and consensual. It's beautiful. And it's none of your beeswax.'

'Christ, Jennifer,' I groaned, fingering Pinatubo, 'he's your father.'

Jonas lay writhing like a worm, gibbering like a loon.

'Go take a Polaroid of your hemorrhoid, Specs.' She giggled. 'Jonas and I have been lovers since my eleventh birthday. I wouldn't trade it for a brand-new BMW.' She examined her father's sawdust-coated face with a slim white finger. 'Speaking of which, Jonas,' she said, licking her finger. 'I get my license in June.'

Jonas's eyes, dull and puffing with broken-nose pain, stared cowlike from a bed of fresh hamburger.

'You okay, Jonas?' she asked, and when he didn't answer she turned to me. 'He'll be okay? Yes?'

'Nothing a little reconstructive surgery won't fix.'

'Well, then' – she stroked my thigh and put a hot hand on my throbbing crotch – 'how about finishing the job? I haven't come yet.'

My nostrils drank her smell. Her twelve earrings winked in the bulb-light.

'Pretty please, with sugar on top? I just love blue-collar guys. I've got a way-big crush on that Kurtis – but you'll do, you mean old ugly old stud you. You remind me of some guys in the mental hospital at Fairhaven. I had an internship there last summer, and those psychos . . . well, they may not be able to tie their shoes but they're all hung like goddamn buffalo. If you don't mind a little spit on your neck a girl can get a damn good hosing. Fuck me, Specs. Fuck me good!'

Well, I didn't fuck her. Oh sure, something in me – make that just about everything in me – wanted to. I saw the long legs and golden hair, the mocking grin, felt the hot hard stroke on my lonely only manstick, and I wanted it, wanted it worse than I'd ever wanted money or a clear complexion or a shiny new car, wanted to sink my teeth into that soft neck, lick those pert pink-nibbed teenage breasts, wanted to make those crazy cornflower eyes rock 'n' roll round that idiotically grinning angel-face, wanted to drown myself in that soft soft sink of sin, lose myself in that sandy Bermuda Triangle at the bottom of her belly. I touched her burning cheek and she pulled my hand down to her soft spongy breast – Oh God, I'd never touched one before! And when I looked at her I was dizzy: It was Muffy! It was Jenny! It was Muffy! It was Jenny-Muffy-Jenny! My fingers tingled, my vision swam like Sahara shimmer, my whole body shook – I felt like one giant quivering hard-on ready to explode.

'Fairhaven,' she said, squeezing my cock. 'Definitely Fairhaven. Have you ever been institutionalized, Specs?'

'Not lately,' I said, the blood pounding in my loins, pimples pulsing with every heartbeat.

But I knew Fairhaven.

I'd called them back in '89 when Mama was basket-case city. After she'd refused to eat her medication and wouldn't leave her couch. After she'd filled her bloomers and sat there frothing like a rabid dog, rocking to-and-fro to some mad sad internal beat, eyes vacant as a bank-possessed house, drool hanging from her chin. She'd struggled against the straitjacket as the whitecoats shot her full of drugs; and in the ambulance I rode along, wiping her sweaty brow; and at Fairhaven, as she was wheeled along the long fluorescent-lit corridors I had to plug my ears to muffle the twisted screams seeping from the locked wards; and after she was hosed down and dumped in a padded room they steered me to an office where a doctor read from her file: Mama had been the State's guest in Fairhaven many times, many years before. Her loving parents had committed her the first time after she burned her Buchenwald tattoo off her forearm with a blowtorch, and then a few years later because she gave up the gruntcakes to every guy who came down the pike, a manic-depressive teenage nympho-maniac runaway. Good old Grandpa Foote – dead of a home-cooked shotgun-supper five years now – and Grandma – fifteen years ago a life-clubbing heart-attack – had committed her again; but once treated and released she'd run off yet again, been committed: two three five eight times over the next years, and finally, the last time, after she'd been found in New York City in the women's prison, caught turning tricks on the streets of Greenwich Village, after the doctors had her back in the hospital, Grandpa authorized the electroshock. But they'd been too late. She'd rolled life's crooked dice one too many times and the cubes had come up snake-eyes. She'd crapped out: was already pregnant with me, her illegitimate bundle of misery. And that's where I'd been born, they told me. Fairhaven. Baby Boy Foote, bastard. My first breaths were taken behind padded walls.

'Asshole!' Jonas lurched to his feet, grabbed my pitchfork and held it front of my face. 'Hands off Jenny, you stupid ugly pizzafaced bastard.'

'No need for name-calling,' I said. But I couldn't argue with his logic. I was stupid, I was ugly, and for certain I was a bastard – and my face – I could feel the flush of blood, the rush of pain, the itch of zits. I softly touched my scaly mug: Pizzaface.

'Go ahead,' I said. 'Stick me, Mr. Gritz.' I felt a pleasant tingling of expectation in my backbone, like when I was a kid, a little cutie-pie kid, and there was a bath waiting and I knew the water was gonna feel nice and Mama's hand would tickle and thrill, but the price for all that warmth and pleasure was all that soap. So what's a little soap? What's a little death?

'Go ahead,' I said. 'You'll be doing me a favor. A big fucking favor.'

'Yes!' cried Jennifer, clapping her hands. 'Do him up, Daddy! For me!'

'This is how it happened.' Jonas mused, his face bloody, his fingers bone-white and tight on the pitchfork – *My pitchfork!* 'My daughter was missing from the party. I came to the barn, looking for her. My darling daughter, who I love more than words can tell.' He touched her head, stroked it and smiled. And if I hadn't just minutes before witnessed their perverse canine coupling I might have found the gesture sweet. He lightly scraped my face with the fork.

'Do that some more, Jonas – I've got an itch.'

'Shut the fuck up, Pizzaface!' he yelled, hooking a prong in my nose and forcing me to my knees. 'I discovered her being raped by the terminally ugly stall-mucker. Oh, I was angry, very angry, like any good father.'

'Oooh, I love it!' Jennifer screeched, rubbing a breast.

'And you, Specs?'

'Save the horseshit for the cops, man,' I said, licking the blood dripping out my nose. Tired. So very tired. 'Get on with it.'

'But of course.' He smiled. 'And Specs, you fucking turdburlgar, do you remember a Christmastime, oh, about twenty-five years back? A snowy night, when a crazywoman – a maid she was – a stupid retarded Jujube maid – was in a car crash? How she claimed another vehicle forced her off the road? Killed her husband? The police didn't believe her. Just a maid. Just a dumb drunk maid. Do you remember? Do you fucking remember, Specs?'

I got up off my knees, the pitchfork prongtips cold and sharp in my face.

Do I remember? Leo dead? A kind man. A hard worker. Hard drinker. Loved Mama. No more games of catch on the beach. No more rides in his pickup. No more cookouts. No family. Mama a wreck. Life changed, changed fucking utterly. No future. No nothing. Just pimples and pain and sorrow and labor. Just sixteen tons of horseshit. Do I remember?

'I remember,' I said to the malicious rich man. 'I remember her baking you cookies and giving you milk and hugs and maybe the only love you ever had in that sorry mother-fucking mansion with those distant fucking parents of yours. I remember her drying your tears when you felt like shit after you stuck a firecracker up a frog's ass or drowned a cat. I remember lots of things, Jonas. We were friends. And my mother loved you. That's what I remember.'

'Your mother, Specs,' Jonas said, smiling horribly, the pitchfork pressing Pinatubo. 'I was driving that other car. Back from prep school.' He laughed and laughed and laughed, then closed his eyes, and a single tear squeezed out and trickled down his face. 'So what do you think about that, Pizzaface?'

I could fucking kill you. I really could.

'I think something tragic happened. I think they ain't coming back and I can't change that. I think whatever happened happened.'

Jennifer Gritz stared at us.

'For real? Wow!' she said, clapping. 'Radical fucking speech, Specs.'

I took the pitchfork. Jonas whimpered.

I could take this fucking pitchfork and shove it in your motherfucking daughterfucking heart. I could. I really could.

I prodded him with the fork.

'What happened to you?' I asked. 'What happened to you, JoJo?' That's what Mama used to call him, her pet name for him. She used to call him 'My little JoJo.' 'What happened?'

'I – I – I . . .' Jonas's face sagged and his shoulders heaved. I pushed him into the corner with the pitchfork.

'I take shoveling shit damned seriously,' I said, poking poking poking.

'I didn't do it on purpose. It was an accident.'

'Accidents can happen. Look at me.' I touched my face. 'What happened to you?'

'You don't want to know,' he whispered.

'Tell me, motherfucker,' I said, prodding him hard.

'I was raped by the whole lacrosse team in prep school,' he said, serious tears coursing down his face, mixing with blood and dripping pink off his chin.

I put the pitchfork down and wrapped my arms around him. *I could crush your fucking spineless spine, you excuse-making motherfucker. Raped by the lacrosse team! I could kill you.*

I started to squeeze and I could feel his ribs giving and his words came out muffled and husky:

'And then this Indian, he was the star, he stuck his stick up my butt,' he whispered with a groan. 'It hurt, Gilbert. It hurt me bad. I hate them. I hate them all. All the Jews and the niggers. All the sand-niggers and gooks, and you . . . you're them. I hate you.'

'You're worthless,' I said, disgusted, letting go. 'Why should I fuck up my karma over you? I forgive you, asshole.'

'So what is this?' asked Jenny. 'A Woodstock reunion? Hey, Specs, that's a radical birthmark on your head.'

'Hey, Jennifer,' I said. 'Why don't you take a hike and fuck one of your grandfather's buffaloes.'

'Well, excu-u-use me,' she said, and walked out.

'Your mother was nice, Specs,' Jonas sputtered. 'She was nice.'

'It's, okay, JoJo,' I said, picking up my ballcap. 'It's time to heal.'

And I held the weeping man. My old friend. My tormentor. The man who killed Leo. The man who married Muffy Snitbread.

Zorro stood twenty hands high in his stocking feet, a giant of a horse who ate like a vegetarian circus fatman, shat buckets and peed like a fire hydrant. But I liked and respected him and could tell he appreciated the hard work I put in every day to make his stall clean and comfortable, and I cringed every time his so-called owner, Big Barton Snitbread, climbed into the saddle. It was a horse-hernia just waiting to happen.

In the nightgloom Zorro was awake.

Bareback I rode. Across fields, over fences, down to the beach. Zorro proud, snorting, sprinting like Secretariat in the damp soft sands. The rain pounded, the wind tore my cap off, I grabbed a handful of horsehair, held on as we flew through the night.

Up the beach a ways. No lights visible. I dismounted and sat in the sand, raindrops falling on my hatless hairless hopeless head.

I pulled the bottle I'd copped from my truck, drank deep. I was tired, so damn tired. Zorro up on the dune, chewing grass. I drank again. Tired. Tired of Cashampton, tired of richfolk and their strange sorry lives. Tired of my own sorry life, my unlucky lackey horseshit life. I had a terminal case of the Cashampton blues. I drank and I drank and I drank. What was keeping me there? With Mama gone, I could split, sneak through a crack in the universe.

Why not? I thought as I stripped my clothes, and the cold rain dripped down from the heavens and spattered my body. *Why not?* I thought, and the sand was cold between my toes as I walked down the slight slope into the ocean. *Why not?* I thought as the freezing water numbed my ankles calves knees thighs, as the roiling moiling foam waves shrunk my balls and cock, as I waded offshore, walking sideways, churning forward, getting deeper, fighting the water's twisting force, withstanding a few wavehits and undertow tugs, as an ice-cold whitecapped green monster knocked me off my feet and tumbled me submerged into a bottom-scraped twisted flesh-ball. *Why not?* I screamed underwater as I swallowed sand and salty seawater and came up gasping and snorting and spitting beyond the wavebreak, sucking air, glasses still around my neck on their frayed string, swimming hard now, putting yards of freezewater behind me with strong strokes, kicking and kicking like a babe in its mother's belly – only this was no warm amniotic life-syrup, this was the cold cruel milkless sea-mother. *Why not?* I thought as I swam – the most natural thing in the world. *Why not?* I thought as I stroked – the thing I'd been working toward my whole sorry life – and I grabbed my unzitted pecker but I couldn't feel it, numb numb – *Why not?* – kick stroke kick stroke kick – *fuckit and fuckit and that's the way of the world* – *Why not? It's the logical solution, the inevitable conclusion – nothing to stop you, nothing to stop you – say it: do it: scream it: screw it –* <u>*SUICIDE SUICIDE SUICIDE!*</u>

The stench of fish was overwhelming. I was down in the boat's hold, lying in a pile of fish, covered with fish, many still

flopping and wriggling: cold scaly slimy fish. I could see sky —
not really sky, just rainy grainy black-gray night.

When my hand had hit the boat I'd thought it was a shark,
and along with the elemental fear of being torn bloody and
limbless there'd been relief: It was over, the long years of
pimples and horseshit were over, but when no jaws chomped
me, no teeth tore me, and I realized it was a barnacled boat I
was caressing and not bigtoothed dumblovely death, suddenly, more than anything in the world, more than anything
else, I wanted to live, I wanted very much to live — to live
and breathe and save my pennies for the laser-surgery. So I
hauled myself up the rope ladder, snuck crawling into the
hold while the rain beat down and the oldtimer fisherman
Zeb Marshall piloted the boat and his son Clem (the same
Clement Marshall who so often in high school had performed
the ritual Whirlie on me) kept the net taut between his boat
and his partner's a hundred yards over.

Outside I could hear the roar of a helicopter and see the
floodlights combing the sea and the boat.

'Damn, Daddy!' Clement yelled. 'What the hell's goin'
on?'

'What I look like, the *'Cyclopedia Britannica?'* the gruff old
Bonacker yelled back. 'You running drugs, boy?'

A bullhorn voice cut through the weather. 'This is the
Coast Guard. Prepare to be boarded.' I could feel the throb of
a powerful Coast Guard cutter and I burrowed deeper into the
fish, gasping for air, tasting bilious Wild Turkey rise in my
throat, feeling fishgook coat my lips.

'What's goin' on?' I heard Zeb ask.

'We're lookin' for a floater, Zeb. Specs Schwartz from the
Upton Riding Club. Someone reported a horse on the beach
and then found Schwartz's clothes by the water. You seen
anything?'

'Nothin' but rain and fish, Cap; but you shouldn't have any trouble I-D-in' Specs when you find 'im. Even with water-bloat. He's unique-lookin'.'

'The description we got said he had bad skin.'

'Bad skin?' Clem hooted. 'That's like saying Lindsay LaRouche has a decent set of knockers.'

'Yeah, well, he's probably fishfood by now.'

Clem chuckled. 'Hope the fish are in the mood for pizza.'

Dripping salted fishslime, naked and shivering, wiener and scrotum scrunched tight, I crawled out of the hold. My age-old dream: a new identity, a new environment. Florida sounded good. Fifty oranges a day and the zits might just quit.

Silent as the shadow of the shadow of a mouse, naked and cold in the wet wind, I made my way to the leeward side. Clem and Zeb were up aft, two yellow-slickered forms staring into the fog-shrouded water.

I lowered myself on the rope, untied the rowboat. The swells took the little dinghy, rocked it away from the main craft, and only when I was safe out in the fog and light rain did I fit the oars into the oarlocks and start to row.

Fogsoup suffocated the beach. Down a ways, dim lights bobbled, shimmered, shook — a search. I left the rowboat and the surf sucked it back, then I jogged up into the ankle-scratching dunegrass. A light burned in the house nearest — a space-age number owned by the renowned Polish novelist and cocktail-party contortionist Nudjerzy Diztantkozinski — and there was Nudjerzy, naked, big-bellied, sitting in the lotus position on the kitchen table, drinking from a coffee mug and stroking his large dark wrinkled phallus.

The potato-field mud squished wet and cold and oozesuck-ing between my toes. A few minutes and I was back at the

Upton farm. I stayed low, approached from the practice fields. The place was empty and my truck was gone, hauled off to the copshop I guessed. I was tired, really and finally tired.

I awoke hungry, the sun stabbing my eyes, buried to the neck in the dumpster full of horseshit.

The weight of the horseshit and pee-soaked sawdust pressed down on me, cold and moldy. I found a damp snot-yellowed Kleenex, wiped my glasses, peeked over the edge: business as usual. The parking lot full of cars, the fields full of horses and clients, a dog eating a fresh-fallen field-turd. Out in one field Hank Upton tutored Musgrove Messersch-mitt on the proper way to hold his butt as the socialite posted up and down in the saddle. In another, Maria directed Marmalind and Portius Pleistocene. Fluffy clouds scudded by in the blue sky. A cold breeze stroked my bare head with freezepop fingers.

The tractor cranked up. Lana the groom, eyes puffy with hangover, was doing my job. The sound loudened, the bucket full of horseshit loomed above, and then the load of fresh steaming turds and pissy sawdust splatted upon my head.

I wiped my face, raised myself over the edge and dropped onto the ground. The impact jangled my chilled stiff bones. I hunkered down and Grouchoed over to the the Pleistocenes' Lamborghini Range Rover, opened the rear door, slid down amongst the suitcases, grabbed a blanket and covered myself.

Smell of food. Fancy wicker picnic basket. Opened it. Crab-salad, deviled eggs. Scooped crab with frozen claws, stuffed deviled eggs into mouth, chewed swallowed chewed swallowed. Found silver flask, guzzled – warm delicious whiskey. Burped. Guzzled again.

Opened suitcase. Frilly lingerie, pink plastic vibrator.

Opened the other. Alligator-logoed socks, leather slippers, striped pajamas. I pulled them all on, burrowed under the blanket, covered my head, waited.

Half-an-hour later I was warm and itchy. The horseshit and fishslime had hardened and caked onto my skin, forming a crust like the Irish oatmeal/sheep embryo mask Doctor Rimjob often plastered my face with.

'Pawww-shuss!' A loud British accent – Marmalind Pleistocene. 'Come, Portius, we must hurry to The City. It's Horgan Yippenskip's birthday and we must be there to shout "Surprise!" Give me your hat and your crop.'

The back hatch opened and I felt a hard clunk on my head. Then another.

The front doors opened and the car listed to the right as Marmalind plunked her bottom into the seat. The weight didn't quite balance as Portius got in the driver's side. The doors shut with an expensive *fwump*, and the quiet powerful engine caught life.

'And what did you buy for Horgan?' asked Portius Pleistocene in his brittle British voice as he popped the car into gear, grinding the clutch painfully.

Marmalind blew her nose with a healthy honk.

'What's the last thing you'd consider an appropriate giftypoo from one top-notch book publisher to another? Give up? I bought him a book.'

'Some surprise. That's like bringing cocaine to Colombia.'

The car sped over the rutted dirt road and turned onto the pavement.

'I considered cocaine, but that too would be like bringing cocaine to Colombia. It's a lovely book. Sixteenth-century Japanese erotic prints.'

'How much?'

'Three-thousand at Sotheby's.'

'Three-thousand dollars for a batch of worm-eaten slant porn!?'

'Erotica.'

'Erotica my arse. At those prices you could buy him a whole regiment of Thai virgins – boys and girls.'

'You would know.'

The silence was long.

'Ahhhhhhh,' sighed Portius Pleistocene. 'I love the smell of horse manure in the morning.'

'Yes,' concurred Marmalind. 'So fragrantly elemental, so life-affirming.'

Portius sniffed audibly and sighed again. 'And the sea. You can still smell the sea. Fish and seaweed. The source of all life.'

I took a whiff and inwardly groaned. It was me they were smelling. Me. I stunk like a fishmarket toilet.

'Portius?'

'Yes, Puss.'

'I'm sorry I was snippy with you.'

'I presume that was love talking.'

'Yes, it was.' They were silent for a long time, sniffing and sighing.

'Portius?' Marmalind said. 'What do you make of that horrible mucker fellow, that Spic Schvartze . . .'

'A tragedy, Puss. That poor spotty bahstard.'

'Suicide is so grubby.'

'The poor Pizzaface.'

'Yes,' Marmalind agreed. 'My sentiments exactly.'

'The authorities are still searching the ocean for the body, but he's part of the food chain I suspect.' Pleistocene lit a cigar. I had to stifle a sneeze. 'It's good to be alive. How about some lunch?'

'Portius?' Marmalind's voice was shy. 'How about a blowie-blowie?'

'Mmmm.'

I heard a zip, the rustle of underclothes, and then nothing but loud shlurps, contented sighs, the occasional '*Rather, Marmie!*' and the squeak of expensive leather as we sped Cityward.

The Pleistocenes parked on 78th Street off Central Park and split. Pinatubo throbbed. I touched her gently. Flakes of dried horse dung fell from my face and shoulders. The skin felt tight and dry. Itching and aching. What I would have given for a long hot zit-softening shower, for a good long pimple-popping session in front of the mirror. I rummaged in the glove box and found a first-aid kit. No Sea Breeze, no Oxy 10, no Clearasil or Stridex or Snitbread Zit-B-Gone. I closed my eyes and sprayed Unguentine: It smarted, oh agonized Christ, it ouched – so I wrapped gauze around my face, mummy-style, to relieve the pressure.

I put on my glasses, took a deep breath and exited the car.

Wearing tight striped pajamas, alligator socks and feet-pinching slippers, face and head wrapped like *The Invisible Man*, I made my way into the park.

Uniformed nannies pushed princely prams. Blue-ribbon rats scampered in and cut of garbage cans, emerging with chunks of pretzel or mustard-crusted stubs of frankfurter. Fifth Avenue fortresses loomed clifflike and imposing outside the park. And behind the bright clean windows: the impossible dream of blonde-bitch-in-your-bed fat-walleted opulence.

I sat there a long long time watching the rich Frisbee-tossing families, the rollerskating yuppies, the Spandexed bicyclists, the slow-walking lovers, the sweet old tortoise-slow couples on canes, the dogs walking their so-called owners. Watching and thinking as the sun fled behind the magic castles to the west.

Onto the street.

. . . Avenues of pain and strain, hurry and worry . . . Cold-faced Easter walkers whizzing by, passing me with a stare or a sneer or a look of fear . . . I needed a drink, needed lots of drinks . . . Lights blinked on up in fancy apartments . . . Uniformed doormen shook their heads with disgust as I wandered by, a striped-suited mummyface with glasses, a hulking psycho in slippers . . . People sneaking quick takes, grimacing when they smelled me . . . Midtown clutter of cars and bars and honking taxis, exhaust-spewing buses – getting colder, getting darker . . . Plaza Hotel . . . limos spitting richfolk onto the sidewalk, bums wandering, a violinist sawing a sad wailing tune into the yellow-skied night . . . Need a drink, need a drink, walking west, need a drink, where to go? what to do? smelling food getting hungry getting cold smelling pizza pizza everywhere don't want pizza pizza bad for skin bad for Pizzaface bad for soul bad joke by cruel jokester universe heading west smell of pizza need a drink need a girl need a life need some weed need a drink need a drink need some shelter – I need I need I need I need . . . therefore I ain't dead yet.

'You shouldn't oughta be on the street in yo jammies, bro,' said a man sitting on a slice of cardboard with a sign that read HOMELESS VET PLEASE HELP. 'You cold?'

I have a layer of thermal horseshit insulation.

'You hungry?' the man asked, reaching into his cup with a brown hand, pink-palmed, face kind and wrinkled. He passed me a buck-fifty.

'Thank you. What can I get with this?'

'Get yourself some pizza, bro,' he said gently.

'Thanks, man,' I said, returning the money. I felt like crying.

Heading west. Women walking. Silk-stocking whispers.

High heels strutting to ruttings. Rustling cloth promising golden gruntcake delights. Lickable lipsticklips. Faces rich, bodies lush. Faces in windows, butter-smooth fancy faces, faces like wax, ghostly, smiling, silent-movie chattering lips, like zoo-animals behind glass — white faces don't see me — keep on walking keep on wandering keep on keepin' on oh invisible wandering Jew son of Buchenwald . . .

'Get out of the way!' screamed a doorman shepherding an old birdlike lady on a cane from a taxi into a building.

Horns honking, cars rumbling, brakes squealing, cityjungle dark now, cold now, wind tearing my balls now, what to do now? what to do?

Roosevelt Hospital Emergency Room.

I entered, sat on a seat. Crowded and loud, the room stinking of misery and pain. Faces black and brown, some yellow, a few white.

'Mothafucka!' screamed a lady with a 40-ounce bottle of malt liquor, holding her nose and moving away from me.

'Pee-yew, King Tut!' yelled another. 'You livin' in the muhfukkin sewer?'

A space cleared around me.

People of pain — oh the moaning and screaming and groaning. The misery. Patients lay on gurneys, moaning and bleeding, bleeding and screaming, holding their heads, gnashing their teeth. Plasma bags hanging, nurses nursing, doctors cutting bullets, thumping chests, stitching knife wounds. Moans and screams and screams and moans.

'Aaaaaaaaaaahhhhhhhhwoooooooooyeeeeeeeeee!!!!!!' came the scream, a huge scream, a scream of massive pain, of monumental suffering. Poor creature, I thought, poor dying creature, poor creature.

'Yaaaaaaaaaaahhhhhrrrrraaaaayyyeeeehhhooooooooo-owwwww!!!!!!'

Lord, what a scream, a world-class scream, the scream of screams. An Easter Day scream.

'OOOOOOOOOOOOOOOOWWWWWWW-OOOOOOOOOO!!!!!!!!'

It was me, screaming right along, singing that song – name that tune. I can name—

'Arrrroooooooooooooooooooooooooooooooooooooooooooo-ooohhhhhh!!!!!' I can name that tune in six-hundred-and-sixty-six notes of pure suffering, Ron. That's our song they're playing, a song for the sorrowful. A lost-my-Mama-stole-some-pajama blues. Shall we dance? A foxhole foxtrot? A woebegone waltz? A Buchenwald boogie? A twisted twist? A slammed-to-the-mat-of-life slamdance?

'Yoooooowwwwzzzzzzzaaaaaaaaaaaaagggggggrrrroob-baaahhh!!!!!!'

A lifetime of pure horseshit was being wrenched from my body like a vomit-for-the-ages.

And then, of a sudden, I realized: I was the only one still screaming.

Everyone was staring.

I laughed. Yes I was crazy. Out of my fucking mind, thank you very much.

'What's wrong with you?' asked the nurse holding a clipboard. Tired face, shabby whites. 'Are you from the flight deck?'

???????????? with my eyes.

'Flight deck – mental ward? Burn unit? Abla Ingles?'

'Thanks, but I'm—'

'You're bothering the other patients. People are trying to die in peace.'

'Sorry,' I said.

'What happened to your face? Name . . . !?'

'My name?'

'You don't know your name?' She marked her pad and sighed. 'Another goddamn John Doe.'

'Excuse me,' I said to the well-dressed white man trying to hail a taxi on Ninth Avenue. 'Could I borrow some money for a hotel room and a shower?'

'I – I – I!' The man's eyes pinballed all over the place. He reached into his pocket, gave me his wallet and ran.

'Thanks!' I yelled. 'I consider this a loan!'

No taxis stopped. Big deal. I had a five-hundred-and-seventy-dollar loan. I entered a deli.

'Outtaheah, bum!' yelled the counterman.

'Hey, pal, my money's green,' I told him, fanning bills. 'Give me a fucking meatball hero and make it snappy.'

Times Square by night. The lights! Oh man, the lights! Neon flashing, neon blinking rainbow sex-dreams, marquees burning bold and bright, honking cabs, smoking manhole covers, trains rumbling underfoot, bodies rushing, tourists huddling, tourists gawking, brothers strutting hawking weed, selling girls selling boys, strip clubs, movie theaters, pornshops, flashing neon fleshpalaces, girlsgirlsgirls, smell of pizza, smell of hot dogs, smell of sweat of peoplestink of hustle of cooking meat, tourists gaping, 'coke dope smoke crack pussy', 'wanna boy?', 'wanna girl?', 'wanna blowjob?', 'wanna fuck?' love and death in one handy-dandy package, and me burping meatball, nipping from a fifth of bar-bought Southern Comfort, digging the action, buying a joint, smoking it up, faces passing, lights wheeling, copping a buzz, gettin' my head all nice and fuzzy, and here it is here it is: DANTE'S SEX WORLD!!!!! Now appearing, Lindsay LaRouche. XXX.

I drain the SoCo, garbagecan the bottle, buy four tokens to enter the flashing neon fleshpalace.

'Live on stage Lindsay LaRouche, the Kissin' Banshee, step right up!' cries the microphone jockey. 'Girls are hot and waiting, titties and clitties, step right up, guys. Stage three a dildo show in two minutes. Hot fresh pussy on every stage! The girls are getting lonely!'

What about the guys? I think, watching furtive men with hands jammed in pockets walking around inspecting the glass-booth girls.

A morose Pakistani pushing a bucket and mop from recently vacated splishsplashshiny splotchfloor booths. Eeyah, the stink of loneliness and desire. The reek of sadness and death. Push your bucketful of sorrow, oh child of India. A breeding ground for serial killers.

Stage three, silver tokens sold for a buck by an aproned brother. Sliding window. Bored six-foot-five Chineseface transseXXXual, big-shouldered, hamhanded, feet like five-toed pontoons, lying on grubby carpet, fingering fabricated fig, cupping phony breast. Windows around the circle-jerkoff stage slide up and down, dim shadowed faces, hidden hands grabbing lonely peckers.

Stage two: girlsGirlsGIRLS!!!

'You tippin' honey?' asks one of the gang of four working the sliding windows – a fake-blonde with a birthmark on her belly, a raised coin of blackness above her razor-sharp dark-jungled pubic bone, sagging hair-nippled breasts framing a gold cross. What are these birthmarks, these little spots of dark? The white body's grudging refusal to forget Mother Africa?

'Two bucks titties, three ass, five . . . Whassamatta? Ya been in a fire?'

'No, but I've got a birthmark too—'

160 • *Michael Guinzburg*

Door sliding down.

Another token. Door sliding up.

Guy in next booth shoves dollars at blonde. She turns, raises a leg, he digs a finger: an explorer. Dr. Livingstone, I presume?

Girls all colors – scars bellies butts breasts fat hair cellulite warts – hands reaching hands grabbing hands poking stroking. It's ten PM, do you know where your children are?

'Safe sex,' says a fleshdoll. 'What's ya name?'

'John Doe.'

Door sliding down.

Puss Parlor, ten bucks cover. Guys in chairs holding on to their johnsons for dear life as up on stage Lindsay LaRouche, my ex-wife, shaking booty, breasts dwarfing all, bump and grind and smile and leer – and the audience lapping it up like thirsty dogs: young men, middle-aged men, guy over there looks like old Billy de Kooning the crazy Cashampton artist, he's grinning and yelling as Lindsay shoves things . . . a carrot an eggplant . . . as she sprays whipped cream from the can onto those mad dreambreasts and licks them – and then to cap it off, her crowning glory trick that rocks the crowd into a frenzy: she shoots ping-pong balls out of her shaved cooter – crowd clapping cheering going wild putting hands together like trained seals as music blares and I'm sick sick sick sick sick puking meatball crab whiskey eggs and a big burly bouncer leads me – gently – no struggle – gently – past the glass-booth babes – gently – down the stairs – gently – out the door – gently – onto the kaleidoscopic neon street of fresh air and exhaust and pizza and hotdogs – gently into the doomed sad American night.

'Sin!' cries the Reverend Doctor Jasper Jurkbaitt in the cavernous 42nd Street Church, a former theater, the XXX posters covered by Christian crosses.

'Sin!' echoes the sea of faces.

'Jesus loves you despite your sin! All around you sex and drugs and violence and suffering – your sin! The rotten teeth of sin! The end is near, children! America is damned, children! Receive Him before it is too late, children! He is calling you, calling you, on Easter Day he is calling you! My children! Give him your tired your poor your wretched soul, come forward come forward come forward and be saved!'

And I surged toward the light to be saved, to be saved and cleansed and forgiven, for I had dreamt of murder and riches and loveless pleasures of the Easter Day flesh; and when my turn in line came, the Reverend Jurkbaitt (who summered on Babylon Circle Road in Cashampton By The Sea) stared at me with big blue eyes in a sweating fishbelly face, touched my bandages with his plastic-gloved hand and said, 'Good Lord, son, take a shower.'

West Side Highway. Mexicans selling flowers. Exhaust gassing air. Near-naked hookers selling quickliptrips. Pale teen-boys selling rectal deathdreams and cigstained lips. Beyond the river, Jersey and America – God's great America, all those miles and miles of field and city, of pain and poverty, of farting cows and struggle and dreams and high-hedged mansions and horseshit – all there to feed the Nightmare City – of rich and poor, of drugs and death, of crime and sex, of pizza and The City. My country 'tis of thee. Damned land of insanity. Of thee I sing.

Eight

WHEW, JOHN. Calm down, brother. Cool thy jets.

I needed a break. There were still some pages to go, but I needed some air. I was exhausted. Exhausted and disgusted. And I needed a drink. Christ, I needed a drink. And I needed people. After living in Specs's tortured head and heart for twenty pages, I needed human company.

I called a taxi and downed a double shot of Wild Turkey. Congratulations, John – you've founded the Death Eating An Onion School of writing. What did those people do to you in Turkey?

The landscape outside the cab window was a green flat blur. The warm clean air felt good in my lungs, but I couldn't shake the Specs Schwartz imagery. It was difficult to imagine anyone wanting to read, let alone publish, John Dough's novel. And his title – *Cashampton* – it sounded like a Sidney Sheldon mini-series. How about *Pimples On Parade* or *A Man Called Horse(shit)*? No matter – it was working for me. I was caring about the characters. I'd been rooting for the fictional Specs – this metaphorical shit-taker – hoping he'd shove his fictional pitchfork into the fictional Jonas Gritz's heart. The section in Dante's Sex World was a bit much, though. Ah, well, I thought, art need not be pretty to be effective – witness Goya, Picasso, de Kooning, Pollock, Bosch, Bacon, Munch, etcetera – and in literature, Selby, Himes, Bukowski, Burroughs, Poe, and now Dough, the Master Of Muck, the Oozemeister General. Through this literary veil of horseshit and pimples, I was really caring for Specs, the poor bastard – his pain was my pain – *our pain* – and I was curious about what would happen to him. Suicide, I supposed. Eventually suicide. It was inevitable. Listen to me, I thought. Talking as if that poor pimpled creature was still alive. What was John doing, inventing a life for a dead man? Why not just end the novella where the real Specs ended it all, in the Cashampton drink? Why extend the misery? What the hell are you driving at, John Dough? What breed of fictional rabbit are you going to pull of your baseball cap? Are you going to pull an Edgar Allan Pough? I mean Poe. John Doe?! John Dough?

Funny guy. Maybe the French would buy it.

'This is fine,' I said, across from Green River Cemetery, in front of de Kooning's house, getting out, paying. 'Excuse me, driver, did you know Gilbert Schwartz?'

'The dead pizzaface?'

'No, the human being,' I said and walked toward the house.

'Ms. de Kooning,' I said, shaking the limp hand and looking about the walls lined with a billion dollars' worth of Abstract Expressionist Art, a stylistic smorgasbord that most likely would be unloaded the day after old Bill kicked the paint bucket. 'I can't tell you how gratified I am for this oppor-tunity.'

'Mr. Lymon,' she hissed, 'cut the glad-handing shit. Just ask your stupid questions and get that gold-digging pair of tits out of here.'

She pointed to the living room. Lindsay LaRouche and Willem de Kooning sat on the sofa, his hands sculpting shapes under her sweater, Lindsay giggling, the TV blaring the Saturday afternoon wrestling show.

'Good afternoon, Mr. de Kooning,' I greeted the obviously enthralled man. Would that every nonagenarian could have a Kissin' Banshee to while away the hours and keep the reaper from the door. Whatever the price.

'Mr. Lymon! Roger, Roger!' he sing-songed, his hands glued to their source of warmth and inspiration. 'Have you met my fiancee, Lindsay LaRouche?'

'Ah, Ms LaRouche,' I said, shaking the hot little hand the buxom bottle-blonde extended beyond the silver head tucked between the cleft of her mountainous chest, trying, but not quite succeeding, to look in her eyes and not at her . . . 'I am familiar with your work.'

'Billbo tells me you're a writer,' Lindsay said, impressed, turning the television's volume down with a diamond-ringed hand as Kamala, a giant, painted-faced would-be-African performed an Atomic Drop on a small white wrestler.

'A mere journalist,' I said, taking out my tape-recorder. 'Ah, Ms. LaRouche, when you accomplished that extraordinary piece of performance art magic at last year's NBA finals – sheer brilliance. Shattering racial boundaries in a single bound by kissing Mr. Jordan on the floor of Chicago Stadium. You did more for the cause of Civil Rights and interracial love than anyone since . . . since Dr. King. My hat is off to you!'

'Thank you,' she said with the true humility of a great artist.

'How long have you two known one another?' I asked, thinking about John Dough's Puss Parlor scene at Dante's Sex

World. That's fiction writing, I mused: taking the actual (de
Kooning's presence at the Terry Tuba party with Lindsay, her
work in porn-performance, and the fact of Specs Schwartz's
brief marriage to the former groom) and linking it with the
fanciful (what might have happened) and the emotional (how
old Specs might have felt about it).

'Not long,' Lindsay said.

'Yah!' de Kooning crowed. 'I feel like Ponce de Leon
discovering the fountain of youth! I am an Action Painter once
again!'

'Oh, Billbo,' cooed the porn-star, drawing him to her
bountiful breast, and then whispering low (but I heard): 'You
make my little cunny quiver.'

'I was somewhat familiar with this angel's cinematic work,'
de Kooning said, his face flushed and happy. 'I am a member
of a quality mail-order video club' – he indicated a stack of
XXX video-cassettes by the TV – 'and I have become a big fan
of this medium. Yah! All the great themes of the day, of art
and life, they are being explored – especially the push and pull
between black and white. . . . Do you know, Roger, that
every color, every shade of the spectrum – even white – has
some black in it? Yah! Painterly questions. Literary questions.
Philosophical questions. Have you seen *A Patch Of Heaven*,
featuring Lindsay and the powerful black actor Boswell James?
What range the man has!'

'That's the one where Bos is a delivery boy from Bermuda
and I'm Princess Di. I seduce him under the dinner table while
the Queen of England makes a speech.'

'Sadly, I missed it.'

'The end of colonialism!' cried de Kooning, clenching a
LaRouchian breast. 'The coming together of the races! Light
and dark! No more fear of the Other! Clarity, not disparity!'

'So how did you two lovebirds meet, Mr. de Kooning?'

'I was in The City one day, seeing the doctor, and I slipped out the office while my jailer – I mean my daughter – while she was reading her *Money Magazine*, and I took a taxi to Lindsay's wonderful exposition at the charming Dante's Sex World. I stayed for six consecutive shows, all night, and finally—'

'I noticed this handsome gentleman in the audience,' Lindsay gushed. 'And then every day for five weeks I got flowers and poems delivered to my dressing-room. I usually ignore such advances, but when Billbo sent a gorgeous lion drawring of my ping-pong ball bit, I said to myself, "This is a true arteest." So the next time I was out here visiting my parents, I looked Billbo up and the rest—'

'Is the history. Yah!' cried de Kooning, climbing the twin peaks and attempting to tickle the Kissin' Banshee's tonsils with his tongue. 'Tristan and Isolde! Romeo and Juliet! Porgy and Bess!'

'De Kooning and LaRouche!' I added, getting into the spirit.

'The wedding is planned for August!' de Kooning announced.

'You have to be there, Mr. Lymon.' Lindsay glowed. 'I'll be Mrs. William de Kooning.'

'Maybe you'll hit it off with one of her bridesmaids,' de Kooning said with a sly wink.

'You'll love them,' said Lindsay. 'Busty Dusty, Candida Royale, Hyapatia Lee, Honey Moons, Christy Canyon, Tiffany Minx, September Raines, and Jeff Stryker. Reverend Jurkbaitt's gonna perform the vows.'

'Tell me,' I said to Lindsay, 'about your ex-husband, Gilbert Schwartz.'

'That poor, poor Pizzaface.'

'I believe,' I said, a bit offended, for I had grown quite fond and respectful of the late stall-mucker, 'that poor Specs preferred to be called Gilbert.'

'Valerie Schwartz's boy?' de Kooning asked. 'You were married to Gilbert?'

'Just for a short time, Billbo,' Lindsay said, taking the painter's hand and placing it back on one of her silicon chest balloons. 'It wasn't like you and me.'

'Valerie,' de Kooning mused, 'was good friends with Jackson. Both loved wrestling.' De Kooning looked wistfully at Mr. Perfect twisting Lex Luger into a pretzel. 'Leo and Val took me once to the show at the Madison Square Garden.'

'I understand Leo and Val were very poor.'

'Yah. Very sad for little Gilbert.'

'Ms. LaRouche, did you ever,' I asked, just for the hell of it, 'see Gilbert, oh, say at one of your shows at Dante's Sex World?'

'He died, Mr. Lymon. He died early April, the Saturday night before Easter – I read the obituary in *Stan's Paper*. My engagement at Dante's began Easter Day. How could I have seen him if he was dead?'

'Tragic,' said de Kooning, looking around for his daughter and then, when he heard her banging about in the kitchen, reaching under the couch and coming up with a pint of gin, uncapping it and drinking. 'To young Schwartz. His loss, my gain.'

Uh-oh, I thought, I'd better zing the Pollock questions in fast. Alz-Well and alcohol, oil and water, the Klan and the Nation of Islam, the—

'Mr. de Kooning, the last time we spoke, you told me that Jackson Pollock had a boyfriend.'

'Did I say that?'

'Something like that.'

'Pollock?' Lindsay asked. 'The guy who made that funny picture you gave me?'

'You gave Ms. LaRouche a Pollock?' It *was* serious. 'Which one?'

'*Number 67, 1950*. It is the prenuptial gift. It will look lovely in the background of her new film. What is the title of the film again, snookums?'

'*Lindsay LaRouche and the Temple of Dendur*. We've already got permission to film at the Metropolitan Museum. I play a curator and I make love to King Tut – as played by Boswell James. It's very artistic and very classy. Billbo has a cameo. I got the idea at Dante's when this guy came to the show dressed like a mummy.'

Christ, I thought. John Dough must have been there that night, saw the guy. 'Do you recall John Dough at your show?'

'The Pearl Man?' Lindsay gushed. 'What a studly hunk!' And then she looked at old Bill and added: 'But I prefer more mature men.'

But de Kooning seemed not to notice. He was sucking on the gin bottle.

'Mr. de Kooning, was Pollock involved in a homosexual congress with a boy?'

'Boy?'

'Or a baby?'

'Baby?' he asked, eyes filming over. 'Baby, yah, baby.'

Paydirt!

'Whose child was it?'

'Baby baby baby!' de Kooning babbled, snuggling up to Lindsay LaRouche, sticking his head under her sweater and playing baby for a while.

'Well,' I said, getting up – stymied by the bottle once again; and Lindsay LaRouche, the future Mrs. de Kooning, smiled with the pride of a fisherman who's finally hooked the big one. 'Well, I'm sure you two will be very happy.'

'Oh shit!' said de Kooning's daughter coming in, seeing her

father clutching a bottle, nursing under the wool. 'Shit shit shit! Get out of here, Lymon – you ratfuck! And *you*, you stupid whore, it'll be a cold day in hell before *you* get a penny. My lawyers will see to that. *Non compos mentis*. He's out of his mind!'

'Waaaaaaaah!' wailed Willem de Kooning.

'Now, look what you've done, you dumb bitch,' Lindsay said to her middle-aged future step-daughter. 'You've upset the baby. I better put him to bed.'

Billy Truck's was dark and cool. A few patrons sat at tables. Hank Upton drank a cocktail with muumuu-clad Larva Shinsplintz and Lasse her chauffeur.

I sat at the end of the bar, two seats down from a pretty lady of about sixty. I stared at the bottles on the shelves, searching . . .

'Good afternoon,' I said to the bartender, an elder gent. 'I'd like a Southern Comfort with a draft beer-back, please.'

The man nodded, made the drink, drew the beer, slapped them down on napkins – this was no Fish Head Danny's.

'Well,' I said, raising the glass of sweet booze through a shaft of sunlight to my lips, 'Here's to Gilbert Schwartz.' And I drank, feeling the sweet warmth charge my still Specs-broken spirit.

'Another,' I called, rinsing with beer and swallowing.

'You're the first guy' said the barkeep, pouring – 'who's ordered that since old Specs.'

'Well, here's to Gilbert,' I said and drank. 'He preferred to be called Gilbert, you know.'

'Oh, I know,' said the bartender. 'My son went to Cashampton High with him. Suicide's a bitch.'

'And then you die.'

'It wasn't suicide,' said the woman a few seats down, her accent seasoned with a touch of Europe. 'This town murdered him. This town and the Nazis.'

'Pardon me, Mrs. Drummond,' said the bartender, easing down the bar to polish glasses. 'You'd know.'

'You knew Specs?' There I was, calling him Specs again, forgetting the man's dignity.

'He was my nephew.'

'Ah, the famous Esther Foote.' I moved closer to her.

'Famous for what?'

'I don't know.' I was drunk. 'For being Gilbert's aunt. For making it through Buchenwald. You and your sister. How did you manage it?'

'You really wish to know?'

I nodded.

'We fucked our way through,' she said brutally. 'Four years of shtupping camp guards.'

'How old were you?'

'We went in eight-years-old and came out three-thousand. And don't think we didn't have shame. When the camp was liberated, the colored troops found us locked up naked, our backs striped by the whip, and they cried and cried. We called them "the black angels." How kind they were . . . And my sister and I, we were plump and well fed. Our fellow prisoners spat upon us, they beat us – the poor skeletons shaved our heads and would have killed us were it not for Josiah Foote.'

'And then Josiah brought you here?'

'Not immediately. We went to an orphanage, but our reputation preceded us. The other "children" beat us, so we ran off to Paris and wrote to Josiah. It took some time for the arrangements to be finalized. So Paris it was. That's where I met the love of my life, Albert.' She pronounced the name 'Al-bear.'

'Albert who?'

'No, Albert Camus.'

Ah, I thought, yet another demented woman. Like Bertha Seward. Was it something in the Cashampton air? 'Have you heard about Big Barton Snitbread's Alz-Well drug?' I asked, as delicately as possible. 'It works like a Roto-Rooter for arteriosclerosis.'

'Are you implying, young man, that I've lost my marbles?'

'Perhaps they're just misplaced.'

'Age is a funny thing. I was not always this silly bag of aches and memories. The body plays its little jokes, but my mind is fine.' And as she drank her martini her sleeve fell, revealing numbers tattooed on her forearm. I drank my Southern Comfort – in one gulp.

'It was May, 1946,' Esther began. 'I was thin and pretty and twelve years old, with breasts' – she held her hands out beyond her chest – 'that made the men in the Paris streets moan and grab themselves when I passed.'

'At twelve?'

'Almost thirteen.'

'Silly me; there's a difference.'

'How do you think Valerie and I made it through the camp, young man? Perhaps it was the stress and strain of facing death every day, but we both grew breasts and started to bleed within six months of our arrival at Buchenwald, and by age nine we were separated from the rest and were servicing all the Adolphs and Rudolphs and Hermans. Early puberty was a gifthorse we did not look in the mouth. Life or death. What would you have done?'

'Whatever it took, I suppose.'

'Where was I?'

'1946. Paris. Breasts.'

'It was a sweet spring night on the Place Pigalle. Walking

free, free as a bird, I was. I was bouncing with youth and beauty in the soft Paris night, wearing a tight striped blouse, a skirt – coming from work. I worked in a matchstick factory. The pimps, they tried to recruit us, and Valerie they got – we were waiting for the papers to be processed, for our hair to grow back, for Josiah to come and get us. I was walking, just walking, when I saw a man leaning over the gutter – he was coughing his lungs out, coughing and spitting and coughing. He was not drunk, no – it was tuberculosis. I knew the condition. My father had been dying from tuberculosis when they took him to the showers.

'I said to the man, he was a handsome man, "Do you live far? Let me walk you home." I helped him home. He was coughing and spitting blood all the way; and up in his little garret I put him to bed. It was Albert Camus. That night we made love, we made love all night. Bartender!' she called. 'Another. And another for my young man here.'

'So you and Camus had sexual congress. What happened?'

We drank our fresh drinks.

'We loved and loved and he coughed and coughed. He was a beautiful man, a deep and understanding man, and I told him about the guards and how my sister and I had survived, and I asked him to beat me, to beat me and whip me, to punish me, but he only cried and cried and coughed and coughed and loved me so very sweetly, so gently.

' "*Merci*," I said. "Oh thank you, Albert. Thank you."

' "*C'est rien*," he said, crying. "It is nothing."

' "Don't cry, Albert," I said. "It only hurts you." And Albert smoked cigarettes, one after the other, crying and coughing. "Don't cry," I begged.

' "Oh no, *chérie Esther*," he said. "It is nothing."

' "Don't smoke," I said. "It makes you cough more."

' "It is nothing," he said, coughing and crying and smoking.

'And the moonlight flooded the room. His stomach muscles were strong from all the coughing. And his manhood rose like a phoenix from the ashes of my pain.

' "That looks like something to me," I said.

' "No, it is nothing."

' "You call that nothing?" I asked. And we made love again. There was blood on his lips, and when he kissed me there was blood on *my* lips, blood on my breasts, blood between my thighs. "You call that nothing?" I asked.

' "It is nothing," he said, coughing and spitting in his handkerchief. "This coughing is nothing. This life is nothing. God is nothing. The love, the struggle to love and the struggle for freedom, these are something, these are the only somethings within the absurd nothing – but then we die. And that – that, too, is nothing. The big nothing. I love you, my *chérie Esther.*"

' "*Oui,*" I said. "*Oui.*" The sweetest word in the French language: *Oui.* "*Oui, Albert. Oui. Oh, oui, l'amour, c'est tout.*" Yes. Love is all.

'And he coughed, young man, he coughed and coughed and wrote by candlelight, coughing always, and we loved and he coughed. For weeks on end. We loved and he coughed. And his stomach muscles grew strong from all the coughing and our love grew strong from all the loving. And the coughing was nothing and the loving was everything. And that is how Existentialism was born. With a cough and a fuck.'

'That's a lovely story,' I said, as afternoon sun lit the bottles behind the bar, as the barkeep polished glasses, as Larva Shinsplintz chortled at her own joke and Hank Upton rubbed Lasse's leg under the table. 'And then what?'

'And then nothing.'

'What about you and Camus? And where was Valerie?'

'Valerie was working for her pimp, and then Josiah Foote, he came to Paris, and Albert, he made me to go. I did not want to leave him, but he forced me. He said America was a young country: He said America would give me back my childhood, my innocence. He was wrong, of course. He had seen too many Hollywood films. But he saw us off at the pier. He was coughing; I was crying.

' "This love of ours?" I ask him, holding him, not wanting to let go. 'Is it nothing?

' "No, *chérie Esther*," he says, coughing and kissing me and gently prying my hands from his neck. "It is something."

'I never saw him again.'

Tears were trickling down her face, and her eyes were bright with memories, memories of love and death and coughing. She was beautiful. I reached a hand and touched her shoulder.

'Did you know Jackson Pollock?' I asked gently, turning my mini tape-recorder on, out of sight under the edge of the bar.

'Yes, I knew him.' She turned to the bartender. 'Please, bartender, another. And another for my young man here.

'I knew Jackson, and I knew his friends. I especially liked de Kooning. He was my lover too.'

'And Valerie?'

'No, Valerie loved Jackson. We were twins, yes, but very different. I married for security; she married for love. Leo Schwartz was poor, but a good man, and he adopted her bastard son. We were not so close then. I offered her money, many times, but she refused.' Esther cried. 'I was saddened by their poverty, and the late Mr. Drummond, he could not deal with their happiness. They were happy because they had a child – and me? I was barren. Barren and miserable. Later, after Leo died, I was devastated by her boy. By his baldness and his skin. His pain was the pain of all the camp Jews. His curse was the curse of the whores of Buchenwald. He was born of a rotten womb.'

'But Pollock and Valerie—'

'Yes, Pollock and Lee and Valerie and Leo. They are all dead now.'

'And Gilbert's dead too.'

'Gilbert and Valerie and Pollock – all dead.'

'And Sp . . . Gilbert' – I had to ask, had to make a stab, had to leap into the ridiculous void – 'was Pollock his father?'

'You seem very eager, young man. What if I told you he was? Would you believe me? Would it matter?'

'Was he?'

'I suppose it doesn't much matter now. They're all dead.'

'This calls for a celebration,' I said, overjoyed. 'You've answered my question. My name is Roger Lymon, Mrs. Drummond. May I buy you a drink?'

'Call me Esther. Do you wish to know about Gilbert's birth, Mr. Lymon, about Pollock's reaction?'

'*Oui!*' I said. Yes! Yes! 'Yes!'

'Then come with me to my house. I will tell you all. And maybe, just maybe, I will teach you the basic tenets of Existentialism.'

She paid the bartender.

'I'm not much for philosophy,' I said, coughing nervously.

'Oh, you'll learn fast enough,' she said with a smile, taking my arm. 'You've already got the cough.'

'It's nothing.'

I was getting good at making love to older women. The truth is, Bertha Seward and Esther Foote Drummond were both skillful and considerate and passionate lovers, not at all like some of the people I slept with to get on the staff at *Artnews*.

'Well,' I said, a bit weary from my investigation and bloated with new strange knowledge, as the taxi pulled up to in front of the Drummond mansion to ferry me back to the Mulrooney Estate (imagining my business card: 'Roger Lymon, Existentialist Snoop'), '*That* was something.' I kissed her hand, rubbing the sad tattoo. '*Merci, chérie Esther.*'

'C'est rien, Roger.'

Eight-and-a-Half

·

C'EST RIEN? It was nothing? Or did she mean, '*De rien*'? –
'You're welcome.' Of course, that *must* be what she meant.

Nine

I HAD THE taxi drop me at Smithers' Pharmacy in Cashampton town. Though it was seven-thirty and the sun was sliding down the sky, the town still bustled with wealthy white shoppers. The boutiques were brightly lit and festive with cash and commerce. Ah, but not so Roger Lymon, Existentialist Snoop – I had one foot in Jackson Pollock's Cashampton, another in Buchenwald, and the third in Albert Camus's post-war Paris. And the whole sad mess shadowed by Specs Schwartz.

Plus a raging headache.

A whole aisle of the pharmacy was devoted to Big Barton Snitbread's products.

'Aspirin, please,' I said to the young man behind the register.

'What kind, what size?'

'Just a two-pack,' I said and paid. 'Do you carry flashlights and batteries?'

'Aisle three.'

'Thank you. Did you, by any chance, know Sp—' I interrupted myself. Enough about Specs. I didn't want to know any more.

I bought the flashlight and batteries (making sure to buy Energizer batteries in honor of the immortal, indefatigable Willem de Kooning), and then sat at the old-style fountain and ordered a Coca-Cola.

It's been quite a trip, I thought. Stranger than fiction. Stranger even than John Dough's fiction. I took my aspirin.

I heard loud clomping from the front of the store, like a squadron of Nazis coming to take their daily pound of flesh from the pre-teen Foote Sisters. The boots belonged to the seven identical Dreckenzorfer Quintuplets and their two cousins.

'Pleaze,' said one to the clerk. 'Pleaze to giff oz azpirin.'

I heard the sale rung up, and then the blonde shock-troops made their way back to the soda fountain.

'Hallo, Rochah,' one said.

'Good evening,' I said, counting. *Seven.* 'Good evening, *Frauleins* Fifi, Bibi, Titi, Kiki, Lili, Mimi, and CeCe.' *My God they're attractive. Why hasn't the Pearl Man had them over for the proverbial pearl jam, with spreadable edible leftovers for his 'little buddy'?* 'How are you splendid ladies doing tonight?'

'Not zo terrific,' one said.

'Zeven Coca-Cola,' another ordered.

'What's wrong?' I asked. *What could be wrong? They're each worth half-a-billion dollars.*

'We haff a headache,' another explained while another handed three aspirins to each of the others.

The Coca-Colas lined the counter – they raised them in unison: like looking in a mirror of a mirror of a mirror of a—

'To Justice Clarence Thomas,' I said, providing a toast.

They drank. Seven synchronized Adam's-apple-bobbing gulps.

'Goodt!' said one. The others nodded agreement.

'What are you Dreckenzorfers up to, tonight?' I asked. *Maybe I can lure the Magnificent Seven back chez Dough for a little synchronized swimming followed by some synchronized gruntcakes.*

'Zee potty,' said one, hiccuping Coca-Cola.

'Zee zweet-zigzteen potty vor Chenny Znitbrett,' said another, hiccuping Coke, blushing sweetly.

'It's tonight?' I smote my forehead. 'I forgot.' *What can I give little Jenny? If John Dough's imagination is on-the-money, perhaps the only suitable gift would be an IUD and a gross of Sensuous brand condoms.*

'Haff you zeen Koortiz?' one asked, blushing. Seven identical pairs of blue eyes and seven blushing freckled faces turned to me, nodding, hiccuping Coca-Cola.

I wonder if there's anything to those stories of women living together in college dormitories or on Israeli kibbutzes or in prison synchronizing their monthly periods? Perhaps this mass blushing and hiccuping and headaching is a case for the medical journals. . . . Ah, they want Kurtis. If he plays his cards right and moves with them to Mormon Utah: Seven brides for one brother.

'Sorry,' I said. 'Have you tried the Luegodagos'? He might be there working on Baby's plumbing.' *Christ, Roger, you're really making these Bavarian babes blush!*

And then the hiccuping became more fierce.

'Are you okay?' I asked the one nearest.

'It iz nozzing,' one said, blushing hard.

'Nozzing,' said another.

'Listen – Kiki, Bibi, Titi, Fifi, Lili, Mimi, and CeCe – I'm a trained Existentialist. I know the difference between nothing and something.'

'It iz nozzing,' said one, her eyes wide and her face dark and the hiccups shattering the pharmacy like anti-aircraft shrapnel – the sharp little explosions coming out fast and furious, like a John Cage chamber orchestra, like a seven-piece dissonant rock band, like a – *I've seen this before!*

Seven world-class sets of jerking heaving rat-tat-tatting rootin'-tootin' Teuton Tetons (thank you very much John Dough for freeing up my prose style), seven big bodies smashing into Snitbread Pharmaceutical product-displays, a small crowd forming as tubes and boxes and cans and jars and bottles clattered and crashed – and then: eerie silence, breath being held, seven elongated necks, seven dark faces—

'Oh no! Oh no!' I screamed. 'Girls, no! No! No!'

Seven sets of arms rising, seven nosebleeds, seven sets of ears spilling, seven eyes bulging, seven eyes popping and plopping and rolling and – *Death be not proud – I have a party to go to!*

I cried. I'm man enough and honest enough to admit that I cried. Take the horror of Auralee Emeraldstein-Bittburg and multiply it by seven. I cried. And I threw up. Yes, I did. And then I started to think. Yes indeed, Ma. I surprised myself how clear and cold and precise my thoughts were. And I had to laugh. It really wasn't funny. But I laughed anyway.

I called Cashampton General, told them to 'send ambulances, lots of ambulances. Seven dead at Smithers' Pharmacy.' I called Big Barton, told him to shake his monumental rear-end over to his old store pronto. I opened boxes of rubber bedwetter sheets (the same brand Specs used for his mother?) and covered the Dreckenzorfers. I crawled the product-strewn floor, wearing plastic gloves taken off a shelf, and collected the errant eyes, put them in my sticky Coke glass. And I hung around, consoling the sales clerk and counterman and other shoppers who were all crying and vomiting. After all, I was an old pro, a veteran of the exploding head wars. I took a pack of cigarettes from behind the counter and left three dollars. I smoked my first cigarette since high school, and I threw up again.

The paramedics showed first.

'Damn, Romeo!' said my smartass ambulance driver, looking at the seven voluptuous covered corpses, blonde hair spilling from rubber sheets. 'You're worse than Julio Iglesias.'

Big Barton came, still in his riding uniform. Police sirens blared in the distance.

'Let's go, Roger,' he said, hustling me out, handing hundred-dollar-bills to the employees.

'But Big Barton,' I said, trying to slow him down, 'it's not every day that seven automobile heiresses experience the joy of an exploding head all at once. Don't you think I should stick around and talk to the police?'

'I think you should come with me,' he said, handing me his wad of hundreds. 'My granddaughter turns sixteen tonight. Nothing short of a nuclear bomb is going to ruin her fun. Let's go.'

I took a good hard look at the cash, maybe two-thousand dollars.

'Money talks,' I said, digging a finger in my ear. 'But I'm a little bit hard of hearing.'

'We'll talk later, Roger. Please,' he pleaded, sweat popping out on his forehead beneath the black dome of his hard-hat.

'I'm sorry,' I said. 'I don't understand.'

'I'm speaking English, man!'

'Speak American,' I said. 'And speak it loud.'

'Please come,' he said, reaching into his wallet and handing me five exquisitely crisp thousand-dollar bills, five perfectly

lovely representational portraits of the dead American president Grover Cleveland. *Now that's art!* 'I promise we'll talk
later. You and me, Roger.'

'Ah, so now you want to talk to little Ralph,' I said, as the
police cars roared down the street, sirens singing. I liked
hearing him beg, seeing him sweat.

'No,' he said, opening the door and giving me a boost up
into his monster-truck Rolls-Royce. 'Now I want to talk to
big Roger, my new vice-president.'

Ten

JENNY'S PARTY WAS in full swing at the Gritz mansion. Outside, on the drive: two brand-new birthday BMW's, one from Jonas and Muffy, one from Big Barton and the ever-snoozy Sarah Snitbread, who, despite the blasting teenage music, was sleeping peacefully in the corner, a pointed party dunce-cap on her head. The younger set was dancing to Nirvana or Pearl Jam or Toe Jam or The Breeders – one of those bands – and us old fogies sat and stood around, drinking and chatting, *yelling* above the din.

Big Barton's secondary gift to his granddaughter, the black-goateed goat (which Jenny had named Axl) I'd last seen being treated for flu by Kurtis, grazed at the buffet table, chipper and hungry, apparently over his illness, packing away The Pregnant Duchess-catered fake-crab-salad before Jenny's brother Clark led him to the dance floor and picked up his front feet for a heavy-metal waltz.

'Do you know the novels of Italo Calvino?' I loudly asked

Tanya Yippenskip, publisher Horgan Yippenskip's sister, who held Jenny's pet female spider monkey Mozart and fed her Viennese cocktail wieners. (Though, truth be told, Mozart seemed more interested in stroking her long simian clitoris than eating Austrian junior tube-steaks.) Talking Italo Calvino was a safe subject. In the Art World, a passing knowledge of the late Calvino can often translate into low-cost highbrow sex. An Italo Calvino novel on your bedside table is as foolproof an aphrodisiac as Spanish Fly or, if you're flying solo, as effective an antidote to insomnia as ten Valiums — form follows function. Since no one is even remotely aware of what goes on in any of his books, you can safely say whatever you want about them without ever having to actually crack one open. All you need to know are the books' titles and the single versatile phrase, 'Ah, Calvino!'

'Know him! He took my virginity shortly before he committed suicide!' Tanya gushed, as Mozart's diddling increased in tempo, her monkey face taking on a look of sheer bliss. 'What's your favorite?'

'Uhh . . . have you tried the crab-salad?'

'I don't know that title.'

'How about some more alcoholic refreshment?'

'Are these newly-published lost works?' she asked, as Mozart reached a screeching climax. 'Have they been translated?'

'Lost works, yes,' I said, seeing a graceful exit. 'And they're still in the Italian. Ah, Calvino!'

'*Ti parlo Italiano?*'

'*Poquito,*' I said humbly, lighting a cigarette. And then, thanks be to the Gods of Literary Folly, Horgan Yippenskip saved my bacon by arriving from his extended trip to the toilet with a fresh round of umbrellaed Mai Tais, Terry Tuba in tow.

'Ah, Calvino!' Tanya said to me with a lusty wink, and took to the dance floor with tubby Terry Tuba, dropping Mozart on Sarah Snitbread's lap.

'So, Roger,' said the dashing young Sylvan Glade Press publisher, sniffling ever so slightly, a few grains of white crystal stuck to an unruly clump of unplucked nose hairs, 'I hear you're penning the definitive biography of Jackson Pollock.'

'You hear right!' I said, almost having to yell above Pearl Jam's jamming. 'I've uncovered certain irregularities in the conventional histories.'

'Sounds fascinating!' His eyebrows danced and begged more. 'You're with what house?'

'Turven Blagden – owned by Shiatsubishi!'

'Turven Blagden! Roger, they specialize in karate books!'

'They do?'

'Fucking right! Unless old Jackson practiced martial arts, I doubt very much if they're your ticket!'

'Well, Jackson *was* into Eastern Mysticism . . .' I said hopefully. 'And he loved wrestling . . .'

'Look, if they end up jerking you around, you come to me. By the way . . .' Horgan's brows were flapping wildly and the single remaining grain of coke clinging precariously to the overgrown nasal forest swayed in the breeze of his rum-breath. 'I understand you're friends with John Dough.'

'Good friends.'

'Did you read the *Enquirer* piece last week about his being an alien from Jupiter and his pearls being interplanetary communication devices?'

'Sorry, I missed that one,' I said, staring at the cocaine particle, salivating a bit.

'I have a proposition for you,' Horgan said, pincering my elbow and guiding me across the dance floor, past Jenny and all the check-shirted rich-kids. 'In here,' said the publisher, at the bathroom door.

'You seem like a nice fellow, Horgan, but I don't do gay.'

'Oh come on, Roger,' he said, pulling me in and closing the door, then speaking above the exhaust fan. 'We're both responsible adults – we're just gonna do some lines and talk some publishing biz, standard operating procedure.'

'In that case,' I said, sitting on the toilet-seat as Horgan lit a joint and set to chopping lines of coke on the toilet-top with his Visa card, 'I'm all ears.' And nose and lungs, I thought, snorting and toking and snorting and toking.

'So, Rog, how about we do a biography of the Pearl Man – authorized or unauthorized, whatever. A biography *and* a film.'

'John's a bit private,' I said, schemes percolating in my sneaky skull. 'But he's an extraordinary fiction writer. Maybe we can do a two-book deal – a three-book deal if the Japanese turn out to be bullshitting me.'

'I love it,' Horgan said, in my face. 'I really, really love it!'

'I'll get back to you,' I said, feeling for the door handle.

'Y'know, Roger, my special friends call me Countess Von Smedley.'

'That's very interesting.'

'How do you keep in such good shape, Rog?' he asked, reaching for my buns as I turned the knob.

'Running,' I said, running.

'Hello, Baby,' I said to my extinguished flame, the Countess Luegodago, who wore a black-fringed cowgirl ensemble and tapped her feet out of time to The Breeders. 'How's the girl?'

'Rog, ya little fuckface – ya still suckin' up ta da Poil Man?'

'Ah, Baby, eloquent as ever. How's the weather in Uruguay this time of year?'

'Stick it up yer ass, peanut-dick.'

'Baby, if I didn't know better, I'd think you actually cared for me.'

'I don't need yer shit, Rog, an' I don't need yer peanut-dick. I got a new pole-man faw my gondola.'

'Yes, so I've noticed. You and Kurtis are healing the rift between the races.'

'Da tip of his prick dwawfs yer whole fuckin' shlong, ya wormy little fuck.'

'My advice, *Countess*, in the spirit of sharing, is that you find an appropriately oversized prophylactic device, perhaps a plastic shopping bag for Kurtis or a garbage-can lid for yourself – you never know.'

'Ya nevah know is right. When I metya I thoughtya had a toucha class. Yer da slimiest little peanut-dick I evah met.'

'Why thank you, Baby. Coming from an Uruguayan countess born in Brooklyn, that's a real compliment.'

'I wonder where the Dreckenzorfers are,' said Muffy Snit-bread-Gritz, in front of a psychedelic Miró painting as Hootie And The Blowfish blew in the background.

'Something probably popped up,' I said. 'I imagine they were detained, perhaps by romance. Where's Kurtis?'

'My husband didn't want him here. Let me show you the house.' Muffy sighed and led me upstairs. 'Where's John Dough?'

'He went to The City,' I said, watching her shapely haunches shift back-and-forth as she climbed the stairs. 'He expected to be back for the party.'

'He hasn't been riding much lately.'

'There are other ways of staying in shape.'

'I saw you all going into the Poon Tang Restaurant last night. Is it serious with the artist woman?'

'No,' I said. 'They're just good friends who—'

'Like to fuck.'

'Why, Muffy!' I said, feigning shock, remembering her salty longshoreman speech in the John Dough novel. 'I didn't think—'

'What? That a *nice* girl like me talks that way? You'd be surprised, Roger. I'm married to a guy who wears his dick on his face and my father's a goddamn . . .' Her eyes pooled and she bolted down the hallway into a room, slamming the door. Her father's a what? A fat megalomaniacal whale? A what?

Axl the goat, his goatee clotted with Pregnant Duchess 'crab-salad' mayo, sniffed my crotch.

'Get lost,' I said, giving him a gentle boot in his goaty ass and wiping the mayonnaise off my crotch with one of the silk handkerchiefs Hiroshi had bought me at Ralph Lauren. 'Go find Countess Von Smedley.'

I was following the trail of art, checking out paintings and sculptures in different second-story rooms: a Monet, a Van Gogh, two T'ang Dynasty horses (odor-free). . . .

I was staring at a Braque, thinking: Old Pablo Picasso had nothing on this boy, when a terrible high-pitched yowling came through the partially open connecting door. I checked it: There was Jonas Gritz, his face a study in concentration, à la Rodin's *The Thinker*, holding a screeching cat (which I assumed to be the aforementioned troubled Tabby), Jonas's right index finger disappearing into Tabby's anus up to the second knuckle.

'Everything copacetic?' I asked.

'Don't you knock?' Herr Gritz threw the cat onto the floor, and it ran post haste, but clumsily, out of the room.

'Sorry, Jonas, I heard what I perceived to be a cry of pain and—'

'I was massaging SnitPrep H onto Tabby's hemorrhoids.' He wiped his finger on his Brooks Brothers corduroy pants. 'They were tender.'

'Yes, of course,' I said, as if seeing a middle-aged millionaire with a digit sunk up a cat's rear-end was par-for-the-course for Roger Lymon – which, I'm afraid, in Cashampton it was. 'I thought it must be something like that.'

'Let's get a drink,' he said, and we walked downstairs to the bar.

'To Tabby,' I toasted. 'May her eight *other* lives be hemorrhoid-free.'

'What's your fucking problem, Lymon?'

'No problem here,' I said, debating whether an anonymous letter to Tabby's Freudian analyst (an anal-assist?) was in order.

'Where's that fucking Pearl Man?' asked Jonas Gritz.

'I am not my brother's keeper.'

'Your *brother* hasn't been around the club lately – thank God.'

'His interest in riding has been in abatement.'

'You don't say. From what I hear he's been riding a horse of a different color.'

'You've got a dirty mouth, Mr. Gritz.'

'And you're a fucking suck-butt phony. You and your *brother*, no class at all. I say the guy's some kind of jewel thief. You can tell he has no class.'

'No class?' I asked, watching him watch his daughter dancing with a boy her own age, who like most of the lads sported a wispy Maynard G. Kerbs goatee (nothing compared to Axl's). 'How can you say that? He rides like Omar Sharif, he's looks better than Fabio, and he drives a Jaguar.'

'A camel-jockey, a wop, and a limey shitbox,' he said, sniffing his finger. 'Three strikes and you're out.'

'I understand that Specs Schwartz's mother was your family's maid.'

'That's right.'

'And Specs – I mean Gilbert – he was your childhood friend?'

'Where'd you hear that?'

'Just around. I understand he once shot a bird and—'

Jonas rubbed his nose thoughtfully. 'Where are you getting this shit?'

'Do you need to blow your nose?' I asked, pulling out my handkerchief, instantly regretting the offer – nothing personal, Tabby.

'No, I don't need to blow my nose,' he said. 'I recently broke it riding.'

'Riding with your daughter?'

'What do you mean by that?'

'Or were you riding Maria?'

'Are you out of your mind?'

'She's a marvelous teacher, very sexy, and she thinks very highly of you—'

'Where do you get these ideas?'

'A little dead wren told me.'

'You stay the fuck out of my business, Lymon,' the rich man said with his central-casting glower turned on full, 'If you know what's good for you.'

'Oh, I don't know,' I said with a smile, thinking about Maria's rough gruntcake potential, and casting a glance at the birthday girl slamdancing with Big Barton.

'What's good for the goose is good for the gander.'

'Goose? I'll goose your fucking nuts off.'

'Oh, I don't think so, cat-lover. You're talking to the new vice-president of Snitbread Pharmaceutical.'

'The what?' he asked, looking at Big Barton, now dancing

close with Jenny, the fully-blossomed blonde lost in the clutches of the massive Dictator of Diarrhea.

'You heard me, *JoJo*.'

'What?' he asked, going white as a slug – and then he walked away, bulling through dancers to speak to Big Barton.

'Are you a lacrosse fan?' I yelled, but I doubt Jonas heard me, what with The Screaming Trees screaming so loudly.

Eleven

'IT WAS A flu medicine we were working on,' Big Barton explained, as we walked over his fields under the cloud-covered midnight moon (we'd driven over from the party in the monster-truck Rolls and parked on the grass), the beer-woozy buffaloes and the camels wandering and chewing, dark humps passing in the night.

'I think with you, Barton,' I flipped on the tape-recorder in my pocket, 'everything's a flu medicine.'

'*Big* Barton's my name, son,' the billionaire said, his usual brio gone.

'Bart, Bartie baby . . . You know how *real* people think AIDS got started?'

'Some say it's a curse from God.'

'Try again.'

'Some say the Africans were having sex with green monkeys.'

'Uhuh. And some say Abraham Lincoln was actually a two-headed woman called Lois from the island of Fiji.' I shook my head. 'A lot of people think it's a Malthusian plot. A plot to wipe out Africa and Asia – population control, Planned Parenthood on the grand scale: No more competition from the Japanese and the Chinese, no more fear of hungry black hordes swimming up to your mansion demanding food and sexual congress from your blonde daughter and blonde granddaughter, no more swarthy homosexuals bending your handsome little blonde grandson Clarkie over a barrel, no more Haitians and Hispanics and—'

'That's ridiculous. The caring professionals at Snitbread Pharmaceutical are working very diligently to find a cure—'

'Hold that thought, Bartie. What most people think – most people whose brains aren't addled to mush by too much TV and liquor and drugs – recreational drugs I mean, not the quality medicines made by the caring pros at Snitbread Pee . . . what most people think is that the US Government was attempting to find a cure for cancer and was conducting top-secret gene-altering experiments down in Haiti, and something went wrong, hugely fucking wrong—'

'That's preposterous.'

'Isn't it? They were probably working on a flu medicine.'

'What do you want?'

'Straight answers – for starters. And Barton, in case you get any bright ideas, my lawyer has a copy of a letter I wrote directly after Cassandra and Sock experienced the joy of an exploding head. Anything remotely curious happens to me, it's time for the Barbara Walters interview. You dig?'

Big Barton swallowed the bullshit and sighed. 'You want the truth?'

'No, I want a job cutting sugar cane in Haiti.'

'The truth is that six years ago we were working on a flu medicine, Roger, a very complex compound comprised—'

'Cut the technical horseshit.'

'The flu drug worked on rats and cats, so we tried it on sheep and dogs and monkeys and goats. It worked on them too.'

'You mean it cured a cat's sniffles and a sheep's sore throat?'

'I mean it knocked the flu right out of their systems. It was terrific, but—'

'This is what I want, the *but* end.'

'But there were some side-effects.'

'Such as?'

'Anywhere from three hours to a month later, the testees started to . . .'

'Experience the joy of an exploding head.'

'That's an accurate, if perhaps overly poetic assessment – but yes. Complete liver failure, followed by recurrent myoclonic jerks, generalized seizures leading to otorrhea, intracranial pressure, severing of the optic nerve, the veins, and arteries – severe proptosis.'

'In layman's terms: The joy of an exploding head.'

'Any animals that didn't die we euthanized, except for a few dogs and goats we kept for observation – I've got a soft spot for dogs and goats – and when we rewarded them with some above-ground time, they got to mating with some of our cancer dogs and goats, and then the cancer testees – they started to . . .'

'Experience the joy of an exploding head.'

'Don't be so callous, Roger. We're really fucking worried.'

'You ought to be, man, it's out there, in *your* community, on *your* fucking doorstep. Eyeballs popping, heads exploding.'

'Please,' Big Barton begged, covering his eyes. 'I was an infantryman in the War, but this . . . this—'

'This is some odious and brutal shit.'

'We don't know how it works, exactly. Transmission is instant, no incubation period . . . the virus gets in the DNA and the carriers don't exhibit any overt symptoms, but the others . . .'

'Experience the joy of an exploding head,' I said. 'But we're not talking about the beasts of the field anymore.' I stopped to pat a red-eyed buffalo with beer-breath. 'This isn't Genesis; it's St. John of The Apocalypse. Alcoholic beagles, Mary's Little Lamb with no wool from chemotherapy, Morris The Cat with an exploding head — and human beings: Dreckenzorfers, Phlebitises, Auralee . . . and who's next?'

'Whoever *he's* screwing.'

'And who's *he?*' Ah, but I knew. I knew the screwer, I knew the screwee — and the screwee was screwed: *Hasta luego, Baby Luegodago.*

'You know who — our human guinea pig.'

'I want to hear *you* say it.'

'Alright,' he sighed, 'it's Kurtis Cash. He was our first and only human guinea pig and then he goes and gets arrested for some godawful stupid rape . . .'

'A rape he didn't commit.'

'Yes, so it turned out.'

'But you didn't testify to his good character at the trial. Kurtis the wounded football player — the hard-working, hard-fucking, hard-luck Kurtis Swimming Otter Cash, working-class hero.'

'You don't understand, Roger. I liked Kurtis, liked him a lot. He means the world to this town.'

'And you showed your affection by setting the poor bastard up. Planned the whole thing. Probably gave the Doberman a hand-job yourself and fucked the girl with a Sensuous brand French tickler.'

'Boy, you've got a dirty mind.'

'No, man, I've got a crystal ball.'

'We weren't sure he had it like the animals. . . . After all, no people had—'

'Experienced the joy of an exploding head.'

'But we couldn't take any chances.'

'So you figured with Kurtis out of circulation he can't harm you. Maybe he gets killed in jail, maybe he just rots there forever – at least he won't be stroking any Cashampton cuties for a while. Give you some time to figure the disease out . . . By the way, what do you call this lovely thing of yours?'

'We call it The Disease. If it isn't stopped. . . . The Disease makes AIDS look like the measles.'

'So what are you doing about it?'

'Testing testing testing. Since Auralee died we've poured so much money into testing that Snitbread stock is heading for the toilet.'

'That's why you were kissing the Pearl Man's ass to become an investor?'

'Right,' he said with a three-hundred-pound sigh.

'What are you doing about Kurtis? He's just a carrier, right?'

'Correct, he's just a carrier; but he refuses to come and take any tests to help us produce a vaccine or find a cure. He's just—'

'Fucking you where you eat.'

Barton nodded.

'So why haven't you taken him out?'

'Out?'

'Don't be cute; this is your new president talking—'

'Vice-president.'

'I just gave myself a promotion.' I laughed. 'And a raise. Say a five-million-dollar signing bonus with free stock and a half-a-mil-a-year salary.'

'And what do I get for all that?'

'Silence, virtue, and cunning. Why haven't you whacked him?'

'Don't think I haven't considered it, but I guess he's seen the same goddamn movies you have: He's got three lawyers holding sealed letters addressed to Pinch Salzberger at *The New York Times*. I've got a copy. He's got us over that barrel you mentioned and he's—'

'Fucking you where you eat.'

'We can't win for losing. We should have euthanized him five years ago.'

'How many people know about this?'

'Just me and Dr. Guberstein and my security director, Lenny Fripp.' He paused and glumly added: 'And my new president.'

'And Kurtis.'

'And Kurtis.' Big Barton stopped, and he looked at me with tired red eyes. 'Why's he doing it? I mean, it's murder. Big murder.'

'No shit.'

'But why?'

'Maybe because he lost his scholarship to USC. Who knows. *Why* doesn't matter, Bart, because now, with the Dreckenzorfers experiencing the joy of an exploding head, now the cops will order extensive autopsies, no?'

'We'll be fucked.'

'The whole fucking planet might be fucked.'

'Maybe if we euthanized him . . .'

'Too late. You think the Dreckenzorfers were Carmelite nuns? Since Kurtis gave them the old Swimming Otter special, they've maybe fucked three or four guys each. Do your arithmetic.'

'So what do we do about it?'

'Work your ass off to find a vaccine or a cure.'

Big Barton sighed. 'We need a live human subject.'

'Not necessarily. The Disease gets in their DNA, right?'

'Right.'

'And DNA survives death, right?'

'Right.'

'Add it up, bigboy. You got a shovel?'

Twelve

GREEN RIVER CEMETERY by moonlight. I was sweating like a pig, digging Auralee's grave. Greatness is thrust upon us when we least expect it.

We'd stopped for a shovel in Big Barton's tool shed, then zipped across Cashampton to the Springs. The billionaire had driven and I'd sat in the back seat – not just because Prince Roger liked being ferried about in high style – of course I did – but because during our informative little chat out in the fields, one of Barton's buffaloes had taken the opportunity to stick his head through the open front passenger-door of the Rolls and leave us a keepsake, a pile of creamy green grass-and-beer vomit.

'I've decided,' I said, pausing from my labor, 'that a presidency of Snitbread Pee is not in my immediate career plans.'

'What is it you want?'

'Money and anonymity.'

'Whatever, Roger. We win this one, I'll give you the goddamn keys to—'

'The candy store,' I said happily, digging my shovel into the cool fragrant earth. 'Now, Bart, I want you to call your security chief. We're going to need some help with the back-up phase of my plan. I'm pleased to announce that Baby Luegodago has just won an all-expenses-paid vacation to Cash Island for a little R and R and some serious fucking testing before . . .'

'She experiences the joy of an exploding head,' he mumbled morosely.

'That's the spirit, Bartie!' I clapped his meaty back. 'Get on it.'

The funeral home had done a bang-up job on Auralee, fitting her errant eye back in its socket – absolutely no trace of sticky guava sorbet – and making the skin bloodless and pale as in her pre-Disease prime, though, running a finger over sharp cheekbones a fashion-model would have died for, I did find it a bit tough and leathery to the touch; but, predictably, the weeks underground had done nothing for her body odor; and I really hate to seem such a nitpicker, but some delicate brown peach-fuzz was marring her once-pristine upper lip.

'Perhaps,' I mused, lighting a cigarette. 'Perhaps *Derma Quarterly* would be interested in a layman's article – a Lymon layman's article! – on the subject of hair-growth after death. What do you think, Barton?'

'I think you're a sick, sick man.'

'How's this for a title: "Fear And Trembling in Cash-ampton – An Exploration Of The Inadequacy of Electrolysis After The Onset Of Rigor Mortis, From the Point Of View Of An Existentialist Amateur Graverobber"?'

'I think I'm about to puke.'

'Well, before you do, grab her feet.'

A minute of lifting and carrying and lifting and hoisting, and Auralee – what was left of Auralee – was in the back seat of the Rolls: a stylish sexy stiff showing plenty of stubbled leg, in a pink Gianni Versace slashed minidress. Gianni would have approved, I think, except possibly for my muddy hand-prints.

'Lenny Fripp's on his way from Forest Hills,' Big Barton said. 'He's had a few DWI's so he's got to go the speed limit, but he should be here in two hours.'

'That's fine.' I looked at my old Keith Haring Swatch watch. 'That'll make it four-o'clock when he arrives, plenty of time to grab Baby and make the Sag Wharf before dawn. Oh, and Barton, I could use a new Rolex, oyster shell variety, in honor of the Pearl Man. Can you arrange that?'

'Whatever, Roger,' Barton said, popping a heart-pill. 'I'm so fucking tired I'll say Yes to anything.'

'That's a good boy, Bartie. Now why don't you climb up in *my new Rolls* and take a snooze while I fill in this grave.'

'Sleep up there with that – that *thing?*'

'Don't be a snob, Barton; that's your old friend Auralee. You could always lay out on the front seat.'

He hesitated. Tough choice: Auralee or buffalo cookies.

'One Mississippi,' I counted. 'Two Mi—'

'Christ,' Big Barton said with a sigh, climbing up into the back seat and slugging from a bottle of Stolichnaya. 'I wish I'd never invented Speed-Lax.'

'I know a certain orangutan on Cash Island who'd agree with you,' I said, giving him a friendly football playeresque pat on his overgrown rear-end and taking the booze. 'Just relax, big guy. Roger Lymon will take care of everything.'

I had a good long guzzle from the Stoli bottle and then closed the coffin, shoveled dirt, shoveled and shoveled and shoveled, and when the grave was filled in and covered with sod I returned to the car to stow the shovel. Big Barton slumped snoring on the back seat, Ex-Auralee's blonde page-boy head resting against his side-of-beef-sized thigh. Young love, so beautiful. Whatever the age.

I tamped the sod with my hands and then stomped the grave.

'What are you doing, Roger?'

'Oh, good evening, Mr. de Kooning.' The great man wore pajamas, a bathrobe and hiking boots. 'You should be at home sleeping or, failing that, testing the envelope of art-theory with Lindsay LaRouche. Rehearsing for *The Temple Of Dendur*.'

'Yah! We worked that out already. She has shown me the Cult Of Isis fellatio technique. It is the Method Acting I think. Instead of tiring me out, it only gives me more of the energy. Lindsay told me to try counting breasts, but that had the opposite of the desired effect. I hope I don't scare that sweet angel off.'

'Oh, I doubt that,' I said. 'She's a hardy specimen.'

'Yah! She has the pioneer spirit.' Old Bill's mouth turned down. 'My daughter has poured out all the liquor in the house. Not even a goddamn beer. She wishes me to return to AA.' He stared at my bottle longingly, licking his lips.

'First we talk Pollock,' I said, taking his arm.

'I love talking Pollock!' he exclaimed. 'I often come here at night for just that purpose.' He looked at my Rolls. 'Is that not young Barton Snitbread's auto?'

'I won it from him in a game of craps.'

'Yah! Good show!' De Kooning cast a sidelong glance at the bottle as we approached Pollock's boulder. 'So what is it you wish to know?'

'Jackson wasn't gay, right?'

'Not possible.' We sat on the cool grass, against the boulder. I rolled Pollock's memorial softball – it was getting dirty and chapped in the elements – rolled it down my thighs and lit a smoke. 'He loved women. Women and liquor and painting.'

'And he wasn't impotent those last years.'

'No, Roger, he wasn't – only with Lee. That was *her* truth, not his.'

'And he had a child, yes? A son.'

'Yes.'

'Gilbert Schwartz.'

'He has dug your grave well, Jackson,' de Kooning said, stroking the grass. 'Better than any previous biographer.'

'But why didn't Ruthie Kligman or Jeff Potter – or Friedman or Soloman or anyone else who wrote about him – why didn't they find what I've found?'

'Because history, it is as much about forgetting as remembering – selective forgetting.'

'That sounds good, but try again.'

'Because time has a way of loosening tongues, of waking the sleeping dogs.'

'If you want a drink, Mr. de Kooning, you'll have to do better.'

The old painter sighed. 'Only a few knew of the child . . . me and Lee' – he indicated the stone at Pollock's feet – 'and of course Jackson and Valerie, the parents, and Josiah Foote and his wife, and Leo Schwartz and—'

'Esther Foote Drummond.'

'Yah, Esther. She was lovely.'

'But if Lee knew, why didn't Jackson cut Specs – Gilbert – in for a piece of the Pollock pie?'

A warm breeze rustled the greenleaved trees and de Kooning echoed it with his own sad sigh.

'Lee would not hear of it. Yah, poor Gilbert. The classic bastard. It wasn't fair for him, for Valerie. Jackson had talked about making a new will – but he was a weak man, under-confident . . . he had nightmares that Lee would bite his balls off! I am serious about this. They had not sexed in years. And he felt strongly that he would die young. Maybe he wanted to die. His life was not much fun. We talked about doing something for Gilbert – we argued like we argued painting . . . Little Gilbert, such a sweet child, so handsome. Poor fellow – what happened to him? But then Jackson told me to fuck off – said he he had a better idea, so I left it at that. We were all poor – it wasn't until Jackson died that the money started rolling, and even then it was nothing compared to now. Warhol and those *putas* changed all that.' De Kooning spat into the night. 'They pissed on the purity of art. They murdered art for art's sake. For them it was art for money's sake. A gang of prostitutes with paint brushes,' de Kooning said sadly, sighing and looking at the bottle with tears in his eyes.

'You want a drink that bad?'

'No, I am thinking about Jackson and Gilbert.' He rubbed the boulder. 'Yah. Sure, Leo Schwartz did a fine job, but that, that was Jackson's boy. And then after Jack died, when the dollars grew large . . . with Lee around, I knew if we tried to intercede, Gilbert would only get pain. And Valerie had Leo, a proud man who did not care shit about Pollock's money. So Esther and I, we agreed to the silence, at least until Lee was dead – if we outlived her. But when she died, I was in the fog . . . And now with Valerie and Gilbert dead, Jackson's legacy doesn't matter.'

'But Pollock was painting to the end.'

'Yah! From what little I saw – strong work. Maybe his best.'

'But what happened to the paintings?'

'Valerie received one – Jackson painted it at the secret studio in the woods the day he died – but she hated it and gave it to Esther; and the rest I never saw – they were lost . . . Am I helping?'

'What happened to the studio?'

'The day after he died, I went to clean the space, but I found no work.'

'So who knew about the studio? Who might have taken the paintings?'

'Whoever took them, they have never been shown or spoken of or written about. Who knew? Esther. Valerie. Myself. Franz Kline. And who else? Maybe one of Jackson's other girls. Ruthie or Bertha Bemon – Seward now.'

'Bertha said she'd show me where the studio was, but she's in the hospital.'

'Yah. She is a good girl. But I think she has started to talk about Pollock lately. You get to be a certain age and memories are important. You don't want to die holding on to your memories. Or lose them to the fog. Memories are like paintings, souvenirs of our lives, meant to be shared.'

'Van Gogh said something like that.'

'Yah, my countryman. Another madman. How about that drink?'

'One more question. The painting that Valerie gave Esther – was it *The Rat King*?'

The wind whispered, the train whistle blew, faraway and mournful in the night, and de Kooning grimaced.

'Yah yah, *The Rat King*. Horrible and beautiful. Essential Pollock. Esther called me after young Gilbert killed himself. Told me she wanted to sell it. It speaks too much about death, and it scares her like it scared Valerie.'

'I've seen it.'

'The toupee man bought it, yah. Esther made him promise not to tell its history until she is dead. The man is a true collector. I do not think he will divulge. But you, Roger, you are a professional teller – a historian. You will tell and I do not blame you. Tell it.'

'I will, Mr. de Kooning.'

'Call me Bill and give me that goddamn bottle.'

'Sure,' I said, taking a jolt of Russian and handing it to him. 'Tell me about *The Rat King*. What does it mean?'

'It is a legend from the Germans.' De Kooning hit from the bottle, just once. 'The sisters told it to me and Jackson the night before the night he died. They brought the legend from the Nazi camp. You know they were child-whores in Buchenwald?'

'Esther told me.'

'Yah. During their first winter there, they were so hungry. They heard noises under the barracks floor. Terrible scuttling squeaking noises. Rats. And then after the winter was upon them, they heard nothing. A woman decided to attempt an escape. So she removed the floorboards and found the Rat King – that is what the guards told the girls it was called. The ancient Teuton barbarians worshiped the Rat King. He was a source of power. From the dark side. And the guards, they killed all the women in that room – except for the sisters – killed them for disturbing the Rat King. It was not a few rats, but perhaps fifty rats, fifty foul diseased rats who had huddled together for warmth and become tangled, their tails tied in knots. They were stuck together, joined by urine and semen and blood. Some had partially eaten each other before freezing – but not freezing to death. Hibernating. Stuck together and stinking. And the Jewish women lifted the Rat King, unstuck the rats. They were going to eat them. But the Rat King awoke. And the Rat King fought with the starving women, and that's when the guards came in and started shooting. And that was the night Valerie and Esther were taken away for the raping. Jackson cried when he heard that story. The next day he painted the picture. It was the battle of the Rat King versus the Buchenwald women. But in the painting – yah, there was the Pollock violence, but there was also the love, the strong real love of Jackson for Valerie. Some say he purposely drove off the road that night. I don't doubt it.'

I felt chilled, and I shivered. De Kooning drank deeply. 'Forgive me, Roger, just thinking of the Rat King makes me want to drink to forget. In a minute I will be a silly old man.'

'Don't say that, Bill. You've got more balls and smarts and class than anyone I've ever met.'

'You did not know Jackson,' he said, patting the grass.

'No,' I said. 'But I know Specs Schwartz, his son.'

'Yah. . . . What is life?' de Kooning asked, sucking vodka, still lucid. 'Each day I awake: I eat my toast and I drink my coffee, and I shit and I paint and I inch ever closer across the street here to my faceless friend death, and I ask myself, what am I doing on this planet? I still don't know. Almost ninety-years-old – still I am asking and still I don't know. Trying to make a neat little order out of all the mess? Impose a form on the formless? Making the little snapshots of eternity? What? I have no answers – only more questions. I am as much in the dark as ever.' He sighed and passed the bottle. 'What does this God want from us? Who is God, Roger? A God that can make Jackson and Lindsay and Esther and Elaine and all the lovely people I have known. A god that can make the Rat King. Is there a God?'

'I don't know, Bill,' I said, drinking. 'Maybe all we're here for is to ask the questions, to ask and ask and ask and provide God with a laugh now and then, because to be sure, we human beings are funny fucking things.'

'Yah!' he said, looking at the moon through the trees. 'Human beings are funny fucking things! Nature makes her own messes and when we try to clean them up we only make a bigger mess.'

And then the greatest living painter on the planet proceeded to cry. He cried and he cried and I held him. I stroked his moonkissed silver hair, and I cried too. His tears soaked into my sweat-damp shirt, and I cried. For Auralee and the Dreckenzorfers and the Phlebitises, for Jackson and Valerie and Leo and Specs, for my dead mother and my dead father, for you, for me – for little Roger Lymon – for all the funny fucking humans I'd ever known, for the funny fucking life we all share, for all the questions, all the unanswered unanswerable questions.

'What's wrong, Mr. Lymon?' It was Lindsay LaRouche, standing in the moonlight in a filmy peignoir, barefoot, her face worried, puffy with sleep, her extraordinary architectural chest panting and heaving and promising an eternity of spiritual nutrition.

'Nothing,' I said, and now de Kooning was sleeping like the innocent baby we all once were and will be again, before life began to play its funny fucking games on us and we started to dream and strive and dance in the long shadows of the dying light. 'Nothing. Bill just had a bit much to drink, but now he's fine.'

Lindsay sat down next to me, her back against Jackson's boulder, and she took a short snort off the bottle.

'I love him, Mr. Lymon,' she said, softly touching the old man's cheek. 'He's a doll. I love all men, but he's special. His daughter thinks I want the money. Sure, I like money, but I *love him.*'

'I can understand why. He's a special guy.' I lit a cigarette and puffed, had a drink. 'Lindsay, when you were with Specs, with Gilbert, why were you so cruel?'

'I regret that now. He was so kind. His ugliness only made

him kinder. I guess I was young, and I was poor and frustrated by this town. I guess it was ambition. I wanted to make it big. And ha ha ha' – she laughed self-mockingly, lightly hefting her domes – 'I guess I did. But now, now I'm sorry I made him feel shabby. If he were alive today I'd give him the finest fuck of his life. I would. Working in the sex-care industry has shown me that sex is a special gift, but it's love that counts. And that man, he loved me. I'm sorry I didn't understand that.'

'And why, working at the Upton Riding Club, why weren't you obsessed with horse penises like the other grooms?' I had to ask, had to find out, for John Dough's novel.

'Other girls dream of horses, Mr. Lymon, but my family were fishermen. When I was a girl, my grandfather used to take me out on the water and sometimes we'd see whales. I fell in love with whales. Like big bald babies – cute but powerful. All that spurting water, all that splashing. And the name – sssssperm whales. You don't think that would make an impression on a girl? I wanted to be filled with a hot giant whale prick, flooded with hot whale sperm. Totally filled up. So horses were just horses, nice little animals. But I've had so much cock the last year . . . I'm sick of people making such a fuss over big dicks. . . . Think how huge the universe is and think how small a man's cock is. Any man. Imagine making a rope out of all the cocks in the world and then climbing to heaven. That's a lotta cock. Then you get halfway there and you realize they're all about the same and you'll never be able to climb them all . . . So what it's really about is love. And if you got love, you got heaven in your hands. You gotta measure a man by the content of his heart, not by the size of his johnson. Sex is just giving. And if you get while you give – great. That's the cherry on top of the banana split.'

'You're the perfect woman,' I said, and I was keenly aware

that my bit of rope thought so too. It was craning toward the moon.

'You think so?'

'God, yes.'

'You're sweet,' she said, touching me down there, her hair fragrant, her lips fat and pouting and yummy, slick with vodka . . . and I kissed them, I licked the vodka off her lovely lips, and our tongues met with a soft wet spark.

'I am the reincarnation of Isis, Mr. Lymon. You would honor me, and you would honor the Goddess, if you gave me your love.'

'Oh, God, yes!' I said, gently laying the sweetly snoring de Kooning on the cool dewy grass, the uncut hair of Pollock's grave, touching one of Lindsay LaRouche's perfect pyramid breasts, peeling her nightie, peeling my pants — kissing and clinging, our bones and cells and flesh melting and tingling and mingling and singing. 'Oh, God, yes!' I said, climbing. 'Oh, God, yes!' I said, entering the moist source of all perfection, 'Oh, God, yes!' she said. 'Oh, God, yes!' I said. 'Oh, God, yes!' we said and we said and we said, starflesh lost in starlight . . . 'Oh, God, yes!'

Thirteen

WHAT KIND OF WORM *am I*? To make love, sweet sweet love, to the Kissin' Banshee, my buddy Bill's woman – to cuckold my friend and to live Specs Schwartz's dream atop his father's dusty bones?

'I told you, Mr. Snitbread, we should've punched Kurtis Cash's ticket five years ago,' said Lenny Fripp, a square-cut block of ex-NYPD granite. (I had gotten Lindsay and a groggy Bill back home before Barton had awakened and before Lenny the Troglodyte had arrived.) 'And whatta we need this bozo for?' He jerked a thumb at me.

'Mr. Fripp,' I said, blowing a smoke ring at the man – we were crowded in the back of the Rolls – Big Barton, Lenny Fripp, Ex-Auralee, myself, and the shovel. 'Have you ever seen The Disease in action?'

'Sure, I seen goats and cats and dogs—'

'Have you ever seen a human being experience the joy of an exploding head?'

'Who's this douche, Mr. Snitbread? I gotta listen to this shit?'

'He's my silent partner, Lenny. Listen to him. And do what he says.'

'Mr. Snitbread needs to be home in a few hours. And so do I. The police will, no doubt, have questions for both of us concerning the seven Dreckenzorfers who exploded in his old store. So after I lure Countess Baby Luegodago from her lair, *you* will take her to Cash Island in *Speed-Lax 1*.'

'How we gonna do that? ''Hello, Countess, your eyeball's gonna jump outta your fuckin' skull if you don't come with us. It prolly will anyway, but we need for you to come and let Dr. Guberstein cut you up and examine your guts to find this fuckin' disease you got.'' That's the plan?'

'I had something a bit more subtle in mind.'

'Baby,' I said, speaking on the pay-phone from dead dark Main Street in Cashampton. Lenny Fripp had nixed the use of a cell-phone — too easily traced. 'Baby, I miss you.'

'Pliz to tell me who ees dees.'

'It's Roger, Baby.'

'Whaddaya want, ya little fuckin' peanut-dick?'

'Baby, I miss you. I need you. I can't live without you.'

'It's faw-fuckin'-thoity, peanut-dick. Yer jus' lucky da Count took some Snitinex an's sleepin'.'

'Baby, I must have you again. I must make love to you. I must.'

'Rog, I toldya, I'm bein' takin care of on dat front — an' reah.'

'Just once more, Baby. I must experience the rapture one more time. Then I promise, *hasta luego*. I won't take no for an answer.'

'No.'

'I didn't want it to come to this, Baby, but my passion knows no bounds. If you don't meet me at your gate in five minutes I'll—'

'Yull what? Kill yerself?' She laughed.

'I'll . . .' I gave her a few crocodile sobs and winked at Lenny Fripp, who spat in disgust. 'I'll tell Diego you're from Brooklyn.'

'What da fuck?' the sleep-grumpy Uruguayan Brooklynite wearing her protective Art-Bra and Art-Girdle asked when she saw the Rolls and Lenny Fripp's company Lincoln Town Car.

'This is my friend Lenny,' I said.

'I always wanted to meet a countess,' said Lenny Fripp, punching the point of Baby's jaw.

Sag Wharf was covered with bright tents. The dawn was sneaking up on us. I let go my end of the Versaced corpse and picked up a sign. It read: 'SNITBREAD PHARM. CRUEL TO ANIMALS.'

'What the fuck's goin' on?' Lenny Fripp asked, grunting, hauling Baby Luegodago along the dock, the Art-Lingerie scraping a trail of divots in the worn wood. Big Barton and I shared Auralee's weight.

'I was warned this might happen,' said Big Barton. 'Someone sent an anonymous letter to PETA about the testing.'

'Goddammit!' I said. Now that I was a stockholder, I deeply regretted my former bleeding-heart liberalism (and that impetuous letter I'd penned).

We made our way to *Speed-Lax 1* and, with some difficulty and more than a few scratches, got a now moaning Baby Luegodago aboard. Lenny Fripp gave her another love-tap – that did the trick, better than Snitinex.

As we got set to hand Auralee to Lenny, Barton's foot slipped on some fresh seagull guano and he hit the dock-deck, dropping his end of the package. Gravity yanked her from my grip and she fell into the bay. Silver flashing fish investigated the pink floater.

'We better get her out of there,' I said. 'Before the horny ghost of Lord Medgar Cash decides to . . .'

'Don't you ever stop?' Big Barton asked, as Lenny Fripp gaffed Auralee.

'I'm a just a full-speed-ahead damn-the-torpedoes kind of fellow.'

'You're a fuckin' asshole,' said Lenny Fripp, pulling the gaff out of Auralee's Versace-sacked butt, and then hauling her dripping onto the boat.

'That may be, Lenny, but I'm your boss. Get Dr. Guberstein on the job,' I said. 'And cut the lip.'

'Will do, boss.'

'And don't start the engine till we're away from the dock.'

Lenny Fripp nodded.

'Well,' I said, waving to the still-knocked-out Countess. '*Hasta luego*, Baby.'

We'd driven only a hundred yards from the wharf when the bomb exploded, lighting the gray sky. Chunks of *Speed-Lax 1* and its ex-occupants rained onto the dock. The check-shirted protesters came out of their tents and cheered.

'That was meant for me,' Big Barton said.

'Look on the bright side,' I said, from the back seat. 'If Lord Medgar fucks with Baby, he's in for a real surprise.'

Big Barton Snitbread was exhausted and worried. We were back at his estate, in the back seat of the Rolls, watching the early sun dappling the ocean and green fields and garish castle.

'Just say that Lenny and Baby were running off for a romantic tryst.'

'What if the police don't buy it?'

'He had a thing for phony South American countesses, he must've kidnaped her, he was a Shining Path guerrilla. I don't know – get creative.'

'What about Auralee?'

'That's trickier. Why did charming Lenny leave the police force?'

'He was caught dealing drugs.'

'Okay, so you say he was stealing samples from you. Say you'd once caught him buzzed out of his skull and having sex with a cadaver you were testing.'

'We don't have cadavers on the Island.'

'Bartie,' I reproached him, showing him my tape-recorder. 'This is your partner, this is Roger.'

'Okay, okay.' Barton sighed. 'Should I call you a cab?'

'What ever for? I've got my new car.'

'Are you serious?'

'I won't even dignify that with an answer. Out.'

Big Barton gave me a tired beaten look and he opened the door.

'What are we gonna do, Roger? We gotta find a cure. We need a subject.'

'Don't whine. We just wait and see who Kurtis takes as his next . . . uhh, lover. Or . . .'

'Or what?'

'You didn't euthanize all your test-subjects, did you?'

'We did.'

'I thought you had a soft spot for goats?'

'So . . . ?'

'So Axl had the flu.'

'Axl? But Axl's been with the company for years.'

'Consider it early retirement.'

'But he's Jenny's pet.'

'Cut the shit. Axl's running away from home tonight. Play it any way you want, fat boy. Put his picture on milk cartons – I don't care. Just get that goat to Guberstein.'

'Okay,' he said with a sigh.

'And Bartie?'

'What now?'

'Are there any paper towels in the car?'

'Why yes, in the glove compartment.'

'Then get busy,' I said, mixing a drink and flipping on the TV. 'I always say, there's nothing like a little buffalo-vomit to ruin a new Rolls.'

Fourteen

AH, LOOK AT me now, Ma! Top of the world! I've made it! Driving a Rolls, living in Cashampton. A respected critic, a businessman, the confidant of billionaires and millionaires. And Pa! Here I am. Wish you were here to count the dollars. The Lehmans are really coming up in the world!

I guess I've never mentioned that the family name was originally Lehman? Have I? Yes, I'm a Jew. Not one of your beanie-wearing bearded fanatics that America so loves to hate, but a fully-assimilated citizen of Jewish heritage whose family changed the name over a century ago. I've never even been inside a Jewish temple. So, I suppose, I thought, fishing a crumpled joint from my shirt pocket as I drove through dawn-splashed Cashampton with the windows wide open and the soft cool air of morning whooshing through my hair, seeing deer grazing in the woods and early birds hopping branch to branch, I suppose it's time to honor my ancestors. So I smoked. For the children of Israel, for the child whores of Buchenwald, for Specs and Leo, I smoked.

I pulled into the Mulrooney Estate and parked on the gravel drive in front of the Schwartz cabin. With the sun coming up I had no need of the flashlight and batteries that I'd been lugging about all night in my jacket pocket. It had been a long and tiring and ultimately very profitable twelve hours, but I couldn't forget my literary interests. Specs, son of Jackson, was still important to me.

The shack was small and sad and only half-there (the fire having burnt the back down). The living room: wounded chairs, a lumpy tattered couch, its center caved in from Valerie's years of manic-depressive tube-watching, a television, a crummy old hifi, 1950s issue, a stack of Charlie Parker and Miles Davis records, a stack of wrestling magazines. In Specs's room: nothing. A few pairs of blue jeans, a few pairs of clean underwear, a few old copies of *Derma Quarterly*. Nothing. The man was an existential cipher. I stood there in the morning silence. Nothing. No clues to Pollock. John Dough had worked a miracle in his book. I couldn't have gleaned a thing from this place. It was like looking in a painting, trying to figure out what the artist ate for breakfast by the play of light and shadow.

I meandered into Valerie's room. Oh, sadness. How heartbreaking the poverty of the dead. Torn rubber bedwetter sheet revealing an ancient brown yellow-stained mattress. Tacked on the wall an Abstract Expressionist painting signed 'Leo' – not bad, not bad at all – and a few framed autographed photos of muscular, pose-striking old-timer wrestlers. 'To Valerie, best wishes, Killer Kawalski.' 'To Val – a sweet kid. Best wishes, Bobo Brazil.' 'To Valerie and Leo and Gil – from your friend the Champ, Bruno Sammartino.' Where were they now? Bruno? and Killer? and Bobo?

Their once proud muscles turned to fat, the glory of the screaming crowd faded into memory. Sad faded memories. Souvenirs. The Schwartz Family souvenirs. Cold as the spaces between the stars.

The kitchen: burnt. The dining nook: burnt.

The bathroom. Specs's bathroom. How many lonely ablutions had he performed here? I turned the faucet on. The water ran rusty brown. I opened the medicine chest. Row after row of old old tubes and jars and canisters – dead cold inert evidence of Specs's valiant losing battle to the many oils and bacteria which flesh is heir to. *How many zits erupted right here?* I closed the cabinet door and looked at myself in the mirror. It was blotched and splotched with the foul crusted evidence of Specs Schwartz's pimple-popping extravaganzas. Damned if he wasn't his father's son. Like Pollock's canvases, the mirror was a tableau of pain. A testament to frustration and suffering, with swirling figurative forms. And each dot and line and drip was a release, an expression of Specs's angst, his twisted fantasies, his Gatsbyesque Muffy Snitbread yearn-ings – the horror of his day-to-day-life. It was a self-contained climate of organic contortion. A world-unto-itself. But most importantly, perhaps – what elevated the piece from just a standard excellent Abstract Expressionist work – was the mirror. When I looked in the mirror I saw, through a screen of Specs Schwartz's anguish, myself. I was Specs. Specs was me. Specs, like his father, the great Jackson Pollock – I should say Gilbert – Gilbert Schwartz was an Action Painter, a brilliant, unconscious chronicler of our times, an immortal link in the chain of suffering: a goddamn genius.

I kicked through the rubble of the kitchen, the sad, fire-blackened mess of dead appliances and million-egged frying pans. Charred cans of lighter fluid – how many! – charred twisted glue-tubes – how many! – charred exploded cans of beer — how many! I searched and I searched, until I found the household tools.

And back in the toilet, very carefully, like an anthropologist, I unscrewed the medicine chest from the wall.

'I'll need evidence,' said Guy Gattling, over a Pregnant Duchess breakfast, after he'd mounted the Specs Schwartz medicine cabinet over his bed, next to *The Rat King*, and after he'd written me a check for ninety-thousand dollars. We had arrived at that figure from what he'd paid for his prized trepanning chair.

'Call Esther Foote Drummond,' I said.

'Thank you, Roger. Thank you,' said the President of the Make My Hair-Day Club. 'You can't know how gratified I am.'

'I know, Guy. You're a true collector.'

'What are you doing with Big Barton's car?' asked John Dough when I finally got home. He was sitting in the den with the door open.

'It's mine now.'

'You look dirty, Roger. You ought to take a shower.'

'Yes,' I said. 'I feel dirty.' Dirty on the inside.

'Natalie said to say *hasta luego*.'

'Thanks,' I said.

'Roger?'

'What, John?'

'You're a very curious man, aren't you?'

'Yes I am, John. Why do you ask?'

'What are these?' He indicated the paper bag of Gilbert Schwartz's effects.

'Those are the late Specs's things. Bobby the cop brought them for you.'

'And what's this?' he asked, pulling a meaty roach from the ashtray.

'It's a roach, John. Light it. We'll honor our ancestors.'

'What's it doing in the office?'

'You must have smoked it doing paperwork.'

'No, little buddy. You smoked it. It's a lousy rolling job. I roll 'em clean and straight. Yours are crooked.'

'Fire it up, John. Stop being paranoid. I'll pay you for your weed.'

'I don't give a shit about the pot,' John Dough said, stroking Specs Schwartz's Valentine's card. 'What I want to know is, did you enjoy my writing?'

'Yes, John,' I said, weary, weary. 'It's good – no, it's better than that: It's a brilliant little book. It scares me and hurts me and I don't know what to say. I'm a professional snoop. I'm not proud of it, but it's what I do. I'm sorry if I compromised our friendship.'

'How far did you get?'

'To the West Side highway, after Specs – after Gilbert gets saved by The Reverend Jurkbaitt.'

'Any questions?'

'Is this a quiz?'

'Don't you want to know how it ends?'

'I know how it ends.'

'How does it end?'

'Suicide, John. Everybody in the Schwartz orbit commits suicide. I even think Valerie did. I'm pretty sure Gilbert's father did.'

'His father?'

'Yes,' I said. 'Jackson Pollock.'

'Ah,' John Dough said, lighting the roach and toking, smoke drifting out his mouth, passing me the roach. 'I wondered about that . . . so it was Pollock, huh?'

'Yes, John.'

'What are you waiting for?'

'Waiting for?'

'Don't you want to see how good old Pizzaface does himself in?'

'John, you may not believe this, but from your novel and from what I've found out on my own, I've grown to care for Gilbert quite deeply. Respect him. I'm not sure I want to see him dead. And I don't like to hear him called . . .'

'Pizzaface ain't nothing but a word. By the way, Roger, the police were by. They want to ask you about the Dreck-enzorfers.'

'You heard?'

'It's on the news. The camera crews are arriving already.'

'Vultures.'

'Yeah, Roger. You're a journalist. You'd know about vultures. Go ahead and read, man.'

CASHAMPTON
(continued)

'AWESOME!' SAYS THE little green-haired baggy-clothed chick with hoops in her nose, her lip, her eyebrow. She dug my pajamas.

'Awesome!' says another, this one with a studded nose – a green stone sitting on the wing of her nostril like some fat green-bottle fly full of horseshit.

Wandering the West Side: I'd seen a crowd in front of warehouse. Joined the crush. Paid twenty bucks. Inside, huge space packed with kids. Banner reading PLATO'S RAVE. Strange kids. All the sweet young things done up like Halloween zombies. Torn clothes, leather jackets, checked shirts, baggy pants (room to hide their guns and genitals, room for their blues – as if their growth was stunted by a toxic world), wacky hats like condoms – multiple earrings, noserings, lipnaveleyebrowrings, multicolored hair, pimples – the whole parade of junior victims: puking from booze, snorting powders, puking, popping pills, smoking reefers, guzzling beers, puking – all wearing combat boots (yeah it's a war out there in here) – dancing wildly to blasting tapes – chainsaw noise, machines grinding, strong kidney-rattling bass lines, electric guitars slicing through the mess, drums pounding jackhammer beats, stitched together with dental-drill whines, water-torture drips, breaking-glass crashes, all variety of explosions – all these sad ragged kids of all races throwing themselves into one another, sharing blood – wasted industrial-society misfit kids: I fit right in.

One room a tattoo parlor. Men and women – boys and girls – showing off inked snakes, inked hearts, inked gardens, inked knives, inked blood, inked slave bracelets, inked rats and cats and dragons and eagles, an inked cup of coffee, inked anything and everything – bodies the field of battle – the tattoo artist inking a nuclear explosion onto a big white breast. Flesh as canvas.

'Awesome!'

'Look at his head! Awesome!'

'But what is it?'

'Hey, you, Mummy Man.'

'Cool outfit. Dig the stripes and slippers. You just out of the hospital?'

'What's that on your head? Locks like a toxic dump.'

I touch my head – the bandages had unraveled. 'It's a birthmark.' I tie them up again.

The chick in the green hair separates me from her sisters.

'Let's dance.'

'I don't dance.' I'd never danced.

'You got cash?'

I'm from Cashampton, ain't I?

She smiles a gaptoothed smile and leads me to a dread-locked boy in the corner. I buy two pills for forty bucks.

'What is it?'

'X. Ecstasy. Eat it, bro, we'll get down nice.'

I pop the pill. She pops hers. Within minutes I'm flying she's flying we're flying – dancing groping stroking – I loved her. I loved the world. I felt as charming as Walter Cronkite, as sexy as Billy Dee Williams, as smart as Albert Einstein. It was heaven.

'I want you, man. I'm Debbie Loo. They call me Devo. What's yours?'

'John Doe.'

'Let's go, John Doe. You got it all.' She climbs into my arms and sticks a hotsnake-tongue down my throat.

'Yeah,' I say, unafraid. I was John Doe, handsome free-spirited John Doe. Money in my pocket. I had it all. 'Let's go, Devo.'

Somehow a cab stopped. We kissed and kissed and kissed and then I paid ten dollars and we were in a stairway kissing. We walked up the stairway. Kissing. Smell of manpiss. A woman on the landing, pregnant, smoking crack. She smoked crack, hit from a Kool cigarette, sipped from a forty-ounce beer.

'Maybe,' I said to her, 'maybe that's not so good for your kid.'

'Yo, mind you own business. I doan tell you how to dress, you fockin pajama freak. You doan tell me nuttin. My baby gotta be ready for life. He gotta know the score before he play the game. Motherfucker gonna need immunities to The City in his system. Don't tell me how to raise my kid.'

Devo's place. Roommates out. Ferrets in. Little long rat-like fuckers crawling all over. But they were beautiful in my high head. Garbage everywhere. Beautiful. Stink strong. Beautiful. And Devo, skinny, tiny, malnutrition-bellied, green-haired, white skin like worm meat, pimples and dirt and stink everywhere – beautiful.

'Do it John. Take off your clothes, your bandages, your glasses.'

I took them off – no shame – and I stood before my Juliet, proud, pimpled and perfect.

'You're beautiful,' she said, stroking the horseshit-scabbed zits of my chest. 'You smell beautiful. Beautiful,' she said, kissing Pinatubo. 'Like a fallout victim. Like a plague victim. That's what we all are.'

And she put her lipringed lips on my zit-free pecker and started licking. 'Beautiful,' she said, gobbing and gobbling. 'Beautiful.'

And I picked her up and carried her around, licking tasting rubbing dirty skin – beautiful – tweaking ringed nipples, ringed bellybutton – beautiful – and then . . . on the ferret-haired floor . . . midst the helter-skelter-welter of pizza boxes and beer cans and old chicken bones . . . I buried my nose in green hair and. . . made love – we made love! Had sex. Oh mad delicious bliss – like the heavens opening up . . .

Beautiful.

So so perfect I had to leave. Had to leave it perfect. Couldn't take a chance the beauty would fade. So I left Devo there. A smiling snoring skull.

Walking the streets – my head deflated – the cold ragged dirty daylight streets – sadness returning to consume joy. I wanted a shower, a long zit-softening shower, a mirror to pop pimples against, a drink, a razor and a soft soft bed to sleep the sleep of the dead.

A dumpy joint called the Hotel Seventeen. My high fading fast now.

'Yo man, Bellevue ain't far,' said the blonde crew-cut clerk behind the bulletproof glass. He wore a few sad beautiful pimples.

'I want a room. How much?'

He looked me over. My bandages back on, I was dirty, and even through the glass I must have stunk.

'Fifty for the room. Fifty for a tip.'

'Fine,' I said. 'I need some supplies. Get them for me, there's another fifty.'

'What do you need?'

'A straight razor . . .' I forked bills. 'I need to shave – and two bottles of Southern Comfort, some soap, a towel.'

'Liquor store ain't open for a while. That razor – you got some coke, I'd be happy to help you dispose of it.'

'What's your name?'

'Miami.'

'Miami, I'm giving you an extra hundred dollars. If you want coke, buy your own. Me, I want privacy. I need to sleep, perchance to dream.'

'Shakespeare, huh? You want me to put that down on the register?' he asked, filling out the room form. 'The owner's Israeli. He won't know the diff.'

'It's John Doe,' I said.

'Oh, Jesus,' he said. 'Another goddamn John Doe.'

I stood there. Stood there naked. In front of the mirror and sink in the shoebox-sized crummy hotel room with red-and-silver striped wallpaper and a cracked ceiling – I stood naked. Clean and naked. Under the brutally honest bare bulb my birthmark-splotched chrome-dome looked like a flock of tar-eating pigeons had used my skull for target practice. The sink was small. An indelible yellow stain ran down its center, the result of a thousand lazy lushes hanging wang and leaking liquor. My glasses reflected the light. I was drooling a bit –

having sucked down a full fifth of Southern Comfort and part of another – and I was lovingly fingering my zitfarm, stroking the angry-red lumps and familiar hunks of gunk, the pesky pestilent protuberances that had persisted on my face and body long past the statute of limitations, way way past adolescence.

Small-town boy. Small-town man. The pimply butt of jokes. The town freak. I had left it all behind me. The faces. The laughing mocking perfect faces. The backbiting whispers and camivorous giggles. The open smirks that had scraped my soul raw, left it oozing, kept me boozing.

Arghh. Enough, Specs. Do it. End this putrid stream of memory.

I took a good long hit on the bottle, shuddered as the syrupy sweetness coated my esophagus, soothing and ripping as it dripped bellyward.

You could stand here forever, drinking and peeing, until that yellow sink stripe cracked, until your sad juices burned through the enamel and rusted the metal. Stand here, pee after lonely pee, ankles swelling, until your liver rotted, until the sink corroded and you were tinkling onto your toes.

I scratched Pinatubo. *Pinatubo!* That's where I'd make the incision. From there would I carve the sacred final smile, the gateway to the other side.

Oh, I was ready. Ready to find out what lay on the other side. Ready to take that plunge. Perhaps I'd hurtle into a void of pure nothingness, where memory and pain would cease and desist. Perhaps I'd be consigned to some loathsome place of toil and terror more demeaning and demanding than this lamentable life, this cruel cruel vale of zits, a place without coffee breaks or comfort, a totalitarian Alphaville where every pimple was a Pinatubo, where every passing specter sported Muffy Snitbread's haunting daunting taunting likeness, where every moment featured a fresh steaming load of horseshit

dumped upon my head . . . Or perhaps – sweet possibility –
I'd fly heavenward, floating free of care and sadness, my soul
as light and merry as a balloon, and I'd find angels – angels
with pimples! angels with hunchbacks! angels with mismatched limbs and eyes on their chins! angels with dirty
faces and beatific grins . . . I'd be at home!

I held the razor to my neck, touched the blade to Pinatubo
and pressed. The blade sank soft into the flesh, yet it wouldn't
truly enter. It was blocked. Hard as a pebble, coated with
gristle, impenetrable as a cast-iron hymen, Pinatubo was
blocking my death. So I cut around her, dug hard, felt the
welcome painsting of sliced nerve and violated flesh, the
warm tickletrickle of blood. I wanted the squirt – the spurt
the splat the mirrorsplash – before I made the slash, before I
chopped my throat and put the lights out forever. I wanted
zitijuice and blood and pain and an end to the anguish. Wanted
it worse than I had ever wanted anything. Anything . . .
except perhaps . . .

. . . Muffy Snitbread, Muffy Snitbread, Muffy Snitbread.

I'd loved her since early childhood when I'd been the
doctor and she'd been the patient and she'd raised my grubby
little hand to her rosy childslit out behind her parents' pre-
Speed-Lax home and said. 'Touch me here, Dr. Gilbert, it
hurts.' And I touched her, touched her gently on the red
petal, and she sighed . . . *But what is this image sneaking into my
memory? this ancient suppressed terror?* Big Barton – Big Barton –
came sneaking up on us, a silent nightmare elephant made
flesh, huge and mean and angry. 'What the hell are you doing,
Schwartz?' 'Playing doctor,' I said, five years old, no pimples,
no glasses, no shame. 'No,' he said. 'I'm the doctor and the
doctor knows what Muffy needs. Muffy needs a lollipop.' And
he unzipped his pants and took it out – huge and horrible and
red – not a lollipop! And he placed it in her mouth and then

. . . then he . . . Big Barton raped his daughter. Muffy screamed, I screamed. He raped her. Ah, Muffy, no wonder you're a bitch.

'Goodbye, Muffy. I have loved you – in my fashion.'

So I took Pinatubo – sweet Pinatubo, shy Pinatubo – I took her between thumb and forefinger and I squeezed – I rolled the walnut nipplezit around, loosening the meat – the whitish-blue head showed, like a baby being born, then crawled back inside the fleshcase – then showed again, then hid, then emerged . . . . . then: blast-off!!!! a hard solid rocket of zitmeat popped forth, bounced off the mirror, bounced back off my chest and clattered in the stained sink, smacking and clacking and bouncing like a roulette ball, and finally coming to rest in the drain.

I let go a giant sigh. I felt the blood running in a warm rivulet. And I plucked what had been Pinatubo from the sink. She was hard, round, shiny, an almost opaque bluish milk-white beauty with pink-rose veins . . . Pinatubo my love, my shining luminescent glowing love – after weeks of zitclot she had emerged hard as a pearl. . . . I laughed. Yes I laughed. She really did look like a pearl. . . . I dropped the razor and set to popping, ping ping bling blang they popped forth, free and easy, shooting from the skin, rocketing all over. I took a deep breath, took a swig of SoCo, splashed some on my face, felt the tingle, the sting, as the blood and booze oozed down my chin. I picked up Pinatubo . . . like a giant pearl! I set to popping. Oh how I laughed as they popped, as other round zitpearls sprang forth. Small ones, large ones, from my face, from my shoulders, from my chest and arms and thighs – pearls, pearls and even more pearls! I reached around and slit into the egg-sized one. The Pearl of Pearls! My face and body were a bloody crazed dartboard mess. I raked my sink full of pearls, ran water on them, drank Southern Comfort, laughed, got on my knees and played marbles with my floorpearls. And as I curled into a laughing bloody ball on the stained threadbare carpet I laughed some more, and as I drifted off into contented sleep I laughed and I laughed and I laughed, and I said. 'Those are the pearls that were his zits.'

Fifteen

'I DON'T KNOW, JOHN,' I said, putting the manuscript down and lighting a cigarette. 'Who's going to publish this? Maybe the French. I don't know. Magical realism is a hard sell. I mean, Christ, Gabby Marquez just did a book about soccer, and Vargas-Llosa's last one was a vegetarian cookbook: *101 Bean Dishes*, which, by the way, Disney has optioned for film.'

'You don't like it?' he asked, his handsome face sad.

'Well, maybe it could use a little rewriting, and I don't think the pearl business is all that credible. And paraphrasing Shakespeare all the time, that's a bit hackneyed. But on the plus side, there's a lot of energy.'

'Roger, you sit there and tell me pearls from pimples is unbelievable when you and I have both seen people with eyes popping out of their heads?'

'But John, now what? Specs comes back to Cashampton in the guise of John Dough? D-O-U-G-H? He becomes you? The Pearl Man?'

'You still don't get it, do you?'

'Get what?'

'I'm him. He's me.'

'I get that part, John. Specs is all of us. He's Everyman. The tragicomic universal loser in all of us. He's the Elephant Man, the Phantom of the Opera, the Hunchback of Notre Dame. He's . . . George McGovern.'

John Dough laughed, he laughed and laughed.

'Logically speaking – about the text, John – what made the pimples turn into pearls?'

'Who knows, Roger. I'm not a scientist. How does it happen in nature? A grain of sand gets in an oyster and irritates the muscle, which builds a protective case. Something like that. Here it's a miracle, a bloody fucking miracle.'

'Okay, I'll buy that, for fiction's sake; but to make that stick you must prop up the credibility of the other textual elements. For instance, John Dough wears a Yankees cap. Specs wears a Cleveland Indians cap. Why switch allegiances?'

'He's a new man. He's no longer a loser. Now he identifies with the Yankees, the winners.'

'Okay, but you have to say so.'

'I just did.'

'In the text, John. This isn't an Italo Calvino book. And why, if Specs lived here his whole life, why doesn't he talk about trees and flowers and animals? Why only horseshit and pimples and blonde-bitched fantasies?'

'Roger, are you a complete fucking lamebrain? The guy is living in an inner landscape. It's all about his inner life. His pain, his futility. The outside world is only there to irritate him.'

'So why the pearls?'

'It's his reward, for all the horseshit. The geek shall inherit the earth. I thought *you'd* understand. That's why Kurtis and I adopted you. Because you're *not* rich.'

'I don't think Kurtis likes me.'

'He likes you okay. He just doesn't trust you.'

'But you trust me, John?'

'I trust you and I like you. You're good company.'

'John, don't take this wrong. I'm honored and flattered that you trust me, and I truly, truly admire your writing – there's even a chance that I can get Horgan Yippenskip to publish it – but I'd much prefer a *real* book, an autobiography, about Turkey and all that. Hemingway said you have to write what you know.'

'I'm writing what I know!' he screamed.

'John, don't get frustrated; you might get a pimple.' I spoke jokingly, but John Dough did not laugh. 'Okay, okay.' I had to placate him. 'It's the strangest, sickest, most ambitious book I've read for a while . . . So how does Specs – Gilbert – how does Gilbert make the transition from hotel room to Pearl Man?'

'He sends the desk clerk out with a pearl, a small one—'

'Not Pinatubo?'

'Don't mock me, Roger. It doesn't matter which one.'

'So Miami sells it.'

'Right. And he buys clothes and food for Specs.'

'And what about Gilbert's face, the scars?'

'The scars heal, the pits in his face and body smooth out. He's as shocked as shit, but it happens – so he accepts it.'

'Fine, another miracle. What about the hair? His once *cue-ball-bald* head grows *your* gorgeous head of hair? Gilbert's brown eyes go green. More miracles?'

'Jesus, Roger, you can be really fucking dense,' he said, leaning back in his chair, touching his eyes.

'No, John, what I'm doing is what any good editor would.

I'm questioning the credibility of your fiction. I mean, I saw your auction at Sotheby's. You were magnificent.'

'Pearls before swine.'

'Alright, that's another good line. Use it. It fits. Keep stealing from the masters; I don't begrudge you that. Honor thy ancestors. But, John, fiction must be *somewhat* believable.'

The Pearl Man chuckled. He held his fingertips to me. They glittered with emerald-green contact lenses. 'Fiction, motherfucker.'

I looked at his eyes . . .

'You have brown eyes.'

'No shit, Sherlock. You want fiction?' He walked over to me. 'Look at my hair, Roger. Look close.'

'It's nice hair, John. As a man who's losing his hair, I'll admit, I'm jealous.'

'Look closely, little buddy. You want fictional horseshit, go with Marquez. Humans with pig's tails and six-hundred-year-old men tied up in the back yard. Look at me, look at my head!'

'I don't see . . .'

'It's a motherfucking wig!' he yelled. 'It's me. I'm me. John Dough is John Doe is Specs is Gilbert is me is me is me! I am the Pearl Man – coo-coo-ca-choo! I'm Specs fucking Schwartz!'

I'd never fainted before. And when I came to, the green-eyed Pearl Man – Specs, Gilbert, *whoever the hell you are!* – was standing over me with a drink. Wild Turkey. The Cleveland Indians cap was on his head.

'Why no Southern Comfort?' I asked – exhausted, depleted.

'Too much of a dead giveaway.'

'Who knows?'

'Kurtis knows. He knew that day in the cemetery.'

'And Kurtis – you know that Kurtis has a disease, a really bad disease and—'

'I know.'

'I don't know what to say . . . Gilbert.'

'Don't say anything. Use condoms. And keep your mouth shut about me. Especially with that Guy Gattling. I went to the Make My Hair-Day Club.' He tugged at his head. 'And call me John.'

'Why are you telling me all this?'

'Because I learned, Roger, that all the pain, all the suffering, it all comes from holding shit in. From not expressing yourself. A man doesn't learn to let go, he doesn't find a release – he drowns in horseshit.'

'So why not announce it? Take an add in *Stan's Paper*. Rub their faces in it. You're not only the Pearl Man, you're Jackson Pollock's son.'

'I don't give a shit about Pollock. That's ancient history.'

'What about his legacy?'

'Roger, I wore his legacy on my face for a lot of years.'

'No, the billion-dollar estate. You're due. Plus, what if I find the missing Pollock paintings? How about if we split the profits?'

'That's *your* ridiculous quest. Me, I want Muffy.'

'Still? After the way she treated Specs – I mean, you?'

'I love her, Roger. I really do. Whatever she is, she can't help it; whatever I am, I can't help it. Pizzaface, Pearl Man, whatever. I love Muffy Snitbread.' His green eyes gleamed. 'What do you feel like doing today, Roger?'

'I don't know, John. All that incest stuff? Jonas and Jenny, Barton and Muffy?'

'All true. The rich are different from you and me, Roger. From Kurtis.'

'How so?'

'They have shit for morals.'

'And Kurtis has morals?'

'Kurtis has ancestors.' He lit a joint. 'Let's go riding.'

I stopped by the Cashampton Police station. *A Current Affair*, *Hard Copy*, *Inside Edition*, the New York news channels – they all had camera crews there. I nodded at Bobby the cop. The station was packed with check-shirted animal-rights activists being questioned about the *Speed-Lax 1* explosion.

I answered Chief Chivas Pugh's questions. No, I told him, there was nothing to connect the Dreckenzorfers to the Phlebitises to Auralee Emeraldstein-Bittburg. Nothing except they all were rich, they all rode at the Upton Riding Club, and I'd seen them all, at one time or another, eating Pregnant Duchess crab-salad.

'Bobby!' Chief Pugh called. 'Get over to The Pregnant Duchess and close that shitbox down. Confiscate all their fake crab-salad. Take it to Cash Island. Mr. Snitbread has offered the use of his lab to analyze anything we need done.'

'Let's grill Snitbread,' said Bobby the cop. 'About the explosion.'

'Leave that poor man alone, Bobby. He's just lost a very expensive speedboat. Have some compassion.'

'Was there anyone in the boat?' I asked.

'Body parts. The coroner is trying to put them together right now.'

'Chief Pugh,' said Bobby. 'Aren't you gonna ask Mr. Lymon why he's driving Snitbread's Rolls?'

'Bobby, Big Barton is a huge supporter of the Retired Bonackers Association. I think that buys him some slack, *and* some privacy.'

'But I'd be happy to explain,' I said. 'I won it from him in a game of craps.'

'You see, Bobby? Now get over to The Pregnant Duchess and take that pollack into custody.'

It was Steve Dunleavy from *A Current Affair*, sticking a microphone in my face.

'Excuse me, sir,' he said. 'Is it a conspiracy? Are the Dreckenzorfer girls connected to the explosion?'

I looked into the camera and shrugged.

'Is it a terrorist plot?'

'No,' I said. 'It's a simple case of food poisoning.'

I stopped by the Cashampton Savings and Loan. Big Barton's five-million-dollar bonus had been transferred into my account. I added Guy Gattling's ninety grand. I was rich now, yes, but like John Dough, like Specs, money was not the high I'd expected. It felt empty. I, too, needed love.

The Pearl Man and I were riding on the beach. I rode King (having received permission from Fergus Frankfurter, who already had a new horse). It was the old gelding's last few days at the Upton Club (he was to be shipped, Hank Upton had said, 'to the clinic in Connecticut' – read that France). Specs – I mean John Dough – John rode Caesar, whom he had bought from the Phlebitis estate.

The day was hot. Families lay browning on towels. Children laughed and played in the placid ocean. Business as usual in Cashampton By The Sea.

'John, the things you wrote about? Were they *all* true?'

'All.'

'The Whirlie?'

'Yes, Roger, I was dipped and flushed numerous times.'

'And Kurtis – the beating he took? Do you think that influenced him?'

'No doubt. Kurtis had it all, and this town dumped a serious load of horseshit on his head.'

'Ask not what your town can do for you, ask what you can do for your town?'

'That's catchy, Roger. Did you make that up?'

'So Kurtis is the victim?'

'The black man in this country is often the victim.'

'Yes, John, I saw *Malcolm X* too. Victim of slavery, victim of bigotry, victim of the drug-dealing government, victim of the gun lobby, victim of the single-parent home.'

'Single-parent home?'

'You never mentioned his father, so I assumed—'

'You journalists like to assume a lot, don't you?'

'I'm trying to figure his psychological motivation.'

'Okay, he's a bastard – like me. And Kurtis and Billy had different fathers. Does that help?'

'Nothing helps.'

Big Barton Snitbread came galloping through the sand on Zorro.

'Ahoy, Pearl Man and Roger.'

'Tally-ho, BB,' I said, watching John with new eyes to see how he treated the man who had jailed his cousin, who had raped the love of his life. Nothing.

'Roger, can I have a word with you?'

Barton and I rode off a little ways, while John got off Caesar and held the horse's reins. Caesar chewed dune grass.

'Here,' said Big Barton, handing me the Rolex of my dreams – oyster-shell variety – and the papers for the Rolls. 'Had to get Sappy Miller to open his jewelry store special for me this morning; and your money will clear in a few days. Thanks, Roger, for everything. Chief Pugh's got The Pregnant Duchess's owner under arrest. Tonight, when I get Axl to the island, Dr. Guberstein's gonna get some goat blood into the crab-salad samples. We might just come out of this one clean.'

'Clean might not be the right word, but that's excellent, Barton.' And then, looking with disgust at 'the man who makes America go,' I couldn't help but ask:

'How's little Muffy?'

'You heard?'

'Heard what?'

'Muffy's in the hospital.'

'No hiccuping, I hope.'

'No, thank God,' he said. 'Her maid found her this morning, sitting on the beach, still in her party clothes – or at least her top was on. It looked like she'd seen a ghost while taking a pee. Her eyes were open and she was stiff as a board, like shell-shock.'

'What hospital? I'm sure John would like to visit.'

'Fairhaven,' he said. 'Jonas committed her to the mental hospital at Fairhaven.'

The barn was a carnival of confusion, horses wandering wild. Big Barton, on damage-control patrol already, had placed a large display in the center of the dirt floor – a sign on a tripod that read 'Help yourself/You can never be too sure' and a basket of Sensuous brand condoms. Fergus Frankfurter was screaming at Lana the groom because his new horse Lao-Tze's stall was unmucked. Huge boulders of fly-coated dung lay stinking in the heat.

'If Lousy gets a hoof infection, Lana, I'll sue the goddamn K-Mart panties off your fat Bonacker ass.'

'Here,' said Lana, bawling, 'Take your stupid ugly bracelet back!' She flung a diamond-encrusted gold bangle at the rich man. He ducked and flew into Lao-Tze's stall. 'At least Sock

Phlebitis could make it twice in a night!' Fergus ran into the shit-heaped stall and searched the sawdust.

'What's going on?' asked Hank Upton, a More cigarette dangling from his lips, pushing a half-full wheelbarrow.

'Lovers' quarrel,' I said.

'Here, Hank,' said John Dough, picking up the pitchfork from the fly-covered hillock in the wheelbarrow. 'Let me help.'

John Dough entered Lao-Tze's stall and with extraordinarily agile wrists forked sawdust-dredged dung and urine-heavy sawdust and tossed it into the wheelbarrow from a distance of five feet. He hooked the bracelet from a clump of horseshit and offered it to Fergus Frankfurter. Fergus took the jewelry, holding it at arm's length. A pair of flies landed on the bauble and started nibbling.

'Fergie,' I said. 'I'd like to buy King from you.'

'Two thousand dollars. The French only offered . . . that's my price.'

'Deal,' I said, pulling my roll of Barton-bills.

'You do that awful well, Mr. Dough,' Hank Upton said, as John Dough ripped a fresh bag of sawdust and sprinkled it in the stall. 'Ever worked in a stable before?'

'Sure,' said John Dough, handing the pitchfork back to Hank, as Fergus Frankfurter made off with my money. 'Back in Turkey.'

Lana was weeping. I put my arm around her. 'Where's Kurtis?' I asked.

'Family emergency,' said Hank. 'Okay, Lana, let's get back to work.'

'Sure, Hank,' said the groom. 'But I don't feel so hot.'

'What's wrong?' I asked, but it was a stupid question.

Lana was hiccupping.

*   *   *

This time the ambulance driver said nothing.

And as John Dough's Jaguar trailed me in my Rolls out the rutted drive, we passed Fergus Frankfurter's Testarossa. Fergus was slumped over the wheel, his arms extended, the bracelet in one hand, his face dark. There were flies on the bracelet, flies dive-bombing his nose, flies investigating his eye-socket and ears. But Fergus Frankfurter couldn't have given a shit.

The Cash house was silent from the outside. We knocked and entered. Kurtis was bustling about. Through a half-opened door I could see his mother lying in bed, her face a mask of pain.

'John, Roger,' said a stressed Kurtis. 'Wash your hands and then carry that bucket on the stove into Billy's room here.'

We scrubbed at the kitchen sink and then John Dough carried the huge pot of boiling water into Billy's room.

Billy Cash lay on his bed, spread-eagled on his distended stomach. The sewing dummies were bare. The walls were covered with fashion photos.

'What's going on?' I asked Kurtis.

Kurtis looked at John.

John nodded. 'He knows, Kurtis, about you, about me.'

'Billy's having a baby, Roger.'

'A baby?' I asked, thinking, how could I – or how could John – write about this? I'd have to lie. Have to make Billy a girl. Billie, I'd call her.

Billy screamed. His face was twisted in agony.

'She's coming!' he cried, and Kurtis unsheeted his brother's smooth brown ass. Billy screamed again. His eyes were mad with pain.

'Push, goddammit,' said Kurtis. 'Push.'

'Push!' said Specs – I mean John Dough – wiping Billy's brow. 'Push!'

My God, I thought, I've only seen this on Public Television – childbirth that is – but this, this . . .

'Here she comes!' cried Billy with a scream – and from his . . . from his backside emerged a . . . it was awful and terrible . . . a huge clot of blood and gristle. Not a baby, no, no – words fail me.

'What is it?' asked Billy.

'It's a girl, champ,' said Kurtis, kissing his brother's sweaty cheek.

After Billy was cleaned up, the sheets changed, and after Kurtis had given his little brother some Wild Turkey and some Snitinex (from the Louis Vuitton bag of Snitbread samples John had given him) and he was sleeping like – like a baby, and after Billy's 'daughter' was buried in the back yard, John Dough and Kurtis and I smoked a joint in the living room.

'What was it?' I asked.

'It's called a blood baby,' said Kurtis. 'They were more common in slavery days. African boys who're gay, they so identify with the female they have these sympathetic pregnancies. They absorb the 'father's' sperm up into their intestines and it clots up with blood and waste. He'll be okay. I wish I could say the same about Clarisse.'

'How's she feeling?' asked John.

'She's sleeping now.'

'What's wrong?' I asked.

'Terminal inoperable total motherfucking cancer.'

'I'm sorry.'

'Yeah.' He rubbed his eyes. 'C'mon, Roger, I want to show you something.'

'Thanks, Kurtis, I've seen plenty already.'

'You ain't seen nothing yet.'

Two men in a canoe. Out in nature, paddling about some glorious wetlands under the blazing Cashampton sun. John Dough had stayed behind to care for Billy and Clarisse.

We drifted in the current. It was quiet and peaceful out there, the occasional bird flying above.

'Who does AIDS *aid?*' asked Kurtis.

'I'm down with you on this,' I said, half-turning and holding my paddle dripping above the water. 'AIDS is a plot, man. A plot or a serious mistake. It helps the ruling class. But what you've got is different.'

'How so? Okay, it's faster, more dramatic, you can get it from French-kissing. A couple of factory-installed extras.'

'How'd you find out you had it?'

'In prison. See, I knew I'd been set up for that rape rap – but why? I thought maybe because I dug white chicks.'

'I thought you hated them.'

'Hate, love – my feelings change moment to moment . . . I had zero idea what I was doing there – not until this little white boy, my bitch—'

'But, Kurtis, you're a ladies' man.'

'People get lonely, Roger. They need warmth. Ricky wasn't gay either; he was married on the outside. He was doing a nickel-plus for a safecracking job. I figured he was safe from AIDS, and shit, he was a cracker – he was my little safe cracker. And, then, two weeks into our thing, he—'

'Experienced the joy of an exploding head.'

'Exactly. He's rolling a joint, he starts to cough – I get pissed that he's spilling the herb – then he's doing the rainbow-face hiccup-dance . . . you know the drill.'

'No investigation?'

'They said it was a brain hemorrhage – sent him home in a box. Another year passes, I cop me a new bitch, won him in a card-game – same thing. I think: maybe I'm fucking them too hard; so when I get me another one, I love him up gentle – *déjà vu* all over again. So I hooked up with some lawyers, I appeal the conviction, win, and when I got out I decided to share the wealth.'

'To spread the blame. The Disease.'

'You ain't lying. It sure as shit is a disease.'

'That's what Barton calls it: *The Disease*.'

'I like it. At least it's less confusing than AIDS.'

He paddled, then stopped, lit a smoke, handed me his matches. I lit mine. He dug his paddle into the cattails.

'Check it out, Roger.'

It was a plastic bag full of syringes and test-tubes and stained bandages, soaked in water, near an open metal drum half-buried in the reedy marsh water.

'Toxic crap from the Island Of The Dead. These barrels are all over. Barton's property comes to the edge of the marsh. He's burying this shit on Indian land. The poison's gotten into the freshwater well on the reservation. We're gonna take that shitbucket for every dirty penny he's got. The papers are being drawn up now. EPA's coming later this week. Peter Matthiessen – the writer-guy – he's helping.'

'Does this have anything to do with your mother's illness?'

'Fuck do you think? Cashampton's nothing but a cancer ward with tennis courts. Fucking white man.' Kurtis spat overboard. 'Nothing personal, Roger. I've got white in me too. I like to think it's that cold-ass European blood that makes me capable of doing what I'm doing. . . . I'm your basic genetic Dagwood sandwich. The jokester God's having a serious motherfucking laugh with my ass.'

'Kurtis, you're beautiful.'

'Think so?' he asked with a sad laugh. 'The Dreck-enzorfers thought so. They were like the punchline to a shaggy-dog story. To them I was the slave. The inferior. But when I was fucking them I was Nietzsche's horse-dick Superman. And afterward, we're lying there, seven living-dead bitches and one seriously whacked-out brother, and I start to cry . . . I ask their forgiveness – but check it out, they thought I had a racial inferiority complex and wanted to whip me.'

'You let them?'

'I may be fucked up, Roger, but I ain't no masochist.'

We lit fresh smokes and drifted out into the water. The sun was hot.

'When I looked in their eyes and I knew I was killing them, then I loved them. God, how I loved them.'

We smoked, the boat drifting lazily.

'Have you heard of the Phoenix Rising, Roger? The cleansing that's coming? All the great religions talk about it. It has to happen. *Has* to. And then life – the whole beautiful crazy-ass shooting-match – it can all start over. Clean slate. . . . It's physics.'

'It's fucking Hitler and Malthus is what it is.'

'Whatever. This time the rich motherfuckers go first. I'm gonna chew the rotten parts off this diseased Earth and teach the next ones to treat her right.'

'You've got a Messiah complex.'

'Better than an inferiority complex.'

'But black people will die too.'

'Lot of black assholes out there too. Anyhow, this is an equal-opportunity cleansing – take it or leave it.'

'I don't see much of a choice.'

'Hey, it's a personal decision: Either wear a condom or don't. Just depends how soon you want to join your ancestors. But if I were you, bro, I'd keep my tongue out of other people's mouths.'

'Well, here we are,' Kurtis said, jumping into the water and running the canoe onto the sand.

'What about Axl?' I asked, as we pulled the boat through the cattails.

'The earth is a wheel. Life is the axle.'

'No, Axl the goat.'

'You mean the rock star? Axl Rose?'

'No, the goat with the flu. You shot him full of what? Antibiotics or—'

'Blood, man. My blood.'

'But why?'

'I remembered him from the old study. I wanted to see what would happen when a carrier gets a second dose.'

'Barton's got the goat on Cash Island.'

'No, Roger, I saw a dream,' he said, lighting a cigarette. 'The old goat-brother is dead. Dead, on the Island Of The Dead. Full-circle.'

'Kurtis, don't take this wrong, but I think you need help. You've got a highly infectious disease. It's terminal.'

'Hey, man, we're born terminal – at least our bodies are. I'm looking forward to dying. It's just a passing to the other side.'

'We're going around in circles here.'

'Now you're getting it. Genesis, baby. Genesis and The Apocalypse. Yin and Yang. The end is contained in the beginning. The shithouse rat eats its own tail.'

Sixteen

FAIRHAVEN IS A huge white-brick monstrosity situated in the unfashionable sector of the East End – unpleasing to the eye, uninviting and austere – not a place to get well.

'Well,' I said to John Dough, as we trod the fluorescent corridors, in search of Muffy Snitbread-Gritz, 'what's it feel like to be back?'

'There ain't no place like home,' he said, as insane cackling and sad groans and mad screams emanated from rooms.

'Click your heels three times and you'll be in Cashampton – nooky and cookies and cash, oh boy!'

Muffy lay in the adjustable bed, pale, stiff, pretty, with unblinking blue eyes. Her mother, Sarah Snitbread, sat with Mariah Frankfurter. They were playing a board game.

'How is she?' asked John Dough.

'She's been traumatized,' said Mariah.

'Will she be okay?'

'Only time will tell,' said Mariah, fingering a string of

pearls. 'You know, Mr. Pearlman – I mean Mr. Dough – John – these are some of the pearls . . .'

'From Turkey,' I said. 'How lovely, Mariah. How absolutely splendid.'

'Yes,' said the daughter of Elliot and Dorcas Quinchard, 'aren't they terrific?'

'Mariah,' I said, offering her a Sensuous brand condom. 'Please take one.'

'Thank you, but I'm on the pill.'

'Uhh, Mariah . . . Fergus sold me King.'

'That's nice. He was a special gelding.'

'Uhh, Mariah. Fergus didn't look . . . uhh, very well at the stable.'

'He's pushing himself too hard. His new game-show's in pre-production.'

'Pull up a chair, boys,' said Sarah Snitbread. 'We're playing "The American Dream." '

'Can you keep a secret, Mr. Lymon?' Mariah asked.

'My lips are sealed with Krazy Glu.'

'The new game-show is a TV version of "The American Dream".'

'Very exciting,' I said, thinking: Fergus had already achieved his manifest destiny – in the front seat of his Testarossa. 'Where's Jonas?' I asked Sarah.

'He had a riding lesson with Maria.'

'And where's Jenny and Clarkie?'

'Clark is at his home playing with the goat. He's got a hangover,' said the grandmother. 'Jenny's around the hospital somewhere. She volunteered here last summer and wanted to see if any of her favorite patients are still in treatment.'

'Ah,' I said, hoping she'd stocked up on freebies from the Sensuous brand condom-display in the lobby. 'You know, Sarah, Clark might well benefit from Barton's Instant AA.'

'Mr. Lymon, why don't you mind your own business and pull up a chair. Mariah's a Guatemalan midget with cooking skills but no English at Georgetown Law School and I'm a Lithuanian prostitute with AIDS just off the boat working in a *Dunkin Donuts*. We're way ahead of you.'

I sat down. John Dough lowered himself into the chair by Muffy's bed, took her small white hand in his large stall-mucking mitt.

I picked a card.

'Who are you, Mr. Lymon?' asked Mariah with a cough.

'It says,' I said, 'that I'm a suicidal Italian novelist with hemorrhoids.'

'Spin the wheel,' said Mariah Frankfurter.

I spun the wheel and it pointed to a purple slice of pie.

'Pick a card,' said Sarah, popping a pill with a Styrofoam cup of water. 'Pick from the purple pile.'

I picked a card.

'What's your first taste of America?' asked Mariah.

'It says, "Drive a taxi in Manhattan, find a wallet with a Lotto ticket, win two million dollars, summer in Cashampton".'

'Bravo, Mr. Lymon!' said Sarah Snitbread, her eyes drooping.

'Who invented this game?' I asked.

'Jasper Jurkbaitt came up with the idea,' said Mariah. 'Jasper and that Italian writer who rented out here back in the early Eighties.'

'Which Italian writer? Umberto Eco? Primo Levi? Mario Puzo?'

'No, it was the depressed one Big Bart gave all the SnitPrep H to,' said Sarah. 'He had a name like a car. Corolla? Camaro? El Camino? Something like that.'

The phone rang. Mariah answered, coughing.

'Calvino?' I asked. 'Italo Calvino?'

'That's the one!' Sarah shouted. 'You know his work?'

A stricken look came over Mariah's face and she dropped the phone, began to hiccup.

'Ah, Calvino,' I said, without enthusiasm.

Sarah Snitbread was asleep and Mariah dead, her body removed from the room (the nurse's aide had found the missing eye under the radiator) and the blood cleaned up, when I went to look for Jenny. John Dough stayed by Muffy's bedside. He stared at her, riveted to her seemingly glued-open eyes.

'John,' I said. 'I'll be back.'

'Uh-huh,' he grunted.

I wondered about Jenny. Who was she fucking? Who wasn't she fucking? She hadn't fucked Kurtis. I'd asked him and he'd answered, 'I wouldn't fuck her with your dick.' She hadn't fucked John Dough, though she had snuggled up to him suggestively at the Upton Riding Club often enough. She hadn't fucked me. She must have still been fucking Jonas.

I found Jenny an hour later — after a depressing search — straddling a psychotic in an unlocked private room on Ward 8. She was angry at the interruption, but the poor slavering raw-dicked loon seemed extremely gratified, jumping out of the tangled sheets and hiding under the bed, whimpering.

'Jesus, Mr. Lymon,' she said, as she wiped spittle off her neck and breasts and dressed her nubile body. 'You really know how to ruin a girl's fun.'

'Oh, I wouldn't say that,' I said, leading her out the room and down the hall, pulling her into a broom closet and unsheathing a Sensuous brand condom. 'You and I need to get something straight between us.'

'Why,' she said, bending over and dropping her jeans,

'that's exactly the same cornball line Grandpa Snitbread used on me only last week.'

'Big Barton?'

'Roger,' she said, guiding me with a practiced hand, 'he's not so big.'

Seventeen

'WOMEN ARE ESPECIALLY VULNERABLE,' said the drop-dead-gorgeous woman doctor wearing the tight white mini-skirt and pink lipstick on the *Today Show*, two-and-a-half weeks later, the day before the much-ballyhooed Pollock premiere. She was speaking via-satellite from Zurich, Switzerland. The graphic identified her as 'Sheila McKenzie-McDougal, MD, former Glasgow prostitute, of the Scottish Prostitutes Education Project.' 'And we must reduce that vulnerability. The Disease—'

The telephone rang.

'Roger,' said Guy Gattling. 'Are you coming to my party tonight?'

'Why not?' I sighed. I was tired, empty — between Jackson Pollock's ghost and The Disease, I was squeezed out.

'Roger, I love my new' — he downshifted to a whisper — 'my new Pollock. Esther Drummond corroborated your story before she died.'

Esther had been felled by a heart-attack only a week previously. Along with de Kooning and Lindsay and John Dough, I'd been one of her only mourners. Green River Cemetery had been dark and gloomy with fog and rain, and in Esther's honor I'd read one of the less depressing passages from Camus's *The Plague*.

'Congratulations, Guy.'

'Isn't it terrific? By the way, I'm also having a small soiree after the Pollock premiere tomorrow, to introduce *The Rat King* to a few select members of the Art World and the press. I'd like you to be there.'

'I'll try.'

The weeks had passed like smoke from a chimney. I was up to two packs of Marlboros a day, which John – I still thought of him as John Dough and not as Specs Schwartz – insisted on buying for me at Dawn Cash's stand. John now spent most of his time at Fairhaven where Muffy was being fed intravenously – no improvement, and Jonas, still taking his daily lessons with Maria, curiously seemed to care not a whit about his wife's illness or the Pearl Man's interest in her. Kurtis was working only part-time at the club, staying close to home, caring for his dying mother, wearing black in mourning for his brother Billy who had hung himself in post-partum depression.

My good dark suit was getting quite a workout from all the funerals.

The 'joy' of The Disease was no longer confined exclusively to Cashampton and its environs, but was spreading like sexual wildfire: In New York, Aspen, Main Line Philly, Newport, Capitol Hill, The Palms (Beach and Springs), in Beverly Hills, Boca Raton, Lake Forrest – everywhere the rich met the rich and exchanged rich bodily fluids, wherever rich men had sex with hookers or servants or Cub Scouts or Girl Scouts – or even their wives and kids – wherever rich women took male lovers or gigolos or other women – or even their husbands – heads were exploding; and in Europe – the French Riviera, London, Paris, Monaco, Sardinia, Rome – The Disease was grabbing headlines, even above the escalating conflicts in Bosnia and Somalia. The rumor holding greatest sway was that it was an advanced form of sexually communicable Legionnaire's Disease – the FBI having tested the goat's-blood pollack salad and found it culpable – an insidious plot against the white power-elite propagated by a Satanic Black-Power Cult – and the owner of The Pregnant Duchess (rumored to be one thirty-second African-American) was in the Riverhead county jail, isolated in protective custody (after being pounded black and blue by other inmates (black and white)), awaiting trial, with bail set at eight-million dollars, taking the fall and bleating innocence. Big Barton Snitbread had found his scapegoat, courtesy of Roger Lymon; and, along with other condom manufacturers worldwide, Snitbread Pharmaceutical was promoting a massive distribution and education program. Sales were sky-high and the stock was enjoying a true renaissance, winging its way through the roof. Big Barton was thrilled (and I suppose, on the level of stockholder, I wasn't displeased myself, though, humanist that I am, I would have much preferred a cure), and he was pumping much of his profits back into the company, testing a new line of impotence aids – brand name Boner Fide. He also informed me that Axl was still undergoing tests (I'd seen numerous flyers posted around town with an FBI sketch-artist's likeness of Axl and the question, 'Have you seen this goat?'), and that the lawsuit filed by the Montauk Indians with the help of Peter Matthiessen had been effectively squelched. Barton had had the toxic drums removed from the Reservation, had greased the EPA, and Chief Of Police Chivas Pugh was quoted in *Stan's Paper* as saying that the whole affair was 'a publicity stunt by a bunch of money-grubbing Indians.'

Reporters continued to hover around town (many filing Jackson Pollock-related stories) – though their numbers had dropped off significantly (and a few had dropped off, themselves) since Disease stories were no longer confined to The East End – questioning, among others, the thinned-down ranks of members and employees at the Upton Riding Club, hoping to catch an exploding head for the eleven-o'clock news. The *Inside Edition* crew almost captured one on the fifth green at the Maidstone Club golf course, but they just missed the ocular blast-off, getting set up only in time to record the WASP bigwig's eye rolling into the flagged cup. Nonetheless, the segment, entitled 'Hole In One', was a ratings smash. Tabloid headline writers around the world were having a field day, exercising their wit at the expense of the wealthy dead. 'AN EYE FOR AN EYE YI YI'; 'WILD BILL HICCUP'; 'HE (SHE) BLEW HIS (HER) MIND OUT IN A CAR'; 'EARIE DEATH'; 'EYELESS IN THE PLAZA' – these were just a few of the banners. But despite all the giddy fun and the jacked-up circulation, the media was still no closer to the real story than before.

Sonja Dreckenzorfer had accompanied the seven coffins back to the Fatherland. Mariah and Fergus Frankfurter had been buried side-by-side in the now-crowded Green River Cemetery, along with Cassandra and Socrates Phlebitis, Marmalind and Portius Pleistocene, and other Cashamptonites, rich and poor. Baby Luegodago – or parts thereof – had been shipped to Uruguay for burial. Lenny Fripp had been blamed for the explosion and for the abduction of both Baby and Auralee Emeraldstein-Bittburg (waterlogged pink Versaced scraps were re-interred at Green River), and Lenny's purported Shining Path connections were being investigated by Interpol, the FBI, the CIA, the NYPD (which, by the way, accorded him the standard high-pomp Commander's funeral) and the intelligence-gathering division of the Daughters Of The American Revolution (who also founded a condom-education group called MATD – Mothers Against The Disease), and his alleged necrophiliacal urges prompted a five-part *New York Times* study by Dr. Ruth Westheimer. The *Times* would not acknowledge The Disease as the cause of any death for another two weeks, until (as the *New York Post*'s Hilton Kramer headlined it) the 'UN-TIMES-LY PASSING' of one of their own book reviewers, a David B. Feinberg, choosing instead to utilize their standard (read AIDS) cause-of-death label: 'died after a brief illness.' Count Hugo Luegodago – real name Pablo Rodriguez, place of birth Guadalajara, Mexico, had died at Baby's graveside, but not before introducing the 'joy' to South America; and The Disease was now building up a head of steam in Rio and other jet-set hot-spots. What else? Not a whole helluva lot. . . . On the home front, except for an increased awareness of the need for condom-use, the talk of the town was the upcoming Cashampton Classic horse show, the recent tragic suicide of Nudjerzy Diztantkozinski and the long-awaited, hugely-hyped Pollock-film premiere. Really, in those first few weeks of the Phoenix Rising, it was business as usual in Cashampton.

The daily phone calls from Hiroshi Koyabashi were particularly irritating. The presses were ready, he'd say. DeNiro was waiting for a script, was considering electrolysis to achieve Pollock's bald head. Streisand wanted to play Lee. It was up to me, Hiroshi yelled. He didn't mean to yell, he'd say, but the pressure coming from Tokyo was immense. *His* ass was on the line.

Meanwhile, Cashampton was seething with what *Entertainment Tonight* (who were doing their show live all that week from Billy Truck's) called 'Pollockmania.' Biographies of

Pollock and posters of his work were being hawked up and down Main Street, in every gourmet store and chi-chi clothing boutique. Gas stations included a free paint-spattered Jackson Pollock beer mug with every fill-up. Bertha Seward – out of the hospital and hopping about quite efficiently on her new prosthesis (her broken leg having been amputated in the intervening weeks) – had opened her Bonacker restaurant and haberdashery, and her biggest-selling item, The Jackson Pollock Look – paint-streaked used blue jeans and T-shirt with an empty pint of Jack Daniel's that fitted into the back pocket – was going for $129.99, matching jeans jacket, with a replica of Pollock's driver's license and a pack of Camels an extra hundred dollars. She was also running tours Pollock's grave, his favorite bars and clamming spots, and his farmhouse and studio – not the mythical secret studio – and the buses were booked solid. And in addition to all that, the enterprising Bertha was hawking grapefruits painted as softballs – $19.95 a pop.

The telephone rang again.

'Roger?'

'Hello, Bartie. How's the big boy?'

'Not so terrific. Is the Pearl Man there?'

'No, he didn't come home last night. Did you try Muffy's room at Fairhaven?'

'Muffy took a powder.'

'Speed-Lax?'

'She's gone.'

'Hiccups?'

'No, Roger, she's missing. The duty-nurse said the Pearl Man wheeled her out early this morning.'

'They probably took a trip.'

'I've checked with the servants at her apartment in The City, the place in Santa Fe, the Palm Beach house – nothing.'

'Take a Snitinex and relax, Barton. I'm sure they'll surface. By the way, I was watching this Scottish Prostitute doctor on the tube. She says she's developed a female-foam that combats AIDS and possibly even The Disease.'

'I'm way ahead of you, Roger. I've got her flying in today to work with Guberstein. We're gonna test the foam on some goats.'

'Axl's got a girlfriend?'

'Sorry, Roger. Axl's in goat heaven.'

'When?'

'The first day back on Cash Island.'

'Hiccups?'

'Yes, bless his soul. I'd known him since he was a kid.'

'Why didn't you tell me?'

'I didn't want to worry you.'

'Worry me, you sonofabitch?' The doorbell rang. 'Look here, Bartie, you sell a few million rubbers you're back on top of the world. I don't like your attitude.' I heard sobbing in the background. 'Who's that crying?'

'Jenny.'

'What, did Grandpa fuck her too hard?'

'Roger, you're like family, but even family shouldn't meddle. She'll be fine. She's just upset that Fred's dead.'

'Fred?' I asked. 'Who's Fred? One of her little loverboys?'

'You know – Fred. You met him. Trigger's grandson.'

'That's truly fucking tragic: the end of a dynasty. Hiccups?'

'Old age. The funeral's just for family, but you're almost like a son to me, so come. Tomorrow at two-thirty.'

'Thanks for thinking of me, but I'm a bit burnt-out on funerals.'

The door-bell rang again. I answered it. It was the postman. The postman always rings twice.

'Good morning,' I said. 'Where's the other postman, the old fellow with the thick glasses?'

'He died. From The Disease. I just got transferred from Patchogue. Look, I found this letter stuck at the bottom of old Jerry's bag. Is this the place?'

It was addressed to Gilbert Schwartz, Mulrooney Estate . . .

'This is the Mulrooney Estate.'

'Right. So sign for it, please.'

'Right,' I said, and signed *Gilbert Schwartz*.

'That'll be twenty-two cents, postage due. Those are 1989 prices; that's when the letter was sent.'

The postage mark read Fairhaven, New York, May of 1989; the childishly-scrawled return address was the hospital; the sender was Valerie Schwartz. So, did I prop the letter by the doorway for John Dough? Did I leave it on the hall table for my good friend and host to read later, at his leisure? Not a fucking chance. I took the letter to the kitchen, turned on the cappuccino-machine steamer and, utilizing a trick we all remember from *I Love Lucy* or some other mindless sit-com, I unglued the dirty envelope. I rolled a joint, lit it, and with great difficulty, read the sad, crabbed dyslexic script.

Dearest Gilbert,
the docotr says it will halp me to get bettor if I stop holding things in. I know that I am damached goods. The Nazis maid sore of that. And my braine is damached from the axident.

You always wished to know who your reel fahter is. The year you were conceeved was 1952, and befor that I hat meny boyfreinds but yer fahter was extra special. Jackson Pollack. Jackson was a good and crazy man, but his marrache was not happy. He was a very poor man but a very great painter.

I was a knockout, Gilbert. A real live knockut. Jackson loved me and he loved you. He did. He wood hold you and kiss you and it maid him vary happy to have a son. But when I was pregnunt with you and he saw other wimmen I ran away. I got arrested in New York when I ast a man for traine fair home. He was a polise and called me a whor and my parents came and got me from the jale and put me in the hosptal eggen. This hosiptal whar you were borne and whar I am now eggen. Bot I still saw Jackson after your birth and he loved you. He still had other girls and he still had a tuf weife and he was two weak to acknoladge he was your fahter to the world. But never forget that Leo Schwartz is your fahter two. He loved you and loved me and he was a steddy man. I loved him two or else I would not have maried him. Your Grampa did not like Pollack and when Jackson kidnaped you and kept you hidden in the cabin and got you drunk and put that terrable thing on your head, Jakcosn called it your birthrite, that tattwo, Grampa Josiah found you both in a bar and beat the hell out of Pollack. But Jackson and I still saw each other, right up until the axidant that killed him.

So all I have of him is you. I love you and beg your forgiveness for the sadnest of are lives. I have been nohting but a hartache mohter, but I love you. I love you my Gilbert. My sweet kind son.

Your mohter.
Valerie Dzirchinski Foote Schwartz.

Ah, Roger Lymon, said I to myself, this is the saddest aspect of the story yet. This poor melancholic delayed letter.

This honest broken woman – 'damached goods' – oh, what a hurtful and heartbreaking world.

I wiped my tears. So that was what the birthmark was. A Pollock. Oh strange ironic life. There was nothing to do except accept, to love Specs and his tragic mother even more than I already did. And it was time to take stock, to look at myself honestly. What had I become, these weeks in Cash-ampton? Just another selfish rich guy, looking for the angle that would put me over the top. A dead soul. Living in Cashampton had inured me to suffering. I'd become immune to sorrow. But this, this misspelled missive from beyond the grave, this touched my heart. So I cried, for Gilbert, for Valerie, and for Jackson, the 'fahter' of Specs Schwartz, the insane melodic executioner of form.

Eighteen

GUY GATTLING'S PARTY that night was boisterous and fun, despite the very real (and exponentially-increasing) threat of The Disease. Servants dressed as dominatrixes in studded black leather, some wearing hoods, all carrying whips and paddles – safe-sex fashion-accessories – walked around serving Bonacker delicacies catered by Bertha Seward's restaurant – hot dogs and potato chips and Cash Bay oysters. I declined (and for declining received a rather gentle spanking with a perforated paddle – which I found still preferable to boiled nitrate-rich Oscar Meyer hot dogs and polluted oysters). Bertha herself was overseeing (by speech) the operation, zipping about quite nimbly, with a minimum of bumping into people and furniture, on her new prosthesis. A few guests, Art World and Hollywood types – Willem de Kooning and Lindsay LaRouche, violinist Po Go Pa, Larry Rivers, Eric Fischl and Clara Spoon (Reggie Spoon had sadly succumbed to the joy of an exploding head), Julia Roberts,

Danny Glover, and Matt Dillon (in town for their Pollock flick, all staying at Terry Tuba's) – were over in a corner playing 'The American Dream,' next to a large display of Sensuous brand condoms.

'Welcome to the party, Roger. Isn't it marvelous?' Guy gushed. 'Have a condom, have a hot dog. Let me introduce you to Julia Roberts.'

'A drink will be sufficient,' I said, watching an actor dressed as Pollock, with an obviously fake bald-wig, splashing paint on a canvas in a corner while a crew of similarly-uniformed fashion models looked on, smoking unfiltered Camels.

'Where's the Pearl Man?' asked Guy Gattling.

'He's with a sick friend.'

'The Pearl Man and Muffy Gritz, eh? I have a surprise for you,' he said, leading me to his locked bedroom door. Once inside he locked the door behind him.

He steered me past *The Rat King*, over to a five-by-two-by-three-foot-large glass fish tank. Ah, I thought, the kinder gentler side of Guy Gattling.

On the pink-graveled tank-bottom, surrounded by tropical fish, lay two twisted shining metal sculptures, like gold-colored scorched total car-wrecks in miniature. Each of the wrecks contained a tentacled red-and-white creature.

'What is it, Guy?'

'In the spirit of Marcel Duchamp and Jacques Cousteau,' he announced proudly, 'it's found-art.'

The multicolored fish swam about – some, I now noticed, were floating dead – chewing drifting tidbits of food.

'But *what* is it?' I asked, not sure I wanted to know the answer.

'It's Baby Luegodago in Kelly Swett's lingerie!' he said happily. 'I paid the salvage crew a hundred bucks a man for them. I can't decide whether to call it *Aquatic Unstill Life* or *Baby Please Come Home*.'

'Either way,' I said, as a small electric-blue fighting-fish wrestled a chunk of meat from the mangled thumbtack lingerie, 'you've taken collecting to new depths.'

'Thank you, Roger. Coming from the man who wrote *Crayola Payola*, that's a real compliment.' He scooped dead fish from the tank with a small net and emptied them in a large abstract gray ashtray. 'But that's not the surprise.'

'Is this the surprise?' I was staring at a newly-hung pen-and-ink drawing of a little boy performing oral sex on a Gestapo-uniformed man.

'Oh no, that's just some of my new Nazi memorabilia. From the art-therapy class at the camp at Bergen-Belsen. Painted on human skin.'

'Christ,' I said, feeling ill. 'Art stinks.'

'Speaking of which: Sharon and Rawlings are in town!'

'They walked here?'

'They certainly did. They should be here in a few minutes to beg their dinner. You'll have to speak with them on the lawn.'

'I can deal with that.' And I could. Since playing whale with Lindsay LaRouche on Pollock's grave I'd had nary a thought of Sharon, and even, one night at dinner at Musgrove Messerschmitt's, had supped upon vichyssoise without the old attendant sadness.

'Now the surprise!' proclaimed the President of the Make My Hair-Day Club as he finished combing and patting his rug in the Specs Schwartz zit-mirror (to which he'd attached a title plaque reading *The Portrait Of Dorian Schwartz*). '*Voilà.*'

He handed me some pictures. I lit a cigarette and smoked while I studied the snapshots.

'Now, Roger, look carefully. What do you see?'

'I see a head, Guy – photographs taken from different angles of a bald head with some sort of substance on it.'

'Yes. I was going through my recent pre-hairpiece files for possible clients to feature in a new before-and-after commercial. Do you recognize the man?'

'Should I? It's not Yul Brynner – he's dead. And it's not Charles Barkley or Captain Picard from that new *Star Trek*. I give up.'

'It's the Pearl Man!'

I looked again. It *was* John Dough – or perhaps I should say, it was John Doe before he became John Dough. John in that nebulous, bald-headed, green-eyed stage between Pizzaface and Pearl Man.

'Well, so it is. But, Guy, I imagine that client-Hair-Day Club-confidentiality is a cornerstone of your business, much like a psychiatrist.'

'It is, Roger,' said Guy, handing me the large ashtray full of little colorful dead fish. It was heavy and smooth.

'What's this ashtray made of?' I asked, stubbing the butt out. 'Part of a Georgia O'Keeffe cow-skeleton?'

'No, it's a Parisian pawnbroker's pelvis, from Dachau.'

'That's obscene.'

'Different strokes for different folks. Aren't you the man who wrote: "Stillman's Francophobia and forced post-anal-retentive experience of sodomy opened up vast new vistas of suffering and creativity"?'

'You really know your Stillman.'

'I'm his biggest fan. Look, Roger, I want you to speak with the Pearl Man. Try to convince him to take part in my new commercial. It would be great for business.'

'I don't know, Guy; John's a very private man.'

'I can appreciate that, Roger. What do you think that dark stuff is on his head?'

'Some glue for his toupee?'

'No, Roger, we use a clear bonding-element.'

'It could be a birthmark. Maybe that's why he got the wig.'

'Maybe so. But it's awfully big. . . . But you must admit, birthmark or melanoma, it's quite artistic.'

'Art is everywhere,' I said, gazing at the *Aquatic Unstill Life* with a sudden strong nostalgia for the earthy earthly Baby Luegodago.

'But what if it's a melanoma?' Guy asked. 'I wouldn't want him doing a commercial and then dying on us. Don't you think he should be appraised of the situation and tested?'

'I'll speak with him,' I said, staring at the pictures of Gilbert's tattoo with dawning comprehension. *It was a map! A map of Cashampton! A map with compass markings, squiggled roads, splotched landmarks. A map! What had Pollock said to Val? That the tattoo was Gilbert's 'bithrite'? A map to the missing Pollocks?*

'Do you mind if I take this photo?' I asked, nonchalantly waving the snapshot of the top of Gibert's head.

'You do that, Roger. If it's cancer, it raises one of my favorite themes,' said Guy Gattling with a smile as he dipped the net into the tank and dumped the one-eyed electric-blue fighting-fish into the ashtray. 'Is art worth dying for?'

I went straight for the bar, had a quick pair of Wild Turkeys to calm my nerves.

'Hello, Roger!'

I removed the hand from my crotch.

'Hello, Bertha.' I kissed her cheek. She was done-up in a Jackson Pollock Look ensemble. 'You look great.'

'No, I don't; I look like wacko Jacko. Whatcha think of the food?'

'Sheer genius, Bertha. I'm sorry I didn't stick around after the opening of the Bonacker restaurant and store.'

'Yeah, well – have you seen Julia Roberts?' I looked. The Medusa-haired actress was dancing with Big Barton Snitbread. She wore hip waders and a torn T-shirt that read 'Retired Bonackers Dive Deeper.' 'Julia bought her outfit from me.'

'That's fantastic,' I said. 'You can even see her curves beneath the rubber.'

'That's the idea.' Bertha smiled. 'She said she'd love to play me in the flick you're writing. Jacko would have loved her lips – she let me feel them.'

'That's wonderful. I wonder how she'll be as Lee Krasner?'

'Who gives a shit? Playing me she'll really get to stretch her acting muscles. Howya like my new leg?'

She unrolled her painter's jeans. The prosthesis was caramel-colored, in sharp contrast to her own abbreviated-at-the-knee, slightly-hairy white leg.

'It's very becoming.'

'It was originally meant for a colored boy, but what do I care? I'm blind.' She cackled. 'His mother won the state lottery and got him a better one.'

'Everyone's a winner.' I gave her a congratulatory kiss on the cheek. 'Bertha, I'd still like to see Pollock's old studio. How about tomorrow?'

'Meet me at Fred Snitbread's funeral. I'm catering the reception. After I show you the studio, I'll take you for a bite.' She winked. 'I'm still eating for success.'

'I'm sure you are, Bertha, but I'm on a diet.'

'Hello, Mr. Lymon!'

'Lindsay!' We kissed – just a social kiss on the cheek. 'You look gorgeous.'

'You look nice too. You haven't been over to see us since Miss Esther died.'

'Well, Lindsay, I've got some very real feelings for you—'

'And I care for you, too, Mr. Lymon.'

'You do?' *Then why do you keep calling me Mr. Lymon?*

She nodded.

'But,' I said, 'I think the world of Bill and I wouldn't want to hurt him.'

'But Billbo thinks you're great too. Why can't we all be close? We'll do a threebie.'

'Thanks for thinking of me, Lindsay, but I'm afraid I don't do gay.'

'That's a shame. I've almost got Billbo warmed up to the idea. He's not drinking and he's painting again. His daughter and I are getting along since he agreed to test Mr. Snitbread's Instant AA.'

'Where *is* Bill?'

'Oh, he's over there arm-wrestling with Matt Dillon.'

'So he is.'

'Come with me,' she said. 'Come with me to the cabana by the pool. The Goddess needs to be honored.'

'Gladly,' I said, following the flying-buttress behind and taking a joint from my cigarette pack, feeling the Sensuous brand condom in my pocket – already my section of the heavenly ladder was reaching for the sky. 'We must never forget to honor our ancestors.'

'Hello, Roger.' It was Hiroshi Koyabashi, looking perfectly ludicrous in an oversized Pollock Look ensemble.

'Hello, Hiroshi, have you met Ms. LaRouche, the noted performance artist?'

Lindsay was flushed and happy. And I was drained and happy. So this is love, I thought – or some facsimile thereof.

'Delighted, Ms. LaRouche. I was lucky enough to catch you at Dante's last spring.'

'Did you enjoy the show?' asked my sweet Kissin' Banshee.

'Enjoy it?! I have been practicing with ping-pong balls ever since!'

'That's so gratifying, Mr. Hiroshi. Imitation is the highest form of flattery. That's what my Billbo says.'

'Ms. LaRouche, do you mind if I borrow Roger for a moment?'

'Not at all,' said Lindsay. 'Bye bye Mr. Lymon.'

'How do you like Cashampton, Hiroshi?'

'Too many Hollywood types. I'm staying over at Jasper Jurkbaitt's.'

'How do you know the Reverend? Root canal?'

'We met at the St. Mark's gay baths some years back.'

He led me to the dining room.

'So, Roger,' said Hiroshi, sitting me in the Andalusian trepanning chair. 'What's new on the Pollock front?'

'Not much. Hiroshi. I'm not sure I want the job any more.'

'You're going solo?'

'Not exactly. But since I found out that Turven Blagden specializes in karate books I've had my doubts about the, uhh, artistic integrity of your motives.'

'I'm disappointed in you, Roger. You must not be reading *The Times*. Shiatsubishi is negotiating to purchase three reputable New York publishing houses. Diversifying. We've bought paperback reprint rights to Gabby Marquez's soccer book, *One Hundred Years Of Goalkeeper Paranoia*.'

'As Jackson Pollock used to say, Hiroshi: "Fuck off!"'

'Have you met my date, Roger?'

'No, Hiroshi. Who's your date?'

'Artie!' Hiroshi called. A large man in a dirty Bonacker farming outfit came over. He was eating oysters. 'Roger meet Artie. Artie meet Roger.'

'Charmed,' I said.

The big man smiled malevolently, revealing large yellow oyster-clotted teeth.

'I've got your face filed, fagoleh,' he said.

'My face?'

'Artie is a great one for faces. I think he was a portrait artist in another life.'

'I'm not sure I understand.'

'Artie belongs to a certain family whose patriarch is a gentleman called Bonzo Mancini . . .'

'Bonzo The Carp?' I felt a chill in the room, and it wasn't the air-conditioning.

'You win a cigar, Roger. Mr. Mancini provides – how shall we say? – security for some of Shiatsubishi's stateside operations.'

'You want me to take him outside, 'Roshi?' asked Artie, sucking an oyster off a shell. 'Teach him the Jimmy Hoffa breaststroke?'

'Not yet, Artie. Roger still has a biography and film script to write, and, dare I say, some paintings to find.'

'Da missin' Pollocks?'

'You like Pollock, Artie?' I asked.

'Love him. His shit looks just like an explosion.'

'Hello, Roger.'

'Have we met?'

The threadbare cream linen suit the old gent wore looked vaguely familiar.

'Now that you're a big-shot you don't remember me?' he asked, blowing his nose on a large raspberry-colored handkerchief. 'I used to have a rather influential gallery in Soho – until The Bakery put me out of business.'

'Oh, yes,' I said. 'How goes it?'

'Not well. I have a touch of age.'

'Ah, perhaps,' I said, looking at the droplet of snot glistening on his now-untidy and snowy nose hairs — 'I can arrange for my friend Barton Snitbread to include you in his Alzheimer's study.'

'It's not my mind, Roger, it's my dingus and my wallet. And I've already met Mr. Snitbread. Look what he gave me.' He pulled a tube from his pocket. 'It's brand-new; I'm the second testee. After Bill de Kooning.'

I read the label: BONER FIDE.

'Well, bully for you,' I said.

'No, Roger, bully for you! Let's take a walk and talk about the first artistic thing that pops up.'

'I apologize, sir, but I don't do gay.'

'That's what you said back in '82, and I seem to remember a little session that resulted in me writing a very favorable letter on your behalf to the editor of *Artnews*.'

'I have a slight memory . . .'

'Well, if you'd like to refresh your slight memory, I could get you a copy of my biography,' he said. 'Turven Blagden is considering it for publication. Tentative title: *Where The Boys Were*. You're in chapter ninety-three.'

'You don't fool me, gramps: Turven Blagden does karate books.'

'Haven't you heard? Last week they put in a huge bid for Sylvan Glade.'

'Do you think,' I said, walking the man out the back door, across a short lawn and into the pool cabana. 'Do you think I might convince you to do some editing?'

'By all means,' he said, unzipping himself and pulling the tube of Boner Fide. 'I'm always open for constructive suggestions. And I hope you are too, Roger.'

I glumly handed him a Sensuous brand condom. 'Be gentle, it's been awhile.'

'You critics can sure dish it out, but can you take it?'

'I'm more of what you'd call a reviewer than a critic.'

'So give me a review afterward.'

'Remember,' I said, leaning over, resigned, feeling the cold familiar intrusion, 'I don't do gay.'

'Appearances,' he said with a surprisingly virile grunt, 'can be deceiving.'

'Hello, Roger,' said Sharon Timlin. A very unkempt bruised-faced Sharon Timlin, handcuffed to a thinned down, equally bruised Rawlings Black. The Cambodian-born video artist Viet Jane Sak was taping the exchange, sipping beer from a Jackson Pollock mug. His battered Chevy Astro-Van was parked in a hedge.

'Hello, Sharon. Would you care for a potato chip or a hot dog?'

'What I'd like, Roger, is a real live raw potato, but Jasper Jurkbaitt doesn't allow me near potatoes or potato by-products. I'll take a hot dog.'

She grabbed two hot dogs from the tray I held, put one in her jacket pocket for later and started chewing the other.

'Hello, Rawlings,' I said to the sad silent monologist. 'How's married life?'

'With this bitch?' he said with a sigh, eating an oyster. 'What a cunt. Now I know why old Pollock offed himself.'

'That good, eh?'

'What I'd give to be back at The Garage, making up stories about my childhood for those schmucks. Fuck the 'Nineties; I miss the 'Eighties.'

'I don't,' I said, feeling a rectal flutter. 'You two don't look so happy. Why the bruises?'

'Dickhead hit me,' said Sharon.

'Yeah, but as usual Spud-Pussy started it.'

'That's because you wouldn't defend me from those black kids back in Bay Shore. Fucking ten-year-olds beat us with rubber hoses and socks full of pennies, Roger, and this dumb-fuck didn't even pull his Buck knife.'

'Whattaya expect? My reactions are fucked.' Rawlings sighed. 'That goddamn Jurkbaitt Nazi won't even let me take my Prozac.'

'That's an excuse?' screeched Sharon, smacking Rawlings in the nose with a balled fist. He held his face in one hand.

'Art isn't always pretty or safe, Sharon,' I said, hoping to leaven the rising domestic conflagration. 'You knew that when you got into the game.'

'Yeah,' Sharon said, licking her knuckles. 'But I thought the dialectical tension between black and white was something only painters were concerned with.'

'Yes, well, art and life run compellingly close these days.'

'Fucking niggers.'

'I'm sure Natalie would be pleased to hear you say that.'

'Where is Nat? I miss her.'

'I've had a postcard from her today. She's been house-guesting with Justice and Mrs. Clarence Thomas outside of Washington.'

'You should have married *her*, you dumb dyke,' said Rawlings.

'Roger,' said Sharon. 'Can I have a word with you in private?'

'I don't know, Sharon,' I said, examining the handcuffs. 'Is that possible?'

She pulled away from Rawlings, as far as their arms would allow, and she put her dirty face close to my ear. God, she smelled.

'Roger,' she whispered. 'I need to get laid. Help me out.'

I checked the EKG of my emotions: nothing there. A flat existential nothing.

'Can't help you, Sharon.' I thought of Lindsay. 'I'm involved.'

'Look, we'll drug Viet Jane and we'll kick the shit out of Rawlings.' Sharon's eyes were wild. 'He doesn't even care anymore. I just need some cock.'

'What if I snuck you a potato?'

'I need cock.'

'I'll have to pass, myself, but if you'd like, I can get my hands on some of Barton Snitbread's Boner Fide cream for Rawlings,' I whispered, feeling an ache in my anus. 'It's guaranteed to make a dead man rise.'

'That's not the point. Scuzzo can get it up, but he doesn't have any bullets. My sweet potato-pie needs live sperm. Olympic swimming-team sperm.' She stroked the hot dog sticking out of her pocket. 'I want to be a mother.'

'Ah, to get the extra hundred G's.'

'That's right,' she said. 'Once we score the NEA grant I'll sell the rug-rat.'

'Sorry, Sharon, fatherhood isn't for me; but I'd be happy to introduce you to someone.'

'The Pearl Man? What a fox. I heard you were best-buds with him.'

'John's a bit occupied at present. I was thinking more about this very handsome black friend of mine. His name is Kurtis, and for sure he's shooting live ammunition.'

'Groovy. Integration copulation. But if he's too dark, then I can't pass the thing off as Rawlings'.'

The party had seeped out of the Gattling house and had gathered around Rawlings and Sharon.

'He's got white blood,' I said.

'Oh, thank you, Roger!'

Viet Jane Sak panned the audience with his camera. Po Go Pa played his violin. Larry Rivers tooted along on his sax.

'Ladies and gentlemen,' said Jasper Jurkbaitt. 'I want to introduce you to Rawlings Black and his beaming bride, Sharon Timlin-Black, who have most graciously agreed to perform for us tonight. Singing for their supper, as it were. In honor of Jackson Pollock.'

The crowd clapped.

'Sharon and Rawlings are really on the right track with their ongoing year-long piece titled *The Sanctity Of Our Vows.* Performance art is an ancient and honorable form of expression. Who can forget that fourth-century performance artist, Saint Simeon The Stylite, who sat on top of a sixty-foot-high pillar for thirty-six years? Who can forget all the flagellants and knee-walkers and cave-dwellers and willing martyrs who honored God with sacrifices beyond the confines of pain, who went cheerfully to torture and death with a smile on their faces and a song in their hearts? Who can forget the great Jackson Pollock? who suffered for his art with such strength and panache? And of course, who can forget our Lord and Saviour, Jesus Christ – the greatest performance artist of them all – who allowed his own painful crucifixion when he could just as easily have levitated off the cross. And in so keeping with these fine examples, I present Sharon and Rawlings!'

The crowd cheered.

'We haven't really prepared anything, folks,' said Sharon, munching her spare hot dog. 'But all of you must know we've been handcuffed together and living homeless. This has really put a strain on our marriage—'

'You're telling me?' Rawlings asked, spitting at Sharon, who then hawked a hot dog lugey and nailed Rawlings in the eye. The crowd clapped.

'This bitch is famous for shoving spuds up her twat,' he continued. 'So what does that make me? A potato-substitute? Modern marriage is what?'

Ah, I thought, this is the Rawlings that rocketed to prominence in the 'Eighties. A pungent, bitter teller of personal truths, a social-philosopher.

'An invention by women to enslave men? A Judeo-Christian shackling of the flesh? The death of the male? The end of creativity? I've begged this bitch for a divorce. I've gotten on my knees, on highways and backroads, in parking lots and outside shopping malls, from Maspeth to Ronkonkoma to Cashampton, begging and begging, but no – Sharon wants the money, Sharon wants the money, Sharon wants the money. Bitch won't let me go until she scores the big-bucks. So what do I say?'

Rawlings' eyes blazed. He pulled his Buck knife from his pocket, unzipped his fly, dangled his penis. He lightly ran the shining blade over the glans and he laughed. The audience *oohed*. Viet Jane Sak hit the zoom button.

'I say, freedom's just another word for nothing left to lose,' he said, cutting the string which held his pants and letting the dirty jeans fall – no underwear. 'I say fuck you and fuck me and fuck it all.' He pulled the hand cuffed to Sharon to his scrotum, held the package tight, and then he chopped.

The crowd screamed.

'Freedom, motherfucker!' Rawlings yelled, holding the bloody flesh-mess aloft. 'Freedom,' he whispered into Viet Jane's camera, as he flung the genitals over the hedge. 'Freedom,' he said, as Musgrove Messerschmitt's poodle Kerensky crashed through the greenery after the discarded potato-substitutes. 'Freedom,' he said, plunging the knife into his heart.

And the crowd, realizing they were in the presence of a latter-day saint – perhaps the most extraordinary performance artist since the great Jesus Christ himself – the crowd clapped politely.

'Freedom,' said Sharon Timlin with a great big sigh, popping a last bit of hot dog into her mouth and chewing, as Rawlings Black bowed gracefully and fell dead on Guy Gattling's lawn. 'Freedom.'

Nineteen

JOHN DOUGH DID not come home that night, nor the next morning. I phoned Big Barton. Muffy still AWOL.

But more important: the paintings. Find the paintings and cut a deal with Hiroshi. I studied Guy's picture of the Pearl Man's head through a magnifying glass and checked it against a tourist map of Cashampton. . . . That thick line running the length of Gilbert's cranium – that was Route 27, the Montauk Highway. South of the highway, beyond the beaches (a blank strip of skin broken now and then by inked jetties), beyond the waves (wavy black inkstrokes) – running to his ears – were tiny dots, like black freckles. Under the magnifying glass they became winged birds, seagulls in flight. It was really quite ingenious, ingenious yet simple. A small tomahawk where the Montauk Indian Reservation would be. Little squares – houses – lining Main Street Cashampton. A line for the Sag Harbor Highway. All roads on Gilbert's head curving in conformity to the tourist map. Of course, things had changed drastically since Pollock's death – there were plenty of new buildings and new roads – but the essentials were there. A three-holed ball where the Bowlarama was built. A small striped cat – a tiger – where Tiger Edgar Cash's Cashampton home still stood. A bunch of skirts and books signifying the high school – old Jackson was not without a sense of humor. A sheaf of dollars and coins forming the shape of Cash Island over by the other ear. A small roaring fire where Fireplace Road started; the scripted word 'Hell' for the farmhouse he shared with Lee; trees and bushes for the woods he loved to walk in; a fish and a liquor bottle where Fish Head Danny's was; and near that, right in the center of the skull – in the woods – a star, a tiny star nestled midst the blotches and dots of trees; a star next to a cabin and a heart. The studio! The secret studio! Where Pollock brought his young girlfriends! Where Gilbert was conceived and tattooed! Yes, I thought, yes! That's where he'd stash the paintings!

To the woods, then! Ah, but Cashampton was jammed with tourists and summerfolk. Traffic barely crawled. I smoked and swore and honked. Benzes and Beamers and Jags – every variety of expensive automobile – clogged the arteries and veins leading to Fireplace Road. Pollock's farmhouse was overrun. I retraced my way. Fish Head Danny's parking lot was packed solid. I parked on the roadside and crashed into the brush. Shall I describe my thrashing, my crashing, my futile wandering through nettles and bushes? All the sweating and swearing? Suffice it to say, I found nothing. Nothing but trees and bushes and a lot of mosquitoes. I had failed. I needed an expert guide. I needed a local. I needed Bertha Seward.

Twenty

FRED'S FUNERAL WAS, as advertised, a family affair. Besides myself, a few servants, including Pancho the butler (who'd told me, upon my arrival, when I asked him where in Central America he was born, that he hailed from Youngstown, Ohio, and had once been a ranked welterweight fighter – hence the flat nose), and The Reverend Doctor Jasper Jurkbaitt, who was to perform the eulogy, the mourners were comprised solely of Snitbreads and Gritzes: Jenny, Clark, Jonas, Big Barton, Sarah, the thirteen head of beerhead buffaloes (their numbers having decreased due to the Snitbreads' fondness for buffalo meat), the two camels, the five ostriches, the Great Dane Speedy, and Mozart the spider monkey.

And a new addition to the Snitbread Magic Kingdom – right in the center of the main field: a thirty foot high whitewashed concrete duck with orange lips.

'It's called The Big Duck,' Big Barton whispered for my elucidation, as the Reverend Jurkbaitt arranged his note cards.

'That took some imagination,' I said, scratching my mosquito bites.

'Used to be a poultry store on the back roads. When Fred died, I bought it for his tomb.' Fred's ashes were in a Ming Dynasty vase next to an eight-foot-high horseshoe-shaped wreath of red roses.

'A Ming copy?' I asked.

'Please, Roger.' Big Barton was offended. 'Fred is family.'

Jenny Gritz winked at me. She was wearing her standard red-checked shirt, jeans, boots, and twelve earrings. Yesterday's grief for Fred had seemingly evaporated into the hot Cashampton sky.

'Nothing but the real thing for me and mine,' Barton said. 'When I go, I was planning on being buried in *Speed-Lax 1*. I guess I'll have to settle for *Speed-Lax 2*.'

'I believe attendance at Green River is a bit overbooked for a coffin that size.'

'Stick around for the reception,' Big Barton said, passing me a packet of Snitex tissues. 'Julia Roberts is coming.'

'Hello, family,' greeted the The Reverend Jurkbaitt. 'We are here today to say goodbye to Fred. Fred Snitbread, beloved son of Erving, grandson of the great Hollywood star Trigger, dearly beloved Fred, who has tragically passed from our midst after a long and productive life. I am not here to celebrate his previous accomplishments – the telegrams Big Barton received yesterday with the condolences of such luminaries as Marlon Brando, Jack Nicholson, Emma Samms, Brian De Palma, and Susan Strasberg, the daughter of his old acting-coach, Lee Strasberg, among others, as well as the beautiful wreath sent by Clint Eastwood, and of course the obituary in today's *Times*, all attest to the high professional esteem and love his fellow thespians and the Art World in general had for him. No, I am here today to speak of Fred the person.

'Fred was a kind friend, a willing companion, even when he was long in the tooth, even when the decay of time had seeped into his jaws. Even then, he loved life and he loved his friends, and for that reason we are all a bit poorer today. Yes, Fred was a giant among horses . . .'

Barton wept. Jenny and Jonas yawned. Clark shuffled his feet. Sarah Snitbread – dressed as Jackson Pollock – seemed asleep on her feet. Mozart diddled her clit.

'Fred knew Clint Eastwood?' I asked Big Barton in a whisper.

'Damn right,' said Big Barton. 'Fred's first film was *Hang 'Em High*.'

'And Fred hung with Nicholson?'

'Yes,' Big Barton said with a sniffle. 'They did two films – *The Missouri Breaks*, Nicholson and Brando, and *Goin' South*, Nicholson and Belushi. Fred and Belushi were great drinking buddies – lots of beer.'

'Well,' I said, patting a yawning buffalo who seemed to have perked up at the word beer. 'Well, I guess those are the breaks.'

Later, the open reception was going full swing. Food was an assortment of Bertha Seward-catered Bonacker delicacies (the demise of The Pregnant Duchess could not have come at a better time for her fledgling business) – Jello, potato chips, baloney sandwiches, and fried Cash Bay clam-strips with ketchup – and a large tub of buffalo Kobe steak-tartare next to a silver tray of complimentary High Octane Speed-Lax. Alcohol was served liberally. The Hollywood contingent, Matt Dillon (and his blonde *du jour*), Julia Roberts (with an unnamed Jackson Pollock-garbed male-model-type), Danny Glover (with his wife), and their host Terry Tuba, were the most obviously touched by Fred's departure, weeping openly.

Ah, I thought, it takes an actor to appreciate another actor's life and death. Everyone filed by the Ming vase and lovingly dropped a red rose on it. And then Matt and Danny, under Pancho's direction, took a camel ride. Jasper Jurkbaitt chatted with his date, the dominatrix who'd spanked me the night before and was clad, appropriately, in black. Who else? Maria the instructor, Hank Upton, Hiroshi and Artie. Who else? A showered uncuffed Sharon Timlin – solo. Bertha selling softball-grapefruits. Lindsay and Bill. Larry Rivers. The usual suspects.

'Roger,' said Hiroshi, garbed in a Bonacker garage-mechanic's greasy jumpsuit.

'Hello, Hiroshi.'

'Say hi to Artie, Roger.'

'Hi there,' I said to the Mancini family-man – done up in a Pollock uniform, chewing clam-strips. Artie smiled.

'Roger,' said Hiroshi. 'The Pollock premiere is tonight and I am quite serious about wanting those paintings. If not today, then soon. And if you don't want to work on the film, I'll take your notes. DeNiro says he can get Fellini for the script and direction. And Julia Roberts has indicated she would like to play Bertha Seward. So plump Bertha's role up. Maybe give her a voice-over narration. Fellini is not in good health, so time is of the essence. If Fellini dies, we'll go for Scorsese.'

'I really am doing my best, Hiroshi.'

'Do better. And find the art – for Artie's sake.'

'Everyone speaks highly of you,' said Jasper Jurkbait to a decidedly heavy-souled Roger Lymon. I was weary. Life in Cashampton had made me tired.

The former dentist was resplendent in a vermilion Armani

suit and his fingers were shiny with buffalo-tartare juice. I couldn't at all tell his chickenfeather-blonde hair wasn't real. On one finger he wore a ring, a large, blue-tinged white stone with red veins.

'That's an interesting ring,' I said.

'It's one of John Dough's pearls from Turkey, the second largest. Liz Taylor outbid me for the massive egg-sized one, but I'm very happy with this. I paid two-point-nine mil.'

Ah, Pinatubo. A pimple by any other name. . . .

'A bargain, I'm sure,' I said.

'Absolutely. You know, Roger – may I call you Roger? – I think now that Sharon's separated from Rawlings, she'll be a real credit to her gender. The American Family needs wholesome examples.' He placed a pale tartare-greasy meathook on the dominatrix's leathered rear end. 'Have you met my friend, Markie De Sade?'

'Why no, we've never met. Are you a professional waitress?'

'Actress, waitress, performance artist,' said the lush-bodied brunette, peeling a softball-grapefruit.

'Ah, but I do remember you – from *Deirdre Does Dublin*. You have some of the most expressive, er, eyes in the performance-art business.'

'Thanks. I agree with Jasper: Marriage and family values are so important. Rawlings just wasn't cut out to be a role-model.'

'And don't forget, we're fighting the good fight against unnatural, ungodly condom use,' Jurkbaitt smiled.

'How could I ever forget?' I asked, as Pancho came by with a bowl full of Sensuous brand condoms. Jurkbaitt took a handful.

'I need these hellish things to illustrate a point in my sermon tomorrow,' he said, putting an arm around Markie

De Sade. 'Abstinence and Platonic love are the only true weapons in the battle against The Disease.'

'Those are pearls of wisdom to be savored in private,' I said, moving on.

Ah, there's Julia Roberts. Now that I'm a rich man . . .

But Julia was chatting with Lyle Lovett, the singer.

The model-type she'd arrived with sat on the grass, drinking a beer, eating a baloney sandwich.

'Hey, man.' I said. 'How's the sandwich?'

'Fuckin' baloney.' The man grimaced. 'First time I get to one of these fancy parties, my movie-star date dumps me for some Texas bumpkin, and what do they serve? Goddamn Bonacker slop. Ain't fit for pigs.'

'It's from Bertha Seward's restaurant. Didn't you get your Jackson Pollock outfit at her store?'

'No, man, I'm a real live Bonacker. I got ten prime acres of potato-field in Cashampton. Finest kind.'

'Listen,' I said. 'I'd like to introduce you to a friend of mine. She's a big potato-lover.'

'She ain't flaky like Julia?'

'No, my friend, she's almost as sane as I am. Finest kind.'

After I'd introduced Rod the Bonacker to Sharon — and Sharon and Rod had gone for a stroll on the beach — I found Lindsay and Bill.

'Bill,' I said. 'Lindsay. How are you two today?'

'Fine, fine, Roger. Congratulate me. I haven't had a drink in over a week and I am painting again.'

'That's great, Bill. I saw you arm-wrestling Matt Dillon last night.'

'These kids . . .' de Kooning said with a shake of his silver-head. 'Yah, I took him two out of three falls.'

'My man,' said Lindsay LaRouche, kissing him. I sighed — involuntarily.

'Bill, how would you like to take a little walk in the woods with Bertha and me? Have a look at Pollock's old studio?'

'Yah, sure — why the hell not?'

And then the warm afternoon party mood that had been so delicately nurtured by the emotional closure put to Fred's life, by the star-fuck hysteria over the presence of the Hollywood contingent, by the weeks and weeks of excitement building up to that night's Pollock premiere — all those sweet summer-time feelings were transmuted to tragic Cashampton horseshit by a familiar, familiar happening: This time it was Maria the instructor who began to hiccup.

Twenty-one

'BILLBO,' SAID LINDSAY LAROUCHE to de Kooning, as we dropped her off at the house across from the cemetery. 'Please don't catch any poison ivy. Principal photography for the *Temple of Dendur* flick starts next week. The last thing I need is to be scratching some disgusting rash on my buns while instructing King Tut in the Egyptian mysteries.'

'Yes, snookums,' he said, planting a long wet kiss on her lips.

'Goodbye, Mr. Lymon,' said Lindsay with a smile. 'Goodbye, Miss Bertha.'

'Goodbye, Lindsay,' I answered, no longer obsessed with her physical spendors, thinking now only of the lost Pollocks on the other end of the rainbow.

'Hold your horses, kiddo,' said Bertha Seward. 'Can I ask a favor?'

'If I can do it, of course.'

'Can I touch them?'

'Touch what?'

'Your famous fucking tits is what. They're the talk of the town.'

'You poor, poor thing,' said Lindsay, drawing Bertha to her breast. 'Oh, why can't they make films in Braille?'

'Holy fucking Christ,' said Bertha Seward, running her hands up and around the oversized mammaries. 'You woulda suffocated poor Jacko.'

'This way,' said Bertha, jamming her Red Sox cap over her ears. 'I'm telling you, de Koo-Koo. You enter the fucking woods a hundred yards past Fish Head Danny's. Right where that boozy lummox crashed the car.'

We'd parked on the roadside, in sight of Fish Head Danny's. The bar's parking lot was full of cars, Benzes and Beamers and Jags – two burgundy Jaguars just like John Dough's. I missed the Pearl Man, but I was glad he'd escaped the Pollockmania.

'What is the shovel for, Roger?' de Kooning asked, swatting a mosquito.

'For artifacts.'

It was hot and airless in the mid-afternoon woods, and immediately I was sweating and huffing, but de Kooning was dry and barely winded, and Bertha, surprisingly agile, limped though the brush like a woodland sprite.

'We should be near Jacko's tree,' said the former Bertha Bemon, fifty feet in.

'Yah! Here it is!' cried de Kooning. 'Hello, Jackson.' Old Bill caressed a tree and spoke softly: ' "I am Nature," Jackson used to say. Yah, old friend, you loved these woods; it is fitting you died here.'

'I'll say he was *Nature*,' snorted Bertha Seward. 'Randier than a fucking billygoat is what he was.'

'Now, look, Bertha,' cautioned de Kooning. 'I have ignored your greed – by selling the grapefruits painted to look like softballs you have stooped to Warhol's level – and you were not even there that day! I have never even scolded you for spilling beans to the collectors, but I will not – I repeat – I will not hear you put Jackson down. He was your friend.'

'Don't be such a sentimental old fart, de Koo-Koo. He wasn't my friend – he was my lover. I was a horny high-school chick and you guys were these exciting famous artists. Not even very good ones, for *my* money.'

'C'mon, you two, ease up. We've got miles to go before we sleep,' I said, paraphrasing Robert Frost.

'Fucking Bubba Frost,' said Bertha. 'Guy had the smallest, softest dick of any celebrity I ever blew.'

We tromped on, Bertha leading the way, occasionally bumping into trees or tripping over logs, swearing like a sailor, clutching her still-sore collarbone and muttering, 'This shit wasn't here back then.' It was stifling hot and the gnats and flies and mosquitoes were biting us all over. I was getting more and more disillusioned by the minute.

'Sshh!' Bertha stopped us on the edge of a clearing. 'You hear that?'

'Hear what?'

'Somebody's fucking,' she said. 'Us blind-folk got extra-strong ears.'

'Somebody's always fucking,' I said. 'That's what makes the world go round.'

'No, moron,' she hissed. 'Somebody's fucking in the cabin. Local kids've been using it as a fuck-nest for years. I heard a chick moaning.'

'What cabin?'

'Over there, idjit! Can't you smell the rotten wood?'

I looked – and oh, dear reader, my heart went pitter-patt and my fingers tingled with adrenaline: Beyond the clearing, squeezed midst the greenery like something in fairy tale, there *was* a cabin! – dilapidated for sure, walls missing boards, roof partly caved in – small and rotted and sad, no doubt inhabited by mice, perhaps raccoons, or even rats (how fitting!) – but there, there it was, in all its faded glory: The love shack! Where Gilbert was conceived. Where *The Rat King* was painted! Jackson Pollock's secret studio!

'Yah!' cried de Kooning, breaking into a run and charging across the clearing – but then tripping and sprawling. 'Shit, shit, shit,' he moaned, clutching his ankle.

'You okay, Bill?' I asked.

'Yah,' he said with a sigh. 'Help me over to the shade. I need to rest.'

I lifted the great Abstract Expressionist to his feet and Bertha wiped his jacket and pants with her hands, straying at his crotch.

'The old salami still working, de Koo-Koo?'

'Yah,' said Bill. 'The old salami still works.'

'You dropped these,' I said, picking up a plastic pill-box and a tube – a tube of Boner Fide. 'This Boner Fide stuff help?'

'Too well,' he said.

'No wonder that brick shithouse fell for you!' cried Bertha, grabbing the tube from my hand. 'You're the Frankenstein of fuck!'

'Bertha,' I said, 'give it a rest.'

'Shut up, Roger,' she said, uncapping the tube and spreading a dab on her fingertip and licking. 'Tastes like fucking cherry soda pop!'

Ninety feet from the cabin, under a tree, we sat de Kooning on a log. Tattered shreds of canvas hung from a single branch above our heads.

'Yah,' said Bill, fondly gazing at the material. 'Jackson's hammock. It used to be much lower. He loved to come here and rest with a bottle. Sometimes Valerie and Baby Gilbert would lie there with him. So peaceful.' Old Bill sniffled.

'Not,' Bertha Seward said with a mischievous cackle — 'when I was in there with him.'

My heart quickened. The ground in front of me was littered with old clam shells, oyster shells, mussel shells, edges soft from years of rain and wind and snow, a rusted ax handle, rusted paint cans — *Pollock liked to use house paint!* — a weathered brick barbecue pit, and beyond: a ten-foot square of raised ground, covered with grass and weeds and daffodils . . . large enough for some paintings?

I sank the shovel into the earth and scooped grass and flowers and dirt.

Bertha kneeled on the ground, resting her forehead against de Kooning's thigh.

'Don't cry, de Koo-Koo,' she said softly as I shoveled, feeling for his face and wiping his tears. 'Jacko would want you to be happy.'

'Yah,' said Bill, sniffling. 'I am too old to sweat, little Bertha, but I am so full of tears. If it weren't for young Barton Snitbread, I would be a vegetable. As you say, I am a Frankenstein.'

'Now you just shitcan the self-pity, old-timer,' said Bertha firmly, kissing his wet cheek. 'Look at me: I'm blind as a bat and I got a plastic leg — you see me complaining? Jacko's dead. We're not. You're a survivor, de Koo-Koo. And you got yourself a swell gold-digger with terrific knockers. So lighten up, or I'll give you a spanking.'

I have to be careful, I thought, working the top layer of ground off the square plot. Don't want to puncture a canvas. That would be millions of dollars down the drain. Oh, but

Pollock would have encased the paintings in plastic, or in a wooden container . . . My shovel clanked against something and I got on my knees and scraped the earth with my fingers, scraped and scraped.

Oh, glorious Pollock paydirt!

'What is it, Roger?' asked Bill, as I feverishly scraped dirt with my hands.

'It's . . . it's . . . the lost Pollocks!' I cried, scooping, finding an old bottle, throwing it aside.

'Lost Pollocks?' Bertha laughed. 'You don't actually believe that old story?'

'Under these bottles,' I said, tossing bottle after bottle. Bottle after bottle. 'The missing Pollocks.'

'Don't be a boob, Roger,' Bertha crowed. 'That was something Lee Krasner made up to decorate the legend. Jack The Dripper was so blind drunk those last years . . .' Bertha laughed and laughed. 'So that's what this is about. An old wives' tale. You poor deluded shmuck.'

'Shut up,' I said, pulling out bottle after bottle, throwing them aside, throwing them. Bottle after bottle. Bottle after bottle. Twenty of them, thirty of them, until my fingers were scraping dirt – nothing but dirt, dirt and worms, worms wriggling off into the grass as Bertha laughed on.

'Look,' said de Kooning, holding up a bottle with three fingers of brown booze in it. 'Jackson missed some.' He licked his lips, opened the cap and sniffed. 'Yah, forty-year-old bourbon. Older than you, Roger.'

'I'm going to check out that cabin,' I said.

'Yah! You do that,' said de Kooning, licking his lips.

'I don't think you should drink that. Liquor doesn't mix with Instant AA.'

'Roger, you really are an alarmist. What is it the youngsters used to say? "Don't believe the hype."'

And he raised the bottle to his lips and drank – then he screeched and grabbed his kidneys, falling to the ground on a bed of dirty bottles, legs bicycling, arms pumping. Then he just lay there, stiff as a board, silent as a mummy, eyes staring through the trees at the sky.

'What the fuck?' asked Bertha Seward.

'He's okay,' I said, bending and feeling the pulse on his neck. It was beating strong. 'Half-an-hour and he'll be himself.'

'Roger,' Bertha whined. 'I'm hungry. Now that de Koo-Koo's out . . .'

'After I find the paintings, Bertha, I'll buy you Matt Dillon.'

'I don't think I can wait that long,' she grumbled.

And, as I approached the cabin, I looked back. Bertha had one hand on de Kooning's fly and the other holding the tube of Boner Fide.

The falling sun streamed through the greenleaved trees, bathing the cabin and framing it with a halo of red light, and as I entered I saw: two naked sweating bodies coiled on the soft ancient timber, hands stroking, lips locked, hair twined, groans coming from deep in their chests, pelvises churning in a Rorschach puddle of love juices – squirming and coiling and crying and then . . . sighhhhhing.

'Oh my God, John!' I cried, recognizing the Man of Many Pearls. 'What are *you* doing here?'

'I could ask you the same thing,' he said, turning his face to look at me.

'Hello, Roger,' said Muffy in a calm voice, breathing hard.

'Muffy . . . you're not in a coma.'

'No shit, Roger,' said the Pearl Man.

'So that *was* your car at Fish Head Danny's' I said, staring at the top of his head.

'Hey, Roger,' he said, shielding Muffy with his body. 'It isn't polite to stare. Give us a moment.'

'I'm sorry,' I said, blushing.

I stepped out of the cabin. *Good God!* Bertha Seward was naked, skewered atop Willem de Kooning, posting up and down on the last of the Action Painters, surrounded by a swarm of gnats, her dark glasses riding low on her nose, her Red Sox cap crooked atop her white hair, her caramel-colored plastic leg planted in the swarm of Pollock's old bottles.

Where's mine? I thought, and then I laughed and stared at the soft blue late-afternoon sky.

John Dough swigged a bottle of Southern Comfort and then passed it to me. He was clothed now, and so was Muffy – in her hospital nightie. She had a loaf of bread and was munching it. The floorboards were cool and soft, rotted in spots, and the sun slanted through chinks in the wall, throwing shadows and beams of light.

'Well, here we are, John,' I said, drinking.

'Call me Gilbert,' he said.

I looked at Muffy and she nodded.

'She knows, Roger.'

'I know, Roger. I know that John here – I know he's Specs.'

'You do?'

'Yes, and I love him.' She stroked his face, and outside a bird sang. 'Thank you, Pearl Man. Thank you, Gilbert. You brought me back to life.'

'And so you two came here?'

'We wanted some time alone,' said Muffy. 'Away from the crowd.'

'Gilbert,' I said. 'This place was your fa – was Jackson Pollock's studio.'

'Was it? Kurtis and I used to come here as kids, to get high and watch the teenagers making love.' He lit a joint.

'Honor your ancestors,' I said with a smile. 'Right?'

'That's right,' he said exhaling, passing the reefer.

'How is everybody, Roger?' Muffy asked.

'They're fine, Muffy. Barton's probably got the FBI and the Retired Bonackers Association out looking for you, and Fred the horse is dead, but other than that, it's Cashampton.' I toked. 'So what happened, Muffy? Why the coma?'

'The night Jenny turned sixteen Muffy saw something that rocked her world.'

'Let me tell it, Gilbert.' Big Barton's daughter took a puff, let it out, passed the joint to John – I mean Gilbert – and then she took a deep breath. 'It was late, Roger, and everybody had left, except for Jenny and her friends who were skinny-dipping in the pool. I went out to the beach to get some air. The first thing I notice up on the dunes is Tabby. The cat. Her analysis wasn't very helpful. She'd been getting more and more neurotic, and when I found her in the dune grass with her insides cut out, I just had a feeling that Jonas had snapped. So I go to the beach. Sometimes I go there by myself at night to just scream. It's very therapeutic, screaming on the beach. Sometimes the whole family gets together, just to scream. But every year there's less and less beach. Erosion. Less and less sand on the dunes. Cashampton is sliding into the sea. By the end of the century we'll be screaming in the house. But what do I find that night? It's Jonas having sex with that goat that Daddy gave to Jenny. I yell: 'Jonas!' But I'm already in shock, Roger, immobilized. And then Jonas, he . . .'

'Tell it, Muffy. You've got to let it out, let it out and let it out, until it's gone.'

'Oh, Roger,' – Muffy sobbed – 'he just comes and pulls my pants and panties off and he forces me . . . he . . . he rapes me there . . . and his penis is still wet with goat-butt . . .'

'The screwy bastard did it, Roger. And Muffy went into a serious fucking coma. I guess I talked her out of it.'

'You loved me out of it. If my husband can fuck a goat, Roger, I can believe anything, even that John here is Specs. Thank you Pearl Man. Thank you from the bottom of my heart.'

'She loves me, Roger!' Gilbert cried, happy-voiced, triumphant. 'She loves me, Schwartz and all!'

He'd found his American Dream.

Gilbert and Muffy left me then, to go back to their lives. And touched as I was by their love, moved as I was by the symmetry and beauty and irony of his dream being realized on the spot where his parents had created him, they weren't gone but three seconds before I was tearing up the goddamn floorboards and digging the sub-cabin earth.

'I told you, Roger,' said Bertha in the doorway. 'There ain't no paintings.'

'So go home. You know the way,' I said. 'And take Bill with you.' I was dirty and sweaty and desperate.

'He's out cold. I screwed him and I ate him and his cock is still hard as a damn rock. That Boner Fide is some dangerous shit.'

'They've got to be here somewhere!'

It was beyond frustrating. And I didn't give a rat's ass about Hiroshi or the potential money or any of the complications down the line. I wanted the paintings. Wanted to see them. Touch them. Art for art's sake.

'There ain't no paintings,' Bertha said again.

'She is right,' said de Kooning, standing behind her, yawning, idly scratching the lump in his pants, holding one of the old paint cans. 'Now I am convinced.'

He put the can down, took the shovel from me and swung

it mightily, splitting the soft rusted metal like a ripe melon, revealing a solid chunk of calcified, rust-wrapped black rock. I picked it up – it was heavy, and hard as a meteor. Dead paint.

'It was my wish that they existed – I had seen the supplies, the canvases and paint cans, but never any work. *The Rat King* . . . it was his farewell, Roger. I think those last years, all of Jackson's creativity went into loving. Yah. It is time to let him rest.'

The two old soldiers in the art wars stood in the doorway, looking at me with pity. I went back to my search.

'Give it up, Roger,' said Bertha Seward. 'Let's all go take a shower and change and see what those Hollywood jerks came up with.' She cackled and snorted. 'Maybe *they've* got your lost paintings – in the flick.'

'And what's this?' I asked, holding a rusted metal toolbox I found under a corner of the cabin.

I took the shovel from de Kooning and tapped the edges of the box, then cracked the rusted hasp. I pulled the lid and it creaked open with an unwilling groan, flakes of rust showering to the ground.

Rags.

Three carefully folded moldy yellowing rags. I held one up to the soft light seeping through the wall-boards. It was a pair of underwear – old-fashioned women's underwear, more voluminous than modern panties, and painted on the crotch was a heart and an arrow, and around the heart an abstract sunrise – or sunset – both sun and moon visible in a sea of stars, and inside the heart, brushstroked in the unmistakeable scrawl of Jackson Pollock, it said: 'Bertha and Jackson forever.'

'What is it?' asked Bertha.

'They're yours,' I said, handing her the panties. 'Your drawers.'

I looked at another – similar. 'Valerie and Jackson forever,' it read.

'That goddamn drunken panty-thief!' cried Bertha Seward, sniffing her old bloomers. 'I knew I left these things out here. Jacko just laughed at me. Here, Roger.' She threw them at me. 'A souvenir.'

I held up the third rag, but instead of a heart, the names were contained within a . . . a softball.

'Jackson . . .' de Kooning said with a smile. 'This is lovely.'

'What is it, de Koo-Koo?' asked Bertha. 'Lemme in on it.'

'That softball game, Bill,' I said. 'The one with the coconut and the grapefruit. You remember what you told me – about Pollock walking off into the woods with a young woman?'

'Roger, you forget: I forget nothing.'

'Yeah. The woman you said he walked off with. It wasn't Valerie Schwartz, was it?'

'I never said it was.'

'And Pollock had a thing for dark-skinned girls.'

Bertha reached and snatched the panties from me.

'Yah, that is true, Roger. He loved all girls.'

Bertha Seward touched the sun and moon and stars, lightly ran her fingers over the letters inside the softball, and read: ' "Clarisse and Jackson forever." '

'The girl that day, Bill, it was Clarisse Cash, yes?'

'Roger, you are a true detective!' he said, clapping a hand to my shoulder. 'You have found your missing Pollocks. Yah!'

Twenty-two

I DROPPED BILL off at home with his women. I dropped Bertha off at the Bonacker restaurant. It was seven o'clock and the sun was hovering fire-red over Cash Bay. I drove over to the Reservation, steering past a gaggle of blonde, rollerblading yuppies who gave me the finger for forcing them to the side of the road.

I found Kurtis Swimming Otter Cash – descendant of African royalty, descendant of Indian chiefs, descendant of Captain Kidd and Tiger Edgar Cash . . . the secret love-child of Clarisse Cash and Jackson Pollock – at home. His tears were falling onto his mother's sweet peaceful face.

'She's gone, Roger.'

'Yes, Kurtis. But it's only a passing.'

'Clarisse,' he said, crying and crying, kissing the smooth lifeless skin and clouding eyes. 'Ma.'

'Kurtis,' I said, touching his shoulder. 'She loved you. She carried you, she gave birth to you, she raised you without a father. She loved you. She was a brave and loving woman.'

'Yes,' he said, getting off the stilled body of his mother and walking into the kitchen, opening the fridge.

'What are you doing?' I asked, as Kurtis took a home-fertility kit turkey-baster full of red liquid. Kurtis didn't answer.

'What are you doing?'

'I'm going to the other side, joining my mother. My mother and my father.'

'Your father was Jackson Pollock.'

'I know,' he said, dropping his trousers. 'Clarisse told me today. She never told a soul before, not even Pollock. It's the last laugh.'

'Kurtis, don't.'

'Leave me, Roger,' he said, flowing tears framing his smile. 'Leave me the fuck alone.'

'Kurtis, don't.'

'Too late. Too fucking late.'

'What's in that thing?'

'Axl's blood. How's that for symmetry?' He laughed through his tears. 'I gave him my blood and I get his. Double double-indemnity. We both get canceled out. See you, pal.'

'Kurtis—'

'See you. And say goodbye and love to Gilbert for me. Tell my brother I'll see him on the other side. You're his only other friend. Thanks for being his friend. Gotta go.'

'Kurtis—'

'See you, Roger,' he said, and plunged the baster up into his ass. 'See you.'

Twenty-three

I DROVE OVER to the Upton Club. There, in a field, riding hard, taking jumps, her long blonde hair flowing in the spectacular sunset air – there was Muffy on McBride.

I tooted the horn. Muffy rode over.

'Muffy,' I said through my open window. 'Where's Gilbert?'

'He's in the barn, mucking stalls.' She sighed. 'Roger, can you give me a ride home.'

'Where's home, Muffy? With John – Gilbert? The Mulrooney Estate?'

'No, *my* home. With Jonas and the kids. Gilbert and I' – she sighed again – 'it just wouldn't work out. We're from different classes.'

'But I thought you loved him.'

'I thought so too, Roger; maybe I did for a moment – and I'll always be grateful to him for getting me out of my coma – he's a terrific fellow . . . but when we got back to Cashampton By The Sea, when I smelled the ocean and I saw the riding club, I knew my place was here, with my family. I have children and a husband and a horse.' She patted McBride. 'And they all need me. I've decided to forgive Jonas. Specs taught me how to forgive.'

'Well, congratulations, Muffy,' I said. 'You and Jonas deserve each other.'

'You'll tell Specs for me?'

'Sure,' I said, the sadness welling up in me.

'And you'll drive me home?'

'Muffy,' I said, wiping a tear, 'you know how to hitchhike. You just stick your thumb out and blow.'

Twenty-four

'IT'S MY FORTIETH birthday today,' John Dough said, scooping a turd from the sawdust in Zorro's stall and dumping it in his barrow. We looked out the open half of the stall door at Muffy riding toward the beach, the dying sun lighting her yellow hair.

'Hooray, John. We'll celebrate at home.'

'She's going back to him, isn't she?' he asked, leaning back and removing his contact lenses, sticking his hand out the window and letting the tiny green films flutter away in the soft breeze.

'I don't know, Gilbert. I think she's going down to the beach to do a little screaming.'

'She's gone,' he said, fixing me with brown eyes, stopping to pat the marvelous steed, leading me out of the stall, wheeling his barrow, clicking the bolt.

'Y'know, Roger, about all that Pollock shit? My father was Leo Schwartz. He may not have been the biological one – but biology is one crazy motherfucking game to get all hung up on. Adios, friend.' He gave me his hand and coughed.

'What do you mean, "adios"? Let's go home and change for the Pollock premiere.'

'There's a will in my desk. My lawyers have a copy. You and Dawn Cash split fifty-fifty. So when you go riding and you see the horseshit, think of me and think of all the fun we had being rich together for a couple months. Oh, yeah, there's an address in my desk. I owe a guy in The City five-hundred-and-seventy dollars. Square it for me, brother.'

'You okay, Gil?'

'Yeah,' he said with a cough. 'I'm fine. Physical pain is horseshit. Where's Kurtis?'

'Kurtis . . . he took Clarisse to the funeral home, but he sends his love. Kurtis – it turns out that Kurtis is Pollock's son too.'

'So we're brothers, of the blood. That's good,' he said, coughing, as we exited the large double doors; and he dumped the wheelbarrow full of horseshit into the tractor scoop and walked toward his Jaguar parked by the dumpster. 'I'm sorry about Clarisse.'

'Yes,' I said. 'So am I.'

'I've got a wicked headache.'

'You want to stop by the hospital?'

'No, Roger. It's over. Fairy tales don't end in hospitals.'

'What do you mean?' I asked, following him past his car. 'What do you mean?'

'I had the money, I had the car, I had the girls, I took care of my mother, I found out who my father was, and . . . I had Muffy.' A dreamy look passed over his brown eyes. 'I made love to Muffy Snitbread, Roger. For a day and a night and another day. Muffy and I were lovers. That's all I ever really wanted out of life.'

'John,' I said, as he climbed up into the dumpster full of horseshit. 'Gilbert. Please tell me you used a condom.'

'No, Roger. That would have meant nothing. They don't let you through the pearly gates dressed for war.'

'But she has The Disease,' I said, climbing up there, leaning over the edge as he lay down, his pitchfork at his side. 'At least she's a carrier. From Jonas . . . Jonas and the goat.'

'I know that,' he said, hiccuping and sighing and groaning, stretching out in the warm fragrant bed of dung. 'I know that and I knew it. And don't cry, my brother.'

'Was it worth it?' I asked, touching his head.

'Fuck yes,' he gasped with a smile. 'I love her.'

'Gilbert,' I said, the tears coming free and fast and hot, and the sobs wracking my body, as my friend lay there jerking and heaving and hiccuping his life away in the stinking dumpster under the setting sun. 'You're worth all those Cashampton motherfuckers put together. You taught me how to love. I love you.'

'Yes,' he said, hiccuping. 'I love you too, little buddy. Love . . . it's the only thing.' He smiled, and his face went dark. 'The rest is . . .' Gasping and hiccuping, his arms spreading like angel wings, the lifeblood rushing out his nose and his brown eyes going large with wonder and his arms reaching for the sky. 'The rest is . . . . horseshit.'

Twenty-five

WE BURIED HIM that night. The night of the Pollock premiere. While the rest of Cashampton was at the theater cheering on the antics of the fictional Jackson Pollock, we solemnly buried the historical Gilbert Schwartz in Green River Cemetery. Buried him with his boots on. In his jeans and jeans jacket and T-shirt. With his Cleveland Indians cap and blonde wig covering his map to the stars. With his pitchfork. We buried him. Kurtis, Dawn Cash, me. I dug the grave.

Kurtis's tears fell hot and many onto the grave.

'Well,' I said, throwing a handful of earth onto the humble pine box, as the stars winked and glittered above Cashampton. 'You were a good man, Gilbert Schwartz.'

And then Kurtis silently walked away, limping into the shadows among the crowd of graves.

'I loved you, Gilbert,' said Dawn Cash, sinking to her knees on the damp turf and weeping.

'You should have told him so.'

'I sent him a Valentine's card, and I was getting my nerve up, but . . .'

'Goodbye,' I said. 'Goodbye, John. Goodbye, Gilbert. Hail and farewell.'

And up on the rise, on Jackson Pollock's grave, a lone dark figure began to hiccup.

. . . THE WREN HAS BEEN designated the little king, the king of birds, the hedge king, and so forth, and has been reckoned amongst those birds which it is extremely unlucky to kill. . . . People believe that if children touch the young wrens in their nest, they will suffer from the fire of St. Lawrence, that is, from pimples on the face, legs, and so on.

Sir James Frazer, *The Golden Bough*